W9-BVK-183

Wheel of the Infinite

WHEEL OF THE INFINITE

Martha Wells

An Imprint of HarperCollins*Publishers*

EOS

EOS
An Imprint of HarperCollins*Publishers*
10 East 53rd Street
New York, New York 10022-5299

Copyright © 2000 by Martha Wells
Interior design by Kellan Peck
ISBN: 0-380-97335-9

Library of Congress Cataloging in Publication Data:
Wells, Martha.
Wheel of the infinite / Martha Wells.—1st ed.
p.cm.
I. Title.
PS3573.E4932 W48 2000   00-21726
813'54—dc21

First Eos Printing: July 2000

Eos Trademark Reg. U.S. Pat. Off. and in Other Countries, Marca Registrada,
Hecho en U.S.A.
HarperCollins® is a trademark of HarperCollins Publishers, Inc.

Printed in the U.S.A.

FIRST EDITION

QW 10 9 8 7 6 5 4 3 2

www.avonbooks.com/eos

To Kimberley Rector,
for being there

Wheel of the Infinite

1

Maskelle had been asking the Ancestors to stop the rain three days running now and, as usual, they weren't listening.

She stood on a little hill, surrounded by the heavy jungle that lined either side of the river of mud that had once been the road, and watched the wagons crawl painfully by. They were wooden and brightly painted, but the roofs hadn't been tarred in too long and she knew it was hardly any drier inside them than out. One of the oxen, straining to keep the wheels moving forward against the tide of mud, moaned loudly. *I sympathize,* Maskelle thought.

Rastim, leader of the little troupe, stumbled up the hill toward her, his boots squelching and his clothes a sodden mess. He paused a short distance from her and said, "O Great Protectress, why is it we're going to Duvalpore?"

Maskelle leaned on her staff. "Because I said so."

"Oh." Rastim contemplated the wagons thoughtfully, then looked down at his shirt where the downpour was making the cheap dyes of the embroidery run, and sighed heavily.

Maskelle would have promised him better, if she made promises.

He glanced at her, brows lifted. "So, there's no chance of just stopping and drowning here, say?"

"No, I think we'll keep moving for now and drown a little further up the road."

"Ah." He nodded. "Then can you come and take another look at Killia's poppet? She thinks she's worse."

Maskelle rolled her eyes to the Ancestors. Rastim was an Ariaden, and they never believed in giving bad news without a lot of preamble, no matter how urgent it was. She started down the hill and plunged back into the mud river.

Killia's wagon was painted with geometric designs in bright red and yellow, now splattered with dirt from the long journey. Maskelle caught the handhold at the back and stepped up onto the running board, which barely cleared the soupy mud. She knocked on the shutter and it was immediately cranked upward. Killia extended a hand to help her in, and Maskelle discovered she needed it; her light cotton robes were so drenched that they added an unexpected amount to her weight. She sat on the bench just inside the entrance so she could wring them out a bit and wait for her eyes to adjust to the dark interior.

Various wooden bowls caught the leaks from the roof, but there were still puddles on the lacquered floor. Overhead, cooking pots banged into empty cage lamps and the bags that held costumes and drapes for the scenery, bundled up to keep them out of the water. Killia's daughter was huddled in one of the two narrow bunks under a mound of damp blankets. Maskelle leaned over and burrowed in the blankets until she touched warm skin. Too warm. She swore under her breath.

"Bad?" Killia asked. She was a tiny woman with the pale skin of the Ariaden and long dark hair caught back by a number of clips and ribbons. Her face had the perfection of a porcelain doll's and to Maskelle she looked hardly more than a child herself, but her eyes were old.

Maskelle shook her head. The priesthood took oaths to the truth, but she had broken all her oaths long ago and Killia had enough to worry about. "I'll have to go down to the river for some more ivibrae—the real river, not the one under the wagon."

Killia smiled briefly at the feeble joke. "Ivibrae for lung rot?"

"Ivibrae is good for any fever, not just lung rot. The girl doesn't have lung rot," Maskelle told her, and thought, *Not yet, anyway.*

Killia didn't look reassured. Maskelle gathered her sodden robes and jumped down off the wagonbed.

Rastim had been walking behind it and the spray of mud as she landed splattered both of them. They eyed each other in mutual understanding; it had been one of those days. She said, "Camp in the Sare if you can make it before dark. If you're not there, I'll look for you along the road."

He swept her a theatrical bow. "Yes, O Great Protectress."

"You're welcome, Rastim," Maskelle said, and splashed toward the heavy dark wall of the jungle.

Two hours later Maskelle wasn't so sanguine herself. The thick clouds made the night fall faster under the jungle canopy, and though the broad-leaf palms protected her from heavy rain, the going was still laboriously slow. She reached the river while the jungle was still a deep green cave, dripping and quiet, and stood on the bank to watch the swollen waters. The river was running high and drunk on its own power, gray with mud and crested with foam. It was the source of wild magic, especially as bloated with rain and powerful as it was now; it would be a channel for any dark influence that cared to use it.

It was none of her business. Maskelle shook her head. *Keep telling yourself that.* The ivibrae proved annoyingly elusive; usually it grew at the very edge of the treeline above the river, but there were no patches to be found in the usual spots, and she found herself having to slide dangerously down the muddy bank. By the time she had picked a quantity and scrambled back up to more solid ground, the green cavern had become a pitch-black hole.

She decided to make her way along the river until she was at the right point to strike out for the road again. She stumbled along, barefoot because no pair of sandals would have lasted half a day in this mess, her patched robes tied up to keep her from tripping, a bundle of stinking ivibrae crammed under her belt, and covered with mud from feet to nose. Her braids kept falling into her eyes and some were fraying apart, revealing how much grey was mixed in with the dark strands. Smiling, she wondered what the court of Kushor-An at Duvalpore would have thought of her now. *Not much, not much,* she chuckled to herself. Rastim was right: their luck was so bad it was beginning to be funny. Perhaps it was the Ancestors, tired of her importunities at last, willing to drown the whole of the Great Road just to inconvenience her poor self. Maskelle smiled at the thought. *Add hubris to the list of crimes, if it wasn't there already.*

The twilight had deepened into night now and the river was a menacing roar to her right; she saw a flicker of light ahead along the bank. Staggering toward it, sodden and chilled, she hoped that it was a river traders' outpost and that there might be such a thing as a cup of warm tea before she had to walk back through the jungle to the road. Or maybe a half-bottle of rice wine. *I'm getting old,* she thought sourly. But that was nothing new. As she drew closer to the light she could hear raucous voices, a great many raucous voices.

She was close enough now for the lamps lit along the balconies to show her the outline of the place. It perched on the edge of the bank, wooden and ramshackle, half of it hanging out over the rushing river and supported by heavy log pilings. Several small boats were tied up under it, and splintered wood, rope, torn sail and the wreckage of fishtraps were caught among them and the pilings. The windows glowed with light and many people moved about inside. *It's a traders' outpost true enough,* she thought, *but it doesn't belong to river traders, not any longer.* Raiders and river pirates must be using it for the night, though they couldn't have been here long—Imperial patrols would periodically sweep the riverbanks to clear them out. She hadn't seen any boat traffic on the river, but had put that down to the rain and rough water. She let out her breath in resignation.

Raiders were as vicious as the moray, the small lizards that hunted the river in packs. Not only drunken laughter came from the inhabitants of the outpost—there were shrieks, thumps, crashes, even roars, like a menagerie. Common sense told her to head into the jungle so she could get back to make the posset for Killia's girl and retire to her own cold supper and damp bed. But this kind of thing had been her business, in one way or another, for many long years, and old habits died hard. There was a crash as a body came flying through the latticework of one of the windows over the dock. That decided her; this she had to see.

She walked up the rickety steps to the nearest doorway and elbowed her way inside. The place was full of river trash, as filthy and muddy as Maskelle herself, except river trash were usually filthy and muddy by choice. Their clothes were tattered rags or pillaged finery, like the torn silk trousers and vest of the one lying unconscious on the floor. They stunk of uncured leather, unwashed person, and rice liquor, and the bad light reflected off sweat-slickened skin and wild dirty hair. They packed the rickety wooden gallery that ran along this floor and even staggered around in drunken battle on the lower level, which was awash in dirty water as the rising river encroached on it. Every one of them was yelling like the mad. *The resemblance to the Court at Duvalpore is striking,* Maskelle thought, watching them ironically. She winced from the din and considered leaving; the place was so smoky from the badly tended lamps that she couldn't see what was happening anyway.

Swearing under her breath, she looked toward the far end of the gallery where there was a raised platform for the upper level loading deck. The giant pulleys and tangled ropes of the old cargo crane hung heavily over it, the arm suspended out over the lower floor, designed to raise bales through the wide doors that opened over the river in the wall behind the deck, swing them inside the building and lower them down to the large area below. Several people seemed to be standing and talking there in almost a sane manner. She started toward them, trying to peer through the smoke and shadow. Frustration made her will it a little too hard, for her view abruptly cleared. *Ah, so they've caught someone.*

The prisoner's arms were stretched up over his head, his wrists bound to one of the supports for the crane. One of the raiders came toward him and he jerked up his legs and kicked his captor in the stomach, sending him flying backward. *Not quite helpless,* she thought, amused. Two other rivermen dived at him, grabbing his legs and lashing him to the lower part of the frame.

He was probably a traveller trapped and caught somewhere along the river. That was why the Ancestors had guided her steps here.

So I'm not too disobedient to make use of, she grumbled to herself, making her way down the crowded gallery and clearing a path with occasional sharp pokes from her staff. The raiders were beginning to point and nudge each other, her presence finally penetrating the haze of liquor and bloodlust. Because of the tattered state of her clothes and her staff, they would think her a travelling nun. Unless they could read the Koshan symbols in the silver embedded in the wood, and she doubted that was a possibility. Maskelle looked around thoughtfully. She didn't think she could kill all of them, and she had taken an oath not to do that sort of thing anymore, but she thought she could manage a distraction.

One of the rivermen standing on the platform was holding a sword, a real one, not one of the long knives the other raiders were armed with. The greasy light reflected off the dark etching on the wavy blade and Maskelle frowned a little. That was a siri. The brightwork on the hilt wasn't much tarnished yet so it must have come from the prisoner. It meant he wasn't native to the river country; several of the southern provinces used the siri and it wasn't common here in the heart of the lowlands.

The Kushorit, the main stock of the Celestial Empire, also tended to be small, dark and compactly built, and the prisoner was tall, rangy lean, and sharp-featured. Maskelle was an aberration herself, having outer reaches blood in her family and being tall and long-limbed because of it. He was about ten or fifteen years younger than Maskelle, which, she was uncomfortably aware, still made him a man grown. He wore a sleeveless shirt and leather leggings, torn and dirty from what had obviously been a hard battle, and the blue and red designs stamped into his leather swordbelt and buskins had faded from long exposure to the sun. His hair was shaggy brown with streaks of blond and one long tightly braided lock hung past his shoulder.

The river raiders wore assorted scraps of leather or lacquered armor and tattered silk finery. The woman who seemed to be the leader had a battered helmet with a crest shaped into the head of a killing bird, obviously taken off some wealthy victim. She was big and muscular, an old knife scar slashing across already harsh features. She strode to the edge of the platform and glared down at Maskelle. "What do you want here, Sister?"

Yes, you're so terribly dangerous, Maskelle thought, smiling indulgently. *I tremble, really I do.* Dangling over the platform, the ropes to control the crane were worn and tangled, and it looked like the counterweight, a leather sack of iron ingots, was the only thing that was keeping the massive wooden arm from collapsing. *That will do nicely.* She leaned on her staff. "I come to offer blessing, my child."

The woman stared, then grinned back at her companions. "We're unbelievers here, Sister; we'd curdle your blessing."

"Not this blessing. It's just what your sort deserve." Maskelle felt a dark surge of power under her feet as she spoke. The river was restless with more than floodwater tonight; it called to her, sensing a kinship. "But I want something in exchange for it."

"What's that?"

"Release that man." The prisoner was watching her warily, without any show of hope, almost as if he didn't recognize her as a Koshan. He didn't look badly hurt, however, just bruised and beaten.

"Oh, so you want him for yourself, Sister?" the leader said. The others laughed and grinned at each other.

If you don't consider the source, it's not a bad idea, Maskelle thought. He was handsome, in an exotic way, which was probably why the raiders had saved him to amuse themselves with rather than killing him immediately. The Koshans only demanded abstinence from initiates during the first three years of instruction, but it was a common misconception that all members of the Order were celibate.

Before Maskelle could answer, the prisoner said, "She doesn't need a club to get company. Some women don't." He spoke in Kushorit, the common language of the Empire, but lightly accented

Maskelle frowned; she should be able to tell what province he was from by that accent, but she couldn't place it. She had been too long from her native land, perhaps, too long among the soft voices of Ariad. The fact that he knew Kushorit was no real clue; it was a common language throughout the provinces too, spoken by traders, scholars, diplomats.

The leader crossed the stained planks to step close to her captive. She grabbed a handful of his hair and jerked his head back. "So you don't like my face?" she said softly.

I wager she didn't do that before he was more securely bound. Maskelle tended to find male bullies merely amusing, but for some reason the female ones always stirred her to rage. *Careful, careful,* she reminded herself. The darkness in the river was so uncontrolled, so near, so willing to be tapped it was hard to resist the temptation.

Voice slightly constricted from the pressure the leader was

putting on his neck, he still said, "Your face I could ignore; it's your personality and your breath that turn my stomach."

This time Maskelle placed the accent; he was from the Sintane. It was a province far on the outer rim, known for fine figured goldwork and weaving. He was a long way from home. The Sintane didn't have deserters or mercenaries like the other provinces; they had outcasts. She looked at the sword the raider was holding. The hilt might be horn or bone, and the ring between the blade and the hilt seemed to be plain silver, all of which told her nothing. The Sitanese sometimes carved family totems into the hilts of siri, and the ring was often an elaborate piece of jeweler's art. Maskelle said, "You must be terribly afraid of him."

One of the raiders gave a short bark of laughter and the leader released her grip on the captive to face Maskelle. "What are you saying?"

"If you aren't afraid, then cut him loose and let him fight your men. If you call them men."

The leader came to the edge of the platform and pushed her face close to Maskelle's. She growled, "I should feed you to the moray, Koshan bitch."

Seen at close range her scar was an ugly puckered fissure across a face webbed with fine lines and darkened with ingrained dirt. The woman was bigger than Maskelle, much younger, all hard muscle, but Maskelle felt no fear; her blood was singing with the urge to kill. She rocked forward on the balls of her feet, looked into the other woman's glaring eyes, and said with utter seriousness, "The moray would choke." Even that was almost too much; if she said one more word, the dam would break and her rage would find an outlet whether she willed it or not. Physical threats always made her lose her temper; in all the years, that had never changed.

The raider blinked, suddenly uncertain, perhaps sensing the danger but not wise enough to realize just what the source was. She stepped back slowly, fingering the hilt of her knife. Maskelle waited, smiling, but the woman shook her head and laughed. "Do as she says. Let him fight." She gestured to the men behind her.

Maskelle took a deep breath that the others probably read as relief. It was part disappointment, part attempt to hold on to her suddenly tenuous self-control.

One of the raiders stepped forward, drawing his long belt knife. The prisoner tensed and Maskelle held her breath; if they changed their minds now there was nothing she could do about it. But the raider slashed the man's bonds and stepped quickly back. The prisoner freed himself from the rest of the ropes, looked around at the raiders, and with admirable self-possession, stretched and rubbed his neck. He caught Maskelle's eye and she flicked a glance at the gallery railing behind her, wondering if he would pick up on the hint. She needed the raiders' attention to be away from the cargo doors and the crane.

He didn't nod, didn't indicate that he had seen her signal, but he suddenly dropped to the platform and kicked the kneecap of the raider who held the captured siri. The man collapsed with a shriek, his leg giving way with a sharp crack. The prisoner came to his feet, taking the sword easily from the raider's shaking hand, ducked a deadly swipe from a bori club as he passed Maskelle and vaulted over the gallery railing.

She leaned over it in time to see him catch an old net that hung over the side and swing down to drop into the water washing over the lower floor.

The gallery audience roared, the leader and her lieutenants shouting and cursing as they ran for the railing.

Down on the floor below, the waving mass of combatants broke into little whirling eddies. In the instant of stillness she saw several rivermen with knives or bori clubs surrounding the one man armed with a sword. The blade flashed and the rivermen scattered.

Perhaps it was the rivermen who were trapped now and not the traveller. Bemused, Maskelle watched the leaping, dodging figures. It was like a game, or an entertainment so primitive it looked like violence to eyes long accustomed to the sophistication of Ariaden or kiradi theater. The prisoner wasn't wielding that blade with deadly intent yet; the plank floor below was awash in dirty water as the rising river encroached on the lower level of the outpost, but not high enough to conceal the dead bodies that would surely be sprawled there if he was. Maskelle knew if he killed some of them that would only fire the others to more fury; it was all or nothing. She was a little surprised he recognized that as well. The crowd pressed in again, trying to rush him, but their nerve failed and they splashed away.

"Well, Sister, where's our blessing?" the leader demanded, trying to recover her control of the situation.

Maskelle tried to decide just which invocation would annoy the Ancestors the most. The Great Opening, the signal part of the Year Rite, would get their immediate attention and hearing the words of it on her lips should elicit the quickest response. She turned away from the railing and stepped up onto the platform, clearing her mind.

As Maskelle faced the room and lifted her staff above her head, the raiders' leader called out, "Attend to the nun, you bastards!" She grinned derisively around at her companions. "She's going to give us a blessing!"

Some of the raiders turned toward this new diversion, but most were too occupied by the fighting to listen. A man almost too drunk to stand on his feet staggered up on the platform muttering, "Kill the Koshan bitch—"

Maskelle swung her staff down and around, slamming him in the chest and sending him crashing backward off the platform. That got their attention.

The shouts and drunken roaring died away. Into the relative quiet Maskelle said, "I am the Voice of the Adversary."

She hadn't spoken loudly, but her words carried across the room. There were gasps and outcries, proving that some of the raiders at least were among the devout. One quick thinker turned and dived out the nearest window. The leader stared around, baffled and angry.

Maskelle spoke the first words of the Great Opening. This was too much presumption for the myriad forces of the Infinite to ignore. All the lamps in this half of the chamber flickered and died.

In the sudden darkness Maskelle swung around to the cargo doors and with the end of her staff threw the latch up.

The doors flew open and wind-driven rain rushed in. There were shrieks and shouts as the rivermen began to panic, shoving and pushing. Maskelle stepped quickly to the crane's counterweight, drawing the little knife she used for cutting fruit. It was too small for the job, but she slashed at the half-rotted ropes until suddenly the counterweight dropped.

The reaction was more violent than she had anticipated. The counterweight smashed right through the floorboards, knocking her backwards. The arm swung and toppled, taking the railing, part of the gallery, and a dozen yelling rivermen with it.

"I meant to do that," Maskelle muttered to herself, stumbling to her feet. The raiders must think the post was under attack by hostile river spirits. They were pouring out the door Maskelle had entered by, blocking it, fighting and snarling like rats. Then a figure tore away from the other panicked, shoving bodies and charged toward her, bori club upraised.

It was the leader. Maskelle met her with the end of her staff, catching the woman a hard blow in the stomach and pushing her away. She staggered back but didn't fall; she must have some sort of leather or lacquered wood chest armor under her silk vest. Maskelle couldn't see much in the half-light, but she assumed the razor-edge of the heavy wooden club was aimed toward her. She kept the staff pointed at the leader, braced to move. The other woman shuffled to the side, trying to get past Maskelle's guard.

Then Maskelle saw that the ropes still attached to the broken crane arm and hanging over the gallery were jerking and twitching; it had to be the rivermen who had gone over the rail with the crane, still trapped in them. Then a head popped up over the edge.

She knew who it was. The trapped traveller had had hair cropped at his shoulders while the river raiders either shaved their heads to avoid lice or grew wild waist-length manes. Grinning, Maskelle angled sideways, making poking motions with the staff, as if she meant to try to break for the door across the gallery. Her opponent, thinking to catch her between herself and the packed door, obligingly stepped backward, closer to the edge.

The traveller hauled himself further up, and when the raider stepped back into reach, he swung his sheathed sword around and struck the back of her knees. The woman toppled backwards with a choked-off cry.

Maskelle turned immediately for the cargo doors, using her staff to trip a flailing, foul-smelling shadow that tried to stop her. Rain and wind poured in, drenching the boards under her feet. She found the ropes for the winch, but they didn't move when she tugged on them. *The other counterweight must be broken, damn it,* she thought, and tossed her staff out, hoping it struck the dock, not the river. She grabbed the heavy rope and swung out after it, getting a confused view of the river below with what little light there was from the cloud-covered moon reflecting off the angry surface. She hoped the traveller had the sense to follow her.

She scrambled down the rope, not quite as agile as a monkey, wishing she was ten years younger. The raiders must have had the outpost longer than she had initially thought, or it had been abandoned before they had ever found it; the rope was beginning to rot, so soft in most places her grasping fingers went right through the strands. But her feet thumped down on the dock before she knew it.

Cursing, she felt around on the scarred wood, feeling holes

and splinters, but not her staff. There were shouts from above and the lamps were flaring back to life inside the outpost. She stood, the wet wind tearing at her hair, took two steps toward the bank, and fell flat on her face. She had tripped over her staff.

"Thank you for nothing, Ancient Lineage," she muttered, her own abbreviated version of the proper Thanksgiving. She grabbed up the staff, staggered back to her feet, and ran for the bank.

Once in the bush she slowed, knowing a fall would only make more noise, though the rain covered most of the sound of her passing. When she had gone some distance, she stopped and crouched in the dark shelter of a dripping tana bush. She heard the thrashing of several people fighting their way through the foliage near her. The raiders wouldn't stay long in the jungle; it was a different realm than the river and they would fear it. *Superstitious idiots,* she thought, squatting in the mud. It was the river that would harbor the evil spirits tonight.

The raiders following her thrashed away and she started to stand. Someone touched her shoulder lightly, a caution not to move; she froze where she was and an instant later heard one more passage through the bush. There was nothing but the rain after that and the tingle of shock through Maskelle's skin and the hackles rising on the back of her neck. Someone crouched in the mud next to her; the air was alive with the warmth and breath of a living body. How she could have missed it before, she couldn't think. *No thanks for the warning,* she thought sourly to the Ancestors. In the thirty years of her apprenticeship and mastery as Their Servant, They had seldom been around when she wanted them. She wished she could say that was the reason she had turned on them in the end, but that was a lie she wouldn't tell herself. Experimentally, she whispered, "Are they gone?"

There was the briefest pause, then he said, "They are now."

Maskelle didn't move and for a moment neither did he. Then a great glop of water from the tana bush struck the back of her neck and she twitched. He flinched, stood suddenly and was gone, though this time she heard him brush against the leaves as he passed.

She shook her head and got to her feet, her knees protesting the movement. He must have climbed out the cargo hatch behind her and followed her into the jungle. He had returned her favor with the warning, anyway. She slogged further into the bush, wondering why a Sitanese swordsman had travelled this far into the Celestial Empire. The problem tickled her brain all the long way back to the road.

She came out of the jungle just where the road broadened out into the Sare. The Ancestors, perverse as usual, had now seen fit to grant her prayers about the rain and it had slackened to a bare drizzle. It was too dark to see much of the Sare now, but morning light would reveal a broad green plain, cut from the jungle in a perfect square, the grasses as clipped and civilized as any park in Duvalpore.

In the center of the plain was a massive rectangular baray, a reservoir of water bordered by broad stone walks. In the center of the baray stood a temple of the Koshan Order, reached by a stone bridge, its conical towers meant to resemble the Mountain of the Infinite, a symbolic meaning in every element of its design, every portal, every inch of carving. Lamps glowed from its many windows and lined the galleries and bridges. To the west of the baray there were three groups of less orderly lights: the campfires and torches of travellers camping here in the safety of the shadow of the temple and the patrols of its guards. In the glow of one campfire she recognized Rastim's wagon and felt her heart un-clench a little. She hated to leave the troupe, even though she knew they had been caring for themselves long before she had ever met them. *I've failed others before. Perhaps that's why.*

She found most of them huddled damply in the wagons, with Rastim trying to keep the fire lit and Old Mali grumbling while she stirred the supper. Voices called greetings from the wagons and Rastim watched her with ill-disguised relief as Maskelle walked up to sniff suspiciously at the cooking pot. Old Mali grumbled something inaudible. From the lumps bobbing in the stew, they had arrived in time to buy some pork from the priests' servants to add to the rice and there was taro root baking in the coals. "Boiling water?" she asked.

Old Mali wrapped a rag around one calloused hand and fetched a steaming kettle out of the coals. "Knew you'd be back," she muttered.

"There was doubt?" Maskelle asked, taking a seat on one of the woven straw mats laid out on the mud. It squished unpleasantly under her.

"Just Gardick again," Rastim said, and gestured disparagingly. "Nothing."

"Hmph." Maskelle took the ivibrae and ground it up with the mortar and pestle used for cooking. Together, and muttering curses at each other, she and Old Mali got the stuff strained into a pottery cup. Old Mali carried it off to Killia's wagon, leaving Maskelle and Rastim to stare at each other tiredly.

"So we'll be there in two days, will we?" he asked.

"Yes." She flexed her hands in the firelight. Her back hurt from the damp and she felt old. More than a half decade over twice twenty years wasn't that old for the Ariaden or the Kushorit. But it was old for a Court Lady, and her hands were almost as calloused as Old Mali's.

"And there'll be good crowds to perform for?" Rastim was uneasy.

"Oh, yes." Though "good" was a matter of perspective. "The best of the best. And generous, too."

"Ah." Rastim nodded, looking out over the dark wet plain beyond the boundary of firelight and wagons. "And the audience with the great priest?"

"He'll speak to you." Maskelle was taking the Ariaden to Duvalpore to see the Celestial One, the highest religious office in the Celestial Empire.

"Two days. If the rain doesn't slow us down."

"It won't," she said, knowing it was true, a Word whispered in her ear by the Ancestors. They were good for something, occasionally.

"Ah."

Old Mali came back from Killia's wagon, a stooped figure on stumpy legs, and thumped her chest and nodded. From long acquaintance with Old Mali, Maskelle took this to mean that Killia's daughter had drunk the posset and it had already relieved some of the congestion in her lungs. With luck, it would help the fever too and Maskelle wouldn't even have to summon the healing spirits.

Maskelle stood and eased the kinks in her back. She wasn't hungry anymore, even for tea, even for rice wine. And she didn't want to answer all the same questions from the others, once the smell of supper permeated the wagons and they began to creep out. She nodded to Rastim and Old Mali and limped toward her wagon. It stood slightly apart the way she liked it, the two oxen unharnessed and dozing over fodder. Old Mali drove it for her during the day, and had opened the light wooden side panels when the rain had stopped, so the interior could air out. Maskelle paused at the dropped tailgate, looking into the dark. She could see the temple from here.

The massive domed spire was black against the lighter shade of the sky, the moon shape of the portal below it barely visible; male and female phallic symbols woven together. The detail of the terraced carvings were entirely lost in shadow. They had passed small sanctuaries along the way, but this was the first time in too many years that she had been so close to a true temple.

She moved away from the wagon, one of the oxen snuffling at her as she drifted past. The temple was calling to her, not the stone shell, but what it represented, and the power that likeness gave it.

She walked through the sodden grass until she came to the

edge of the baray and stepped up onto the stone bank. The Koshan priests had the custody of the temples, but they were only static forms. It was the End of Year Rite that remade the universe in its own image, and that was only performed by the Voices of the Ancestors. The End of Decade rites were even more crucial.

This year would be the End of a Hundred Years rite.

Maskelle lifted her staff, holding it above her head. An echo whispered through her, a reflection from the Infinite through the structure of the temple. After all these years, it still knew her. "I helped another stranger tonight," she whispered. "I didn't kill anyone to do it. Not intentionally, at least. Is that enough for you?"

A slow wave of darkness climbed the temple wall, the lamps in the windows winking out one by one.

She lowered the staff and let out her breath. No, it wasn't enough. *And now they will all know you're back.* Oh, the delight in the power never died, that was the curse, and her true punishment, whatever the Adversary had decreed. She shook her head at her own folly and turned back to the camp.

She reached the wagon and climbed up the back steps, closing the panels that faced the campsite. She sat on the still damp wooden floor, looking out at the temple and the silver surface of the baray in the distance.

She was facing the right direction for an illusion of privacy, though voices from the other campsites, oddly distorted over the plain, came to her occasionally. The night breeze was chilly on her wet clothes, the drying mud itchy on her legs. And someone was watching her. She knew it by the way the oxen, caught in the firelight from behind the wagon, cocked their ears. She found his outline in the dark finally, about twenty feet away, sitting on his heels just out of reach of the light. She might have walked within ten feet of him on the way to the baray. Again, the shock of being so taken by surprise was like ice on her skin. She waited until it drained away, then quietly she said, "Come here."

The breeze moved the short grass. He stood up and came toward the wagon.

Her staff, as much a part of her as her hands or feet, lay on the wooden bench of the wagon. He stopped just out of arm's reach. Her arm's reach. She was within easy range of his sword.

He stood in the shadow where the wagon blocked the firelight, but the moonlight was strong. The heavy siri rested easily on one lean hip.

Maskelle stretched out her foot, her toes finding the staff where it lay on the rough planks and gradually easing it toward her hand.

"What did you do?" he said.

He couldn't be asking her what she thought he was asking her; after a moment she realized he meant the lamps in the temple. "I'm a Voice of the Ancestors." That was still strictly true, if it didn't actually answer the question. "What were you doing in the outpost?"

"Getting killed. Did it look like anything else?"

Instead of taking the bait, she said, "That's a fine way to say thank you."

"I was going up river and walked into them."

"That's still not 'thank you.' " Though it could well be the truth. If he had come up the Western Road from the Sintane, he could have crossed the river at the fords at Takis. But why move along the bank instead of going on to the Great Road? *Well, the Great Road has regular patrols; the river doesn't, not in the rainy season.*

He didn't take the bait, either. He said, "You're a wizard?"

"No."

Silence, while the damp breeze made the water in the baray lap against the stone banks and the temple cattle lowed in the distance. Why did she suspect it was the silence of disbelief? Almost against her will, she added, "I receive the Ancestors' Will, when they have any, and translate it for others. In return, They allow me to manipulate the power of the Infinite." An enormous simplification of the process, but she didn't think he wanted an hours-long philosophy debate.

More silence. The disbelief was so thick it was practically dripping off the wagon. Finally, he said, "Are all the Koshan priests wizards?"

Ancestors help me, Maskelle swore under her breath, then gave in. "To some extent. But none of the others are like me."

He didn't make any response. He was standing with his arms folded, but she had seen how fast he could move. Annoyed, she said, "If you don't believe me, you can ask the priests at the temple."

He jerked his head toward the camp. "Those priests?"

"What?" She sat up, startled, and the staff thumped loudly on the wagonbed.

He stepped back as Maskelle grabbed her staff and stood up. She could already hear the bells on the priests' sistrum. Another moment, then he turned and walked—*strolled,* Maskelle thought, a brow lifted ironically—into the dark. She could hear his steps on the wet grass. Not magic then, and no power about it. Just skill at moving quietly.

Voices from behind the wagon recalled her to the current problem. Swearing under her breath, she dragged her wet robes off the bench and clambered down to the ground.

There were three Koshan priests standing near the fire, their cobalt blue robes caught up to keep them out of the mud, and a young acolyte with a sistrum behind them. Beyond the priests, half-surrounding the wagons, was a group of temple guards mounted on the small, sturdy horses of the lower plains. The guards wore dark silk overrobes sewn with chain and breastplates of tightly braided plates of lacquered iron, their crested helmets fitted with masks to make them faceless and terrifying.

Old Mali was still crouching stubbornly by the cooking pot, but the others were hiding in the wagons, peering anxiously out.

Their eyes followed Maskelle as she crossed the campsite. Rastim was standing before the lead priest in an attitude of abject fear. *Damn overdramatic Ariaden,* Maskelle thought. Shaking her head in resignation, she approached the tableau.

The priest's eyes flicked over her dismissively as she moved around the fire, then came back to her in growing astonishment as he saw her staff. The light was catching the old traces of silver left in the carved letters of the sacred text. The sparks jumped from word to word as the text wound up the length of the fine smooth wood like a snake around a pappas tree. The letters were worn down from years of handling, but they could still be read. Until they faded from sight, the staff would still have power. *Not unlike me,* Maskelle thought ruefully.

The priest was young and fine-featured, but the shaven scalp under the hood of his robe was marked with colored designs of the first rank. The men with him were older but not so high in honor. He stared hard at her, looking for what was left of her tattoo, but her hair had grown over it, obscuring all but the border of the design at her hairline. The staff told him that her rank was Voice, but not which Voice. He wet his lips, and said, "You shame us, lady. You should shelter in the temple."

She leaned on the staff, mud and all. She hadn't ever really expected to arrive in secret. "Thank you for the offer, my son, but I can't."

His eyes narrowed, alert for insult. He said, "You have a reason for refusing our shelter?"

"I'm forbidden the temples," Maskelle said, watching his eyes.

He stared at her, frowning, and his gaze swept over her, seeing for the first time past the worn robes. He would have trouble estimating her age, she knew. Country people always thought her younger, city people used to courtiers who spent all their time lying in the shade and rubbing oils and creams into their skin always thought her older. His eyes went to the staff again. *But there are only so many Voices,* she thought. And the chance was he would know where all the others were.

She watched with interest as the blood drained from his face. "You . . ." He did not step back from her, though the tension in his body told her he wanted to. He drew in a breath and said coldly, "So the rumors were true. You've been summoned by the Celestial One."

"Rumors fly fast." She smiled.

A muscle jumped in his cheek. "I have something to show you."

Maskelle lifted her brows. She hadn't expected that response. "You know there are very few rituals I'm allowed to perform."

He turned away without answering, his attendants hastily parting for him. Maskelle followed, baffled and trying—successfully, she hoped—not to show it. *What does he want? If this is a trap . . . If this is a trap, he's mad.*

The priest led her through the dark, crossing through the muddy flats with no concern for his robes, one of the guards hurrying forward with a lamp to light the way. After a moment she realized he was leading her toward the temple's outbuildings, the stables, storehouses, and the quarters for the monks and servants that stood near the end of the causeway that crossed the baray to the temple. He turned through a narrow gate in a stone wall, pausing to disperse the guards with a wave. Only his priest attendants followed Maskelle through the gate.

Inside was a courtyard, the few lamps hanging from hooks along the walls illuminating muddy ground and more gates leading off into the rambling structure that loomed over them in the dark. Two guards stood outside one of the gates, and one quickly reached to pull it open as the priest strode toward it.

Inside was a warm close room, the damp air smelling strongly of goat and the ground littered with straw. The other priests had remained outside, but the one guard with the lamp had followed them in. The head priest took it away from him and held it high over the occupant of the wooden pen.

Maskelle took a deep breath, despite the smell. "It's a goat." *The man is mad.*

It was an ordinary brown goat, staring up at them with opaque brown eyes. The goat turned its head and bleated, and Maskelle saw what was hanging out of its side. It was the rear half of a moray lizard. She stepped closer and leaned down, swallowing a curse. The moray were about a foot long, with tough gray green hides and a ridge of distinctive spines along their backs to complement their sharp teeth and clawed feet. This was distinctively a moray, or at least the back six inches of one. It was stuck against the goat's side as if it had grown there, the two back legs dangling, the spiny tail hanging limply. Baffled, she looked up at the priest, who was watching her with a grim lack of expression that was impossible to read. She said, "It's strange, but such things happen. Animals born with extra limbs or . . ." *Other, completely different animals hanging out of their bodies.* No, she didn't think she had heard of that before. She forged on anyway, "They aren't always omens, though people think . . ."

He was shaking his head. He pointed toward a stone block set back against the wall of the stall, and angled the lamp so the light fell more fully on it. Hanging out of the stone was the front half of the lizard.

Maskelle wet her lips, feeling a coldness in the pit of her stomach. She said, "All right, that one is, uh . . . odd." The front half of the moray hung limply out of the stone, its front legs and the wicked oblong head like some bizarre decoration. The stone itself was a square block with cracked mortar on the sides, as if it had been broken out of a wall.

"Could this be the result of your curse?" the priest asked.

Maskelle lifted a brow, but she found the bluntness rather refreshing. "A dark power, following in my wake, you mean? It's possible. When did it happen?"

"Six days ago."

She shook her head, a little surprised. "I wasn't in this province yet. We've been travelling hard."

He turned away, the shadows falling over the monstrosity in the rock as the lamp was withdrawn.

Maskelle followed him out into the relatively fresh air of the court, where the other priests still waited outside. One of them must have realized she wasn't just an ordinary, albeit eccentric, Voice travelling the Great Road and told his fellows; the tension emanating from them was palpable now. The lead priest stopped and eyed her narrowly. He said, "When I saw you, I had hoped for an easy answer."

She resisted the impulse to say something philosophical about easy answers. She didn't suppose him to have any more patience with such platitudes than she did. Instead, she said, "If it's an omen, it's a frightening one. I'll tell the Celestial One of it when I see him."

"If it is a dark power . . ."

It would be simpler if it was a byproduct of her curse, a wandering dark power that corrupted whatever it touched, following in her wake. "If it's a dark power, I'll deal with it. I haven't been with the Adversary for seven years, but He does take care of His own."

There was a stifled noise of shock and fear from one of the other priests. The lead priest glanced back at them, frowning. He turned back to her, and she could see him recalling what she was, despite everything. He hesitated, then said, "I offer you our hospitality . . . The guesthouse . . ."

His companions were badly startled, but evidently their fear of her was still an abstraction, whereas their fear of him was firmly founded, and they made no open protest. She smiled, badly tempted, and she knew she hadn't quite left the desire to cause chaos behind. She shook her head. "No, we both know how that would end."

He misunderstood and his grey eyes turned angry. Maskelle sighed. She had forgotten what it was like to deal with the young of the well-born. She said, gently, "You can stand bond for everyone in your temple, but you aren't their conscience, and I don't have the time to waste in fighting."

He still watched her grimly, no sign of any bend in that stiff spine. Then he stepped back and gave her a full sixth-degree bow, only one degree less than the rank actually due her. He turned away and his retinue followed with less grace, one of them sneaking her an abbreviated bow behind the backs of the others.

Maskelle walked slowly through the dark, back to the wagons where Rastim and Old Mali waited for her by the fire. Rastim let out his breath in relief when he saw her and Old Mali grunted in eloquent comment. "Trouble?" Rastim asked her.

She nodded and leaned her cheek against the staff. Trouble. She had known it would happen, but perhaps she hadn't thought it would be so soon. *Maybe I am too old for this,* she thought. *Too old for war, too mean-tempered for peace.*

"Should we move on tonight?" Rastim sounded worried.

Maskelle looked around. A few other members of the troupe had broken cover. Firac with his two young sons, who worked the apparatus on the largest of the puppets, and Therasa and Doria, who played the speaking women's parts. The travel had been difficult and their oxen weren't in the best of shape. She shook her head. "No, we'll stay the night."

2

Despite her assurances to Rastim that all would be well, Maskelle had sat up the rest of the night on watch. The priest of the Sare had kept his word. Nothing had disturbed the peace of the plain, or the serenity of the temple.

From the time Maskelle had been a young initiate she had been used to sleepless nights. The Year Rites could last for days, and once the Wheel of the Infinite was constructed it had to be guarded, until it could be dispersed into wind and water to strengthen the supports of the universe.

Now she sat on the wagon seat next to Old Mali, thinking of the upcoming Hundred Year Rite. The sky was overcast and a slight breeze stirred the thick vegetation on the edge of the jungle to either side of the wide road. The damp air clung to her skin and she felt badly in need of a bath. The universe didn't seem in any great need of support, but perhaps she wasn't as attuned to it as she used to be. She couldn't tell if the uneasiness she felt was inside or outside of herself. *You are getting old. Your soul wasn't so divided in your youth,* a nagging voice said. *Yes,* she told it ruefully, *much easier to do damage with a whole soul.*

This stretch of the Great Road, leading deeper into the well-occupied outskirts of Duvalpore, was fairly safe from bandits and they weren't alone on it. A large wagontrain of merchants was only a few hundred yards ahead of them, and single wagons or small groups of travellers had passed them several times throughout the morning. They were moving into the country where what had been brackish swamplands had been drained and brought back to life by freshwater canals to make the rice-growing land that supported the capital. Duvalpore was a city of water: canals, barays, moats, all necessary to support life during the dry season. It still surprised her how much she was looking forward to seeing it again.

Old Mali elbowed her in the side, and Maskelle said, "I know, I know. I saw him an hour ago." Of course, he was closer this time, standing next to the milestone near a stand of rain trees, looking up the road.

The swordsman had been pacing them all morning, just in the shadow of the jungle. He had stayed near their wagons all night, a silent companion to Maskelle's lonely vigil. He hadn't slept either, and he hadn't tried to approach her, though she felt reasonably certain he had been conscious of her presence. He had kept moving most of the night, perhaps to keep himself awake, making a wide circuit around their camp almost as if he was on watch too. Near dawn she had watched him strip and wash in the temple's baray, an act of irreverence that would have shocked the priests and which Maskelle regarded with wry amusement. Or maybe her reaction to it was what she found amusing. The Court would consider her past all that, but obviously her body still thought she was twenty.

Old Mali made a lewd noise and Maskelle became aware she was staring. She eyed the old woman sardonically. "Don't be disgusting. I'm a priestess, remember?" This sent Old Mali into such paroxysms of laughter Maskelle had to pound the old woman on the back before she choked.

The rain didn't return, except for a misting drizzle in the late morning, making Maskelle wonder how this luck was to be paid for later.

In the late afternoon the Great Road met the Great Canal, which it would parallel for the rest of the way into Duvalpore. The jungle gave way to a plantation of large-leafed breadfruit trees, papaya and banana, and a large outpost with two- and three-storied wooden buildings that went up to the bank of the canal and extended over it to the other side. Maskelle stood up on the wagon seat and shaded her eyes. There was a large passenger barge moored to the pilings and several smaller trading or fishing boats bobbed on the still-swollen waters. It wasn't as bad as the untamed upper river, but it still didn't look good, and many of the boats were obviously waiting until the water level dropped.

There were many signs of normal activity: boatmen lounging on the steps to the canal near the crates and barrels of offloaded cargo, boys and girls on the bridges under the outpost checking the fish traps, and a large group of colorfully dressed people sitting down to a meal on one of the balconies overhanging the water. The merchants' wagons that had been ahead of them all day had drawn up on the trampled ground near the outpost, and there were several light, fast-travelling wagons there also, including one bearing the symbol of the Imperial Mail.

Rastim jumped down from his wagon and came back to consult with her. "This looks all right, hey?" he said hopefully.

She hesitated. She had wanted to press on to the temple of Illsat Keo, which was within the city's outermost boundary, but it was a few more hours of travel at least. Over the years she had grown used to avoiding people; she had no intention of delivering any innocent bystanders to her curse, and she knew the Illsat Keo was safe from that. But the Ariaden needed to make their living, and to them this post would look far more like the beginning of civilization than the temple on the Sare. People and travellers meant possible audiences, and therefore money. If they pressed on, they might have to camp on the road.

As she was considering this, a wagon pulled by two steaming

oxen trundled out of a narrow track between the trees, loaded down with several happily shouting children, an aged farmer, and a large load of taro. She swore under her breath. She had forgotten how populated this area was. There was no avoiding people now; there would be small farms and larger plantations everywhere along the road. She nodded resignedly. "It'll do."

They drew the wagons up in a clear spot just far enough away not to encroach on the territory already staked out by the merchants, and Rastim and Firac went in to conduct negotiations. Maskelle tried to help Old Mali unharness the wagon, got cursed at for her pains, and left the old woman to it in disgust. She went to sit on one of the fallen logs above the water steps, not quite sure where this feeling of impatient distraction had come from.

A few of the boatmen came up to get her blessing on their keel-tokens and she gave it, since her blessing was still worth what it was worth, even though it wasn't currently sanctioned by the temples. The sky had lightened, but the canal water was a dull brown, the current fast-moving, and branches and other debris were catching in the fish traps and around the pilings. Something drew her eyes to an old barge pulled up on the bank of the canal for a repair to its aging hull. There was someone stretched out asleep on the flat roof of the cabin. Not exactly an unusual sight; there were plenty of boatmen doing the same on their beached craft or in the shelter of the pilings. Then she recognized him and she realized what she had been looking for.

He had disappeared earlier that day and she had admitted to none of the initial disappointment, growing irritation, and progressive worry she had felt throughout the afternoon. She shook her head at herself. Obviously he must have taken the direct way through the trees when the road curved, beating them here.

She wasn't sure where this sudden obsession had come from. He was just following them because they were going the same way and were indisposed to interfere with him; he had already discovered the perils of travelling alone.

Maskelle looked up, frowning, as Rastim and Firac came down the steps from the post and squelched across the muddy ground toward her. Rastim's face was stony and Firac was muttering angrily under his breath.

"I take it things didn't go well," Maskelle said as they approached.

"There's a problem," Firac said grimly.

"What?"

"We can't afford it." Rastim folded his arms, looking away at the river.

Maskelle gazed up at the Infinite, begging it for patience. None of the Ariaden had ever been this far into the center of the Empire before. The Temple of the Sare had probably charged next to nothing for the food and fodder they had used, and nothing at all to camp in its protection. The outpost must charge city prices. "You didn't offer them a show?"

"They don't want one," Rastim said stiffly. He had obviously been mortally offended.

"Not just that," Firac clarified, outraged. "They won't let us perform for the merchants or these others." He waved an arm around at the boatmen, now watching curiously, and the other travellers and traders in the compound. "The merchants' head driver already asked if we were performing tonight—"

"Oh, Ancestors above." Maskelle stood up. That was enough. Rastim looked startled, then aghast. She ignored him, going around to the front of the post and up the steps to the doorway, her irritation boiling over. Inside she found her way through rooms smelling strongly of fish, lit by smoky lamps or propped-open windows. Firac was all but cheering her on, but Rastim was at her elbow, worriedly muttering, "Your temper, your temper."

She found the factor in a long room that opened onto one of the balconies, sitting at a table, arguing with traders.

A Koshan nun wasn't an unusual sight, but the room fell silent when Maskelle entered. She went up to the table and slammed her staff down across the scattering of coins and papers. Everyone stared, gap-jawed with shock. Her eyes on the factor, she said, "Stand up."

He was a large man, his head half-shaved and the rest of his hair braided, his face plump and good-humored, a temperament belied by the steel in his eyes. He smiled placatingly, and said, "Now, Sister—"

"Revered," she corrected coldly. She had held the title once and was still due it by the rules of temple precedence.

He hesitated, calculating. She held his eyes. The calculation gave way to uneasiness, and he said, "Revered," and stood up. Several ranks in the temple were addressed that way, and none of them could be offended with impunity.

She said, "These people are players and can't afford your extortionate prices for shelter unless they can perform." Her voice sounded soft and very angry. "Is there any real reason they shouldn't?"

The factor spread his hands. "No, Revered, but if I let every band of beggars who said they were entertainers—"

That stung Rastim to speech before Maskelle could interrupt. "We're not beggars," he said heatedly, stepping forward. "We do Ariaden and classical kiradi theater. We've come all the way from Ariad and we haven't had a chance to perform since Sakili."

"It was a misunderstanding, Revered," one of the other men suggested worriedly.

"If the Revered wishes it, then they can perform," the factor said with a stiff smile.

Maskelle looked at all the anxious expressions and wondered what they were seeing. A heavy silence lay over the room, surely too heavy for a dispute like this. But that was her own conscience behind that thought; they couldn't know what she was. *Had been*, she reminded herself, *had been*. "The Revered wishes it," she said, and turned away.

*   *   *

Rastim and Firac's announcement that they had won the battle and would be able to perform was greeted less than enthusiastically by the rest of the troupe. Gardick swore at them and Therassa pretended to collapse in a dead faint.

Even Firac was hesitant when Rastim wanted to break out the scenery and do a full-scale Ariaden production, maybe *Conquest of the Inland Sea* or *Dawncallers*. Since they had no money to hire extra stagehands, this would have left everyone exhausted and in no condition to travel the next day. Maskelle was alarmed; it was more important that they reach the safety of Duvalpore soon than it was to rub their victory in the post factor's face. She wished she had realized that before starting the whole thing. But Rastim and Firac were voted down by the others and it was decided that they would do a kiradi comedy of manners, which could be read without scenery or costumes. Knowing Rastim, he would still try to work in a few puppets.

Maskelle would have thought a kiradi comedy a bit too sophisticated for this crowd, except that the merchants who were to be the primary audience turned out to be from Mahlindi.

The Mahlindi had nothing like theater in their native country and it had proved wildly popular with them when they encountered it in other lands. Maskelle had once seen a group of them sit for four hours enraptured by a Ventredi morality play performed in a language that none of them could understand. While they might know nothing of the subtle mores of kiradi noble society that the comedy was drawn from, they were certain to give it all their intelligent attention and appreciate most of the jokes.

The Mahlindi were even willing to pay in advance, a copper coin for every member of their party, including the hired wagon drivers and guards, whether they wanted to see the play or not. This enabled the Ariaden to afford fodder for the oxen and overpriced pork buns and rice for themselves. Old Mali saved them money by buying taro cheaply off the back of a farmer's wagon, and fled cackling from the factor's assistants when they came to shout at her for private trading in the post compound. But everyone was in a better humor after a hot meal and almost looking forward to the performance.

At twilight they lit torches around a flattened spot of ground between the merchants' wagons and theirs. The Mahlindi brought woven mats to protect their brightly patterned robes from the grass and proceeded to arrange themselves in orderly rows without having to be asked. There were only three chief merchants, identifiable by the clan markings on their cheeks and foreheads, but they had each brought at least a dozen apprentices and servants. Their guards and drivers arrived in a grumbling, reluctant group behind them.

Maskelle moved back out of the torchlight, back to the open area between the two wagon camps, where she could see the stage, the front of the outpost, the place on the bank where the boats were drawn up, and the road where it curved past the trees. She sat on the wet grass, feeling the damp seep up through her robes. The life and torchlight around the makeshift stage seemed like an isolated pocket in a night of wild darkness. The wind had risen again, tossing the tops of the trees and sending fast-moving clouds across the moon. The lights in the post were dimmed by shutters and the inhabitants had withdrawn from the balconies.

Rastim walked out to the center of the stage, made the odd Ariaden bow that was the same for everyone, whatever their rank, and the play began. Maskelle gave it only part of her attention; she was listening to the night. She had the growing feeling that it was trying to tell her something.

The Ariaden had been unable to resist including puppets, and Firac's sons Thae and Tirin appeared each with one of the big walking puppets. These were elaborate contraptions that fastened to the operator at the feet and waist, and could be manipulated with rods held in the operators' hands. The troupe owned larger ones that took two operators, one sitting on the other's shoulders, but these were relatively small and only towered a few feet over the boys' heads.

The appearance of the puppets, the light wooden bodies brightly painted and the distorted heads with their clacking jaws, brought the curious boatmen over. Drawn by the laughter and applause of the Mahlindi, a party of wealthier travellers, probably passengers from the barge that was weathering the bad currents, came down from the post. Most of these people had never seen the elaborate Ariaden puppets before and there was much whispered commentary in the crowd. Someone else was drawn by the noise as well.

Maskelle looked for him, and saw him finally just beyond the reach of the torches, sitting on the grass and watching. It gave her more information about him, though it was nothing that made any particular sense. She wasn't sure how a Sitanese outcast could have seen kiradi theater before, but he got the joke that even passed the Mahlindi by, the one that appeared to be an innocuous remark about idle hands and was actually a subtle innuendo implying masturbation, to the point where he actually fell over on his side with laughter.

A burst of applause made Maskelle glance at the stage. At first she thought the figure crossing in front of Therassa and Doria's scene was a child, escaped from some parent in the audience. It was a puppet.

"Great Days in the Dawn of Life," Maskelle swore, starting to her feet. *How did that damn thing get out?* She circled the crowd hastily, coming up on the wagon that formed the stage right entrance. She caught Rastim as he pelted into her and dragged him behind the wagon.

"I don't know," he whispered frantically, answering the question she hadn't had the chance to ask yet. "Thae and Tirin got the Aldosi out of their boxes, but they know better, they would never—"

"I know they wouldn't." Maskelle leaned around the wagon

to peer at the stage. The animate puppet was standing, staring out at the audience, the painted face expressionless. Therassa and Doria were still saying their lines, but they were casually putting distance between themselves and the puppet. The crowd still thought it was part of the show; to people unused to puppets, the one that was walking by itself was no more miraculous than the two that had been controlled by the young boys. Firac and Gardick were standing out of sight of the crowd near the wagon marking the opposite end of the stage; Firac was holding a net. Maskelle shook her head. That wasn't going to do much good.

All the Ariaden puppets had names: the Aldosi were the two big walking puppets Thae and Tirin were working. The one that was working itself had been Gisar, a clown puppet manipulated by strings pulled from above. Gisar had had the misfortune to be on stage during a performance that had offended a powerful magister in the eastern province of Corvalent. It was how Maskelle had first met Rastim and the other Ariaden.

Gisar now lived locked in a box hung beneath Rastim's wagon and sealed by all the protective symbols Maskelle knew to put on it. It had been getting stronger, the particular nature of the curse put on it making its malevolence grow with time instead of fade. It must have been able to manipulate one or both the boys from inside its box, so when they had thought they were only unpacking the Aldosi puppets, they had opened Gisar's container as well.

"You'll have to go and get it," Rastim whispered.

"I know that." It hadn't done anything yet, but possibly it was biding its time, waiting for her. Across the length of the stage she caught Firac's eye. When she had his attention, she stepped out away from the wagon.

"Wait," Rastim said urgently. He gestured rapidly to the others on stage. Ariaden actors had a sign language, used for communicating silently during the complex performances. Doria suddenly clapped her hands and gestured extravagantly stage left, saying something about the townspeople's dancing festival. Firac, Gardick, and Killia gamboled onto the stage, followed by the two boys with the Aldosi puppets. Firac whirled the net over his head, looking as much like an escaped madman as a celebratory dancer.

The puppet Gisar stared at them, backing away from the trap. Maskelle darted onto the stage in the confusion and it sensed her presence immediately, turning to come at her with its hands upraised and wooden fingers curved into claws. It ran at her, and she thumped it in the chest with her staff, sending the light body tumbling back. Firac dropped his net over it, and in another moment, Maskelle, Firac, and Gardick were dragging the creature offstage. The audience applauded happily.

Rastim and Old Mali ran around behind the other wagons to join them, and between the five of them they managed to drag the thing back to Rastim's wagon and bundle it back into its crate without drawing any unwelcome attention. Almost everyone in the post must be watching the play by now and assuming any odd activity to be connected with it.

Maskelle drew the seals again, in wax and in coalblack, trying to ignore the knocking and rustling inside the heavy box.

"How did it get out?" Gardick demanded, still breathing hard from the struggle. The puppet had managed to bite his hand and Old Mali was digging the splinters out for him.

The noises quieted as Maskelle made the final sign and she sat back on her heels. "See where the last seal was scrubbed off? It made someone do that and then made him forget what he did. With the unpacking you all were doing for the play, it could have been anyone. It's not such a hard thing, when someone's opening boxes, to make him open just one more."

"Not such a hard thing," Firac muttered uneasily. "Then why didn't it do it before?"

Maskelle glanced at Rastim's worried face. "It's getting stronger."

Gardick swore and Firac moaned. "But we're closer to Duvalpore and the chief priest," Rastim said quickly. "In a few days it'll all be over."

Gardick said grimly, "If we're still alive then. Ow!" The last was to Old Mali, who must have dug a bit deeper than strictly necessary for the last splinter.

"What we need," Maskelle said, cutting across the growing argument, "is a lock with a key. I'll keep the key."

"Use the one on the moneybox," Firac suggested. "There won't be much to steal, not after we pay our fees here."

Swearing under his breath, Rastim fetched the lock and Maskelle fixed it on the box's latch. Further discussion was put off by Doria and Therasa, repeating their last exchange at a shout so Firac and Gardick would hear their cues. Everyone bolted off and Maskelle followed more slowly, shaking her head. She would like to think that the puppet's escape was the source of her earlier disquiet, but she had the feeling it was only a portion of it and the greater part was still to come.

Maskelle went back to her position at the rear of the audience. She looked for her swordsman, but he was nowhere to be seen.

Near the end of the performance, when most of the Ariaden were on stage, something drew Maskelle's eyes to the bank below the outpost. The light from the lamps along the balconies didn't fall there and the shadows were deep. . . . *The light.* Maskelle sat up abruptly. There should be smaller lamps attached to the pilings, so a boat passing down the river during the night wouldn't be in danger of striking them. There had been lamps, the last time she had noticed.

She got to her feet, her knees cracking in protest at her long immobility, and made a wide circle around the audience, out of the torchlight. The boatmen were playing dice with the Mahlindi's guards and drivers in the very back, and none of them looked up as she passed.

It was very dark near the bank, the shadow of the outpost blocking what little moonlight escaped past the clouds. She only knew how near she was by the sound of the river and the mud squelching underfoot. She found the water steps that led down to the bridges under the post, crept down them to the first piling. She ran her hands around the rough splintered surface until she felt the cracked globe of the lamp; the glass was still warm.

So something came out of the river and put out the lamps, she thought, finding the steps again with her staff and climbing back up the bank. *But where is it now?*

The play had ended and the troupe were taking bows, the Mahlindi thumping their feet and shouting to show their appreciation. Maskelle moved away from the outpost as the crowd dispersed. She saw the factor's assistant gesture emphatically at the pilings, calling an order to someone, and others ran to relight the safety lamps.

Maskelle withdrew all the way to the edge of the trees where she had a view of the whole camp. There was a group around the factor's assistant now, pointing at each other and talking angrily; she took it that some blame was being passed around for allowing the lamps to go out. It would be nice to believe it was an accident or negligence, but she didn't think she was so lucky.

It was late and the camp quieted down rapidly. The Ariaden were the first to retire, cranking down the shutters on their wagons against insects and the threat of rain. The boatmen went back to their boats, and the Mahlindi and the other travellers gradually withdrew into their own wagons, the drivers wrapping up in blankets and stretching out on the seats or tailgates. The factor's guards were all stationed inside the post; the Mahlindi had sentries, but they were all watching the merchants' cargo wagons.

Maskelle paid special attention to a trader's wagon nearby. Before retiring he filled a lamp with oil from a large gourd which hung on the sideboard of his wagon. He had also banked his cooking fire badly. Water spirits could be driven off by fire, especially if they could be lured too far away from a source of running water.

A little time passed and the lights inside the outpost went out, one by one.

Sitting on the damp ground under a breadfruit tree, in the dark and quiet, Maskelle began to feel the night come alive around her. She felt the wind breathe through the heavy leaves above her, felt the impatient river water lap and tug at the pilings and the ropes, felt the weight of the wagons on the ground, the stamp of the oxen's feet. Felt that she wasn't alone.

He was about twenty feet from her, crouching at the base of a tree at the edge of the compound. *Hah,* she thought, easing silently to her feet.

She made it to within five feet of him before his head turned sharply. "Surprise," Maskelle said, a barely voiced whisper.

She had surprised her swordsman this time, she felt, and annoyed him too, though it was too dark to read his expression. He was sitting among the knobs at the base of an old cypress, the sheathed siri on the ground in front of him. This close to him she could still sense the scent of the Temple of the Sare on him, from when he had bathed in the sacred baray. He didn't say anything as she settled next to him, but after a moment he evidently decided not to hold it against her, and whispered, "It hasn't moved since it came out of the river."

Maskelle hadn't expected to see whatever spirit had come ashore during the play, at least not until it moved into the compound. "How long have you been watching it?"

She could feel him looking at her. "Since the middle of the play." Shifting to face forward again, he added, "I saw the lamps go out too."

She decided not to correct his impression that she had seen the lamps blown out and not belatedly noticed the absence of light. She scanned the bank, but still couldn't see where the damn thing was. Giving in, she said, "Where is it?"

There was a snort of exasperation and he leaned closer to her to point. "There, next to the boat with the broken hull, in the reeds," he said.

She squinted. She could see the beached boat, a narrow-hulled slip used for quick travel. There was a crack in the hull and it had been left abandoned in the reeds on the bank, far from the occupied boats. After a moment she was able to discern a shape crouching near the bow. She gave the man next to her a sideways look, impressed. She had known it was somewhere along the bank, but she would never have seen it on her own, not without the Adversary's help.

"What is it waiting for?" he asked, still watching her.

"Me," she said, and stood slowly.

As soon as she stretched her senses toward it, it moved. It stood too and came toward her up the bank. A large dark shape, at least the size of a big man and roughly human-shaped, but its form seemed to flow and shift with the shadows. Maskelle frowned, staring incredulously. Water spirits were small, the size of children. They were little, gray-green creatures, dangerous to sleeping people or animals, but easily frightened by fire.

The man beside her stood, his sheathed sword in one hand. "Magic would be helpful now," he suggested, eyeing the thing that stalked up the bank.

"I'm not a wizard, I'm a priestess," Maskelle said, not taking her eyes off the creature. *It's not a water spirit.* It was something new. *Ancestors, what a thought. After all this time, I'd have sworn I'd seen everything.* It was within thirty feet of them now and she hastily rearranged her plans. "Get it to follow you back through the trees."

"Fine." He sounded exasperated.

"It's not human," she cautioned him, as he started to move away.

There was a lamp hanging from a post at the top of the water steps, one of those the factor's assistant had relit. As the shape from the river drew near it, the light reflected off and through it, as though the creature was made of black glass. The flame winked out as the thing passed.

Her swordsman stopped long enough to say, "No, really?" before slipping away.

Maskelle moved back into the trees, watching his progress. He went down toward the river, coming at the creature from the side and slightly behind it. She saw him bend and scoop up something from the ground, then shy it at the creature's back.

Maskelle glanced upwards, appealing to the Infinite. *He threw a rock at it. Rastim could have done that.*

The creature didn't so much turn around as reverse its direction, moving with the smooth rapidity of rushing water, abruptly closing the distance between itself and the man. He dodged backward, made sure its attention was focused on him, then bolted for the trees.

Maskelle moved rapidly herself, tucking her staff back among the cypress knobs and running toward the compound. She went to the sloppy trader's wagon she had spotted earlier and found the large gourd tied to the sideboard. Sniffing it to make sure it contained lamp oil, she cut it free, slicing a finger in her haste and need for silence. Then she found a metal cup abandoned nearby and scooped up a quantity of coals from the banked fire.

When she came back around the wagons, she saw the creature had halted at the edge of the trees, but the swordsman stopped and threw another rock at it, and it couldn't resist the challenge. It flowed forward, losing some of its shape as it crossed the invisible boundary into the forest.

Very good, Maskelle thought. At least it behaved like a water spirit. Maybe it also scented the temple on the swordsman, just the way she had. She followed hurriedly as it moved further into the trees, wedging the gourd under her arm so she could work the cork out while still keeping hold of the cup, which was steadily burning her hand.

She caught up to them just as her swordsman turned at bay in a little clearing. The creature rushed for him, still eerily silent, and he ducked and dodged, turning and catching it with an upward stroke of the siri that would have disemboweled a man. The metal split the black surface with no discernible effect. *Rastim couldn't have done that,* Maskelle thought, impressed.

She crouched down, dumping gourd and cup on the ground,

knowing he couldn't keep that up for long. She tore her sleeve off and shoved it into the open neck of the gourd, then held the cup up to it. *This better work.*

She looked up in time to see her swordsman bowled over backward as the water creature rushed him. It towered over him, and she shouted, "Over here! You've got the wrong one!"

It hesitated for a breath then rushed back toward her.

She had time for the thought that it hadn't seemed to move this fast when it was after someone else. The rag caught when the creature was right on top of her and she slung the gourd into it, throwing the cup after it for good measure. The gourd dissolved when it passed through the creature's surface, the oil spreading out in a cloudy wave over it. She ducked an angry swipe from a limb, and for a moment she thought the oil hadn't had time to catch. Then fire swept up the surface and the creature tore away, thrashing and whirling.

Maskelle scrambled back. The creature was a cloudy mass of dark swirling vapor, fire running in glowing rivulets over its surface. It heaved and struggled, losing more of its shape every moment, until it burst and vanished in a spray of water.

Maskelle scrubbed the droplets off her face with her remaining sleeve. The water tasted muddy and foul, like the bottom of the river. Across the clearing, her swordsman rolled to his feet and came toward her. He stared at her, breathing hard, then said, "That wasn't enough heat to boil away all that water."

Maskelle sighed. She would have preferred to be admired for her cleverness instead of questioned for her lack of logic. Sucking on her cut finger, she said, "That was its own stupidity. It panicked and dissipated itself." She shook her head. "It shouldn't have followed you in here, it should have stayed out there and made me come after it. But there's not much brain mixed into all that water." *Thank the Ancestors for once.* "It wasn't an ordinary water spirit, so we're lucky this worked at all."

He looked down at the disappearing puddle, then knelt and

ran his hand over the grass curiously, cupping the water in his palm. "How does it kill people?"

"The little ones lay down on sleeping people and drown them. This one . . . could do just about anything it wanted, I think."

He glanced up at her, then shook the moisture off his hand.

Maskelle started to speak, but the words caught in her throat. The sense of alarm was urgent again, was more intense with every breath. *Idiot, this was a distraction.* "There's something else."

He stood. "Where?"

She was already running back toward the compound, crashing through brush and tripping over roots. She swung by the cypress to grab up her staff, then ran flat out across the open ground toward the Ariaden's camp. As she reached the edge of it, she heard the tailgate of a wagon creak.

As soon as she rounded the bulk of Firac's wagon, she saw it. There was a figure standing on the now open tailgate of her wagon.

She was too far away. The figure turned toward her, raised its hand. Then her swordsman tore around the back of Rastim's wagon, coming at the intruder from behind, catching it in a tackle and dragging it off the tailgate.

She reached them a moment later. Her swordsman was holding the furiously struggling figure face down. Maskelle moved around, trying to get a better look at the intruder as he twisted his head back and forth in the wet grass, choking with rage. And it was a "he" she saw, and not an "it." He was dressed in torn and dirty trousers like a fieldworker and he was wire-thin, the bones standing out in his outflung arms. There were no old rank designs on the scalp beneath the stringy dark hair, and there was no disguising the rough and calloused skin from long hours at outdoor labor. One of his outstretched hands was clutching a small silver-glass globe.

Maskelle's brows knit. "Bastard sons of pigs," she muttered.

The Ariaden, the Mahlindi, the boatmen, everyone inside the post, they all would have been killed. She could feel the power inside the glass straining to break free, even as the fieldworker strained to break free from his captor. She stepped close and caught a handful of the boy's greasy hair. He twisted away and spat at her, but she had already seen what she needed to see. The pupils of his eyes were as silver-grey as the surface of the globe, opaque and solid, not like human eyes at all.

Rastim tumbled out of his wagon and moved to stand beside her, scratching his head and looking down at their unwelcome visitor. Heads were peering out from the other wagons. She stepped back and said, "Kill him."

There was a shocked word of protest from someone and Rastim stared at her.

Maskelle ignored him, looking down at the man who had caught the boy, preventing him from breaking the globe and setting the curse loose on the compound. He hadn't bothered to draw the siri, which was sheathed again at his belt. He had his knees planted on the boy's shoulders, keeping him pinned to the ground.

The others were silent now, aghast or baffled. The boy hadn't reacted to Maskelle's words, though she had spoken in Kushorit, except to make the same gasping, snarling noises he had made since he had been caught. Of course, in *Teachings,* the philosopher Arabad had theorized that speech was impossible without a soul. *So the old fool was right about something,* Maskelle thought dryly. *I should write him a letter.* She said, "Whoever sent him here tied his soul to the curse in the globe. He's already dead, his body just doesn't realize it yet." It was an old magic, older than the temples, and a foul one.

Even though she had just told him to do it, the swiftness still surprised her. The snap of the boy's neck was audible. The swordsman stood, stepping casually away from the now limp body. She recalled that this was the third time he had surprised her, and according to all reputable authorities three was a highly significant number.

She sat on her heels and pried the globe out of the boy's hand, bending the dead fingers back to work it loose. She turned it over curiously. The glass was free of defect, the silver-grey pigment blended with it evenly. She knocked it against the wagon wheel.

The glass shattered and the contents spilled out on the grass. There was a general scramble among the Ariaden to move back. When nothing immediately disastrous happened, Rastim returned. "Dried snakes?" he asked, baffled. The globe had contained a bundle of what did appear to be small desiccated snakes, each no more than an inch or so long.

"Not snakes," Maskelle said. "Tela worms." The wisps that looked like dried skin were actually their wings. They swarmed like bees and their poison burned into the blood and made the body jerk and spasm. A few of them could kill a large man in minutes. It would have been an unlovely death for all of them. "If the globe had broken while he was still alive, his life would have fed theirs and they would have swarmed over everyone in the camp."

"Gah," Rastim said, or something like it.

Old Mali, ever practical, was approaching with a straw brush and a small shovel. Maskelle nodded for her to go ahead and the old woman swiftly scooped up all the dried worms. "The fire," Maskelle said. Old Mali gave her a disgusted look, but took the shovel to the cooking fire anyway and tipped its contents in.

Maskelle got to her feet again, unconsciously brushing her hands off on her robes. She turned and found herself eye to eye with the swordsman; they were exactly the same height.

He was watching her with an air of irony. He said, "The priests sent him to kill you because you're a wizard."

"The priests didn't send him," she said, mock patiently. "And 'wizard' is a barbarian word."

He cocked an eyebrow at her, then suddenly turned, drawing the siri, facing the open area beyond the wagon. Maskelle stepped back, but she heard the footsteps and shouts a moment later. "Damn it, that's the post guard," she said.

Rastim was at her elbow. "Hide the body?" he asked, worried.

Maskelle hesitated. The Ariaden didn't look like much of a match for an armed troop, but their profession made them quick-witted and used to moving swiftly in concert. Having seen them in action when the upper-level scenery had started to come apart during the climax of the performance of *Otranto* in Hisak City, she had no doubt of their ability to hide a fresh corpse from even a determined troop of guards. "Yes, hide the body."

Rastim whirled around and gestured quickly. Her swordsman hopped out of the way as Gardick, Vani, and Firac descended on the boy's body. They swept it away and into Rastim's wagon before the first of the guards came into view.

There were about ten of them, surrounding the wagons at a run. The Ariaden, who knew what part they had to play, milled around near the fire, looking as if nothing odd had happened.

One guard came forward and Maskelle went to meet him, leaning on her staff.

If he was the captain, he was surprisingly young. And he had intelligent eyes, not something she was glad to see. He said, "There was report of a disturbance here, Revered."

"Oh, you mean, the screaming and thrashing around? They were rehearsing their next theatrical, that's all," Maskelle said, smiling, gesturing casually back at the Ariaden, who were doing a good imitation of a disturbed henroost. A rehearsal in the middle of the night, after a grueling day's travel and a long play. At least it wasn't pouring down rain.

Not surprisingly, this explanation failed to satisfy. He eyed her a moment, then said, "Who is that?"

"What?" Maskelle glanced behind her and almost dropped her staff. She had fully expected the swordsman to disappear; he had had more than enough time. But he was standing a few paces behind her. He had, at least, sheathed the siri. "Oh, him." She looked back at the guard captain. "He's—"

Rastim materialized beside her. "We hired him to protect us on the road."

Maskelle bit her tongue and managed to retain her smile. She had been about to say that he was just another traveller in the compound, drawn by the commotion. She reminded herself to tell Rastim that she had been lying to authority before he was conceived.

The guard captain said, "Then you don't mind if we look around?"

"Not at all." Maskelle shrugged.

Rastim gestured expansively. "Go right ahead."

He turned and called to his men. "Search the wagons."

So that's how it is. Maskelle still kept her smile, despite the irrational urge to anger. She had planned for this, hadn't she?

The other guards moved forward. Maskelle turned back to the wagons and found herself facing her swordsman again. He was looking at the guards with an intent expression that she had previously seen only on cats waiting for unwise lizards to venture out of woodwork, and he had his hand on the hilt of the siri. She waited until he met her eyes, and said, "Don't draw that."

His expression said plainly that she was mad, but he took his hand off the swordhilt. Maskelle walked back to the fire, aware he was following her.

He stood a pace behind her and to the side when she stopped by the fire, and she recognized it as the position someone who was acting as her bodyguard would rightfully adopt. Maskelle had only managed to keep soul and body together for the past few years by staying one step ahead of everyone else, or at least convincing them that she was. He had been helping her since she had found him with the raiders, and he seemed to think she should know the reason why. Pride and years of conscious and unconscious deception kept her from simply turning to him now and asking. Maybe pride, and maybe the fear that if she asked him, he would leave. It was almost funny.

The post guards weren't all as diligent as their captain. Or as polite. Some of them were only desultorily poking around at the bundles and chests tied to the outside of the wagons, others were pushing their way inside. If that kept up, Maskelle was going to be very unamused.

One of the men was trying to enter Killia's wagon and she was blocking him, trying to explain about the sick child inside. He refused to listen, grabbing her arm to shove her out of the way. Maskelle strode across the camp. "Leave her alone," she said, giving him a prod with her staff.

The guard let go of Killia and stepped back, unhurt but startled.

"She's afraid and I've just got her back to sleep," Killia was explaining, exasperated. "They can look in if they just don't wake—"

It happened so quickly Maskelle didn't see it. She felt someone brush against her, and when she looked the guard was already on the ground, the bori club clattering off the wagon wheel. It was her swordsman who had pushed past her, who was standing with his back to her, between her and the guard who was now scrambling to his feet. The guard must have reached for her arm or, Ancestors help him, made to swing the club at her.

The other guards were drawing weapons. She thumped the swordsman in the back to warn him, and he ducked as she swung her staff up.

Unlike the river raiders, the post guards knew what that meant. They hesitated, and that gave the captain time to react. He ran between them, flinging up his arms and shouting, "Stop!"

She realized her arms were trembling, and not from the weight of the staff. Her heart was pounding and the anger a lump in her throat. *That was a little close,* she thought, sense returning. She lowered the staff. She said, "You've searched. Now go."

The captain shook his head, breathing hard. He said, "What's in that wagon?"

"A sick child," Killia said, standing up and slapping the dirt off her pantaloons. She was too good an actress to sound angry, but the blood had drained from her face. "I told him he could look. I just didn't want him to climb inside."

The matter was settled an instant later when a round, wan face peered over the top of the tailgate at them and whimpered.

"See?" Killia said, dropping the tailgate and lifting the little girl into her arms.

The captain sighed and waved his men away. Some of them had the grace to look foolish, though the one who had started the trouble was belligerent and reluctant to withdraw. The captain waited until he had walked away before he said, "Sorry, Revered. It was a mistake."

"It was almost a deadly mistake," Maskelle told him, thinking, *I'm not doing well at this so far. Haven't reached the city yet and I've almost broken my oath twice.*

He stared at her a moment, uncomprehending, then shook his head and followed his men. As the guards returned to the post, Rastim let out his breath. Maskelle asked softly, "Where is he?"

"Firac's wagon, in the lower bed."

"I thought they put him in yours."

"We did, but they were going to search it and we had to shift him."

She shook her head. She hadn't seen them do it, though she supposed they had taken advantage of the distraction. "We'll give him a farewell tomorrow, after we cross the dike." A funeral on the eve of entering the Temple City was not auspicious. She went back to the fire.

There was a very worried group of Ariaden gathered there.

All told, they were not a prepossessing lot, but then for the Ariaden theater that hardly mattered. Killia hovered near the tailgate of her wagon, a blanket wrapped around her, obviously not wanting to stray too far from her child.

From the expressions on their faces, the way they kept sneaking looks past her, the swordsman had followed her and was standing a few paces behind her again. She realized that was the third time he had moved to defend or protect her. And there was that number three again. The Infinite had been producing a large number of odd conjunctions lately. It could feel free to stop at any time, as far as she was concerned.

She said, "Well?"

Gardick, who always had something to say, said, "Can we expect more of that tonight?"

"No, not tonight."

There was an uncomfortable stirring. Firac, Doria, Vani, the others, familiar faces after all these months. They were nine in all, not very many to perform some of the more elaborate productions, but the Imperial capital of Duvalpore would appreciate the intricacy of Ariaden theater where the provincial cities hadn't. One or two wouldn't meet her eyes, others looked worried, others merely tired.

Rastim cleared his throat. "I think we all know what sad condition we would be in but for the . . . but for Maskelle."

She pushed her ragged hair back from her face, to cover her momentary smile. Her name still sounded odd, spoken in an Ariaden accent. More proof this land was in her blood; she had been foolish to ever leave.

Gardick said, "No one is saying different." He looked around at the others, his expression combative. "But we don't have to pretend to like it."

Maskelle laughed. Sometimes she liked Gardick.

Then Gardick said, "And who's that?"

He was pointing past her, at the swordsman. Maskelle pressed her lips together. And sometimes she didn't like Gardick at all.

Rastim saved her from the embarrassing admission that she had no idea by stepping forward and saying, "Now, that's Maskelle's business, isn't it? Why don't we all get some rest? We have more travel tomorrow."

That little speech should have occasioned a revolt, if not a small riot, but the troupe had become accustomed to accepting the impossible along with the unpleasant in the past few months, and all they did was stamp and grumble, or exchange tired looks and roll their eyes.

As the others drifted back to their wagons, Rastim leaned close and out of the side of his mouth whispered, "Who is he?"

"I don't know," she whispered back.

He grimaced at her and she grimaced back. She patted him on the back and made shooing motions. Rastim went reluctantly, casting doubtful glances over his shoulder.

She turned back to her swordsman. He was ignoring the curiosity of the Ariaden and matter-of-factly studying a long slice on his forearm. The bori club must have grazed him. *Well, you did tell him not to draw the sword.* "Come with me, I'll clean that up for you," Maskelle said. Old Mali had left a brazier near the fire and she used one of the wicker pads to pick it up.

He gave her an odd look, but followed her back to her wagon obediently enough. She climbed in and lit two of the hanging cage lamps with the coals from the brazier, then set it in the padded holder on the shelf. He was sitting on the tailgate, looking over the interior of the wagon. It was furnished with cast-offs and hand-me-downs and oddities collected in travel, frayed blankets and cushions of faded Tiengan weaving, a battered copper tea server, Nitaran puzzle boxes. He was looking up at the curved roof where about a dozen puppets hung, their painted faces pointing down like an audience of human-headed bats, their features lifelike in the dim light. They were being stored here because

Maskelle had few possessions and the other wagons were overfull. There were also pieces of scenery folded up in the chests and under the bunk. Maskelle moved a stage tree aside to get to the clean rags and salve.

"You're a healer too?" he said, somewhat warily.

"Not really." Old Mali had made the salve. Maskelle wasn't going to mention that in case he had seen the old woman outside. Old Mali's appearance didn't exactly engender confidence in her skills as a physician, and she knew the Sintane was fairly civilized for the outer reaches. She looked up and saw he was still sitting on the tailgate. She lifted a brow. "I could toss it to you."

He came further into the wagon, taking a place on the bench almost within arm's reach. But again she had no sense that he was afraid, just careful, like a strange cat that had chosen her for a companion.

She took his arm and wiped the blood away. He felt him react to the contact, just a slight start, perhaps because her hands were cold. His skin was very warm and she was more aware of the pulsebeat in his wrist than she should be. She noticed he was clean, or at least not more filthy than she was from long days of travel, then remembered the midnight swim in the baray. That didn't help her concentration any.

She was uncomfortably aware that the last time she had been this close to a man had been two months ago when she had helped hold Rastim's son down so Old Mali could lance his boil. Before that . . . Well, she wasn't going to add up the days, but it had been a long time.

He had said nothing, and under the pressure of that silence, she found herself saying, "What's your name?"

His eyes flicked up to meet hers. Green flecked with gold. "Rian."

Caught unprepared by his willingness to give up that information so readily, she stared at him and he grinned at her, obviously conscious of having surprised her. Again. Inwardly cursing her susceptibility, she said, "Is that all? No family, no clan?" If she was remembering rightly, the Sitanese took the name of their local lord for a family name.

He turned his head and she noticed his right earlobe had the marks of at least four piercings for ornaments; she knew the Sitanese denoted rank in their warrior caste with ear studs, but she didn't know what the number signified, if anything. He had laid the sheathed siri next to him on the bench. She had thought it without ornament, but this close she could see the ring and the hilt bore deep marks and gashes—not signs of use, but places where stones or figured metal had been removed. Had he sold everything valuable during his long journey, or carefully removed any mark of rank before he left? *Maybe both,* she thought. He was wearing an amulet around his neck, next to his skin. She knew it must be important to him, since he had sold or otherwise gotten rid of any other ornament. It was a small disk of fine white stone on a faded blue cord, inlaid with lapis in a runic figure. *That doesn't tell you much,* she thought in wry self-disgust. *Your education in the customs of lands outside the Empire might have been just a little better.* But then she had never expected to have to wander them. He said, "Things are less complicated in the Sintane."

"If the Sintane is so much better, why are you here?"

"I didn't say it was better, just less complicated."

When she released his arm the warmth of his skin seemed to cling to her fingers. She took a tana leaf from the wrapped bundle under the salve jar. He watched with a somewhat bemused expression as she worked the sweet-smelling salve into the leaf. "You don't want to know my name?" she asked.

"I know your name. You're Maskelle."

For an instant, she felt cold. "How do you know that?"

Instead of betraying any guilt, he gave her that look she was beginning to be accustomed to, the *what is wrong with your wits* look, and explained, mock patiently, "You answer to it when the others yell it at you."

"Oh." *Idiot,* she told herself. "The others are the Corriaden Travelling Grand Theatrical, from Ariad."

"But you're from Duvalpore."

"Yes." She took his arm again and laid the leaf along the cut, then bound it in place with a clean strip of cloth. She had to grit her teeth to hold back the impulse to explain that the tana had healing properties too; his opinion that she didn't know what she was doing was as palpable as the dampness in the air. It had to be intentional.

He looked at her staff. "What's a Voice of the Ancestors doing on the Great Road with a travelling Ariaden puppet show?"

"It's not a puppet show."

He looked up at the puppets suspended from the wagon's ceiling, one eyebrow lifted in eloquent comment. "It's not an ordinary puppet show," she explained, tying off the bandage and aware she sounded like a fool. And that they had somewhat strayed from the subject at hand.

She looked at him. He looked back, still with that same air of ironic comment. He wasn't afraid of her at all. Careful, but not afraid. That might be ignorance, but he had called her a wizard, and if she understood what the Sitanese meant by the word, then he should have been. "Why did you follow me? You were avoiding the road, weren't you? Why come to the Sare and risk the temple guards?"

As if she hadn't spoken, he said, "If it wasn't the priests that sent that boy, who was it?" Since she had left Duvalpore years ago, no one had spoken to her with this sort of directness. If they believed her guise as a travelling Koshan nun, they treated her with the difference due a religious under the protection of the Celestial Empire and the temples. If they knew who or what she really was, they were afraid. Even Rastim and Old Mali, her best friends among the Ariaden, never questioned her like this, possibly because they dreaded to hear the answers.

No one in years had told her she was wrong, or so much as inferred that her judgment was wanting. She found herself grinning. "It wasn't the priests. One of the most sacred duties of the Koshan is to serve the Voices. That's why the head priest of the Temple of the Sare offered me hospitality, though he knew what he was letting himself in for, from his own people and from the one who sent the boy."

He stared at her. She knew she had had the satisfaction of finally really startling him, though she wasn't sure how. He said, "Are you a nun?"

"Once. Not now." She adopted a bemused expression, though she hadn't much confidence in it.

"Are Voices celibate?"

"No." She had actually opened her mouth for an explanation of the Koshan Order and how the Voices were lifted above it when they were chosen, when he kissed her.

A persistent rapping at the side of the wagon interrupted them. Maskelle sat back from Rian and saw an eye peering cautiously at them through a gap in the partly closed flap. Rastim's voice said, "Excuse me."

Maskelle got up and tore the flap open. "What, what, what?"

Rastim stepped back, pointing across the compound. "The guards are still watching us," he whispered urgently.

She looked past the wagons toward the post and saw several of the guards at the bottom of the stairs, apparently in idle conversation. Stepping out onto the tailboard, she could see the flickering lights of small handlamps around the compound between the Mahlindi's wagons and theirs and also at the edge of the trees and up at the road. Rian leaned on the gate beside her and pointed out, "They would have to be moon-crazy not to watch us."

"That's true," Maskelle said, trying not to be distracted by the warm presence next to her thigh. "They'll keep anything else from coming into the camp tonight, Rastim."

"I did realize that, thank you both very much," Rastim said through gritted teeth. "But there's something else."

Damn Ariaden anyway, Maskelle thought, resting her forehead against the rough wood. "Just tell me, Rastim, really."

Rastim cast a worried look at Rian, then lowered his voice and said, "It's knocking."

"What's . . ." Maskelle frowned. "Oh. It." Of course it was knocking. The damn thing had an instinct for when to cause trouble.

"I'm afraid they'll hear it," Rastim elaborated.

"Yes, I've got the idea now."

Rian looked from one to the other. "Hear what?"

She let out her breath. "All right. Let's go do something about it."

Rian jumped down from the wagon behind her and followed them over to Rastim's wagon. Within a few steps, Maskelle heard the knocking. If it got any louder, the post guards would hear it, too.

Firac and Therassa stood near the box where it hung beneath the wagon. Maskelle folded her arms and contemplated it with annoyance. The knocking was slow and paced evenly, with a funereal quality. She glanced at Rian, who stood at her shoulder. She wasn't sure if he had seen its performance during the play or if he had already left to stalk the river creature by that point. She said, "It's a puppet."

Rian frowned at the box, then looked at her again. "It's moving."

"Well, they don't in the normal course of things, that's true," Rastim said, sighing in resignation and scratching his head. "It's . . ."

"Under a curse," Maskelle finished, knowing how long it could take Rastim to get to the point. Some of the provincials the Ariaden performed for had seen so little of puppets they hadn't yet grasped the fact that the wooden constructions needed a human actor to move; she had thought the Sintane would be among them, but evidently Rian knew better. "We need to shut it up." The knocking was getting louder already.

"We could wrap blankets around it . . ." Therassa suggested. "Or bang the drums, that would cover the noise."

"And wake everyone? Again?" Rastim asked. "The traders would kill us—and who could blame them?"

"Maskelle, can't you do something?" Firac asked, worried.

"The puppet that walked out by itself during the play?" Rian persisted.

"Yes." Maskelle rubbed her forehead. If she used her power, it would just draw more unwelcome attention from the spirits of the river and the jungle, and there was too strong a chance of other attacks tonight as it was.

Rian folded his arms. "If you tell me why it's cursed, I'll tell you how to stop the knocking."

They all stared at him. Maskelle raised a brow and looked at Rastim, who shrugged doubtfully. It was obvious he didn't think Rian could fulfill the bargain. She said, "They were performing in Corvalent and had heard stories of a man called Magister Acavir their whole way through the province. He had a reputation as a penurious tyrant."

Rian looked at Rastim, who muttered, "I thought it was just a myth."

"The Ariaden treat their rulers with less deference and it's very common to make fun of them at public plays and festivals. A sense of humor is considered very important in any high official. So one night, to please a balky audience, they substituted the name Magister Acavir for some bumbling court official in one of their Ariaden plays. It worked, the audience did love it. And guess who was there in the very town they were performing in."

There was some feet shuffling and Therassa sighed. "The knocking?" Rastim prompted.

Rian shook his head, as if reconsidering his association with them. "Put the box underwater. It'll muffle the noise."

Maskelle rubbed the bridge of her nose. *Good. Now I feel like a fool, too.* Rian didn't realize the full efficacy of his suggestion. Water wouldn't only muffle the sound, it would provide a barrier that the curse's power couldn't penetrate. "Not the river." Running water would be best, but she didn't want to see Magister Acavir's curse and the river in its current state brought together, and they needed to be able to move quickly. Stagnant water would eventually lose its power to seal the curse in, but it would buy time to get away from the post before the creature thought of a way to bring the guards down on them. "If we unloaded one of the bigger puppet's boxes, and filled it with water, we could put Gisar's box inside it." All the puppet boxes were proofed with tar and lined with padded silk to keep water out; they should keep water in just as well.

Unpacking one of the larger puppets and hauling out its box presented no problem, but filling it with water and lowering Gisar's box into it was problematic, or at least the Ariaden thought so. The water trough allotted to their camp was about twenty yards past their wagons, in the direction of the post. The oxen had been watered earlier and were hobbled nearby.

Rastim and Gardick carried the large box over to the trough and filled it. The others brought Gisar's box, singing to cover the increasingly frantic knocking inside, Firac banging on the lid in apparently impromptu accompaniment.

Maskelle stood in the shadow of Rastim's wagon, shaking her head. If the post guards thought the inhabitants of the Ariaden camp more than a little deranged, now they had ample proof to support their opinions. Rian leaned against the sideboard next to her. "They're overdoing it just a little," he commented. It was too dark to read his expression, but the sardonic note in his voice said everything.

"They always overdo things. It has something to do with being actors."

"Why are you with them?"

She glanced sideways at him. "I met them in Corvalent."

Firac and Killia pretended to stagger, and Gisar's box tipped into the larger box, splashing Rastim and the others. The guards, watching from the steps of the post, didn't react except to exchange glances. *Probably struck dumb with amazement,* Maskelle thought.

"The performance that Magister Acavir objected to?" Rian asked.

"Yes. I was in the audience too." Acavir hadn't wanted to listen to reason and Maskelle had had to frighten him a little to discourage him from violence. Another small violation of her oath. Perhaps the Ancestors would consider it small, as well. And perhaps it had escaped the Ancestors' notice how much she had enjoyed it. *Not likely.* Rian was still looking at her. "He wanted to kill them. The curse was a compromise."

The Ariaden were carrying the large box back to the wagons slowly, ready to burst into song if the knocking was still audible, but the water muffled the noise admirably. Maskelle knew they would have a needlessly elaborate story to explain their actions if anyone asked. She glanced briefly upward in wordless appeal to the Ancestors. *Who are probably laughing themselves sick,* she thought. "They've made too much out of this since it happened. You'd think a cursed puppet was the end of the world." She needed to stop trying to think of a way to lure Rian back into her wagon and focus on the present situation. The continued interest of the post guards was a problem, considering the activity of Gisar the puppet. Putting it in the second box was a good stop-gap measure, but it would only work until the creature thought of something else.

"Why are they going to Duvalpore?" Rian asked.

"To get the curse on the puppet removed." She watched him carefully, and added, "I'm going to Duvalpore because the Celestial One asked me to."

Rian shifted against the wagon. "And you thought no one would look for you in a troupe of play actors."

"No one did, not all the way from Corvalent, and I had had a great deal of trouble before then." She let out her breath. The dark spirits that hunted her had been confused by the presence of so many other living beings around her; they had been long used to her travelling alone, and it had taken them until now to find her again. She added, "So I'm dragging them along with me for their own good and mine, whether they like it or not."

Rian said nothing for a moment, then, "Why don't you use your magic?"

Maskelle smiled to herself. The night was turning wild, the wind was up, and the river still rushed through the pylons supporting the post. She said, "It's not mine to use," and walked away.

4

Rian watched Maskelle walk back toward the fire. He had had a long journey, made longer by the fact that he didn't know where it would end. Travelling through the lowland jungles had meant unfamiliar and dangerous animals, raiders, poisonous plants, and strange people with inexplicable customs. He had been hunted by the savages that lived in the deep jungle, chased by the ten-foot tall flightless gankbirds that populated the hills, and then lately drowned in the near constant rain, which had driven him to the point where he would have been ready to sell his body for dry clothes, if only someone had given him the opportunity. The journey had almost ended on the river fighting those motherless drunken raiders and cursing his own stupidity. Instead he had found a woman worth following.

She was also a woman who thought a curse that could make a thing of painted wood stand up and walk was a minor annoyance. He had seen what the priest-shamans of the Sintane were like. But she had saved his life, and it wasn't as if he had anything to lose. *Nothing matters, remember? You gave up your honor,* he reminded himself. At least she could have the courtesy just to admit that she was a powerful wizard, but from what he had seen of the Kushorit and their Koshan priests since crossing the Empire's boundary, they were none of them entirely sensible people.

The leader of the Ariaden had come back from disposing of the puppet's box and now stood staring at Rian, his expression a grim glare. Considering that he was nearly a full two feet shorter, Rian didn't find it a particularly daunting sight. Rastim said, "I don't know who you are, but you watch your step. She's an important lady in the Celestial Empire. A powerful lady."

Rian shook his head and looked away to conceal his grin. *No, really?* When the obvious eluded him to that extent, he would lay down in a hole and the little actor would be welcome to cover him up. "What's the Adversary, and how is it different from a Voice of the Ancestors?" He had been hearing people swear by the Adversary most of the way through Gidale Province and more and more since he had crossed the border into the Empire proper, but he had never heard what it was or that it had a voice. Rian had learned Kushorit back in Riverwait, to speak to the provincial traders who travelled across the Sintane to the mountain caravan trails, and who often brought important news of what the other Sitanese Holder Lords were up to. He knew enough of the language for everyday conversations, but had never learned the subtleties, and he had been unable to tell if the people were afraid of the Adversary, or worshipped it, or both.

Rastim looked cautious, as if the question held a hidden trap. "What are you talking about?"

"You heard me. To the priests at the big temple, she said she used to be the Voice of the Adversary. What did she mean?"

The Ariad's face went still and sincere, by which Rian took to mean that he was about to hear a very big lie. He wasn't disappointed. Rastim glanced around, as if checking for hidden watchers, as if the rest of the Ariad weren't staring curiously at them from across the little circle of wagons, and said in a whisper, "The Adversary's a demon, the demon of all demons."

Rian folded his arms and looked bored, because he knew that would annoy the little man more than anything else. "That's pig shit. The Koshans don't believe in demons. We know that even in the Sintane, play actor." Nobody was really sure what the Koshan religion was, but they knew what it wasn't, and it didn't have anything to do with the grubby cult of demon worship that had spread in some of the outer provinces, with its curses and witching dolls and trading blood for supernatural favors. The odd thing was the Koshan temples in the provinces hadn't tried to stamp it out, the way the Dial priests had. The Koshans had simply treated it with a supreme indifference that was more damning than any attack.

Rastim glared. "All right, all right. It's some Koshan thing, like some spirit of bad luck and vengeance, or something."

"Bad luck?" Rian sounded skeptical, though he thought Rastim might be telling the truth now, at least as he saw it.

"Bad luck and bad things that happen, something like that. And taking revenge on people. And justice. If it was part of any sensible religion, they would call it a demon. They all get together and draw lots for who has to be its Voice. A symbol for it is carved into the base of every doorway of every temple, to scare other demons away."

The last part sounded inexplicable and Koshan enough to be true, at least. Rian drew breath to pursue the question, but from across the camp Maskelle said, "Rastim, we can't stay here."

She was standing by the banked fire, her arms folded, staring off into the night. Rastim muttered, "I was afraid of that," and went to her.

Impatiently she pushed her dark hair back from her face and in the glow of the firelight Rian could see the loops and whorls of the Koshan tattoo, just at the edge of her hairline. She said, "We have to push on to Illsat Keo tonight, or we'll just have more trouble."

Rastim shook his head. "What good will that do? It will be just as bad there as here."

"Not there. Illsat Keo is a Temple of the Adversary."

"Oh." Rastim said, shifting uncertainly. Rian noted that he

didn't look quite so unconcerned about the Adversary as he had implied before. Maybe the Ariaden believed more of that demon story than he had thought.

Maskelle was looking up at the cloud-heavy sky. "When we get up on the road, move the body to my wagon."

Grumbling, but not too loudly, the Ariaden made ready to leave. They were so afraid of the cursed puppet Rian knew it must have done much worse than walk out during plays or knock on its box. Rastim seemed to be the only one nervous of the prospect of visiting a Temple of the Adversary; but then the others seemed to know little of the Koshans. Not that Rian knew much of them either.

Until crossing the river he had avoided even the small villages, in case the hunters the Holder Lord's Heir had sent dared to trespass so far on Imperial territory. One night not long after he had crossed the border he had stumbled on what seemed to be a small abandoned shrine, and driven by pouring rain and exhaustion, he had spent the night on the stone flags under the dome, looked down on by the hundreds of faces carved into the walls. In the morning he had realized what he had been too dazed to notice the night before: the shrine had been empty but clean swept, undisturbed by animal droppings or even blown leaves and dust, and he knew it wasn't abandoned. He had fled, not wanting to be seen by even some lonely Koshan monk-caretaker.

As Rian helped harness the oxen, he watched the post guards watching them. The factor came out on a balcony, wrapped in a sleeping robe and a disgruntled air, but no one attempted to interfere with them. Either the post guards weren't inclined to pursue a problem that seemed to be leaving of its own accord, or the factor wasn't anxious for another confrontation with Maskelle. From the gossip Rian had heard from the boatmen, everyone who worked in the compound agreed that she had gotten the better of him in the first one.

Once clear of the compound, Maskelle's wagon took the lead

with Old Mali at the reins. It was so dark up on the road that even though each wagon had a lantern hanging from the box, the Ariaden called Firac still had to walk ahead with another lamp. The breeze had died and there was an odd kind of suspended silence in the night that Rian didn't particularly like. The cool air was still heavy with water, but the rain hadn't returned, and without it the jungle at the edge of the road was almost too quiet. It wasn't true jungle; Rian knew there were farms and little villages all through here, and the belts of trees concealed cultivated fields, but for all that they could be in the middle of wild nowhere.

He walked back down the road a short distance past the reach of the lamplight and then returned to stand beside Maskelle, who was leaning on her staff and watching the wagons crawl by from the muddy verge. "They're not following us," Rian said, not that he was much reassured by it.

"But something else might be?" Maskelle asked, watching him.

He shrugged, feeling he was being tested. Maybe she wanted to know how much of the night's ambient tension he could sense. "It just feels wrong, like something's breathing down my neck."

She smiled pityingly. "The Infinite touches everyone," she said, but her tone was more self-mocking than anything else.

"Tell it to keep its hands to itself," Rian suggested, and went to check the other side of the road.

Maskelle went up to ride on her wagon next to Old Mali and Rian walked beside it. They kept moving at the same slow pace, seeing no one else on the road. Rian still felt they were being followed, though he knew there were no wagons or horses on the road behind them, not for several hundred yards at least. He had spent most of his early life either hunting or being hunted by raiding parties of the nomad tribes in the mountains above Tarkat. His instincts told him something was stalking them, and if it wasn't the post guards sent by the vengeful factor, then it was something worse, from the river. In the dark he could see

Maskelle's head that kept turning toward the dark belt of trees, which didn't help either.

The time passed and they travelled quietly; only the occasional snuffling of an ox or a sleepy murmur from one of the other wagons disturbed the peace. After a time, Maskelle climbed down from the wagon and walked along the roadside next to Rian, the glow of the lamp tied to the wagonboard lighting their way. She muttered, "If it has any wits at all, it has to know we're making for the city boundary and Illsat Keo."

Rian assumed "it" was another water demon, following them along the river's course. If it was something worse, he wasn't going to ask. "If it could stop us and it doesn't, there's got to be a reason for it," he said, thinking of an ambush somewhere ahead in the dark.

"So say it doesn't want to stop us." She halted on the muddy bank and leaned on her staff, thoughtful. The wagon with the lamp pulled ahead and Rian couldn't read her expression in the dark. Sounding frustrated, she said, "I can't tell if it's self-aware and following us out of some intelligent motive, or if it's just a remnant of what attacked us before, tied to the boy's body and trailing it. Or if it's both."

"When are you going to get rid of the body?" Rian asked her. The corpse had been rolled in an old blanket and placed in one of the canvas slings that hung underneath the wagon, which were used to haul fodder for the oxen.

"When we pass the dike that crosses the road and marks the outer boundary of the city. It's not far now; we've already passed the first of the Passage Markers." These were waist-high square stones carved with protective symbols that stood on either side of the road at intervals of twenty-one feet, and would apparently continue all the way to the city. Rian had seen them on the roads that led to the smaller shrines and temples; they were another one of those things Koshans thought necessary.

"Does it make such a difference whether we dump the body

inside the boundary or outside it?" Rian knew little about magic and less about religion, but he had been here long enough to know that the Kushorit never put anything anywhere, not a road, not a water trough, and probably not a pig sty, without a reason involving spirits and the Infinite.

She nodded slowly, looking off into the dark.

Rastim's wagon drew even with them, and he peered down from the seat. "What is it?" he asked.

"I almost made a mistake," Maskelle told him.

An hour later the road began to rise and Rian knew they must be nearing the dike. In country that flooded during the rainy season, the city would need massive dikes as well as canals to control the water. Maskelle was riding on the driver's bench of her own wagon, and when the upward slope became more dramatic, she tapped Old Mali on the shoulder. The old woman guided the oxen to the side of the road without a word and Rian waited beside it. The other wagons rolled slowly past them, the sleepy faces of the Ariaden peering curiously out; only Rastim knew what they meant to do.

When the last wagon passed, Rastim reined in and said worriedly, "Are you sure about this?" He tipped his head toward Rian significantly. Rian glanced upwards in annoyance.

"Yes, yes," Maskelle said impatiently, shooing a grumbling Old Mali across the muddy road to Rastim's wagon and glancing over her shoulder back toward the river, as if she could feel something watching them from that direction. "Just hurry and go."

Old Mali climbed up onto the bench and settled herself with a gusty sigh. Reluctantly, Rastim pulled a battered shovel out from under the bench and tossed it down to Rian, then he shook the reins and the wagon rolled on.

Rian moved ahead, finding a good spot at the side of the road. Maskelle cut the ties holding the sling to the underside of the wagon bed as he started to dig. Rian had pointed out that burying the sling with the corpse was a waste, but apparently once it had been in contact with the curse living in the boy's remains, it couldn't be used to carry food anymore, even food for animals.

As Maskelle came back toward him, she froze suddenly. Rian dropped the shovel and reached for his siri, but she wasn't looking toward the jungle. She stood with her head tilted a little, as if listening intently to the undercurrents in the night.

When she shook herself and moved forward again, Rian picked up the shovel again. He felt obligated to point out, "This is still a stupid way to get rid of a corpse. When it rains again, which will probably be in the next hour, it'll wash right out of this bank."

"We're not hiding it from the Imperial Constabulary," she told him impatiently, "we're laying a curse." She helped him dig, scraping the muddy dirt out with her hands. The night was very dark with just the one lantern, and Rian could almost feel the stalking presence buried in the jungle himself.

"Wouldn't it be better to dump the body into the canal?" Rian said, but he didn't stop digging.

"This body is still cursed. If we dump it in the canal, something else will inhabit it."

Rian grunted, acknowledging that that was a good enough reason. "But burying it is different?"

"Farmers in the outer reaches bury their dead this way, giving the body to the earth spirits after the soul is fled to the Infinite. This boy's soul was long gone before his body stopped living, and this just might protect it from being used again." She stopped to look around at the surface of the muddy roadway briefly, as if expecting to see something appear on it. "Earth spirits usually accept the offerings gradually, over time, but then the ritual is usually performed by laymen and not consecrated Voices."

"So it's better to bury him," Rian muttered, trying not to think about demons living in the dirt under his feet. *If I learn any more about the Koshan view of the world, I'm going to be afraid to touch anything, water, dirt, trees.* They kept digging, Maskelle reminding him, "It doesn't have to be deep, just enough that we can cover him completely." Rian nodded; he could hear branches and palms thrashing somewhere in the brush and thought, *It's close.*

Finally, Maskelle said, "All right, that should do it," and sat back on her heels, breathing hard.

Rian tossed the shovel aside and ran for the body, dragging it in the sling back toward the hole. Maskelle helped him bundle it in. He grabbed the shovel again, but she held up a hand. "Not yet."

He hesitated, glancing toward the trees and the heavy brush. The thrashing was closer, as the intruder in the jungle fought its way toward them. What it was fighting, he had no idea, except that it was obviously fighting something. Rian dropped the shovel and drew his sword, putting himself between Maskelle and the edge of the trees. Whatever she was going to do, he didn't want it interrupted. "What else is out there?"

"The trees, the rocks, the moss, the birds, everything in the jungle. The spirits that live there resist the intrusion." Maskelle spoke hurriedly, clawing through the pile of dirt. She had dropped her staff beside the pit, and in their haste they had buried it.

Maskelle uncovered the staff and scrambled to her feet. Rian could hear her whispering something, not in Kushorit, but some language that sounded very like it.

The thrashing came to the very edge of the brush, just within the deep shadow. Rian tensed and one of the oxen lowed in alarm. But the noise abruptly ceased. The ground grew warm, a heat Rian could feel through his worn boots. He risked a glance over his shoulder and saw a low ground mist creeping over the open pit. It was swirling around his feet. He swore under his breath, tried to ignore the prickle of unease crawling up his spine, and faced the dark trees again.

The smell of rot came up from the pit, heavy and sickly sweet in the damp air. Maskelle stepped back from it. "Now we can cover him up."

Rian watched the edge of the trees, wary for a trick. "It won't try something else?"

She shrugged, looking around for the shovel. "It might. I've never seen a dark water spirit so strong before. Whatever cursed the boy's body must have done something to it." She paused and added, "But for now it's going back to the river."

Rian waited another moment then shook his head, sheathed the siri, and took the shovel away from her. It didn't take long to cover the pit, and soon they had the wagon moving again.

Illsat Keo wasn't visible from the road, but Maskelle had described the marker at the head of the track that led to it to Rastim and all he and the others had to do was follow the short trail through the trees to the temple's gate. When she and Rian reached the marker, she could tell they had been here by the deep ruts in the mud, which told a story of a wagon wheel sunk deep and freed by hard labor. "Looks like they made it all right," she said, then noticed Rian was looking up at the marker post.

It was a round pillar, the stone stained by moss and wrapped about by a few vines. At the top was a carved image of a gashwing, the largest of the flighted birds in the central lands and a carrion-eater. The gashwing was one of the Adversary's incarnations and a common symbol for it. She said, "Let's go," wondering if Rian would comment, but he said nothing, just guided the wagon off the road, turning it to avoid the spot where the Ariaden's wheel had come to grief.

The clouds had cleared enough that the moon was visible, making it easier to drive the wagon. It was a short track through the jungle and soon the lamps on either side of the temple gate were visible. The wall around the temple compound was so low a tall man could easily see over it. There were three small shrines inside, the tallest of their delicate towers barely thirty-three feet high. There was also a library and quarters for the handful of monks and nuns who lived here, a low series of buildings on the opposite side of the compound from the shrines. The Ariaden's wagons were drawn up outside next to the low wall, near the stone-paved edge of the little canal that watered the temple. There was no room for wagons inside, but they wouldn't have fit through the narrow gate, anyway.

There were more lamps burning inside the compound, and as Rian drew their wagon up to the others, Maskelle swung down from the box. A blue-robed nun was coming out of the gates, carrying a handlamp. She lifted the lamp, revealing a wrinkled face and the faded designs of her rank on her shaven skull. She said, "Ah, Sister, your friends said to expect you. We haven't much hospitality to share, as most travellers don't stop here, but we welcome the company—"

Maskelle held the hair back from her face in a lank tangled handful, and said, "Barime, it's me."

The older woman stopped, staring, screwing up her eyes to see, as if she had to read the remains of Maskelle's rank design, barely visible at the edge of her hairline. "My child, it is you," she said finally. She put the lamp down with a shaky hand and came forward to embrace her.

Maskelle managed not to hug her too hard, feeling her eyes prick with foolish tears and annoyed at herself for it; the old woman felt as light and fragile as a dry wisp of grass. She said, "I had to come here, Barime. It wasn't safe on the road." She laughed, though it wasn't funny. "Do you think He'll mind?"

Barime drew back, smiling and shaking her head. "If He does, that would be Answering us at least, one way or the other." Rian was unharnessing the oxen and she waved at him, the gesture taking in the others already in the compound. "Your companions are all most welcome."

Old Mali appeared in the gates and hurried toward them, taking the lead oxen and the harness away from Rian and batting at him when he tried to help her. Barime took Maskelle's hand and led her to the temple.

The compound was awash in light, the stone lamps set on the pillars and the edges of the shrines' platforms all lit now, revealing the pinkish gray tint of the stone and chasing shadows through the filigree of carvings. Parrots and tigers and female figures wove through the three-tiered pediments and the heavy decoration around the doors. A group of seated figures that managed to combine the grotesque with the whimsical—men with the heads of monkeys, another one of the Adversary's incarnations—guarded the small open court in the center, life-sized and lifelike in the flicker of flame. On the packed dirt of the open space in front of the monastic quarters, Firac was giving an impromptu demonstration of Ariaden theater with one of the small string puppets, a curious group of monks and nuns gathered around him. Maskelle saw with relief that most of them were too young to remember her. They didn't look at all upset at having their rest disturbed, but then Koshans were used to going without sleep when the rites required it. Killia was sitting on one of the low walls, her daughter in her lap. The little girl looked much improved, and curious about the men and women with their shaven heads and colorful tattoos and vivid blue robes.

"You're tired," Barime said, looking up at her. "There's time to talk in the morning." She looked at the group around Firac. "I'll send them back to bed. It's not often we get visitors, and never foreigners with such interesting toys. Will you take vigil in the shrine?"

"Yes." Maskelle sighed. "For all the good it will do."

Barime embraced her again and went to chase the others back into their quarters. Rastim came up to her, his face drawn from exhaustion but his expression holding nothing but relief. "It went well, then, getting rid of the you-know-what?" he asked.

"Yes, it went fine." She saw Rastim glance suspiciously at Rian, who was standing a short distance away and looking around at the compound. She said, "You're wrong about him, you know. He doesn't mean me any harm."

Rastim gave her a doubtful look, but said, "Maybe so." The temple's inhabitants were retiring to their quarters, the Ariaden straggling back out to the wagons. He added, "You were right, we should have come here and not stopped at the post. Gisar stopped his knocking as soon as we got past that bird thing out on the road."

"Was it your wagon that was stuck?" she asked.

"Yes, why?"

"No reason." She was glad she had sent them on. If Gisar had had enough power outside his box to trap the wagon wheel in the mud, then they had gotten here none too soon. But Gisar was only a minor creature and would have no wish to draw the attention of the Adversary. "We'll be in the city tomorrow. You should get some sleep."

"So should you. You look tired to death." Rastim patted her shoulder and followed the others.

"Thank you," she called after him. *I didn't need that.* Not that there was really time to do more than nap; it couldn't be more than two hours until dawn.

Barime returned as the Ariaden went back to their wagons. She said, "It was time you were back. I'm only glad that I was here to see it." She gave Maskelle the full bow that was due her rank, then turned to Rian and gave him the courtesy bow due to honored strangers. Rian seemed startled at having his presence acknowledged, but managed to return the gesture.

Barime embraced Maskelle again and then went back to the temple living quarters. Rian stepped up beside Maskelle, watching Barime leave, and asked, "Can all the Koshans do magic?"

She rubbed the back of her neck and let out her breath. "Yes and no. The closer you come to a full understanding of the Infinite, the more your ability to manipulate the spirits of earth, water, and air increases." She leaned on her staff, looking up at the temple platform. The lamps had been left lit for courtesy to the visitors and the three shrines looked larger without the people to lend perspective. "And the less your need becomes to use that ability." She shook her head. "It has nothing to do with rank. There are monks and nuns, living as hermits in the deep jungle, who are more powerful than the Priest of the Sare or any of the higher ranks."

Rian regarded her, suspicion in those green-gold eyes. "So Koshans don't use their magic."

"Not the way you think of it, no."

"Except you."

"Except the Voice of the Adversary." Maskelle went up the steps to the central shrine, past the guardian monkey men, and stood in the open doorway. The interior was dark, the intricate carving of the Adversary's various incarnations lost to shadow.

It was not very spacious or lavish, but no Koshan temples were. The sizes and shapes of the buildings were important, the heights of the towers and the doors, the curves in the carving, the number of paving stones in the floor, that invoked the spirits of the Infinite, not what was inside. This one was empty except for the niches in the walls for offerings of fruit and flowers, brought by the villagers and farmers in the surrounding country-side. It smelled of damp stone and must and the moss that grew on everything during the rainy season despite the constant efforts to scrub it off.

Rian was standing at the bottom of the steps. Patiently, as if prepared to wait all night. For someone who could be as sarcastic as he was, it was a little surprising. She leaned in the doorway, the rough stone cool against her back, and said, "What were you in the Sintane?"

He shifted from one foot to the other, eyed her warily, then said, "I was a *kjardin* for the Holder Lord of Markand."

"What's that?"

"A retainer, a personal guard. There aren't the right words in Kushorit."

She motioned for him to come up and he hesitated. "Why is there a demon carved above the door?"

"It's the aspect of the Adversary that eats evil." She shook her head. "The Adversary isn't a demon. The Adversary eats demons for dinner." She turned and moved into the little shrine. There was nothing here, just so much empty stone. *You expected something else?* she asked herself. The shrine was as empty of any spirit presence as the jungle and the river were crowded, but Maskelle could sense it was a recent vacancy. The temple had the feel of a room warmed by a living presence who had just stepped out the far door, just before she had stepped in the near one.

Rian had climbed the steps behind her and she glanced back at him. She couldn't see his expression in the dark, but he was looking up at the shadows where the ceiling extended up into the tower. She said, "The word in our language for 'Adversary' translates to the word for demon in some of the outlying provinces. That's where those stories come from. The Adversary is the only Ancestor, the only humanlike spirit, that never lived in this world as a human. Before the rise of the Koshan temples, it was thought to be the god of luck, both good and bad. But that's a misunderstanding of its purpose."

"So what's its purpose?"

"To destroy evil." Maskelle moved to the open doorway at the back of the shrine.

There were steps here too, leading up to a round stone platform at the back of the temple. It was within the boundary of the low walls, but high enough to be awash in moonlight and screened by the thick green of the treetops, cut off from the light of the court and compound by the stepped tower of the shrine. The breeze had died and the night was quiet except for the calls of nightbirds. She sat down on the smooth stone, still warm from the day's sunny intervals. She heard Rian step onto the platform behind her and said, "This is a moon-viewing platform. It's important to some of the rituals to know the exact shape of the shadow patterns on the moon."

He moved up beside her, looking up at the full moon. There was a mottled pattern of dark and light across its surface tonight. Without referring to the texts that recorded all the permutations and their meanings, Maskelle could only translate it as far as "portentous events." With the approach of the rainy season Equinox and the culmination of the Hundred Years Rite, that was only to be expected. Rian sat down next to her and relaxed into a sprawl.

"This is one of my temples," Maskelle said, "or it used to be." She shifted around to face him. "Why did you come to the Empire?"

He let out his breath and started to pull off his buskins. "It's a long story."

"That's no reason not to tell it."

He wrestled with a recalcitrant knot in the bootlace. She didn't think he would answer, but then he said, "The Holder Lord died."

She frowned. She could see that prying information out of Rian was going to be no easy task, even under the best of circumstances. "You were much attached to him?"

"More so than I thought, apparently." He managed to wrench the buskin off, gasping in relief, and stretched out on his back.

Maskelle gave up any attempt at subtlety. "I can see why it's a long story, if you tell it like this."

He sat up on his elbows. "All right. I'd only been at Markand Hold a year. I was part of a treaty between Markand and Riverwait."

"Part of a treaty? They trade . . ." She hesitated over the word he had used, then settled for "personal guards?"

"Not usually, but when the Holder Lord of Markand's legion is on the border and he's naming treaty terms and he points at you and says 'And I'll take that one,' nobody has much choice about it."

She watched him thoughtfully. "So Riverwait gave you up to an enemy."

"The Lady Holder of Riverwait gave me up." He looked away. "The Holder Lord of Markand had been coming to her hall for years and I was the first of her cortege. We didn't get along. He chose me as part of the treaty because he knew what it would cost her in honor. She didn't have a choice. Refusing to give me to him would have been refusing the treaty, and Markand would have overrun us within a month."

"But she gave you up."

"I know that part, we don't have to go over it again," he said, some annoyance in his voice. "I spent a year at Markand serving the Holder Lord."

She frowned. "Serving how?"

He sighed. "As a *kjardin*. A personal guard."

Maskelle sat back, wrapping her arms around her knees. She could imagine it all too readily. From what she had seen of Rian, he would have made no secret of his dislike when the Holder Lord had come to Riverwait on his earlier visits. The Holder Lord of Markand must have been something of a sadistic games-player to demand the favorite bodyguard of the Lady Holder as part of a treaty in the first place. And it must have been an interesting year at Markand for Rian, a virtual prisoner in the guise of a trusted retainer, and of course everyone else in the Holder Lord's court would have known.

Rian was watching her face and must have followed her thought. "I made sure he didn't enjoy it too much," he said. "There are ways."

"I can imagine."

He laid back down and stretched, brows lifted ironically. "I think I overdid it, though."

It was a nice sight; she had always been attracted to lean

men with flat stomachs, even if his skin was a little light for her eyes. "Oh?"

"There's an old custom, that when a High Holder Lord dies his best guards and servants go to the grave with him."

"Go to the grave?" Maskelle repeated blankly.

"Continue to serve him in the sunland," Rian explained. Seeing that she was still baffled, he spelled it out. "Get killed during the funeral, so the relatives can prove how much they really did honor the old bastard."

She looked away to conceal her reaction. To a member of a religious order which had debated for ten years on whether it was acceptable to allow cut flowers as spirit offerings, the idea of a living human as part of burial goods came as something of a shock.

Rian added, "It's fallen out of favor. But the priests read the omens and said the Holder Lord needed company on the journey into the sunland. Everybody, the family, the bodyguards, the wives, the clan leaders, the Guild Chiefs, all got together to decide who it would be. Guess who we picked?"

"I see. And I suppose the Holder Lord left detailed instructions about this to his priests before he died." Intellectually Maskelle could appreciate the final refinement of cruelty, but then she had been told often that she seldom did much of her thinking with her brain. *The Holder Lord of Markand is dead,* she reminded herself. Which was fortunate, because otherwise she would have to go to the Sintane and kill him herself. "How did you get away?"

"I survived the funeral games, which they let me know was very inconvenient for them. The Holder Lord's Heir wanted me put in the tomb alive, the way they used to do it. The guard captain, who was my lord officer, thought they should strangle me, which is also an old custom. But the chief priest decided to be magnanimous and had them give me a drug that would keep me unconscious through the burial rites, so I'd wake up just in time to suffocate."

"Small favors."

"Very small. But they didn't get as much of the drug down me as they thought, and it took so long they were late for the beginning of the rite, which starts in the Hall of the Hold. I pretended I couldn't stand, moaned and thrashed around, and they left me in the funerary chapel attached to the burial mound, with only a couple of guards outside. I was just conscious enough to put a finger down my throat and get rid of the rest of the drug. It almost took too long, but I was finally able to wake up enough to take one of the guards from behind and the other when he turned around. I got out of the chapel just before the procession came into sight. There was nowhere else to go, so I headed for the border into Gidale. The Heir sent hunters after me, so I had to keep going." He sat up, unbuckled his belt, and half-drew the siri to show her the hilt. "See that? This isn't mine, it's the Holder Lord's. I took it from the offering table. It had panthers and stags worked in gold; I sold those in Tirane."

Maskelle grinned in appreciation of the irony, though she suspected Rian had regretted giving up the sword's ornaments. "Why didn't you want to tell me this, why make me pry it out of you?"

He set the sheathed sword aside, though still within easy reach, and laid back down, propping himself up on one elbow. "You're a religious and I've been condemned as a sacrifice by priests, how did I know how you were going to take it?"

"I see." If she was going to do what she knew she wanted to, it was time for a little honesty. "It's not half so bad as some things I've done."

"And what's that?"

"I killed one of my husbands. Well, some people believe I killed all of them, and in a way, that's true."

Being Rian, he frowned and said, "You had husbands?"

"Three. The first one, Ilian, died because he trusted me too much. He followed me into danger and I couldn't protect him. I killed Sirot, the second one, myself, because of a vision I had."

She looked up at the enigmatic face of the moon, framed by faint faded stars. She had gone over this so many times in her own thoughts, but she realized this was the first time she had spoken of it aloud to anyone in seven years. "I thought it was from the Adversary, but I made a mistake. I was using too much power, relying on it and not the words of the Ancestors." Regret stung her again and she had to stop speaking to control her voice. She had hated Sirot by then, and everything had been a good deal more complicated than she was making it sound, but the essentials were really all that mattered. "My husband's son, who was only a boy at the time, was one of the heirs of the Old Emperor. The vision told me that if he took the throne, the Celestial Empire would disappear in a storm of darkness and chaos." She looked at Rian. "So I tried to stop that from happening, any way I could. My husband fought me and I killed him for it. The third husband, Vanrin, was a man who supported me out of love and folly and ambition, and he was killed in the fighting afterward."

Rian was watching her worriedly, his brows drawn together in concern. "But you stopped the boy from being the heir?"

"No, he was made the heir, and when the old Emperor died, he took the throne. And nothing happened." She laughed a little, bitterly. "The vision was a lie, a trick of the dark spirits, but I believed it completely." She shook her head. "I've been in a great deal of difficulty and most of it's my own fault. I betrayed my sacred duty to the Koshan Path. The Adversary will no longer speak to me, but while I still live there won't be a new Voice to replace me, so the Empire has been denied the Adversary's counsel for the past seven years. In the fighting I used too much of my power and gained the attention of the dark spirits, the things that live in the shadows. Like the river when it runs hard and wild like this, and whatever it was that killed that boy and replaced his soul with something else." She smiled wryly at how long the catalog of her folly was becoming.

"They punished you for it?" Rian asked cautiously.

"No, I made my own punishment too, my own curse. Now whenever I manipulate the Infinite, use the power that most people call magic, it draws the attention of the dark spirits and they can find me again. And I can't hear the Adversary. It's like being blind and deaf." *Or worse, because no one's made blind and deaf because of their own idiocy.* She added tiredly, "At first I was evil, then I was an annoyance. Now I'm just pathetic."

His voice serious, Rian said, "Not pathetic."

"Maybe." A wind stirred the trees somewhere past the temple, the sound coming to them like the distant rush of water. Rian was watching her, a faint worried crease between his brows. She said, "But of all the things I've done, I've never given up anyone to an enemy." She leaned over, slid a hand into the soft warmth of his hair and kissed him.

When she drew back, he said, "I knew that when I first saw you," and pulled her down to him again.

Maskelle had time to remember that her bones weren't twenty anymore, no matter what the rest of her thought, and that the stone beneath them was unyielding, but none of it mattered enough to give her pause. It had been a long time since she had been with a man and longer still since she had been with one she wanted this much, one who wasn't afraid of her, whose humor and stubborn temperament matched her own. All thought dissolved into lean hard muscle under her hands, first through tight fabric and then only hot bare skin.

At one point Rian managed to gasp, "Is the Adversary going to care that we're doing this on his moon-viewing platform?"

"No," she told him, laughing, "it's a very ancient, very honored form of offering."

Later, her head pillowed on Rian's back, Maskelle drifted into sleep. He didn't make a very good pillow, having no comfortable softness about him, so her sleep was light and the transition from waking world to dream was almost imperceptible at first.

The dream landscape was much like the real one, though the moonlight seemed to penetrate the heavy shadows of the trees overhanging the wall to a greater depth, so that she could make out the rough knotted boles hung with moss and the vines entangling the branches. Her physical awareness of Rian's body was still intense; she felt she could have traced every line of muscle, every curve, every old scar. This melded with the dream until she could feel his breathing and his heartbeat as if they were her own. He lay on his stomach, his head pillowed on his arms, drowsing just on the edge of sleep and kept from slipping fully into unconsciousness by a need to listen for anyone or anything approaching. This gave her the freedom to move further into the dream, rising above the moon-viewing deck to a point near the top of the stepped tower, so that she could see the whole of the temple laid out below her in the dark. The three shrines were much as they were in the real world, as were the statues of the seated monkey men and the quarters for the attendants. But the lamps were not lit in the court and the wagons and oxen didn't stand outside the wall.

I'm seeing it at another time, Maskelle thought. *But is it later or earlier?* Then she saw a figure step out of the second shrine and go down the steps, and despite the moonlit dark she recognized herself. She could see that her head was still shaved so that her rank tattoo was visible. *Ah, so it's earlier.*

Then a wave of darkness like a silk drape covered everything and Maskelle found herself looking at an entirely different landscape.

Intimacy on the threshold of the Adversary's shrine had been used as an offering for generations since the Koshan Order first battled the worship of blood demons for the hearts and minds of the people of the lowlands. Some later Koshan philosophers contended that it had been some wily priest's device to attract converts accustomed to the excitements of human sacrifice, that the spirits of the Infinite, not being anthropormorphized deities, were indifferent as to whether their followers had sex or not. But it appeared that those particular philosophers were dead wrong, because with Rian's help she had gotten herself a dream vision straight from the Adversary.

The moonlight was the same, but the jungle and the canal were gone and in their place she looked down at a great dusty plain, limitless and vast, the purple-grey clouds of a recent storm overhead, the air dry and cool. The plain was empty except for strange small mountains that thrust upwards at intervals, towering several hundred feet above her. They were all oddly unmountainlike shapes, the nearest formed like a mushroom, with a round base supporting a domed top. And while her slow wits insisted that those couldn't be mountains, that there was no sort of stone that could take these forms naturally, she saw pinpricks of light on some of the farther ones. She focused on the nearest clump and suddenly her vision altered as her brain transformed the image into reality. They were buildings, as large as the greatest temples of the Kushor-At in Duvalpore, carved out of smooth grey stone. The plain under them was not grey sand but grey stone, seamed with the even shapes of paving blocks. Miles and miles of paving blocks.

Then she was walking on those blocks, very near one of the buildings, her feet bare on the warm stone. She looked up at the great shapes towering over her, saw that the surfaces of them were rough and worked with strange unfamiliar carving, the shapes of the openings square and well-defined. There were balconies on some of them, or open galleries. A bridge high overhead connected two of them. She walked toward the door of the nearest, a round high opening in the base, wide enough to drive four or five wagons through side by side. She was too far to see anything of the inside but the flicker of yellow firelight.

Then she was on the Adversary's moon-viewing platform again, her head pillowed on Rian's back, the wall of the shrine and the trees and the nightbirds and her own sky above.

Maskelle lay there, the feeling slowly coming back into her numbed limbs, and knew that her spirit had truly left her body, that it had been a real vision, and not just wishful thinking. It was baffling, it was inexplicable. *It's the first time the Adversary's spoken to me since I left Kushor-At,* she thought. *Why now? What's changed?*

There were no answers in the night.

5

"I've had a letter from the Celestial One," Barime said, pouring tea from the heavy pottery jug, "but he didn't tell me about sending for you."

"He hasn't become less cagy in his dotage. He didn't tell me why he sent for me either," Maskelle said. She felt a little light-headed, as she always did the third sleepless night in a row, but they would be in the city by late this afternoon and she could sleep in the wagon on the way.

They were sitting under a vine arbor on a little terrace off the monastic quarters, on braided grass mats and soft faded cushions. The sun was just rising and the Ariaden were still asleep in their wagons, though the temple attendants had been awake for the past hour. It was cool and the air was fresh, birds and monkeys chattered in the greenery just past the low wall, and the day prom-ised more sun than rain.

Barime had made them as free of the temple's quarters as if Maskelle had still had the governance of this and all the other temples of the Adversary and had a real right to be here. This had included the use of the bathing room, and even though the water was pumped cold from the canal and there was no hypo-caust, it had been quite civilized compared to the arrangements possible on the road. Rian had already managed to shed the dressing she had put on the bori club-cut on his arm, and she had replaced it with materials supplied by the temple's infirmarian.

"I can see why he didn't want to spread the word of your return, but I would have thought he could have trusted you with the reason for it," Barime agreed. Besides the tea, one of the young monks had brought fruit, warm flatbread baked in the temple's ovens, and spiced fish paste. It was a welcome change from taro and dried pork.

Rian was trying not to eat like a starving man, but Barime was hardly fooled and kept passing the bowls to him. He was sitting behind Maskelle and to the side, where he could watch the gates and much of the compound, and the door into the quarters. He had hardly gotten within three feet of Maskelle since Barime had come out, but she didn't think Barime was fooled by that, either. It did give her an idea of the circumspection required by a Sitanese Lord's personal guard, though.

"Maybe 'trusted' is the wrong word," Maskelle pointed out.

"It must be the Hundred Year Rite," Barime said, ignoring that serenely. "He wants your help with it."

"There are so many others he can go to. The provincial Voices, the seventh-level priests. And he sent for me over five months ago, before the rite started." She shook her head, watching the leaves settle to the bottom of her cup. The Celestial One had been her friend when she had left Duvalpore seven years ago, the only friend remaining to her in the city. But she wasn't sure if that was still the case. So much had happened since then and the Koshan temples had suffered from the lack of the Adversary's council. *And everyone knows whose fault that is.*

"Perhaps he simply wants to see you." Barime watched her thoughtfully.

Maskelle looked away. It was a possibility, she supposed. She smiled a little wryly. *You were hoping for something more interesting, weren't you?* She knew Rian was watching her too. "How have things been at Court? Is Chancellor Mirak still our best enemy?"

Barime made a gesture of annoyance. "He is as always, if not worse. I've never met the man, but I feel as though I know him from the descriptions I receive in my letters, and it isn't pleasant knowledge. Kiasha wrote me of a new presence at court, some foreign emissary, who seems to have an undue amount of influence." She looked at Maskelle seriously. "You know Mirak won't welcome your return."

"I would be disappointed if he did welcome it. Much of the attraction of it comes from the trouble it will cause Mirak. And the others." She glanced back at Rian in time to see him look away, his jaw muscles tightening to suppress a smile.

Barime smiled. "You haven't changed."

Maskelle made a warding gesture, only half in jest. "Don't say that."

"You know what I mean."

Some hours later Maskelle climbed out of the dim interior of the wagon and into the brilliant sunlight. She stood on the seat next to Old Mali and surveyed the road. Rain had come and gone throughout the morning, but the heat had set in with afternoon. The road had grown more crowded as the day had advanced and she had not been able to sleep much. She was covered with sweat and after being jolted in the wagon her head felt as if it was stuffed with straw. It hadn't helped that Rian evidently slept in increments, waking up when no more than half an hour could have passed and getting out of the wagon, then coming back in not much later. He was a few wagons down the line now, walking beside Rastim at the side of the road. She couldn't fault him for wanting to stay alert, or for the driving need to do so, but she knew they were already well within the active influence of the temples in Kushor-At and there was no chance of attack. *Or at least,* she amended, *no chance of attack from restless water spirits, even strangely powerful ones.*

She let out her breath and sat down on the wagon bench, resigned to being awake. Old Mali grunted at her and she grunted back. The road rolled on, hot and bright under the sun, the mud hardening in spots and wet and stinking still in others. There were more and more travellers, and they even had to stop several times and wait for the road to clear. They passed merchants, farm wagons, an Imperial courier, and a party of Imperial guardsmen escorting an embassy from Kutura-clane.

"I thought we were close," Rastim said, for perhaps the third time. He had jumped down off his wagon and run up to hang off the running board of Maskelle's.

"We are," Maskelle said, not patiently. They were skirting the edge of Duvalpore now and had been for some time. To the west, past the rice fields and hidden by the band of trees, was a scattering of temples, canals, and a residential and merchants' quarter bordering the giant western baray. They could have gotten into the city proper faster by taking any one of the several turn-offs they had passed, but Maskelle wanted to go directly to the Temple City.

Perversely, she said nothing when the road dipped down through stands of palms and fruit trees and they passed over the second dike. Past it the trees fell away to a stretch of open fields that led up to a belt of sago palms at the base of towering stone walls. They glowed golden in the sunlight, stretching for miles on either side. Someone in one of the wagons behind theirs shouted with excitement and Maskelle smiled tightly.

Rian swung up onto the wagon suddenly and Maskelle jumped so violently she almost fell into Old Mali's lap. She ignored the quizzical look the old woman gave her; she hadn't realized how tense she was. Rian settled onto the perch at Maskelle's feet and didn't appear to notice her nervous start.

I love this city, she thought. Maybe she had forgotten how much. The huge gates stood open, heavy logs reinforced with metal cladding, and traffic swarmed through. There were five gates in this section of the city wall; this one was called the Gate of Reunion. Well, there were many reunions soon to come. She wasn't sure what was unnerving her. There were no enemies within these gates that she feared. *Except yourself,* she thought, watching the walls loom larger. *Except yourself.*

Rian was watching the guards. "Will there be trouble getting in?"

"No, they won't stop us," Maskelle said. There were two guards dressed in the livery of the Imperial Constabulary, high buskins, loose trousers, and short red jackets open in the afternoon heat. One of them was swinging a bori club idly, but they appeared to be more interested in gossip with the travellers and traders gathered at the side of the gate than with stopping any wagons. The Hundred Year Rite would culminate at the Equinox, coinciding with the secular Water Festival and also this year with the annual lunar holiday. The celebrations would be huge and people were streaming into the city for it. She said, "This is civilization now, remember?"

Rian leaned back against her legs and looked up at her, cocking an eyebrow. "Does that mean they'll let us leave, too?"

She ran a hand through his hair. The dampness in the air was making the ends curl. "It's an open city."

He looked unconvinced, but no one gave them any notice as the wagons trundled through the gate onto a broad paved area. Ahead the view opened up to the western approach to the Temple City.

Maskelle heard a loud startled exclamation from one of the wagons behind her. At the edge of the pavement a few hundred yards away was a wide moat. The afternoon heat shivered off the calm water, which was separated from the river by a system of canals. There were a few boats, some flat cargo barges, but most were pleasure crafts, with people in white gauzy robes shaded by colorful awnings or parasols.

At first, in the light and heat, the grey shapes beyond the water looked like a mountain range in small scale. Then the eyes resolved the mountains into giant stepped domes covered with carvings and statues, some topped with slender spires. The temples. Maskelle's heart started to pound.

Past the moat, a long terrace with three gates made the formal entrance to the city. Beyond that was a vast open space of paved court, dotted with groups of brightly dressed people. Past that, dominating the view on a rising mound of stone, were the five giant conical towers and the long pillared galleries of the Marai, the Temple of the Mountain.

The road was dipping down toward a broad stone causeway lined with guardian stone lions that bridged the moat. Old Mali halted their oxen for a moment as the wagons in front of them slowed in rolling out onto the causeway. Travellers new to the city and inexperienced jostled other wagons and lost each other, and peddlers hawked their wares at the top of their lungs, anxious to separate the newcomers from their money before they saw the greater markets further ahead. Maskelle glanced down at Rian. He was shading his eyes, studying the view.

Rastim took advantage of the stop to come up and climb onto the running board on Old Mali's side. His round face was shiny with sweat, but he looked more excited than anything else. "Is that the palace?" he asked.

"What?" Maskelle realized he meant the temple. "No, that's the Marai, the Temple of the Mountain. This is Kushor-At, the First City, the Temple City. The Palace is in the Principle City, Kushor-An, over that way." She pointed to where another great stone causeway led off to the west, bridging ground, canals, and another moat to reach the city's second heart.

"The Celestial One lives in the temple?" Rastim persisted. He must be having visions of vast audiences. This was undoubtedly the largest city the Ariaden had ever seen.

"Close enough," Maskelle told him. There were hundreds of temples spread throughout the First City and the Principle City, each with a precise role in the system that made up a network as complex as the canals and barays that provided water and transport, and she was in no mood to give a lesson in either architecture or history. "Just calm down. We'll get there, all right?"

"I know that, but what's—" The traffic in front of them started to move and Rastim was forced to run back to his own wagon.

They rolled onto the causeway, a breeze lifting the warm damp air. The odor coming off the water was as fresh as that of the wild river, heavy with nothing but the scents of the jungle vegetation creeping along the banks and the spices and incenses on the boats. It was often a source of amazement to foreign visitors that water carried in man-made channels remained so clean, and they attributed the phenomenon to the holy nature of the barays and canals. It had more to do with the skill of the original builders of Kushor-At and Kushor-An, who had learned everything there was to know about moving water from one place to another in building the dry season irrigation ditches for the rice fields.

The boats nearby were all pleasure craft, wide and flat-bottomed, guided by poles fore and aft, the passengers protected from the sun by the awnings. Watching the nearest glide by, Maskelle was struck by a memory with almost the tangibility of a vision: a long-ago afternoon on one of those boats, drifting in the heat of the sun down the canal that led past the palace complex to the western baray, the prow filled with flowers and the breeze playing through the bells. Annoyed, she shook her head, banishing the image.

The wagon rolled off the causeway and onto the plaza in front of the terraces. It was even more crowded with other wagons, milling people, oxen, horses. Old Mali made worried grumbling noises.

"We need to get the wagons out of here," Rian said, standing up on the perch to get a better vantage point.

Maskelle dragged herself out of the past and said, "That way."

There was a walled post house to the far right of the plaza, a huge one with room for dozens of wagons. They made their way to its gate without running over anyone and Maskelle climbed down to do the bargaining. Rastim hovered worriedly at her elbow while she spoke to the attendant at the gate.

"We can only afford one night," he said after she had finished and handed over a couple of coins to secure their entrance.

"We'll only need one night," she told him, and thought, *one way or the other.*

As large as it was, the post compound was still crowded. Wagons of all shapes and sizes, from a light two-wheeled peddler's cart to huge two-storied wheeled houses with shuttered windows and roof platforms crowded the enclosure and oxen, onagers, and horses were tethered everywhere. The noise of the animals combined with the babble of voices speaking in dozens of languages to make a bewildering din. Rian seemed to take it in stride, though with him it was hard to tell. The Ariaden were in a state of bewildered excitement; the city was everything that had been promised and the variety of the people could only mean that some of them might want to see theater. Maskelle's presence as an apparent travelling nun gained them polite attention from the attendants, and with a little help from them they found a spot to draw the wagons up.

The others ran around setting up camp and Maskelle stepped back out of the way, looking toward the Marai's towers, easily visible over the wall of the compound. *Better get it over with,* she thought sourly. Now that she was here, her nerves were making her stomach jump. The attendants were already bringing fodder for the oxen, and Rian and Firac were trying to figure out the system that filled the troughs with water from the channels crossing the compound. She caught Rastim's arm as he bustled past, and said, "I'm going to the Marai."

"Oh. To pray?" he asked, looking up at her, nonplussed.

"You could call it that." One of her braids chose that moment to fall in a lank length over her face. She pushed it back, thinking sourly, *You can be sure no one will recognize you.* "I won't be gone long." She turned away.

"Ah, well, take care!" he called after her.

She hadn't reached the gate of the compound when she realized that the person behind her was not another traveller on his way out. Rian was following her.

She said, "I didn't ask you to come with me."

"I know that."

She stopped and faced him, giving him the look that had frozen the blood of lower-ranking priests and made her the terror of the Court, even before she had given them real reasons to fear her. She said, carefully, "I don't want company."

He folded his arms and gave her a look right back, the expression of someone long accustomed to the powerful and who had become somewhat bored by their idiosyncracies. He said, "After last night I'm not going to be easy to convince."

Maskelle started to make a sharp reply, but took a deep breath instead. *Well, that's a point.* "None of this is going to be easy. We're here now. There will be plenty of people needing to hire guardsmen. You don't have to throw in your lot with me."

He looked away, nothing but annoyance in his face. "Are you done?"

Maskelle knew that in the Sintane this was probably all some terrible insult, but she didn't care. She said, "Are you sure?"

"Yes," he said impatiently. "Are we going?"

"Yes, yes. Ancestors help me," Maskelle snapped, "we're going."

They left the compound. She had chosen the road and this

gate because it would bring them into the city at the point most convenient for reaching the Marai; she had gauged the day as well, knowing the Celestial One would be spending this phase of the moon in the Marai for the Hundred Year Rite. But as she crossed the plaza toward the second set of inner gates, she found herself wishing that the Celestial One was in the Baran Dir and she still had half the city to cross.

There were quicker ways, but she found herself lingering in the market that had sprung up at the inner gates. It was a small affair of carts and awnings, here to take advantage of the travellers entering the city, but even so it boasted bolts of colored silks and cottons, incense and spices and trade goods from provinces half the world away. There was food too—fruit, sweet confections, shellfish, and roast pork with honey, kept warm over braisers set up on the paving stones of the plaza, the odors thick in the air. She found her steps slowing almost involuntarily.

Rian was looking at a display of metalwork, wary and watchful, though no one in the cosmopolitan crowd seemed to have more than a second glance for a Sitanese swordsman. She looked at the trader's wares, spread out on woven mats under an awning. Her eyes passed over the copper cooking pots and fancy knives and on to the goldsmith's work, beads, rings, and ear and belt ornaments.

She knelt down for a closer look. Much of it was Sitanese, little figures of stags and mountain panthers, animals strange to the heart of the Empire, and winged figures and sea beasts and other creatures from foreign myths. She nudged an ear stud out of the glittering array. It was small, exactingly shaped into a hunting cat's head. She remembered that the Sitanese believed that decorated objects contained all the powers of the subjects represented. "How much?"

The trader, a wizened old man with very bad teeth, seated cross-legged on the mat, bowed his head to her and said, "For the nun, two five-foil pieces, no more."

"That's far too much." She had no idea of the proper price

of gold or any other precious metal or stone; when she had last lived here, purchasing such things had been the province of servants. But the time on the road had taught her how to bargain. She flicked another ear stud, a plain gold bead, out of the pile. "For the nun, both these at one five-foil piece, no more." It was the most she could afford.

He grinned and bowed to her again. "My apologies, I thought you a travelling nun, lady, newly come to the city."

Maskelle grinned back, feeling that luck, and possibly the Ancestors, were with her just this once. "I'm travelling, but I've come—" *home* "—back." She handed over the coin.

Getting to her feet, she found Rian watching the crowd. She handed him the ear studs. "I noticed you were missing some."

He stared at her like she had suddenly grown another head, or a third eye. "Don't look at me like that," she said, pushing on through the crowd.

She came out of the forest of awnings near the bridge across the Marai's moat and started up the wide flight of stone stairs to the causeway. From the top the view of the temple was wonderful, the multiple levels of pillared galleries clearly definable beneath the five stepped domes. More of the city was visible from this angle, a sight that would have probably made Rastim swoon. Small tile-roofed wooden buildings standing on pilings filled the gaps between the causeways and bridges and the bright silver surfaces of canals. Green belts of foliage and tamed plots of jungle wove in and out among the major temples, which towered above the other structures, some atop large platforms or stepped pyramids, some with graceful domed pinnacles. She could see the towers of the Baran Dir from here, though at this distance the details of the carving were lost. The small market had whetted her appetite for the city and she had the strong urge to postpone the visit to the Celestial One and go over to the far side of the eastern baray, where there were markets and pleasure gardens and every other imaginable form of entertainment. Then she remembered she had only one or two coins left, and of all the things she needed from the Celestial One, a loan was not the least. She let out her breath and started across the bridge toward the Marai. She glanced back to see if Rian was still following her. He was. He had also stopped to put on the ear studs and the gold looked good against his skin.

The entrance to the Marai was very near and Maskelle was forced to admit that the disturbance in her stomach was pure nerves and not a desire for dinner sparked by the odors of the market. The Temple of the Sare had reacted to her presence, but this was the Marai, one of the two pivotal temples in the Kushor-At and the Celestial Empire. Surely in a place teeming with life, at the center of so many lines of earthly power, she would go unnoticed.

The broad bridge crossed the Marai's moat, a span of almost four hundred feet. It was a common spot for people to gather on their way to or from the temple, and they passed priests and temple servants or workers, and a few groups of wealthy nobles dressed in silk robes and shading themselves with parchment parasols. Back against the balustrades carved into the forms of guardian snake spirits there were even a few peddlers, selling plaques with temple dancers drawn on them for foreign visitors. They had passed the center point, where stairs watched over by stone lions led down to the water on each side, and were almost to the gate in the outer wall when Rian said, "Are they going to just let us in?"

"Of course. The temples are open to everyone; what would be the point, otherwise?" She stopped at the bottom of the steps that led up to the first gate and bowed a greeting to the blue-robed doorkeeper priest, who returned the bow and went back to his discussion with two tonsured students. From the doorkeeper's mildly preoccupied expression, she doubted he recognized her, not unless he was a better actor than Rastim. Maskelle knew someone would recognize her soon enough, but she wanted it to be after she had seen the Celestial One. She wanted this quiet reacquaintance with the Marai first, before she dealt with its people.

Through the gate was the Marai's outer court. The temple looked confusing from any distance, but the layout was really very simple: a series of squares, one inside the other. The innermost square had the giant mountain towers at its four corners and in the center. The outer court was as wide as the moat they had just crossed, but covered with soft green grass, still wet from the last rain so that Maskelle could feel the damp heat rising from it. A walkway crossed it, elevated some twenty feet above the ground, dividing the lunar court on the left from the solar on the right, and leading between the first two library buildings and the two reflecting pools, then reaching a terrace that bordered the outer pillared gallery. The court was mostly empty at this time of day, though she could see a few Koshans of different ranks scattered about in the shade of the library porticos, giving lessons to acolytes and whoever else wanted to listen.

She reached the terrace and the shade of the tall pillars of the gallery and paused for a moment. The inner court just beyond was smaller, paved with white stone. Several sets of stairs in the walkway that crossed it led them higher and higher above ground level. There were a great many steps; to keep its bond with the Infinite, the temple's resemblance to the Mountain had to be more than symbolic.

Rian was uncharacteristically silent. Maskelle started across the walkway, feeling the sun burn into the back of her neck. To distract herself, she asked him, "Are priests so feared in the Sintane?"

He glanced at her. "They aren't feared. But they're powerful and they keep their secrets."

"Secrets?" They reached the flight of steps up to the second gallery. *So far so good*, Maskelle thought. Her awareness of the temple was growing more intense. She could sense the diminishing of the solstice alignment with the end gateways, the growing nearness of the equinox alignment with the great domed tower in the center. "What secrets?"

"Secrets about the sanctuaries. If too many people saw the inside of one, they might start to realize there's nothing there worth paying tribute coin to."

They had started up the last flight of steps and the words of the meditation ring were passing through Maskelle's mind, drilled there by years of habit. There was a different meditation for each step in every temple. It was part of the Celestial One's duties to complete a meditation ring in every temple in the city, and the Marai was always done during the Year Rites. She said, "Why should that be a surprise? There's nothing in the Marai, or any of the other temples. Nothing of note, anyway. People, dust, bats, crickets, mosquitoes. The temples are just symbols of the different faces of the Infinite. It makes more sense to look at them from the outside than in. In fact, the further away you are, the easier the Infinite is to understand."

Rian made a noncommittal noise. Maskelle smiled to herself. She knew his wits were too lively for him not to realize the Koshan were different, but he wanted more proof first, and behaving as the ultimate skeptic was probably a good way to elicit information. It was eliciting information from her. She asked, "Does no one believe in the priests, then?"

"No one with any sense," Rian said, his voice dry.

She laughed, surprising herself. They reached the top of the steps and the second pillared gallery. A breeze swept a little dust past the pillars and she could hear a sistrum somewhere inside. There was a priestess, a young one, coming along the gallery, and when they had passed the ritual of bows, Maskelle asked where the Celestial One was.

The young woman gestured back toward the first solar tower, the one that sat in the upper right-hand corner of the square. "He's on the Sky Bridge, Sister."

Maskelle thanked her and the priestess passed on, managing to be too serene and reserved to glance curiously at Rian, but only just. They came to the end of the gallery and Maskelle took a deep breath and stepped into the first solar tower.

Carvings of mountain spirits spiraled up the inside of the dome, which was honeycombed with narrow bridges and balconies. It was thankfully dark, daylight coming in only through the entrances at the different levels, and empty.

Empty of everything. The past, the future, the Infinite, like a hollow shell. Maskelle hesitated, really fearful for the first time in years. If such a powerful temple as the Marai was dead to her . . .

Up on one of the narrow walkways a shadow passed. The shape was that of an older priest, a common enough sight in the temple, but his sandals made no sound on the stone. Maskelle breathed out in relief. She could feel the stirring of life in the Marai now, its link to the Infinite.

She moved further into the tower. A passage led off from the opposite wall, becoming an open gallery washed in sunlight as it left the dome. Another shadow crossed it as she watched, this one a woman, dressed in an elaborate style of court dress a few decades out of date.

She glanced back at Rian. He was standing in the doorway, looking around curiously. He hadn't seen the shadows; to see them one had to be fairly well along on the path of understanding the Infinite. She crossed the mosaiced floor to one of the interior spiral stairs, saying, "The parts of the temple are named after the corresponding parts of the Mountain. Sky Bridge is a pass on the eastern side."

He followed her up the stairs. "Is this a real mountain or a Koshan mountain?"

Maskelle smiled. "A real mountain, much further west. It's the symbol of power for the spirits of earth and stone."

The stairs wound upward to an open gallery facing the east and looking out over the outer court, the outer gallery and the moat. She stopped to stand against the railing, the warm wind tearing at her braids. The view was magnificent. The spires of Alamein Kitar, impossibly light and insubstantial, more like a dream or vision than solid stone. Arkad, with its green copper dome. The towers of the Baran Dir, the second hub of the city, with the dark waters of the western baray behind it.

Rian stepped up beside her. She thought he was looking at the Baran Dir, which was always what caught the attention of those newly come to Duvalpore. It was a forest of massive towers, larger than the Marai, all surmounted by carved stone faces, so large they were visible even at this distance. The Baran Dir was a symbolic map of the heartland of the Empire, with each tower representing a temple or a Koshan hospital. But he said, "I didn't realize how big it was."

He had been looking at the sprawl of the buildings, canals, gardens, causeways and tree-lined avenues that seemed to stretch to the horizon. She said, "It's been a city for a long time. Our records go back over seven hundred years, when the irrigation canals were first built, but there were people living here even before then. The records of the Rite go back longer." She glanced at him. "Why did you decide to come here?"

He shook his head. "When I ran this was the only way I could go, and I had to get far enough away that they wouldn't bother to follow me. Then there wasn't much point in not going on."

"Now I know why you wanted to come with me. You're almost as rootless as I am." She looked at the Baran Dir, the shadows crossing the stone faces. "You know we might be leaving here today with an angry mob at our heels."

"Mobs are easy to get away from. No organization." Rian leaned back against the pillar and studied her thoughtfully.

"I suppose attempts on the Throne happen more often in the Sintane?"

"The Holder Lord executed two brothers, a sister, and a

cousin for trying to take the Markand Hold, just in the time I was there, and that was a slow year."

"I keep forgetting what savages you all are over there."

Rian looked down at the city again, but a smile tugged at his lips.

Maskelle let out her breath and looked again at the serene faces of the Baran Dir. So little had changed. *That's what I'm afraid of,* she thought again. She pushed away from the railing. "Let's get this over with."

She turned back into the tower and followed the stairs all the way up to the top of the dome. The round chamber had windows looking out over the city in every direction. Framed in one was the Illsat Sidar, the only Temple of the Adversary within the city. Caught by the image, she didn't see the ancient little man, seated cross-legged on the far side of the room just below the window facing the western baray, until he turned his head.

He was a very old man, with a once strong frame emaciated by age, wrapped in a blue Koshan robe. The rank tattoos on his scalp were faded and obscured by wrinkles, but his dark eyes were still bright. He said, "My daughter."

To anyone else the mask of his beneficent expression would have been impenetrable, but Maskelle knew him better than that. She thought she had surprised him, and she wondered if he had not expected her to come after all. "My father."

"Your journey was arduous?"

She stepped further into the room. He wasn't alone; seated on grass mats nearby was another old priest and a young woman in dark green court robes, with strings of amethyst and opals braided through her hair. "It was agreeable enough, once we passed the boundary."

His brow lifted, and he turned to the others. "I must ask your indulgence while I greet my friend who has travelled a great distance to meet with me."

"Of course." The priest stood immediately and reached down

to help the courtier to her feet. The upper rank of priests were all considered equals, so they used no honorific with the Celestial One. And since the Celestial One always gave up his names when he assumed the office, the priests called him nothing at all. "We will return at some later day, at your convenience."

The woman stood a little awkwardly, obviously not used to the spare comforts of the temple, and obviously not as anxious to leave as her escort. But she bowed her head and said only, "Celestial One." The priest escorted her to another doorway, and Maskelle felt her glance rake them.

When they had gone, the Celestial One smiled wryly and gestured for her to sit.

Maskelle took a seat on one of the mats, laying her staff down behind her, fighting down that sense of too-powerful familiarity again. Most of all she was conscious of an overwhelming sense of relief. She had dreaded this meeting and now, at least, she would be free of that anticipation. She noted Rian, correctly guessing that to remain standing while they sat would be judged rude, had taken a seat on the floor a few feet behind her and to the side. She hid a smile. The number of doors in the cupola had given him an instant's pause, but he had still managed to pick the spot where he could see all of them at once.

The Celestial One, she thought, had noted it too. He said, "Who is your companion?"

"He's Rian, from the Sintane. They're mostly agnostics." She felt Rian glaring daggers at her back.

The Celestial One smiled at Rian. "Then why does he wear the sigil of Taprot?"

Maskelle turned to look at Rian. His expression was wary. Considering that the amulet was currently tucked inside his shirt, it must have at least some presence in the Infinite for the Celestial One to be able to sense the traces of its presence. Resigned, she turned back to the old priest and asked, "And what is Taprot?"

"A spirit of protection, who casts favor on those whose duty is to protect others, to lay bare falsehood, or to pursue criminals. The Sitanese depict it in the form of a hunting cat, the Gildane as a monkey, and the Versatin as a crocodile. There are other forms, but those are the main ones of interest."

That was enough of that. The polite conversation, as if she had gone off on a retreat or a meditation ring and had just now returned to the city, had to stop. "Well, you've got me here. Now tell me what you want."

His eyes narrowed. "The Voices have spoken of danger to the Hundred Year Rite since the beginning of this year, but there was nothing specific, only vague warnings. I wanted your help with the interpretation of their warnings."

He's not telling me everything, Maskelle thought. She widened her eyes ingenuously and said, "All the other Voices and the seventh-level priests have all gone incompetent? The ones that weren't already, I mean."

"No." He frowned. "But I suspected there would be interference with the Rite."

The silence stretched. Maskelle gave in and said, "What do you mean, interference?"

He betrayed a moment's exasperation. "If I knew the source of the interference, I should have related it in my letter."

"Oh, I doubt that. Then you would lose the upper hand." Maskelle propped an elbow on her knee and rested her chin in her hand. "I suppose you realize what it cost me to come here."

His gaze softened. She wished she could tell if it was sincerity or acting. He said, "That I realized. I would not have asked you if I had not thought it serious." He sighed. "But I wish I had asked you sooner."

She frowned and said slowly, "I believe you think it's serious, but that's all."

The Celestial One let out his breath, and stared grimly into the distance. This she knew wasn't acting. He said, "Then I will show you, and let you judge for yourself."

*   *   *

Rian wondered how the Celestial One would negotiate the way through the Marai and for that matter, how he had got up into it in the first place. The steps were too steep and some of the passages too narrow for a palanquin or a litter. It turned out to be a simple solution; a large young priest came in at a summons and picked the fragile old man up to carry him easily down the stairs.

Rian wasn't sure what to think of the Celestial One. He had never met such an exalted religious before, but he had the feeling that in this case even prior experience wouldn't have helped. The Koshans weren't like anybody else, and the Celestial One even more so. The sigil of Taprot, which he had only kept because it wasn't worth selling, thumped him in the chest as he started down the stairs after them, and he wondered why the Celestial One had mentioned it.

Following Maskelle and the priests through these narrow halls that opened unexpectedly into galleries with sweeping views of the city, Rian thought again how strange this place was, built not for human convenience but to some other design. It was a design alien to the fortresses of the Sintane, which were built for defense and to withstand long harsh cold seasons, but the overall affect was not unpleasant. There was no surface that wasn't carved and not all the subjects were religious. Just in the stairwell there were rows of lotus buds, sinuous dancers, a forest hermit being chased up a tree by a tiger, a market scene.

They passed several men waiting in a wide pillared hall, some dressed in elaborately draped and colored silk robes, two with the swordbelts of guardsmen, though they had the bearing of high rank. They all made gestures of respect as the Celestial One passed. Rian wished he had bothered to learn more about the Empire—he wasn't even sure of the Celestial One's real status, if he was a secular as well as a religious power. But this place had always seemed more than half myth, even in the more cosmopolitan Markand. And he had had other things to worry about.

They entered an inner courtyard that must be raised some thirty or forty feet from actual ground level, considering all the stairs they had climbed in crossing the two outer courts. In the center was the fifth tower, an even larger imitation mountain than the ones which stood at each corner. Rian gave up even looking at the carvings; the detail was too much to absorb and he didn't want to be distracted. Four covered passages crossed the court, wide pillared corridors each extending from one of the long galleries to the base of the middle tower.

Clouds had covered the sun, and though the reflection off the polished stone was muted, it was still temporarily blinding after the murky dimness of the tower. The young priest set the Celestial One on his feet as soon as they reached the bottom of the stairs and the old man crossed the wide paved court under his own power, leaning on his staff, his fragile body bent forward determinedly. There were several other priests standing in the shade of one of the porticos, who bowed to the old man as he passed.

He was going toward an open archway in the portico around the base of the central mountain-tower. Maskelle made no move to follow him, muttering, "What does he think he's doing . . . ?"

"Trouble?" Rian asked her.

She shook her head impatiently. "That's where the Year Rites take place. I'm not supposed to . . . Oh, damn it."

Rian glanced at the watching priests. He read more curiosity than hostility in their bearing, but perhaps they didn't realize who Maskelle was. Yet. He wished he knew enough to sort the truth from the self-deprecating exaggeration in everything she had told him, but that would come later. The only sensible course now was to look on everyone as a potential threat. *That shouldn't be difficult,* he thought grimly. It was a habit that he should have no trouble falling back into.

Maskelle hesitated another moment, apparently oblivious to the curious eyes of the other priests. Then she shook her head at herself in annoyance and followed the Celestial One. Rian trailed after her, cursing his fate. If she had qualms about entering the place, then he should stop her, but doing the thinking was not usually the place of a *kjardin*, no matter how witless or stubborn the person to be guarded. Not that Maskelle was witless. But he had seen enough of her to know that her idea of what was dangerous was different from that of sensible people; it didn't mean she couldn't be killed by a dagger between the ribs from some mad but lucky enemy.

They entered the tower through an archway that led into welcome shade. Like the other towers, spiral stairs curved up the inside walls to reach the other levels, but at first it looked as if there was nowhere else to go on this floor, though he knew from the size of the place this couldn't be the only chamber. There seemed to be nothing except for a massive carving on the far wall, a stylized ocean populated by strange creatures. Then Rian's eyes adjusted to the sudden dimness and he realized there were two walls, one in front of the other, their designs interlocking, so the smaller barrier seemed to fade into the larger one behind it. The Celestial One crossed the room and went around the edge of the smaller wall. His attendant priest was standing in the archway, apparently ready to wait patiently, but Rian followed Maskelle.

Once around the wall there was a wide doorway, framed by more of the large carved snakes. Rian knew they were guardian spirits like the lions, but their resemblance to demons was hardly reassuring. As Maskelle started to step through the doorway, she stopped abruptly and whispered something under her breath. Then she stepped inside.

Rian started after her, but found he had stopped in the doorway too. The air in the large chamber was hot and still and something in it made the hair on the back of his neck stand up. He made himself move forward.

The floor was carved of one very large, very flat stone, its grey surface almost as smooth and soft as pearl. The reason for this extravagance was apparent when he saw what lay in the center. It was a round, complex, colorful design, about twenty feet across, obviously incomplete. At first he thought it was being painted onto the stone, but then he saw it was three dimensional, raised as much as an inch off the floor. *Colored sand,* he thought. Or powdered shell or glass. The only break to the floor's seamless stone surface was a raised lip that enclosed the section where the design lay.

Maskelle circled it to the right, still swearing under her breath, and Rian followed her automatically, hanging back a few steps to keep out of her way. *It's a map,* he thought, though he had never seen a map that wasn't flat lines drawn on parchment or hide. But in the ridges and depressions and flat stretches marked with tiny dark green protrusions he was sure he could see mountains and lakes and the jungle on the lowland plains. It was a more complete map than any he had ever seen, showing things that in the Sintane were only trader's tales. Then a closer look showed him these weren't lakes and forests but complex designs, like the carved arabesques and patterns of lotus buds on the temple walls outside.

He shook his head, a little dazed. There was something strange about being in the same room with the thing. Or maybe breathing the same air as it; there was something about it that seemed alive. It gave the impression of taking up all available space in the large chamber, as if walls, any walls, were too small to contain in it. Rian realized a moment later that it was a map again. He could see the mountain borders of the Sintane, a deep blue ridged depression that must represent the waters of the In-land Sea.

The waters were moving, waves crawling up the white sand beach . . .

Rian rubbed his eyes and looked again. It was just meaningless shapes now, nothing but complicated patterns in sand.

He swore softly. He didn't need to be told this was a powerful magic. Frustrated by the elusiveness of the thing, he tried to follow the pattern with his eyes, starting at the incomplete areas and following the spiral of several layers of built-up colored powders, all with intricately sculpted symbols. He resisted the urge to make them into towns and valleys and roads and hills. He made it past several turns, ignoring the branches that led off to more complex arrangements towards the center, but as the spiral neared another incomplete section, it dissolved into dark sand, the designs ceasing to resemble those on the temple walls and becoming something ugly and dark. Rian looked away, a sudden constriction in his chest. When he looked back at it, it was a map again, and the section of dark sand was a living storm, worse than any rainy season monsoon, tearing up the terrain that lay helplessly under it. With a sudden, bone-deep certainty, he knew that whatever this magic was, something was terribly wrong with it.

Maskelle stepped carefully back from the edge of the design, taking Rian's elbow and drawing him after her. Even a step or two away from the thing, the air was a little easier to breathe. Her voice shaking just a little, Maskelle said, "How did it happen?"

The Celestial One's voice sounded resigned. "We don't know."

Rian started guiltily. He had had no awareness that there was anyone else in the chamber at all. He looked around and saw there were three other priests in the room, all older men, the complexity of their scalp tattoos denoting high rank. They carried carved staffs like Maskelle and they didn't look pleased to see her. "You don't know," Maskelle repeated, sounding as if she was hovering in some state between utter stupefaction and disgust. "Haven't you tried to remove it?"

The Celestial One sighed and leaned on his staff. One of the other priests said, "We have removed it every time."

She turned to stare at him.

The man, a grim-faced priest with hard eyes, nodded. "Since the twentieth night of the Rite when it was first placed there. Every day we remove it, every day it forms again. Sometimes in the same area, sometimes elsewhere."

Maskelle shook her head and turned away, almost fleeing the chamber. Rian gathered his scattered wits and went after her.

The Celestial One's attendant stared worriedly as Maskelle stormed past and they came out in the inner court between two of the covered passages. The sun had appeared again and the reflection and heat coming off the white stone was temporarily blinding, but at least the air was fresh. "So what happened?" Rian asked impatiently. "What is it?"

"It's supposed to be the Wheel of the Infinite, the most important part of the Hundred Year Rite." She ran her hands through her hair, completely undoing her braids, and stopped with double handfuls of hair, as if she was contemplating pulling it out. "What it is now, I don't know." She shook her head, biting her lip. "The End of Year Rites— Each year the highest Koshan priests, the Voices, make a . . . a model of the world. Through it the world is remade in its own image. The culmination takes place at the rainy season Equinox, and the sand that was used to make the model is collected and dispersed to wind and water, which strengthens the bonds that hold everything together."

Rian looked at the tower. *Everything?* The utter stillness of the air in that chamber, so different from the wind-cooled passages in the rest of the place, the raised lip of stone around the center portion of the room, made sense now. "That design, that was the model?"

"Was, yes."

"The black storm-looking . . . thing. It comes back all by itself?"

She nodded grimly. "What I want to know is how it got there in the first place."

The Celestial One hobbled out of the covered walk and over to them, raising his hand to shade his eyes against the glare. He said, "That was why I wanted your advice."

"How did this happen?" Maskelle demanded again.

"On the twentieth night of the Rite, Master Igarin fell suddenly ill." He looked at Rian and added, "The rite must end on a certain day and delay can't be allowed, so if one of the Voices can't continue, someone must take his place. A young priest called Veran, who was training to be elevated to Voice, took over the duty while the others present carried the sick man out to the court and summoned healers. Veran was alone in the chamber for perhaps a quarter hour, no more. When the others came back to return to their task, it was as you see it. This was eleven days ago." He shook his head. "I should have obeyed my first impulse and written to you earlier. If I had, you would have been here in time."

"Veran, Veran," Maskelle muttered to herself. "He's a new one. Where is he now? What explanation does he give?"

"He is in the care of the healers, under watch. He is ill himself now and can tell us nothing of how this happened."

Maskelle's expression was dubious, as well it might be. Ignoring the fact that he probably shouldn't be cross-questioning the Celestial One, Rian asked sharply, "What happened to the other priest, the one he replaced?"

"He is dead."

"Poison?"

"There was no sign of it." The old man's face was wry. "The convenience of his indisposition had occurred to us."

Maskelle grabbed handfuls of her hair again and paced rapidly up and down the court. The Celestial One watched her hopefully, which worried Rian more than anything. The old man really had no idea what had happened to their Rite, and no idea how to fix it. Maskelle stopped and said finally, "The disruption that forms every day . . . It's the same size as the first one, that Veran made."

"Yes."

"There's more there than one person could do in a quarter hour."

The Celestial One winced. "We realized that."

Rian asked, "How is the Rite made?" Since no one had bitten his head off for asking questions, he didn't intend to stop.

Preoccupied, Maskelle answered, "You drop the sand from your palm and then guide it into place with your breath, using a small wooden tube to make it more accurate. It's not as hard as it sounds; anyone who was clever with his hands could learn to do it." She looked at the Celestial One. "But what are you doing about it?"

"The highest masters remove the offending section of the pattern, while the others continue with the undamaged section. They thought they had established the boundaries of the affected area." The Celestial One regarded her steadily from under his heavy grey brows. "But they have not been entirely successful. Sometimes the spot changes its position to avoid them."

Rian looked from one to the other. *I take it they can't just stop,* he thought. *Or sweep it up and start over.* If it was that simple, then surely they would have done it already. And if it really worked as they thought it did . . . If that was really the world in there, spread out on the floor in colored sand with that disruption, that dark design of fire and storm and yawning void in it . . .

"Taking it apart . . ." Uneasily, Maskelle said, "I'm not sure that's a good idea."

The Celestial One looked away. "I was afraid you would say that."

6

The clouds had returned and a light rain had begun by the time they left the Marai. Crossing back over the causeway, Maskelle still wasn't quite sure how things stood between her and the Celestial One, if he was really serious about expecting her to stay here and help him. She thought he had hoped, somehow, that she would look at that . . . thing that was forming out of the sand in the Year Rite and tell him how to fix it. *Fond hope,* she thought sourly. But she didn't suppose he had really believed that she would solve his problem so easily. As she and Rian reached the end of the causeway, she realized she had forgotten to ask the Celestial One for money. Well, he had said he would send someone to the post house with word for her tonight; she would ask then.

She stopped at the end of the causeway and took a deep breath of the warm damp air. Darker clouds now streaked the grey sky and the foot traffic had increased as people hurried to finish their errands before the rain turned heavy. More awnings and cheap oilpaper water shades had sprouted over the little market while puddles formed in the paving. She looked at Rian, who was standing with hands on his hips, surveying the passers-by at the base of the steps with a disgruntled air that was increased by the rain soaking his hair and sticking the thin fabric of his shirt to his chest. They exchanged a look. He said, "The Rite . . . It really remakes the world?"

She nodded, gathering her sodden robes around her. At the edge of the market there was an open-sided wooden building where water steamed in copper pots over braisers and a rough stone oven smelled strongly of sweet bread. Having breakfast with Barime that morning had awakened a craving for real tea, not what passed for it in the provinces or among the Ariaden, and she led the way under its shelter.

Maskelle went to the back, away from the other customers, and sat down on the damp matting that covered the pavement. Rian took a place where he could watch her back and the approach from the market. The Kushorit didn't believe in eating out in public streets and avoided it whenever possible; except for the woman preparing the food and the boy helping her, the few other customers under the shelter were foreigners. They stared curiously at the old nun and the young Sitanese, until Rian unhooked the siri's scabbard from his belt and laid it within easy reach, then gazed meaningfully at them. That made them shuffle nervously and go back to their food and conversations.

The boy brought them tea in brown clay cups and a banana leaf full of little buns rolled in palm sugar. Maskelle gave him the last silver bit she had. She watched Rian taste the tea and wince. Kushorit tea was an acquired taste. "I don't know how to explain the Rite without using ritual language," she began slowly.

"I could see it was a making a map." Rian frowned, rolling one of the buns around in the scattered sugar. "But I could also see that's not all it is."

"The symbols are the reality. When I was first learning the Koshan way . . ." *An eon or so ago,* she reminded herself. "There was an old story that back when the Kushor-An was still being built, before the Celestial Court moved here from Tel Adra, that word came to the Voices from the outlying islands that the Emissary of Sakkara had sent an invasion fleet."

Rian's brows draw together in puzzlement. "Sakkara?"

"I'd never heard the name before either. No one has. When the Voices heard of the invasion, it was near the Equinox when the culmination of the Rite occurs. They were still constructing the Wheel of the Infinite and they hadn't yet reached the Aspian Straits, where the fleet would have to pass to reach the Rijan Gulf and the delta, to sail up the river to Duvalpore. The armies of the Empire were very small then, barely enough to protect the villages and the roads from bandits. They knew the Sakkarans were sending hundreds of ships. So, when the Voices built the symbols for the Aspian Straits into the Wheel, they changed the symbols, just slightly, so that the Aspian Straits were closed. And that's what made the Inland Sea."

"What happened to the Sakkarans?"

"No one knows. One story is that the Voices didn't build the Wheel fast enough, and they closed the Straits with the fleet inside it. The Sakkarans were so struck by the loss of all the ships and people that they never recovered, and dwindled away to become nomads, or went north to join the Batiran Cities. I've heard the Celestial One say that he thought it more likely that in changing the shape of the land, what they actually did was change everything about it, its shape, its history, its reality." *Its reality.* Could the alterations to the Wheel already be affecting the world, even before the Rite was culminated? It might explain the monstrosity the Priest of the Sare had shown her, and the power of the water spirit. The thought was not comforting. She continued, "They changed the whole region to someplace else, that looked a great deal like the places where the Sakkaran cities used to be, and they sent the Aspian Strait and the cities somewhere else, that looked the same, but with no Celestial Empire to attack. Which is why we don't try to do that anymore."

She sipped her tea thoughtfully. "We don't know what all the symbols in the Wheel mean. The ones that show the bottom half of the world aren't even visible unless you look at them through the Infinite, and we don't even know what geography half of them are meant to represent except what we can see in the Wheel itself."

"There's a bottom half to the world?" Rian sounded a little skeptical.

She nodded. "The lower ranks of Koshans travel and make maps and bring them back here, so the librarians can record them and the Voices can try to identify what the still unknown symbols might represent. It doesn't always match exactly. The theory is that the Wheel shows us what the world would look like if we could see it from the Infinite."

"The Holder Lord thought the Koshan monks were spies, though he was never stupid enough to kill one."

"That would have been stupid," Maskelle agreed. "That was the kind of thing I used to be sent to deal with."

Rian looked out at the dingy market again, the rain splashing on the pavement, the stalls and awnings, and the grey walls and towers of the Marai floating above the rain-mist in the distance. He said, "If that story is true, then the Kushorit rule the world."

"In a sense. If you can destroy a thing, I suppose you can be said to rule it." She should have realized he would see it that way. The Sintane might be behind the rest of the civilized lands in many ways, but in understanding the uses and abuses of secular power it might well be ahead. "It's not called the Celestial Empire for nothing."

"But no one knows."

She shook her head. "The Voices know. That's the last part of the elevation to Voice, the revelation of what the Rite is actually capable of. The entire Koshan priesthood is based on locating the people who can be trained and trusted to be Voices. It's safer if no one else knows." She took a deep breath. "Though it's not as if anyone could build a Wheel of the Infinite, even if they knew how. It takes years of learning, not just to know how to make the symbols, but how to weave them in and out of the Infinite.

And you have to learn how to listen to the Ancestors of the Marai, so they can guide you if you go wrong." She glanced up at him and demanded, "Why are you smiling?"

"I was thinking of how the Holder Lord would have shit himself if he knew." Rian cocked an eyebrow at her. "You had that power in your hand, but instead you tried to take the throne?"

"I didn't want the world. I had a reason for trying to take the throne. Besides, one person can't build the Wheel, or bring the Rite to a culmination at the right time." She added wryly, "In the Infinite, timing is everything. For a long while now, mine has been terrible." She set her cup aside reluctantly. "I suppose we'd better get back."

They went outside and started down the steps to the lower plaza. As Maskelle reached the bottom, her eyes were on one of the stands in the other section of the temporary market. Piles of gourds and melons lay on wicker mats and the market woman was looking around as if gauging the crowd and the possibility of packing up early. Maskelle saw the woman glance her way, saw her eyes widen in shock. Her own self-consciousness almost betrayed her, and it took her an extra heartbeat to realize the woman was staring not at her, but at something just behind her. Maskelle swung around, belatedly bringing up her staff. She was in time to see a raggedly dressed man only two steps above her, raising a short club. Before she could move, Rian melted out of the group of tradesmen hurrying down the steps around them and caught the upraised club. The man managed a strangled yell before he met the steps face-first.

The crowd scattered with startled exclamations. Maskelle stepped up and leaned over the attacker as Rian held him pinned to the wet stone, one of his arms twisted into an easily breakable position. The man glared up at her with nothing but wholly human malice and fear in his eyes. She glanced up at Rian. "He's not under any influence." She looked down at the captive speculatively. "Except political. Are you Mirak's? Or did Disara send you? Or Raith himself?"

The man sneered at her but said nothing. Rian said, "Do you need answers?"

A little more fear crossed their captive's face. Rian's matter-of-factness was more threatening than any amount of shouted threats. "No." Maskelle straightened and leaned on her staff, the wood and silver slick from the rain. "It doesn't matter. Let him go."

Rian looked exasperated, but hauled the man up and shoved him away out toward the plaza. The man fell, rolled, and bolted off through the crowd.

"A thief, Sister?" one of the men from the market asked.

A small, somewhat bemused crowd had gathered. Parts of Duvalpore could be rough going after dark, but not here, in the Temple City and at the very base of the Marai. And a Koshan nun should be safe anywhere. These people would find it difficult to believe that a Koshan could be attacked in their own city; even if they had seen the man about to deliver a blow obviously intended to be fatal, they might discount the evidence of their own eyes. Maskelle said, "Yes, a thief."

With narrowed eyes Rian watched the man run away. "You have a lot of enemies here," he commented

"Well, yes," she admitted.

The crowd, seeing that nothing else seemed likely to occur, began to go back to their business. Rian said, "They were quick to find you, unless somebody at the post house recognized you and warned them." He looked at her and added thoughtfully, "Or the temple."

Maskelle started to deny it, then realized she knew nothing of how the currents of power had shifted in the past years. "Maybe. Maybe not. Did you see where he came from?"

"He was clumsy. I saw him as soon as we got to the causeway.

He was waiting on the other side of the wall between the grassy court and the moat."

Maskelle nodded to herself. If the man had been that close to the Marai, then he couldn't have been under any kind of influence. It was barely possible to work dark magic within the boundaries of Duvalpore, but the power sink in the Infinite that the Marai formed would overwhelm any lesser force. She turned to go through the market, where the people huddled under the awnings and shades watched them and discussed the matter animatedly as they passed by. That should discourage the man's friends, if he had any. "Didn't he see you?"

Rian nodded. "I hung back at the top of the stairs so he'd think we were splitting up. He was anxious and went for you right away instead of waiting to be sure." He rolled his shoulders, shedding tension like water. "That he came for you here means they don't know where we're camped. If we're lucky they won't have a chance to follow us back, but don't count on it."

"Oh." *Well, you could have told me he was there.* It didn't appear to have been any of her business. Rian was drawing more attention now; it wasn't usual to see a nun with a guard attending her, especially one who was obviously from the outer provinces. It occurred to her that she might have stopped and thought a moment about the logistics of having a Sitanese *kjardin* who was also her lover. She hadn't asked for the guard, but she had wanted the lover. Or maybe she had just wanted a friend. *No, let's be honest. I definitely wanted him as a lover.* Everything else seemed to have come with the territory. *If I had stopped and thought, I'd still be here in Duvalpore, in the same circumstances, but with a nice lump on my head and lonely into the bargain.*

They reached the posting house to find that the Ariaden were already giving a performance. Inhabitants of Duvalpore typically went to ground during the hard rains of this season, but the travellers in the post house hadn't learned that kind of resignation.

Walking up on their camp, Maskelle saw the wagons had been arranged in a semicircle and they had taken the giant oilcloth that could be draped on posts to form a mountain backdrop and stretched it from the top of Rastim's wagon to Firac's. Under this shelter, a small group of travellers and their children crouched on the muddy ground watching Gardick, Therassa, and Doria doing an abbreviated version of an Ariaden comedy play. Lamps hanging from the wagons made it an almost cheerful scene.

Rastim was sitting on the tail board of his wagon, watching the performance with a self-satisfied expression. As Maskelle made her way over to him, he said, low-voiced, "This is a good place for theater. We only passed the word within the compound, and look how many people came, even with the rain."

Maskelle sat next to him. It wasn't dry, but the oilcloth deflected the worst of it. "That's good, because the rain isn't going to stop anytime soon."

Rian, leaning against the wagon and surveying the camp, muttered darkly to himself in Sitanese. Rastim gave him an annoyed look. On the makeshift stage Gardick was making an elaborate pantomime of pretending to sneak up on Therasa, who was doing the same to Doria. The audience laughed appreciatively. Rastim asked, "How do we approach the chief priest about—" he lowered his voice cautiously "—the curse?"

Gisar had been quiet since the Illsat Keo and wouldn't have any opportunity to make trouble within the city boundary. Maskelle had been planning to draft Rastim and maybe Firac to help haul the cursed puppet to the Marai tomorrow to get the Ariaden's problem taken care of. She started to say this, but caught sight of indigo silk, visible even through the drizzle and mist, coming in through the gate of the post compound. It was a large palanquin. Rian had seen it too, and gave her a worried glance. She said, "No, blue means it's from the temples."

As the palanquin approached, they could see it was attended by temple guards on horseback and a number of priests, all clutching oilcloth parasols. The traders and travellers who hadn't ventured out of their wagons for the entertainment peered out now as the palanquin passed.

The play stumbled to a halt as the Ariaden caught sight of it and their audience turned to watch. The temple guards spread out, forming a loose barrier between the camp and the rest of the compound. Beside her, Rian stirred purposefully and Maskelle leaned over to take his arm and pull him toward her. He came reluctantly, and she felt rather like a handler hauling on the harness of a two-hundred-pound hunting cat and hoping it chose to pay attention. He settled against her, watching the guards warily.

The curtains of the palanquin stirred and the priests gathered around it, two of them helping the occupant out. It was the Celestial One. He shook the priests off, leaned on his staff, and picked his way through the mud to the oilcloth shelter. The awestruck audience shifted to make room for him. Undoubtedly many of these people, newly come to Duvalpore, did not know just who the old man was, but it was obvious from his attendance and method of arrival that he was important. Carefully, the Celestial One made to sit down, one of the younger priests hurrying forward to whisk a rattan mat under him before his robes touched the mud. The old man settled himself comfortably, then gestured to the actors. "Continue."

After a moment the Ariaden rose to the occasion. Doria stammered her next line and the play continued. "Who is that?" Rastim whispered.

"The chief priest," Maskelle told him.

Rastim stared at her in horror. "This play isn't fit for him!" he whispered tensely.

"He won't care."

Rastim moaned, then subsided into a choked silence.

After a time, when the temple guards did nothing but stoically sit their horses in the rain and the other priests huddled uncomfortably under the edge of the oilcloth, Rian settled against her a little and she felt some of the tension in him uncoil. He said, "Does he do this often?"

"No," Maskelle said. She saw Rastim was listening alertly too. The Celestial One was watching the play with polite attention, though he hadn't reacted to anything the actors said or did. He was probably deep in meditation and had no idea what was happening on the makeshift stage. "It's uncomfortable for him to go too far from the temples and the connecting canals." She hesitated, not knowing how to explain without using the Koshan words that neither man would understand. "Here in Kushor-At, the symbol is almost the same as the reality, and the temples are very powerful symbols. The Celestial One is a symbol, too, and after being a part of that for so long, it's not easy to be just a man again."

Rastim scratched his chin thoughtfully. "How did he become Celestial One? Was there a vote among the other chief priests?"

A vote? Maskelle thought, bemused. The Ariaden were a strange people. "He died."

Rastim and Rian both stared at her. "Died?" Rastim repeated.

"To become the Celestial One you have to become so close to the Infinite, so at one with it, that you can merge with it and return at will. One morning he died, and later when they were preparing him for his funeral, he sat up and asked for tea." She smiled wryly. "There are probably at least one or two other Koshans in the city who can do it and some very advanced penitents hiding out in the jungle. They just aren't careless enough to let someone see them and force them to take on the duties of Celestial One."

She could feel Rian and Rastim exchanging a look behind her back, their enmity temporarily forgotten. Then Rian asked, "How do you become Voice of the Adversary?"

Rastim stirred uneasily, nervous of what her answer might be. Maskelle said only, "That's a long story."

Abandoning the death issue and returning to the earlier topic of conversation, Rastim said slowly, "So, the chief priest stays in the city?"

"Always in the city, usually in one of the temples. It's easier for him to travel on the canals than on the streets."

After a moment, Rian said, "You're part of that too, aren't you? The temples and the boundaries. Is it the same for you, when you leave it?"

The question was too perceptive by far. She ran a hand through his hair as a poor attempt at distraction and said, "Not anymore."

Rian was still watching her, brows drawn together. Rastim said worriedly, "Then why is he here?"

Maskelle saw the gates of the compound opening again, and her eyes narrowed. "That's an easier question. Look." She nodded toward them.

There were three more men on horseback there, dressed in the lacquered iron breastplates and crested helmets of the Palace Guard. They saw the Celestial One's palanquin and the temple guards and stopped in the gate. One of them leaned down to question the compound's attendant, who shrugged elaborately. One of the temple guards spotted them and turned his horse toward them, so the interlopers would be sure to know they had been noticed.

"Are they here to arrest us?" Rastim asked nervously.

Maskelle shook her head. "They can't. Not unless they catch us stealing or killing someone. I imagine they were sent to ask us—me—politely to leave."

After a moment, the Palace Guards turned their mounts and left, the attendant swinging the gate closed behind them. Maskelle said, "The Celestial One never travels in state. He came here like this so he could be seen here. To make it plain to certain people that I—we—have his protection."

Rian was still looking grimly toward the gate. "Whoever sent them won't go against the Celestial One?" He looked at her again. "Not even for something they want very badly?"

Maskelle started to reply, and for an instant thought she heard the whisper of the Ancestors across the outer edge of her consciousness. She hesitated, but if they had really spoken to her, their message had passed too swiftly for her to understand. She said, "No. No, they wouldn't. Not for any reason." Her mouth quirked at the irony of it, but she told herself it was surely true. "Not even for me."

After the play, the audience hurried back to their wagons through the rain that now fell more lightly but from a steadily darkening sky. The Celestial One stayed planted on his mat, looking around at his hosts with a beneficent smile. Their purpose accomplished, he sent away the temple guards and the priests, with instructions to bring the palanquin back in time to return him to the Marai for the next meditation ring. When the Ariaden realized that the old man meant to spend the rest of the evening with them, they panicked. Rastim, quietly hysterical, practically dragged Maskelle behind his wagon to ask what they could possibly serve their guest for dinner.

"The same thing Old Mali was planning on serving everyone else. Oh, I meant to tell you, don't buy anything from the post house; there's a market right across—"

"We found the market! But he's a— A—" The little man gestured helplessly, speechless for once.

"The Koshans are ascetics, Rastim. And he's over a hundred years old, there's not much he can eat anymore. Some melon or taro will do just fine."

Rastim calmed slightly, peering cautiously around the wagon to where the old man sat. Killia's daughter, ordinarily wary of strangers, crouched next to him showing off her wooden dolls. The Celestial One was studying them with grave attention and the little girl looked about to climb into his lap. Rastim said,

"The highest personage who ever came to our theater in Ariad was the Protector of Orad-dell."

"All right." Maskelle had never understood the Ariad's hierarchy. "It's a good thing the Celestial One came tonight, anyway, whatever the reason. I need to ask him for money."

Rastim stared at her, aghast.

It took some time for the compound to settle down after all the excitement, but eventually the other inhabitants retired to their own wagons and makeshift shelters, and smoke from braziers and cooking fires mingled with the rain and the mist. The Ariaden hauled out all their mats and some rugs to cover the muddy ground around the fire, and the Celestial One sat down to dinner with them. Old Mali had been to the market, and relatively fresh melon and some papaws were added to the usual baked taro and rice. As Maskelle had predicted, the Celestial One found nothing unusual in the plainness of the fare and ate very little of anything.

Maskelle finally managed to interpret Rastim's winking and brow-furrowing and realized he wanted her to bring up the subject of Gisar. Obligingly, she turned to the Celestial One and said, "My friends have a little problem. One of their puppets is under a curse."

"Ah." The old man nodded, as if this was a problem commonly brought to his attention.

"In Corvalent, by a magister named Acavir."

"Corvalent," the Celestial One said, in a tone of mild exasperation. "They are very unwise in their use of power, in Corvalent."

"And no sense of humor," Gardick muttered, from over by one of the wagons.

"It was very active before we arrived in the city." Maskelle shrugged. "One lunar cycle in the outer gallery of the Marai, while you're present for the Rite, should take care of it." The Ariaden were all leaning forward in breathless suspense.

The Celestial One nodded. "Bring it tomorrow and I will have it placed there." There were some gasps of excitement and

Rastim buried his face in his hands in pure relief. The Celestial One added, "You will do me the honor of coming to a temple guesthouse tonight."

All the Ariaden now looked at Maskelle. Rian, sitting at the edge of the firelight, shifted uneasily.

Maskelle eyed him thoughtfully. She said, "All of us?"

"Of course."

There was a stirring among the Ariaden, mixed alarm and curiosity. Rastim rolled his eyes with weary resignation. Maskelle shook her head. "We've been travelling all day and we're not going to move again tonight. We'll come to the guesthouse, but tomorrow."

The Celestial One raised his gray brows, frowning slightly. "Tomorrow?"

"Tomorrow."

They eyed each other a moment, then the Celestial One sighed. "Very well. But I will leave some of the guards here, to make sure you are undisturbed."

Maskelle couldn't tell what Rian's reaction was from her place near the fire, but she would bet that he wasn't happy. She said, "You think there's that much danger?"

"Perhaps, perhaps not." The old man gestured impatiently. "This is too important. I don't want any . . . unresolved situations from the past to interrupt the progress of the Year Rite."

Considering how the Year Rite is progressing, interrupting it could be the best thing, Maskelle thought grimly. "All right."

Later that night, the palanquin and its attendants returned for the Celestial One. The priests departed with it, but the temple guards remained, one in the shelter near the post house gate and five others scattered through the Ariaden's encampment. Rastim pulled Maskelle aside and asked anxiously, "What is this place we're going to?"

"A temple guesthouse. They're for Koshans travelling in from the provinces. Or anyone who comes to speak to the Celestial

One and doesn't have anywhere else to stay." Rastim still looked worried. It finally dawned on Maskelle why. "They won't expect us to pay for the use of it."

"Oh, that's all right then." Rastim looked relieved. "Can we give performances there?"

"Probably. The court should be big enough."

Rastim returned to the others to take them the good news, and Maskelle retired into her wagon to let them talk it out amongst themselves.

The camp settled down gradually. After a time the wagon board trembled and creaked and Rian hauled open a shutter and climbed in, muttering under his breath.

Maskelle steadied the swinging cage lamp. She was sitting on the faded blankets covering the bunk and had shed her wet clothes, wrapping herself in the last dry robe she had. It was from Meidun, neither white nor Koshan blue, but red with black embroidery on the collar and cuffs. The night had grown cooler as the rain grew harder, and she was glad for the robe's warmth. She asked, "What were you doing out there?"

"I was making sure they'd let us leave," he said. He sprawled on the floor of the wagon, dripping muddy water onto the worn boards.

"They're here to protect us," Maskelle said earnestly, though she couldn't quite keep her lips from twitching with amusement.

Rian consulted the ceiling for a moment, apparently asking it for patience.

"They will keep out any uninvited guests," she pointed out more reasonably.

He sat back on his hands, looking sour.

She eyed him thoughtfully. "You're getting mud everywhere."

"There is already mud everywhere. There is nowhere, from the Rijan Pillars to the Gulf of Mais, that is not covered with mud."

"There's no mud in this bed, and there's not going to be."

That worked.

Later, when Rian's clothes were a damp pile on the floor and he was stretched out next to her in the narrow bunk, she stroked his back and came to terms with the fact that she was not going to send him away. It was selfish of her, perhaps. Not perhaps. Acknowledging one's faults was an important step to the acceptance of wisdom, but she seemed to have stalled at that point instead of going on to do something about them. She asked, "Can you read?"

"Read what?" His head was buried against her neck and his voice was muffled.

"Anything. Anrin, maybe?" It was the written form of Kushorit, the everyday language of the Celestial Empire which just about everyone but the half-wild people of the deep forest tribes learned to read and write, either from their village priests or the travelling penitents. The outer provinces had their own written scripts, but she knew that few outside the noble or religious classes there had the skill.

"What's that?"

"You'll have to learn it." If they stayed long in Duvalpore, and it looked as if they would, he would need to know. *You're being overconfident again,* a warning voice whispered.

Rian groaned and nuzzled her neck, apparently in an attempt to distract her.

"Reading is a skill required of personal guards here."

His muffled snort was eloquently doubtful, but he didn't argue with her.

She asked, "So what is Taprot in the Sintane?"

He finally stirred enough to lift his head. His hair was tousled and his eyes wicked. He said, "It's the patron of justice, of catching thieves, punishing murderers."

She ruffled his hair. *That is . . . oddly coincidental.* The Koshan Order taught that there were no coincidences. The Adversary and the other Ancestors put the pieces on the board, but they didn't give away the game.

Rian sat up on his elbow, watching her thoughtfully. "Tell me how you got to be Voice of the Adversary."

"That was a very long time ago," she said forbiddingly.

He settled in more comfortably, apparently willing to wait however long it took for her to bring herself to tell the story. She sighed and gave in. "When I was a girl I lived in Rashet, a village some miles west of here. No one knew at the time, but a cult was growing in the area, centered around a man-witch who had learned dark magic from somewhere to the east. He had a galdani—"

"What's that?"

"A spirit of the Infinite that has become polluted and crossed back into our world. He was—"

"A demon."

"All right, a demon," she agreed, pulling at the blanket and shifting around in annoyance. "The witch was keeping it by sending his followers out to attack travellers on the Eastern Road and anyone else who was out after dark. It fed on hearts and kidneys." The memory was unexpectedly fresh; her first experience with violent death. She shook her head and went on. "No one knew why this was happening. There were just all these mutilated bodies found in the ditches and the rice fields. The governor had called for extra troops to patrol, but it took time to get them and people were starting to panic. Then the Adversary spoke to me for the first time."

Rian was silent a moment, watching her. "What did he tell you?"

She smiled. "He doesn't always speak in words. It's difficult to explain, exactly. And you have to remember, he's not really a 'he.' He's a spirit, a force. Spirits don't have language, they can't speak like we do, they don't even think like we do. He showed me the witch and the galdani, and what needed to happen for

the galdani to die. I went there, and I made those things happen."
She lay back and looked at the wagon's ceiling, the candle flame
staining the hanging puppets with light and shadow. "I was very
lucky that first time. Or maybe it wasn't luck. In Duvalpore, the
old Voice of the Adversary had died. I didn't know that, either.
I didn't know anything. But in searching for the new Voice, the
Ancestors sent the Celestial One and the other priests to Rashet,
and there they found me. And a lot of dead cultists."

Rian drew his fingers through her tumbled braids. "That's
how the Voice of the Adversary is chosen? The old one dies, and
the Adversary picks a new one?"

"Yes. We all agreed later that it would have been better to
choose a Koshan who had come up through the ranks in the
ordinary way. When I did my service as a penitent, I was not
exactly in a humble frame of mind."

"But what—" Rian started to say.

"No more questions." Talking about it had brought everything back to her, more vividly than she had thought possible.
She leaned forward and stopped his mouth with hers, and for
once he obeyed her and proceeded to distract her from any serious thoughts.

Another priest came early the next morning, waiting in the
center of their camp with a couple of acolytes as attendants. The
Ariaden had never been good at getting an early start, being more
used to giving performances in the evening and travelling through
the afternoon. After long association with them, Maskelle was
starting to lose the trick of it herself. She found it easier to stay
up for days on end than to rise early after a night's sleep.

The rain had let up, as it often did in the mornings of this
season, and the Ariaden staggered around packing the oilcloth
and bundling their other belongings into the wagons. The priest,
an old man who had a sixth level rank by his scalp markings and

must be accustomed to the Celestial One's more unusual orders, watched them calmly.

The guesthouse was not far and the streets not very crowded this early in the morning, so they managed to move the wagons with only a little difficulty. The temple guards were dismissed, leaving them escorted only by the aging priest. He walked beside Maskelle's wagon to show them the way, scandalizing the Ariaden and startling Rian. When they turned into the wide tree-shaded street lined with large houses behind wooden palisades, Rastim, who was riding up with Maskelle, muttered that they must have taken the wrong way.

The priest stopped to open the gate of a house directly behind the Marai, the wooden palisade that surrounded the house backing up against the canal that enclosed the temple. Maskelle saw Rian eyeing that palisade, and knew he was noting the fact that it was meant for privacy and to keep out casual thieves; any healthy adult could easily scale it. Over the wall they could see the house was two stories, a veranda running along the upper level shaded by the high-peaked roof and the tall trees in the court. The street was lined with similar houses, the homes of wealthy tradesmen and city or court officials.

The gate opened on a courtyard of packed dirt, shaded and to some extent protected from the rain by the broad leaves of the trees. An open area in the back had space to park the wagons and a pen and roofed enclosure for the oxen, as well as a gate that opened out to the canal to what was probably the house's private water stairs. A wooden shelter to one side covered the stone oven and firepit of the outdoor kitchen.

Maskelle climbed down from the wagon and stretched, letting the priest have the job of persuading the Ariaden that this was the place they were supposed to be and that it was all right to put their wagons in the back area and to feed their oxen on the bundled fodder stored in the roofed pen. She walked up the path of paving stones that led to the house.

Thick pillars supported the upper part and divided the lower into pantry, storage, and bathing rooms. She climbed the staircase that led up to the veranda on the upper floor. The mats that hung between the pillars to shield the veranda from rain and sun had been rolled up, probably recently since the interior still smelled a little musty.

There was a large main room for eating and socializing, then a number of smaller sleeping rooms to accommodate large groups or families. The appointments were those of a fine house, the carving on the doorframes and lintels precise and skilled, the colors in the lacquered wall paintings soothing and delicate. The subjects were all domestic, appropriate for any taste: elegant gardens, beautifully garbed ladies weaving cloth, children playing in courtyards, servants working in well-appointed kitchens, boats on the canals. Bronze lampstands would shed light over the mats and rugs and low tables in the main room, and the other rooms all contained large sleeping cushions rolled up for storage, with piles of extra cotton blankets and small wooden chests to hold clothes and belongings. It felt very odd to walk these rooms, even though she could sense that this was a place of temporary abode only, no one's permanent home. It had been a very long time since she had been in a house like this. *Seven years.*

She was in the main room looking out over the court when Rian came up the stairs. He said, "Rastim wants to know how many other travellers are staying here with us."

She smiled. "Tell him forty or fifty."

Rian came further into the room, looking around with wary approval. "This is a guesthouse?" he asked.

"Yes," she said slowly. "The different temples all have several." Which he already knew from their conversation last night.

"There's a carving of the Adversary's demon face above the door."

Maskelle sighed. She didn't see what he was getting at. "That's just one aspect of the Adversary, and it's not a demon face. Most buildings have that carved somewhere, for luck." That the Adversary's mark was so prominent on this house's pediment was perhaps the reason it had been chosen for them.

"So this wasn't your house?"

"What? No." Now she knew what he meant. She turned away. "My house burned down."

Firac's son Thae came bounding up the stairs, then stopped in the doorway to gaze around in awe. Recovering, he saw Maskelle and said, "That old man is here again."

That, she supposed, *means the Celestial One.* She went out to the veranda and down the stairs, Rian behind her. The water gate stood open to a view of the canal and the back façade of the Marai. A passenger boat was docked at the base of the steps. It was a wide flat-bottomed craft sheltered with a white awning and hung with white silk side panels. The breeze played the tiny bells in the fringes. Several boys—acolytes or servants, it was hard to tell the difference when they all wore grubby breechclouts—leapt down from the boat and began to roll up the panels.

Maskelle went down the steps into the thick damp warmth rising off the canal. The Celestial One was sitting in the boat, clutching his staff. She leaned on one of the support poles for the awning and said, "I don't suppose you're here to help us greet the sunrise."

"I came to bring you to the Marai. There is much to do," the old man said, glaring at her.

Maskelle didn't recall agreeing to spend the day staring hopelessly at the ruined Rite, but it was as good a plan as any. She stepped back, nearly trodding on Rian, who was standing at her elbow. "Rastim, get Gisar; we're going to the Marai."

Rastim and Firac ran for Gisar's box while the other Ariaden jumped for joy and the Celestial One sighed and rearranged his robes. Maskelle leaned on the boat, trying to think constructively. Starting at the beginning would be good. She ducked her head under the awning again. "There's something I want to do first."

"What now?" the Celestial One demanded.

"I want to see Veran, the one who started all this."

The young priest was not in the Marai but in the hospital attached to the Gila Stel, a smaller temple that stood about two streets over from the Marai and formed part of the interconnecting web of canals and temples that concentrated its influence. With some grumbling, the Celestial One had taken Maskelle and Rian down the canal to the Gila Stel in his boat, then sent word to Niare, the priestess in charge of the small temple, to meet and accompany them. He had then taken a nervous Rastim and Firac to the Marai to see to the disposition of Gisar's box.

The hospital occupied three levels of a long stone building that stood just to the west of the Gila Stel. Koshans had always believed that the free movement of air was almost as essential as the free movement of water for the health of the body, and the hospital's walls were lined with windows, their cloth panels standing out at angles to keep out the rain and the sun's heat but still allow in the breeze.

Niare met them outside on the lower gallery, near the square fountains on either side of the entrance that brought in drinking water and fed the channels that surrounded the building and aided the healing power of the place. She was a young woman for her office, and Maskelle supposed she had still been a nun or a lower rank when Maskelle had left the city. Niare greeted her with a wariness that showed she knew exactly who her visitor was, however.

Inside was a large room, cool and quiet, the pillars carved with the plants that medicines could be made from and the names of the Ancestors and spirits associated with healing. The sick lay on pallets near the walls, with a brazier beside each bed for warmth during the night. In the area near the entrance many of the patients were sitting up, talking or playing at diceboards. Others toward the back of the chamber lay quietly, wrapped in blankets, sleeping or silent with pain. One of the blue-robed attendants came to greet Niare and lead them toward the stone stairs at the far end of the chamber.

Following their guide Maskelle realized that Rian was looking around as if he doubted his sanity. Finally she asked, "What is wrong with you?"

"Who is this place for?"

She shrugged. "Everyone." There were a few Koshans of various ranks among the sick, but most of the patients were tradesmen from the markets in the area or people who lived nearby. Some were probably beggars, but since daily bathing was required and clean clothing supplied to those who didn't have their own, it was difficult to tell.

"It doesn't even stink," Rian muttered.

The place was hardly immaculate; one attendant was collecting dirty crockery and another was dealing with the soiled bedding of someone who had been messily ill. "I'm beginning to be very glad I never went to the Sintane," Maskelle said as she started up the steps.

The chief healer waited for them at the top of the stairs. He was an old man, though not nearly so old as the Celestial One. She had known him once, years ago, when he had first been made chief healer here. His expression was grim as he nodded to Niare. Maskelle wasn't sure if the grimness was for her presence or the state of his new patient.

The young priest was at the far end of the second level, separated from the other patients by some painted wooden screens. There was an attendant with him, a young monk who squatted patiently beside the pallet. A jug of water and a basin of soaked cloths stood nearby, giving off the scent of ivibrae and saffron and other healing herbs. The brazier was full of coals and the young priest wrapped in cotton blankets, but he still shivered and tossed his head. His eyes were open and staring and his breath came quick and hard, as if he was running a desperate race.

Maskelle knelt beside the bed. Niare asked the chief healer, "Is there any improvement?"

He shook his head. "He seems the same. He is so fevered that he shivers and seems to be cold. But he doesn't have the other symptoms of any of the illnesses that usually cause such fevers. None of the usual remedies for such things seem to help. He speaks, but much of the time we can't understand him, and it is hard to tell if he is even aware of what he says."

Maskelle looked up at him. "What does he speak of?"

The chief healer frowned. "Of being pursued by something, some creature. Also of the Year Rites." He gestured helplessly. "Nightmares are often caused by these fevers."

Maskelle laid a hand on the young man's forehead. His skin was dry and hot to the touch, as the healer had said. His eyes turned to her, bloodshot and vague. Hair pricked her palm from where it had already begun to grow over his shaven scalp. She felt nothing of the darkness about him, nothing of that restless power that had taken the farmboy's mind and soul and sent him to their camp with death in his hand. *But if it was there, it wouldn't stay. It couldn't, not in this place.* But before this she would have said that it was impossible for such a thing to enter the city at all, let alone the Marai or any other temple. And the powers that stalked her hadn't the conscious wit to attack the Hundred Year Rite. *Circle a myrrh tree three times for luck,* she thought, *I hope they haven't grown wits.* Then she shook her head at herself in exasperation. *Not everything is about you. Examine the problem from all the paths.*

"Do you know where you are?" she asked the young man softly.

His eyes darted aimlessly, then focused on her. He whispered, "The Marai."

That's interesting, she thought. Was it delirium or something else? "What Day is it?"

"The twentieth Day of the Rite. The Hundred Year Rite."

Veran tried to sit up suddenly and Maskelle grabbed his shoulders and held him down. The attendant moved to help her and she shook her head at him. "It's coming," the young man whispered. "I have to be here. But I shouldn't . . . It's not my time—it must be a dream."

It's not his time. Veran had replaced the Voice whose turn it was to work on the Rite. "I think he's reliving what happened." Perhaps over and over again?

"We thought so too, but he won't answer questions," Niare said, sounding weary. "The Celestial One tried for hours."

Veran tossed his head and muttered, "I shouldn't . . . I shouldn't . . . It's coming. . . ."

Maskelle leaned forward and caught the young man's chin, turning his face toward her, waiting until the bloodshot eyes focused on her. "What do you see?"

He gasped, tried to pull away from her.

She said, "The Adversary commands you to speak."

There was a shocked stirring behind her, but she ignored it; this was what the Celestial One had brought her here for. She had no right to invoke the Adversary, but in the state Veran was in she doubted he knew that. The young man's eyes locked on her; his dry bitten lips tried to form words.

"Tell us what happened when you were alone in the chamber with the Rite. Tell us and accept the Adversary's protection."

He opened his mouth, but his voice was a choked exhalation.

"The Adversary defends the just. He—" Watching him intently she looked, really looked, into the young man's eyes.

It was then she realized he wanted to speak. He wanted very much to speak. She saw past the veneer of fevered delirium to awareness, and intelligence, and overwhelming desperation. He knew what had happened and he wanted to tell them, but something prevented him. She heard a whisper of the Ancestors, but again it faded before she could understand the words.

"It's all right," she said quickly, wiping the sweat from his forehead. The instant of clarity was passing and he looked like just another man being driven mad by some illness of the brain, but she knew better now. "I see it. I know. You're trapped and you can't get out."

He slumped back with a strangled cry, but it was a cry of relief. She said, "Try to rest. Don't try to talk anymore. We'll think of some way to help you."

She stood slowly. Niare was watching her, worried and still shocked. The chief healer and the attendant just looked shocked. Maskelle said, "It's not fever or any natural sickness. It's possession."

"Possession?" The chief healer was incredulous. "Here?"

"Here," Maskelle said grimly. "Use tamarisk, sandalwood, myrrh—"

"I know what to do for possession," the healer interrupted. He looked down at Veran, his face troubled. "Are you certain? How—"

"I'm certain," she said. "But if I'm wrong, it won't do him any more harm, will it?"

Niare lingered to speak to the chief healer, and as Maskelle and Rian made their way out, Rian asked, "Will he do what you ask?"

"Yes. He doesn't like the idea, but that won't stop him." She added wryly, "He wants the boy to get well more than he wants me to be wrong."

"I thought demons couldn't get past the city boundaries."

Maskelle stopped just outside on the hospital's portico, out of earshot of any of the patients inside. The sky was lightening a little and it looked like the morning rain might hold off for a time. The Gila Stel stood across a square of grass and shade trees, its golden stone a little dulled by the weather. It was a small temple compared to the Marai, only about a fourth the size, with two stories of galleried courts supporting a three level stepped pyramid, and five small, elegantly proportioned shrines atop that.

Birds called in the trees and Maskelle could hear the bustle of a market just beyond the street wall. "They can't. So whatever caused this isn't a demon." She looked at the Gila Stel and the morning mist rising from the canal behind it. "The Voices who are conducting the Rite would like to believe that whatever Veran did to the Wheel came out of his madness. I think that's a fond and foolish hope. It's far more likely a deliberate act by something that used Veran like a tool." She started along the path toward the temple. "But I'm more used to looking for evil than they are."

"That's why the Celestial One sent for you," Rian pointed out.

That, she thought, *is true.* She added, "And the problem with looking for evil is that you then have to do something about whatever you flush out."

There were two women coming up the path from the Gila Stel, both dressed in casually draped robes, though the richness of their jewelry marked them as Court Ladies, and probably High Court. Pearls hung in garlands from their belts, gold draped their necks and banded their arms and ankles. Their hair was elaborately dressed, plaited and wound up in buns, held in place by gold pins. One was young and very lovely, with high cheekbones and skin so fine it was almost translucent. After a moment Maskelle recognized her as the Court Lady who had been with the Celestial One when they had arrived at the Marai yesterday. She would have been an extremely beautiful woman, but there was no warmth to her beauty, no spontaneity in her gestures in her conversation with her companion. *The spirit dancers carved on the temples have more life to them,* Maskelle thought.

The second woman was older, grey woven through her hair, her robe more modestly draped. It had been seven years and Maskelle had managed to stop searching every face she saw for old enemies, so it took her a long moment to recognize the second woman as Disara.

Maskelle stopped where she was on the path. Disara's eyes

passed over her without recognition; she was speaking to the other woman, and foreigners and other strange people were always to be found near the hospitals. There were people sitting under the trees near the far side of the temple, probably the women's attendants and servants.

Rian was watching her closely. "What's wrong?"

She shook her head minutely. Disara might not recognize her, with her hair grown out and her face and body hardened by seven years of travel. She wanted to see if Disara would know her and how the older woman would react.

The two women reached the portico, just as Niare and the chief healer stepped out of the hospital. There were polite bows and greetings back and forth, then the chief healer stepped back inside, gesturing the women to follow him.

As Disara stepped up to the portico, her eyes met Maskelle's. Maskelle saw the shocked recognition in Disara's face, saw her expression harden to revulsion and anger an instant later. She swept on into the hospital, leaving the other woman behind.

Sounding relieved, Niare said under her breath, "That went as well as could be expected."

Maskelle almost smiled. So she wasn't the only one who had been curious about Disara's reaction.

Instead of following her companion, the young woman was looking Maskelle and Rian over frankly. Since they hadn't been introduced and no one was making any effort to do so, Maskelle stared back at her, hoping she looked as rude as she felt. Undeterred, the woman said calmly, "You are the Voice of the Adversary, lately returned to the city?"

Niare shifted uncomfortably and started to speak, but Maskelle said first, "No, I no longer hold that title. I lost it when I was cursed and exiled from the Empire."

"Ah," the woman said, unruffled. "I was misinformed." Her eyes went to Rian again with a detached curiosity, as if she was examining a statue and not a person.

Maskelle said, pointedly, "I think your presence is required somewhere else."

The woman stared at her a moment, expressionless, then made a sixth-degree bow that might be intended as a subtle insult and continued into the hospital. Maskelle shook her head and Rian muttered something under his breath in Sitanese. Maskelle guessed from the disgruntled tone that he didn't approve of the young woman either. She turned to the path that led past the Gila Stel to the canal.

Niare sighed and turned to walk with them. Maskelle asked her, "Who was that High Court flower?"

"That is the Lady Marada. She comes from the Garekind Islands and is visiting at Court." Niare hesitated. "She has the Celestial Emperor's favor." She was watching Maskelle carefully. "It is even rumored that he may make her a consort."

Maskelle's brows rose. "Really," she said dryly. Perhaps manners were different in the Garekind Islands, then, and the woman had not intended rudeness. It was far to the south, a long and difficult voyage across the Rijan sea, and few of its inhabitants ever visited the capital. "And she visits the sick when she isn't astonishing the High Court?"

"No." Niare's voice was amused. "She only visits Veran."

"Veran?" Maskelle frowned.

"She had asked for instruction in the Infinite, and Veran was teaching her. Informally, of course. She has a great curiosity about the Path, but I don't think she fancied the required service as a penitent."

Well, that's common enough, Maskelle thought. And Veran must have many friends who visited him in his illness. There was no reason why she should feel uneasy at the thought.

Niare left them at the Gila Stel. There were a few boatmen, dicing on the stone bank near where their boat, its white silk awning trimmed with flowers, was tied up. Four women, dressed well but without the profusion of pearls and gold, were sitting on the benches under a stand of palms, fanning themselves and talking animatedly. Maids or waiting women, their eyes slid curiously toward the strange travel-worn nun and the Sitanese outcast. Maskelle could see the Celestial One's boat coming down the canal toward the temple's water steps. Waterfowl took flight, disturbed by the boat's passage, and she saw the Celestial One had come for them himself. She gazed upward in mute appeal to the Ancestors. *Does he think I mean to try to escape?* Rian asked, "Who was that other woman, who looked daggers at you?"

Maskelle glanced at him. He was ostensibly relaxed, but not without that edge of tension. She said, "That was Lady Disara, my husband's mother. The husband I killed."

Rian stared at her. "You could have told me before." He looked sharply at the people who had come with the two Court Ladies and managed to lower his voice. "How can I protect you if you don't tell me these things? What is wrong with you? Were you run out of the Empire for being crazy?"

"That was one of the reasons." Maskelle sat down on a bench under one of the trees to wait for the boat. She sighed and rested her arms on her knees. "I think maybe I might need a *kjardin* after all."

7

As the Celestial One's boat slid up to the water steps, Rian scanned the boatmen and the others near the canal, alert for betraying tension, a body deliberately held to conceal a weapon, any abrupt movement. Markand had been good training for this; everyone there, no matter how long in service or close in relationship, could be a potential assassin. Compared to that, looking for threats in a place where everyone was a stranger and he had no idea of the alliances, factions and undercurrents was almost easy.

Again, the Celestial One was unaccompanied except for the boys who poled the boat and the young priest who helped him up and down steps. Maskelle grabbed one of the support poles and swung easily down into the boat. Rian followed her.

"You didn't have to come after us," she said to the Celestial One with some asperity. "Did you think coming here was a ruse for me to escape?"

"It crossed my mind," the old man said grimly.

Water gurgled as the boys pushed the boat away from the portico. Rian saw Maskelle glare at the old priest and he automatically gauged the distance to the bank, which was lined with terraced wooden buildings with carved gables and pediments, in case they had to leave the boat suddenly. There were children playing on the water steps they passed, so the canals must be free of the predators that made the rivers so dangerous.

Still watching the Celestial One almost angrily, Maskelle said, "I'm an outcast. The upper ranks are going to object if you try to include me in the Rite, especially in a Rite as important as this one. Especially a Rite this . . . damaged."

"That's why you must no longer be an outcast." The Celestial One was looking away, at the gardens along the opposite bank. He said quietly, "You've been punished enough."

She said, "That's not your decision." Her hands were gripping the bench tightly, the blood draining from her knuckles.

The Celestial One frowned, showing a hint of the crotchety old man Rian suspected lurked just under the serene surface, and said, "It is my decision as far as the Order is concerned."

She turned a sardonic gaze on him. "I took that road and I can tell you it doesn't lead where you think it does."

The Celestial One pressed his lips together. "Don't lecture to me, child."

Maskelle leaned forward, and this time the edge in her voice was dangerous. "I'm not your child."

Rian shifted his weight unobtrusively. The boys poling the craft were far up in the bow and the stern and couldn't possibly reach them quickly enough to interfere. He braced himself to · dump the young priest, who was watching the confrontation with open astonishment, over the side.

The moment stretched. The Celestial One sat back, smiling slowly. "You have not lost your fire."

"Don't pretend that was a test, old man." Maskelle eased back on the bench but didn't relax. The young priest was saved from a swim in the canal, but Rian didn't relax, either. Sounding more peevish than angry now, she added, "There's always the chance my intervention would just make things worse."

"I can't think how," the Celestial One said frankly. And unnervingly, Rian thought.

Maskelle shook her head in exasperation. "Why didn't you just tell me what had happened when I got to the Marai yesterday? Why take me in to see it unprepared? Did you think I had something to do with it and you wanted to see if I looked guilty?"

The Celestial One sighed. "I wanted you to see it for yourself." He looked at the far bank, rheumy eyes narrowed. "I wanted your conclusions to be untainted by any preconception. I have looked at it so much in these few days since it happened I no longer trust my own judgment."

I must have heard wrong, Rian thought, *that sounded almost rational*. Maskelle must have agreed, because she grumbled, "Why didn't you say so in the first place?"

"You wouldn't have listened to me then. You wanted an argument. Now you've had one. Perhaps you can be content now that you understand my reasons for all this."

Maskelle just looked at the old man. Rian was a little reassured by the fact that the Celestial One could evidently be a real bastard when he set his mind to it. *Maybe the Koshans aren't that strange after all.*

At the Marai, the Celestial One led them straight to the inner court, where the central tower stood. In the portico around the base of the tower, Maskelle paused to tell Rian, "You can't come in this time. We're going to be doing some things that can't be disturbed." As an afterthought, she added, "And arguing. But mostly alterations to the Rite. You should go home."

Rian ran a hand through his hair, frustrated. There were some servants sweeping the court across the way and a few priests talking in one of the colonnades, but no one was within earshot and no one was paying more than the ordinary curious attention to them. "Who else is in there?"

"Just the Voices, a few other priests, probably." She smiled at him, somewhat fondly.

Rian swore under his breath. "This isn't a game. You know

something's trying to kill you and you have enemies here." He suspected that was a mild estimate of the situation.

"Yes, I know," she said, glumly regarding the polished stone under their feet and dragging the toe of her muddy and travel-worn sandal over the edge of the step. "I'll be with the Celestial One."

"What's that worth?"

"If violence takes place in the Celestial One's sight, the whole Order and anyone outside it who follows the Path will have to go through a purification ritual."

To the priests-shamans, at least the ones in Markand, "purification" involved fire, iron, and screaming, usually by a nonpriest. "Does that involve pain?"

Maskelle snorted. "No, worse. Fasting, abstinence, complicated meditation rituals. No one wants to go through that, not even to get rid of me."

I'll never understand these people, Rian thought. He looked at the entrance into the tower. He hadn't had a chance to explore it yesterday. "Is this the only way in?"

"No, there are a couple of others at the upper levels. I think." At his expression she shook her head. "Rian, if anyone is going to make trouble, it will be me. Really. I'm the most dangerous person here." Her mouth quirked wryly. "Especially to myself."

"That I already figured out," he muttered. There didn't appear to be any other choice. "Fine. If you get killed, don't send your shade crying to me."

"I promise, on what's left of my honor, not to haunt you."

Rian didn't think much of that promise, but the Celestial One, who was waiting in the archway, thumped his staff impatiently and glared. He let out his breath. "All I'm saying is just watch your back."

"I will, I will." She made shooing motions at him. "I was nursemaiding myself a long time before you came along to do it."

She and the Celestial One disappeared inside the tower and

Rian paced the court for a while, trying to judge how safe the temple really was. It wasn't a bad place to wait, all things considered. The clouds had settled in and a light rain fell off and on, steaming off the smooth grey stones of the court and dripping from the figures of the Ancestors and spirits and hero priests and priestesses of the past carved into the walls and galleries and columns around him. A variety of people seemed to come and go in the court for various purposes, and few except the Koshans approached the central tower. It gave him time to think about what they had heard at the hospital, about poor spell-maddened Veran and the dead Voice Igarin.

Something or someone had assuredly poisoned the Voice. Rian mortally hated poisoners. It was an indiscriminate weapon and he had seen too many innocents fall victim to it. The worst time had been when poisoned must cakes meant for the Holder Lord had accidentally been sent to the rooms of his favorite concubine. The young woman had shared them with all the servants who happened to be with her that afternoon, and it had killed all of them, including an adolescent lamp girl and two pageboys so young their voices hadn't changed yet.

Rian had smelled a poison murder as soon as the Celestial One had spoken of Igarin being so conveniently taken ill. People never took ill at convenient moments, and all these priests seemed to live to vast ages and be as hardy as cart horses. The Celestial One had said there had been no sign of poison, but Rian wondered how much these people really knew of such things, for all their herbs and magic. They didn't seem much interested in killing each other.

Rian stopped, watching a group of priests walk along one of the covered colonnades that divided the court, the dark blue of their robes flicking in and out among the grey pillars. He had been shocked to realize that the temple guards the Celestial One had brought with him to the post compound really had been for their protection, that the highest priest in the Celestial Empire apparently went anywhere he pleased without guards, with only the boys who paddled the boat or the young priest whose main duty seemed to be to help him negotiate steps. *It's not the Sintane,* he reminded himself again. That observation was a triumph of the obvious. Maybe no one in the city wanted to kill the old man. It was remotely possible. Maybe Rian had just been too long at Markand, with a lord whom most rational people looked for chances to murder.

A young Koshan woman was coming across the court with an armload of some kind of wooden packets. Rian watched her with idle curiosity, until it became apparent she was heading directly for him. She stopped a few paces away. Rian didn't know how to read the rank tattoos yet, but hers looked fairly new on her shaven scalp. She cleared her throat, looked up at him uncertainly, and said, "My name is Sister Tiar. I was sent to give you instruction in reading Anrin."

Oh, really? On close observation he saw that the things she carried were books with wooden covers. Rian shot a glance at the entrance to the Rite's tower. "Sent by who?"

"By—" She hesitated, then finished less confidently, "The one who was the Voice of the Adversary."

Rian made a noncommittal noise. So Maskelle had remembered her threat to make him learn to read. He just stood there and stared at the young nun, hoping to scare her away.

It didn't work. More determined than she initially appeared, she stepped briskly past him to the shelter of the tower's portico, sat down on the step, and awkwardly deposited her armload of books. She picked one up and opened it, saying brightly, "Shall we begin?"

"Women," Rian muttered under his breath in Sitanese, then gave in gracefully and went to sit next to her.

While she was explaining the basics of what she meant to teach him, he listened with half his attention, picking up one of the books and paging through it to look at the drawings. These

Koshan books were strips of very thin smooth wood, written on with a variety of colored inks and then lacquered over to protect the surface, the strips then bound together with cords. They were kept in oilcloth cases to protect them from the ever present damp, though it seemed only the binding cords suffered from it. The drawings in this one were the same sort of scenes that were carved on the walls of the Marai. He hoped every book in the pile wasn't about religion.

The nun Tiar was looking past him toward the archway into the tower. Now she said, "Do you know if there's any progress? Everyone is very worried and no one will tell us anything."

If such a thing had happened in Markand, there would have been panic and bloodshed in the corridors of the Hold. Here, everyone was "very worried." From what he had heard, the Koshans hadn't made much effort to conceal what had happened, but they hadn't tried to spread the word, either. The knowledge was probably still confined to the upper ranks of the temples and the lower who were attached to the Marai. Rian said, "They don't tell me anything either."

She turned the pages of the book, running her thumb along the wooden edges, biting her lip. If she was trying to decide where to begin, it was evidently a taxing decision. Then she said slowly, "We've been wondering . . . Not many of us who are in the lower ranks now knew the Voice of the Adversary before she left, and . . ."

Rian waited unhelpfully. He wasn't sure what she was getting at.

She finally looked at him, her face worried, and said in a rush, "Are you with her voluntarily?"

He stared at her, surprised. *So what did they think? That I was kidnapped, under a spell?* He grinned slowly. "Yes. She's tried to get rid of me a couple of times, but it didn't take."

Her cheeks darkened and she looked away, embarrassed. "It's

just that there are so many stories about her and . . . Some of the others speculated that she had . . ."

"Trapped me?" Rian finished, fascinated. There were a lot of questions itching at him that he couldn't possibly ask a strange Kushorit woman who was a nun and barely out of girlhood into the bargain. And anyway she probably had no idea how many men Maskelle had had in the past and if any of them were better to look at than he was.

"Yes," Tiar said hurriedly, and grabbed another book off the pile at random and launched into the lesson.

Rian sat pretend-patiently through what the various symbols in the written version of the Kushorit language meant. After Tiar had gotten over her attack of self-consciousness, he asked her, "Do you know Veran?"

"Yes." She selected another book, troubled. "I hope he'll be all right. He worked so hard. He would have advanced to the seventh level this year and many thought that eventually he would be made a Voice."

So the disaster had ruined Veran's chances for advancement, even if he did recover. It didn't sound like the man had much reason to act against the Rite on his own. "That's why they let him near the Rite?"

"Yes, there are always a few initiates to the seventh level who are given the opportunity to participate in the Rite in a minor way. The Voices perform the most important parts, but the others are allowed to take their places occasionally, to add to their knowledge." She shook her head. "Veran was the youngest who had ever been given that honor."

Rian leaned back against the pillar, watching Tiar sort through the books. If Maskelle was right, then something had gotten to Veran at some point before he had entered the tower to take the dying Voice's turn at the Rite. If Veran was an involuntary partici-pant, then it must have caught him unawares; if he had made some sort of deal with it, then regretted it later or been betrayed, it might make things more difficult. A guilty man would take steps to cover his trail. "He was teaching a lady from the Court named Marada?"

"Yes, the foreign lady." Tiar shook her head, as if recalling something she found baffling. "He said she was very strange. He thought at first . . . Well, he thought she was more interested in him than in learning the Path. But he told Nasir later that he must have been mistaken." She colored again and added, "I imagine I'm not supposed to know that but things do get around. Veran told the others that it was very hard to understand what Marada meant by the things she said and did. I suppose that's because the people of the Garekind Islands have very different customs."

He thought Marada wanted him, but he was wrong, Rian wondered. *Or she tried to seduce him and he refused.* Or the young priest had been just as confused as Rian had by that strange, direct way of looking someone over that Marada had. "So she really did want to learn?"

"Yes, she came to study with him quite frequently, every day as arranged. He gave the lessons on the terraces outside the library of the Myad Keo."

"When was the last lesson?"

"Not long ago." She frowned. "Only a day before he became so ill, and all this happened." She gestured back toward the tower.

"Are you certain?"

"I saw them there myself." Tiar was not stupid. Rian didn't suppose one could get through all the learning it took to be a Koshan and not have wits. She frowned, watching him carefully, and said, "Does that mean something?"

Rian shrugged. If Marada was a poisoner, he didn't want to see Tiar in the hospital on a pallet next to Veran's. "It could, but probably not. He must have seen dozens of people that day." Yes, dozens of people. Family and friends and other Koshans and market vendors and servants, people he had seen every day of his life without coming to harm, and none of them foreign visitors with suspicious manners who had quickly managed to place themselves close to the Celestial Emperor. He pointed to the book. "What does that one mean again? The one with the bird's head . . ." By getting half the symbols she had shown him wrong, he managed to distract her back into the lesson.

"Are you ready to try now?" Vigar asked.

Kneeling awkwardly on the floor, eye level with the Rite, Maskelle knew that no one else but another ninth-level Koshan could have heard the tightly restrained annoyance in the man's tone. It was buried under layers of training, discipline, and meditative calm. Dryly, she said, "Yes, I've just been standing on my head all this time for the joy of delaying you."

Vigar didn't swear, didn't sigh, and probably didn't even twitch an eyelid. He and the other Voices did not want her here, but the Celestial One's word was law where the Rite was concerned. They had not spoken one word of their disagreement and would not; they were all too far down the Path of the Infinite to express such petty sentiments. Maybe that's why she preferred the Ariaden, who expressed petty sentiments with a refreshing forthrightness. *The Sitanese aren't bad at it either,* she thought, smiling to herself, remembering Rian's outburst at the Gila Stel.

She sat up and rubbed her eyes. The many lamps made the chamber even warmer than usual and the still air felt stale in her lungs. The patterns of the Rite existed both in this world and the plane of the Infinite. Following the design as it wove in and out through here and there made her eyes ache all the way down to her toes. In building the Rite all it took was an awareness of the Infinite and the Rite's shape both in it and this world. Untwisting that complexity was a far greater task than building it in the first place. She said, "It's actually intersecting with the edge of the First Mountain. I don't like that."

"You don't? I find it delightful that the excrescence is almost touching one of the focal points of the power of earth," Vigar said, his tone just as arid as hers.

Maskelle looked up at him, surprised at the show of temper. Smiling, she said, "Really, Vigar, I didn't know you had it in you." The other Voices, standing or kneeling around the chamber, all gazed at him in mild shock. There were fourteen of them here. With all the confusion, Igarin had not yet been replaced, and though the others had been summoned when the disaster occurred, most were still en route from the Temple Centers in the rest of the Empire.

Vigar smiled sourly. "I take it you concur with our deductions."

She sighed. "I agree it's not just a random disruption with dark-colored sand. It's woven in the Infinite, just like the rest of the Rite." The new part was still forming symbols, as if continuing to delineate the landscape as the rest of the Rite was. But without knowing what the symbols meant, there was no way they could tell what landscape it was. It might be another way of representing the section of the basin below the First Mountain and the edge of the Western Sea, which was what should be occupying that area, or it could be something totally unknown. "I don't see anything you haven't already seen." She gestured helplessly. "Whatever it is that makes it rebuild itself after you remove it . . ." She had thought about this all night, and the only reasonable possibility that occurred to her wasn't all that reasonable. Still, it was better than no theory at all. "There could be a second Wheel of the Infinite." Because of what the Wheel was, in this world and in the Infinite, the two Wheels would in effect be the same one. Changes made to one would affect the other. "When whoever built it makes their adjustments to the design, we see them reflected here. When you restore the original symbols, their Wheel changes to match."

They all stared at her. She could sense the disbelief settling over the room like a chill fog. Arela, the only other female Voice who was present, said carefully, "Who could do such a thing?"

"Don't ask 'who,' " Maskelle said, meeting her eyes deliberately. "Ask 'how.' Once we know that, then we'll know who."

Arela's eyes went hooded as she turned over that thought. She and the other Voices were considering the idea, that Maskelle could tell, but Vigar was the only one who was staring at the Wheel instead of at Maskelle. She waited, saying nothing, seeing the calculation in his eyes. After a time he said slowly, "It would have to be situated on a power center, somewhere in Kushor-At." He lifted an ironic brow. "Perhaps the Baran Dir?"

She smiled back. She had to admit, it didn't seem likely. The power centers were all carefully mapped, all supporting temples or other places of importance in the Infinite. All it would take was an unoccupied room of good size, protected from stray breezes, but there would be too many opportunities for discovery in the temples. "Perhaps not. But this entire situation is unlikely."

Vigar's brows drew together as he considered. He shook his head slightly. "It seems difficult to believe, but . . ." He turned to the other Voices. "We will order a search of the major temples."

There were no sighs or mutterings of disagreement, but Maskelle could tell the others were not convinced. Vigar ignored the potential conflict and looked to Maskelle again. "Now that we've addressed the question of 'how,' perhaps we could examine 'why.' What is our opponent attempting to do with his Wheel? What is the purpose of these disruptions?"

For the first time, he had admitted the existence of an opponent and was not trying to pretend that this was some sort of natural occurrence. Maskelle met Vigar's eyes, willing him to understand. "You may have to let one of them grow a little, so that we can see what it's trying to make."

Vigar didn't reply, but his mouth twisted ruefully as he looked at the Rite. Arela said, "We had thought perhaps you would recognize the symbols, if this was the creation of a dark power."

So that was it. "One of my dark powers, you mean?" Maskelle said, lifting a brow. *Now we get to the heart of the matter.* This was undoubtedly why the other Voices had agreed to her presence here. "Unfortunately not." The strange symbols had been laboriously extracted from the Rite over the past three days. According to Vigar, there was a group of monks and nuns set to making copies of them onto wooden tablets, which were then taken to the various temple libraries, where other groups searched for clues among the accumulated wisdom of the Koshans and the Celestial Empire.

Vigar looked even more depressed. "Then we will trace it again, from the Angle of Ascension of the Southern Range, and see if that illuminates the situation any."

Well, that's something anyway, Maskelle thought. Vigar agreed with her and was now willing to admit it, if not in so many words. The others didn't sigh or groan, but from the general air that hung over the chamber, they might as well have.

8

By afternoon, Rian had gleaned a good deal of information about temple life from talking to the nun Tiar, the servants who came and went in the court, and a group of young priests who had come out to discuss some obscure point of Koshan philosophy and instead had taken the opportunity to find out if Rian knew anything about the progress of the Rite. From them Rian had also found out a great deal about Veran and his relations with the Lady Marada, and it all made him that much more impatient to discover how the Voice Igarin had been killed.

One of his new acquaintances, a non-Koshan who was paid to manage the Marai's stores of food and lamp oil, had told him that the seventh-level priest who acted as Temple Master and supervised its day-to-day running would have had charge of Igarin's body.

By wandering around the lower levels and asking people, Rian tracked the Temple Master to a room in the outer libraries that faced away from the causeway. He was not a young man, but he wasn't old either, and had a bullnecked build more like a laborer or a wrestler than a scholar priest. His face was round and bland, his expression deceptively mild. He was seated on a mat near a window, with several lacquer tablets around him and his fingers stained from charcoal writing sticks. He looked up inquiringly when Rian stopped in the doorway and said, "Yes?"

Rian realized he still didn't know the complex system of bows for the different ranks, or even what respect was accorded a man who was a seventh-level priest and also had charge of the whole Marai, so he just launched into what he had come for. "I wanted to ask about the Voice who died. They said he hasn't been buried?" He suppressed a wince at the baldness of the question. *At least if I offend him too much I can always play dumb foreigner.*

Being a Koshan, the priest didn't react to this admittedly bizarre query other than to say, "It's our custom to sit vigil for seven days when Koshans of an advanced level die. This is to make sure they haven't joined the Infinite temporarily and mean to return." He looked regretful. "The body has begun to decay, so it doesn't appear Igarin will be coming back to us."

"Oh," Rian said, somewhat caught off guard. *And I thought she was making that up.* So maybe the Celestial One really had died and come back to life. But the Temple Master hadn't called for guards or thrown him out yet, so he forged on. "Could I see the body?"

The Temple Master eyed him thoughtfully. "Why?"

Good question, Rian thought. "Maskelle told me to," he said, thinking it was worth a try.

The man's expression immediately changed. Rian realized he might just be able to get further with the implication that if he failed to follow Maskelle's orders something terrible would happen to him than anything else. The Master set the tablets aside and gathered his robe to stand. "Very well."

It turned out that the dead man was kept not in the Marai itself but in the living quarters attached to it, which were in the second gallery on the west side. The rain had started again, harder this time, but the quarters could be reached by walking through the outer galleries that formed the great outside square around the main temple and separated the outer court from the inner.

The living quarters were two levels of stone cells opening onto the long porticos facing the temple. The Master led Rian to a

room on the lower floor where several young monks sat just outside. They stood up to make bows as the Master approached. He
motioned them to sit again and stepped past them into the room.

Rian glanced around, trying to keep his expression blank. If
this was the room Igarin had lived in, then Voices didn't get much
for their service. Surely the man had had a house somewhere, and
this was only the room he used while he was at the Marai. The
walls were carved with forest scenes and spirit dancers, but otherwise it was bare except for a brass incense burner and a few bowls
filled with flower petals. The dead man lay on a dark blue silk
mat on the floor of the chamber, wrapped in formal Koshan robes.
The candles were lit in all the niches and the bronze holders,
casting a soft glow on the corpse. There was hardly any smell of
decay and the man didn't look as if he had been dead more than
a day. Rian looked at the Master, suspicious. "This is Igarin?"

"Yes."

"This man's been dead four days?"

"Yes." The Master explained gently, "The Voices have strong
ties with the Infinite. Their souls are woven within it, and when
they die, it takes some time for those ties to unwind. Their bodies
decay very slowly."

Rian circled the corpse, playing for time and wondering how
he could manage to get a closer look. It was hard to tell what
Igarin's age had been. His features had already taken on the same-
ness of death and he was wrapped up to his chin in the robes.
The Master was watching him closely. Rian asked, "How exactly
did he die?"

The Master's round face was grim as he remembered. "He
had difficulty breathing. It came on suddenly. One moment he
was working as usual, the next he was gasping for breath. They
carried him out of the Rite chamber, thinking it was the heat.
While they were trying to revive him, he died out in the court."
He gestured, trying to convey the hopelessness of those final moments. "It happened very quickly."

"Were you there?"

"Not when it first struck him." The man shook his head. "I was working in the Solar Library. The shouts for help summoned me to the court, but I only reached it in time to see him die."

If that was all true, then it had to be something quick, something given to the old man not long before he died. "He wasn't ill beforehand?"

"No." The Master eyed him thoughtfully. "He had had nothing to eat or drink since the evening before, almost an entire day. The Voices fast while they perform their parts of the Rite." He added, "We thought of poison, too."

Rian scratched his head, studying the corpse. "In the Sintane there's a poison called thisock, that can be given through the skin. Assassins treat the outside of a cup with it, and if the victim picks it up before it dries, he's dead." This was all true, though irrelevant, since thisock took forever to work and didn't cause the difficulty in breathing Igarin had experienced.

The man's brows drew together. "I hadn't heard of that. Is it a plant that grows in the lowlands?"

Rian shrugged. "No. But it has to be dried and ground to powder before you can make the poison from it." He added carefully, "It leaves discolorations on the skin."

Frowning, the Master stepped forward and stooped to inspect the corpse's hands. Rian knelt next to him, trying not to show undue haste, and said, "Better check everywhere."

The Master unwrapped the corpse's robe and began to examine the cold waxy skin. Rian watched carefully. He wasn't sure what he was looking for; something that made as little sense as all the rest of it, something strange. Despite the slowness of the decay, there seemed to be nothing out of the ordinary. Then the Master turned the corpse's head and Rian said, "Wait."

"What?"

"There, is that a bruise?" Rian pointed to the back of the corpse's neck.

"I can't tell." The Master stood and took down one of the candles. As he held it carefully over the body, the light fell on the neck and head.

Rian turned the head a little more. *That's it.* There was a distinctive round bruise at the back of the neck. He lifted the chin and there it was, though it shouldn't be there. A thin line of bruising across Igarin's throat. He sat back, thinking it over, distractedly rubbing his hand off on his breeches.

"What does that mean?" the Master demanded, frowning.

"Strangling marks." Rian pointed to the long bruise across the throat. "That's where the cord caught his neck. A thick, soft cord, by the look of it." On most of the strangled corpses Rian had seen it had been done with wire, which cut the skin and left a far more visible mark. "The bruise on the back of the neck is from the killer's hand."

The Master squinted, moved the candle around to throw the light from different angles, trying to deny the evidence of his own eyes. Finally he shook his head, baffled. "It's there, but it can't be there. He was struck ill in front of fourteen Voices of the Ancestors and the Celestial One. He died in the court of the Marai, in front of a dozen Koshans and servants and guards. There was no one near him except those who were trying to save him."

"I know," Rian said, not helpfully. He sympathized, but it was only one of the impossible things he had encountered in the past few days. "I just find them, I don't explain them."

The Temple Master sent the monks outside the chamber running to bring various seventh-level priests to consult, then stood outside the door to Igarin's room, staring thoughtfully into the distance.

"What will you do?" Rian asked him, curious.

He shook his head slightly. "Consult the temple libraries to see if this or anything like it has ever happened before."

"It'll be in there?" Rian rubbed the back of his neck, trying not to reveal how unlikely he found the idea.

"If a Koshan was present when it happened, or heard of it, it will be in the libraries." The Temple Master smiled briefly, as if he wasn't the least bit fooled by Rian's tone. His expression sobering, he added, "I hope they find something. Otherwise, it's a foreign magic."

Rian looked away across the grassy court. It was a green so deep, even under the grey sky and the misty drizzle, that it almost didn't look real. He knew he should get back to the court outside the central tower. The Temple Master had this in hand and there was nothing else he could do here, but he hesitated. Finally he said, "I have a question about Koshan philosophy."

The Temple Master gestured. "Ask it."

"What is the Adversary?"

The Temple Master flicked a glance at him, but didn't seem to feel the need to inquire about the reason for the question. "It's almost easier to tell you what the Adversary is not," he said slowly. "The Adversary is the only Ancestral spirit that was never a living being. It was created by the other spirits to destroy evil. The other Ancestors speak to the Voices, giving advice and council, and they are also tied to specific places. Many of them are tied to the place where they lived, when they existed among us as people. There is no absolute proof of this, since they lived so long ago there are no written records, only stories and myths. But the Baran Dir was built on the place where the Ancestors that are associated with healing were said to have made their home, and it is a fact that their Voices are always the strongest there. Since the Adversary was never a living being, it is personified only in its Voice. So the Voice of the Adversary is not just the Adversary's voice, but the Adversary itself. Or herself."

Rian found himself staring at the carving on the nearest pillar, a scene of some human-shaped spirit giving audience to a host of warriors. He was beginning to recognize the subtle differences in the face and the relative size of the figure that marked the way the Kushorit portrayed the Ancestors as different from ordinary humans. He said, "So they hear spirit voices in their heads." He glanced at the priest and saw the man was watching him alertly. "And what the spirits say is always true?"

"Always. But it can be misunderstood. Learning how to understand the meaning of the Ancestors' messages is one of the primary reasons for the years of instruction in Koshan philosophy. It is the reason there are Koshans at all."

Two blue-robed priests were crossing the court at a hurried pace, probably the first of those summoned by the monks. Rian nodded to the Temple Master and vaulted the balustrade, landing on the ground below and starting back toward the main temple.

Maskelle didn't emerge from the tower until very late in the evening. Somewhere behind the clouds the waning moon would be rising and the stars coming out. The rain had stopped and the air was heavy and warm and still. The lamps set in niches and hung from the galleries and windows on the upper levels of the court threw stripes of gold on the slick pavement.

She stretched, feeling the ache in her shoulders and lower back. This was only a temporary respite. She was going to have to go back in a few hours, when Vigar would make his final decision whether to remove the damage to the Rite or not. She wasn't looking forward to that. She looked up and saw Rian sitting on the wide balustrade of the side gallery's portico, under the carving of entwined spirit dancers, and started toward him. "Were you here all day?" she demanded.

He countered. "I found out some things."

"What?"

He hopped down from the balustrade and as they left the central court through the west wind passage, he told her about Marada's visits to Veran and the marks on Igarin's body. "The Temple Master said he was going to try to find out if anything like this has ever happened before. He thinks it'll be in the libraries somewhere if it has."

They were in the outer gallery by the time he reached the end of the story and Maskelle stopped to look back at the Marai. Lamps lit in the windows and between the pillars outlined the stepped domes and the upper galleries. Her thinking was still fuzzy, half her mind still in the Rite and the Infinite. If Igarin's death had been caused by a spell, and it had to be a spell, then it was of a kind she hadn't encountered before. "So it acts like poison but kills like a garroter. And why would Marada, if it is her, want to do this?" She used both hands to scratch her head vigorously, feeling two or three braids come loose, trying to get her wits to work again. "Is she a sorceress sent from the Garekind Islands looking for a war?"

"There's nothing that says she came from the Garekind Islands," Rian pointed out. "Nothing except her word."

Maskelle stopped, her hands in her hair, frowning at the temple. The Ancestors were talking a lot tonight and she couldn't understand one word. "What makes you say that?"

"Givas said the story he heard from the Quay Arbiter's servants is that she came off a boat from Telai, with a retinue of unfriendly maids and guards who supposedly can't speak Kushorit, with nothing to prove she was from Garekind except a letter with the seal of some High Sea Lord."

Telai was an island port at the mouth of the Great River. Ships from all over the world docked there. *She could be from anywhere. Or she could have taken a ferry across from the mainland to buy passage on a river barge, and just claimed to have arrived on a seagoing vessel.* Obviously Rian was thinking along the same lines. "Who is Givas?"

Rian jerked his head toward the temple. "He's the old man who takes care of the lamps in the lower passage on the west side and sweeps the big court in the middle."

"Oh." Maskelle digested this. "The Garekind Islands isn't the end of the world. They have an embassy at the Celestial Emperor's court, the ambassador must have heard of her—"

"Maybe he would have." Rian regarded her with a brow lifted ironically. "But he died, three days before she got here, and no replacement's come yet. His family and servants have all left to go home, and the few Garekind Islanders who are staying to wait for the new ambassador have been here so long they're almost Kushorit now themselves, and wouldn't know the difference if she said she was their own long-lost daughter."

"How nice for her." Maskelle shook her head. "I'm no good, I can't think. Let's go home."

They walked back the long way around, Maskelle oblivious to the light rain. The Marai was at the intersection of several major canals, causeways, and streets; there were still people about, still lamps lit at market stalls or carried in the hands of servants lighting the way for palanquins, some of which were elaborately decorated and had awnings stretched into fantastic shapes, sailing ships or giant garuda birds. When they reached the gate of their house, Maskelle stopped abruptly.

After their initial reluctance the Ariaden had made themselves comfortable. The place was as bright as a bawd's house, every lamp lit in the house's upper floor and the outdoor kitchen. From the collection of clothes and bedding hanging in the open areas of the lower floor, they had also been catching up on their washing. The scent of roast pork and baked taro still hung over the court, and on the upper level gallery Old Mali was on her hands and knees scrubbing the floorboards—apparently for the sheer pleasure of having a floor again, since it had been as clean as possible that morning.

In the open area under the tallest trees they had put up a rough scaffold, with hooks and a system of levers and pulleys to lift heavy scenery and puppets. It was knocked together out of cheap materials and in a frighteningly haphazard manner. The ground of the court bore evidence of the presence of a large number of people by churned up mud, scattered flower petals, and torn fragments from straw mats and rugs. Maskelle shook her head wearily. "I seem to remember rashly assuring them they could give performances here. I had no idea they'd put up the whole damn stage and start tonight."

"Is that what that is?"

"Yes. You haven't seen Ariaden theater before in all its glory?"

Rian shook his head. "I've seen kiradi. They used to come on the Trade Road over the Riadur Pass." When he noticed Maskelle staring at him in surprise, he added defensively, "It was something to look at."

"They had kiradi theater at Markand?" Maskelle asked, bemused. She had pictured the place as something like a wild boar pit, only with people.

"The Holder Lord liked to pretend to understand foreigners," Rian said, as they started up the stairs into the house. "And they had kiradi theater in the High Lord's Hold at Belladira, so we had to have it too."

The main room now looked as if the Ariaden had been living in the house for years. Wooden puppet cases were stacked up just inside, and rugs from the wagons had been strewn across the polished floorboards. Their own lamps and battered crockery were piled on the low table and the lacquered chests. Most of the actors were gathered here, discussing the success of their first production in Duvalpore with a lot of gesturing, yelling, and rice and palm wine. Rastim stood up to greet them, his steps wobbling a little.

"Did it go well?" Maskelle asked him.

Rastim gestured happily. "It was wonderful. There was a very good crowd. Wealthy people and their servants. There's some important officials from the districts outside the city staying in the houses along this street, and they came with their guests. A man even asked us to perform at the festival that's coming up!"

Maskelle stopped. "The Equinox?"

"Yes."

"What was the man's name?"

Rastim thought about it, weaving back and forth slightly. "Giaram Kisnel Something . . ."

"The G'Ram Kisnil?"

"Yes, that was it." Rastim beamed. "He's going to send his people to make the arrangements tomorrow. He said we should perform in the Grand Plaza in front of the Outer Court. Is that a theater?"

"Sort of. You'll like it. Lots of room for the stage," Maskelle assured him.

Rastim turned to give this intelligence to the others and Maskelle and Rian escaped down the passage to the sleeping rooms. Keeping her voice low, she explained, "The G'Ram Kisnil is the warden of the public festivals. It's a post appointed by the High Minister, to organize entertainments for the crowds to keep them under control while the priests are performing the Rites. The grand square is the plaza in front of the Marai. Rastim has just agreed to make Ariaden theater a principal part of the entertainments for the largest festival of the year."

"I hope that's a good thing," Rian muttered.

"It's what they came for," Maskelle said, smiling a little to herself. "It doesn't surprise me. They tell the stories very differently from the traditional plays that the Kushorit are used to. I just hope Rastim and the others don't mind performing in front of several thousand people. I don't think they're used to crowds that size."

"You mean after the festival we could have half the city lining up to get into our cow yard?"

"Well, yes." Maskelle found the room where Old Mali had brought her things in. Her faded Tiengan blankets had been laid out on the bed pad. "I hadn't thought of that." She pulled her muddy sandals off and dropped down onto the cushion. "Maybe

I should find somewhere else for them to do it. I could get the Celestial One to give them another house."

Rian sat behind her and started to rub her shoulders. It was even harder to think with his fingers digging into the tense muscles of her shoulders and neck, but she made herself ask, "It would make more sense if we knew why Marada wanted to do this, if she did do this."

"Why has to be somebody else's job. I just know who. There's too many coincidences. She's the Emperor's concubine but—"

"She's not a concubine," Maskelle objected. *Surely the Emperor's not old enough for that,* she told herself. She hadn't been gone that many years. "She's a Court Lady."

"Whatever you want to call it. She comes down to the temples to make friends with priests, and out of all of them she picks Veran, and out of all of them Veran's possessed by a demon."

"Well, when you put it that way," Maskelle said thoughtfully. She remembered she had responsibilities to her little household, whether it chose to listen to her orders or not, and asked, "Did you get anything to eat today?"

"The Temple Master fed me. He feels sorry for me because you brought me here against my will and everything."

"Oh, thank you. That's all I needed," she grumbled. She felt warm breath on her cheek, then his teeth in her earlobe. At that less than opportune moment Firac strolled in with a Koshan priestess following him. "Someone wants to see you," Firac said brightly.

The priestess looked startled. Maskelle sighed and Rian sat back on the cushions, propping himself up on one elbow. Fortunately the priestess was only second level, so it would take at least a day or two for the story to spread all over the city. Firac ducked out of the room and the woman cleared her throat and said, "I was sent from Niare of Gila Stel."

"Yes?"

"The young priest Veran is dead."

Maskelle said sharply, "When?" at the same time Rian sat up and demanded, "How?"

The woman looked from one to the other and opted to answer both. "He died not an hour ago. Late this afternoon, after the chief healer changed the treatment, he slept quietly and seemed much improved. The monk who was watching him said he woke and asked for water, and when he gave it to him he lay back down, and the next moment he was dead. The chief healer came from his quarters to examine him but . . ." She gestured helplessly.

Rian flung himself to his feet, an abrupt move that made the priestess start and eye him a little nervously. He paced across the room, muttering to himself. Maskelle demanded, "Was anything wrong with the water?"

The priestess turned back to her. "No, nothing. The chief healer tried it himself."

"Tried it himself—" Maskelle rubbed her face. *Foolish, lucky* . . . There were a great many words to describe the chief healer's action, but there was no point in saying them to this woman. "All right. Is that all?"

"Yes. Niare says she will come to the Marai tomorrow to speak to you herself."

"Very well. Thank you."

Rian managed to contain himself until the woman had left, then he said, "It was Marada. She was there today. Why can't the Celestial One just order his guards to go get her?"

"Because we don't have any proof," Maskelle said, exasperated. "Just because she's in the right place at the right time, and she can't prove she's who she says she is, and her circumstances at court are suspicious . . ." She was hardly convincing herself with this, and Rian's expression told her it wasn't working on him, either. She added, "And anyway it's not the Celestial One who has to be convinced, it's the Emperor." If Marada had been a Koshan, the Celestial One could have questioned her himself. If she had been any ordinary Kushorit citizen, the Celestial One could have dragged a Magistrate out of bed for an order to have the Constabulary watch her home. But as a foreigner in the Celestial Court, she was under the Emperor's protection. It was more frustrating for Maskelle than Rian realized. If she had still been able to wield the temporal power of the Voice of the Adversary, she would have been able to go to the Celestial Home and arrest Marada herself. "And if she's as influential as rumor says, he'll be hard to convince."

Rian flung himself down on the cushions next to her. "Then let's get proof. I know where she lives. Givas told me."

Maskelle buried her face in her hands. *I took an oath not to meddle with the Celestial Court. I should tell my suspicions to the Celestial One and not pursue this myself.* But she asked, "What do you expect to find?"

"I don't know. Something. They always forget something."

Maskelle considered it. "You don't think she's clever enough to cover her tracks?"

"I've seen lots of clever people who didn't and ended up stretched on an execution rack with buzzards eating their innards." Rian shook his head and looked toward the doorway. Maskelle could read impatience to be out and away in every line of his body. "She has a private guesthouse like this one, to the west in the Principle City, near the big east-west canal. She doesn't live in the palace and the Emperor's men don't search her rooms. Why shouldn't she keep her poisons or her magics there?"

"The Emperor wouldn't have men search her rooms even if she did live at the palace, not unless she did something to warrant it," Maskelle corrected, but there was sense in what he said. *And another grim little window on life in Markand,* she added to herself. Her oath warred with logic and instinct, and logic and instinct won. *If we're wrong, then we've caused no trouble and nobody will be hurt.* "I can't go tonight, I have to go back to the Marai soon. We'll have to wait until . . ." She hesitated, frowning. She had no idea when or if the work on the Rite would give her leisure to run about the city sneaking into people's houses.

"It's better if I go alone," Rian pointed out. "I'm less likely to be recognized. Nobody knows me."

"Hmm." He was probably right, for more reasons than that. She was not exactly accustomed to acting by stealth. "It'll be better to wait another couple of hours before you go. The homes of courtiers and government officials are down there. They'll entertain until late at night, and it's not far from the pleasure garden district."

"If she's there I can't search the place. As it is, I may have to try a few times before I can get in."

"Very well." Maskelle gave in, not too ungracefully. He spoke with the confidence of someone who did this every day. *I hope* kjardin *isn't also Sitanese for "housebreaker."* "Just don't get caught."

9

This was the first time Rian had been out of the First City. He had familiarized himself with the layout of Duvalpore by talking to the porters and servants at the Marai and the post house they had stayed in the first night. With the canals and the long avenues, and the Kushorit fascination with east-west and north-south axes, it wasn't a difficult plan to commit to memory.

Kushor-An, the Principle City, had five major entrances, and Rian found the causeway that led to the nearest by going past the Marai and the smaller satellite temples beyond it. At one point he passed through a market where many of the stalls were still open and found himself pausing in front of a cloth vendor. The lengths of silk and cotton and brocade sparkling with gold thread were displayed to advantage in the light from dozens of brass lamps. He found himself wanting to buy something for Maskelle, though for a *kjardin* to give a gift to his lord was unthinkable. But then, he wasn't *kjardin* anymore. And Maskelle made the Lady Holders of the Sintane look about as formidable as the frazzled woman at the other stall selling gourds. *You don't have the money, anyway*, he reminded himself, and kept moving.

The causeway to Kushor-An turned out to be a sight worth seeing in itself.

Walking down its broad paved length in the cool damp night

air, he passed between stone giants, each more than thirty feet tall. In the light of the torches mounted between them, he could see some were meant to look benevolent while others were grotesque six-headed monsters. In another place he would have thought they were meant to represent gods, but here, there was no telling. In the darkness beyond the barrier of the giants there was sometimes the water of a canal, sometimes marshy ground. It was too dark to see if there were any buildings there.

Even at this time of night there were still people out: porters with yokes over their shoulders, peddlers with exotic goods or food, idlers, guards, and servants forming processions for the palanquins of the rich. Even in Markand and the High Lord's Belladira, the two largest Holds in the whole Sintane, the streets would have been dark as pitch and empty of everything but demons, thieves and murderers at this time of night. Duvalpore still pulsed with life.

Rian wasn't the only foreigner out late, either. He saw several Medara Islanders with clan marks painted on their faces and other travellers who could easily be from any of the outer provinces, though there was no one who looked Sitanese. A party of Mahlindi merchants in their brightly patterned robes stood under one of the giants, gesturing up at it and talking excitedly. Rian crossed to the other side of the causeway in case these were the same Mahlindi who had been on the Great Road with them, but they were too occupied to notice him. Then a procession escorting some noble from Kutura-clane came down the causeway guided by a Kushorit official and some men in city guard livery. The Kutura-clane wore bright feathered cloaks and tall headdresses and even the Mahlindi stopped to stare at them as they went past. Rian felt less conspicuous every moment.

Maskelle, fortunately, had not thought of the argument that there were not many Sitanese in Duvalpore and that she and Rian had been seen together all over Kushor-At, so he was just as likely to be recognized at this point as she was. *And she thinks you're not going to find anything,* he thought. Just because Maskelle wasn't likely to leave damning evidence strewn about didn't mean the Lady Marada was as careful. People who thought they were clever enough to plot secret killings often made the same mistakes as half-witted petty thieves. *And,* he told himself, *it's been a long time since you caught somebody you didn't wish had gotten away.* His oaths had forced him to send dozens of men and women to traitors' deaths for trying to kill the Holder Lord, something he had wanted to do himself, probably far more than any of them had.

At the end of the causeway was a gate guarded by two stone elephants, each large enough to do battle with any of the giants. Their tusks looked like real ivory, and on their harnesses gilt and gems glittered in the torchlight. Past the gate a wide avenue led up to another great temple, its lower levels hung with lamps, but most of it lost in darkness. That had to be the Baran Dir. From seeing it at a distance in daylight Rian knew it was a truly massive structure, larger even than the Marai, and that all the towers were topped by benign stone faces. The Palace was somewhere up there too, to the west of the temple. There were dozens of large buildings around the Baran Dir, some wood, some stone, visible only as lighted windows in shapeless masses in the night. The avenue leading toward the temple stretched between two canals where pleasure boats still drifted, the lamps on their bows revealing people in bright silks lounging on cushions and drinking wine.

He found the street he wanted halfway down the avenue to the Baran Dir and crossed a bridge over the canal to reach it. The street was lined by large palisaded houses, hanging lamps glowing golden on roofs ornamented with heavy carving and widely extended beams, shade trees and palms growing in their courts. Maskelle had been right, several houses were brightly lit and noisy, with richly dressed people and servants going in and out of the gates and small caravans of palanquins crowding the street in front of them. Rian counted down and found the one that should be Marada's. It was dark except for a muted glow of light over the palisade, probably from the outdoor kitchen.

He went down the street cautiously, staying away from the lighted gates, his boots making little noise on the soft ground. There was another canal at the far end—he could glimpse reflected light on the water between the buildings fronting it. The wideness of the street and the flowering bushes planted along the palisades made stealth easy. The house compounds were set apart from each other, with alleys between them leading over to the next street. He slipped down the alley next to Marada's guesthouse and saw that behind it on the other street was what must be the manse of some high official or noble: it was three stories high, with lamps glowing and people moving on all the balconies. He hesitated, but the noisy house's courtyard was large, and a stand of trees blocked the direct view into the alley. If he waited and came back tomorrow there would be every chance the owner would be holding an entertainment then, too.

Rian jumped and caught the top of the palisade, hauling himself up to look over and scraping his hands on the rough wood. The court was empty, the house dark. On the far side there was firelight and a couple of lamps near the kitchen hearth, but if anyone was there they were keeping quiet. Marada only had a few maids and six or so menservants; considering the size of the processions that Kushorit nobles routinely dragged along to their entertainments, she would have most of them with her. If her servants were anything like those in the Sintane, any left behind would be dozing until their mistress returned. Drums and cymbals made a counterpoint to unfamiliar stringed instruments from the noble's house as Rian scrambled over the top of the wall and dropped to the packed dirt below.

He crept toward the back of the house. On the lower floor the screens had been dropped between the pillars, closing off what should be storage and the bathing area and quarters for the servants. Rian didn't mean to go up through the inside of the house anyway. He froze as a voice spoke softly from the kitchen area and another answered. *Two at least,* he thought. The words were incomprehensible but then according to the gossip Marada's servants couldn't or wouldn't speak Kushorit.

Rian waited long enough to be sure the two weren't about to jump up and investigate any suspicious noises, then he continued to the back of the house. There he climbed up the outside of the great corner pillar, feeling for hand- and footholds in the carving. The wood was slick with damp and it was hard going. It occurred to him that being caught sneaking into the chambers of a foreign noble lady who was a guest of the Celestial Emperor himself was a transgression likely to badly upset even the usually serene Kushorit. The explanation that he was only looking for signs that she was a poisoner and a murderess was not likely to be well received either. *Worry about that when it happens,* he told himself.

He reached the railing of the veranda and climbed over, dropping down to a crouch. The house stayed quiet and dark, and the low mutter of voices continued from the outdoor kitchen. He slipped into the nearest doorway.

A small cage lamp had been left lit in the inner hall and he picked it up. If he stayed away from the doors and windows on the far side, the light wouldn't be seen from the kitchen area just below. He skirted the edge of the common room, the light gleaming off the lacquered woodwork and the colors in the wall paintings. The room was bare except for the low table and the cushions that must have come with the place. He passed on into the sleeping rooms.

The house was larger than theirs but not so well laid out, the individual rooms bigger but not so many of them. The first few he looked into were also oddly bare. The bed cushions had been unrolled so he supposed they were occupied, but their owners had left little sign of their presence behind. The Ariaden had moved into their house in force with puppets, stage paraphernalia, children's toys, dishes, and discarded clothing. This house looked like theirs had the day they had arrived.

Then he reached a large chamber at the back and paused in the doorway, baffled. It was anything but bare. The floor and the bedding were littered with silk wraps in jewel-like colors, the wooden chests covered with scent bottles and tangled jewelry, jade and pearl gleaming softly in the light from the lamp.

He took a slow step into the room, by habit careful not to disturb anything, though it looked as though an ox had already trundled through. *So she has the laziest servants in Garekind, or wherever she comes from.* Funny that she let them get away with it. Rian had lived in the private chambers of both the Lady Holder of Riverwait and the Holder Lord of Markand, and been well acquainted with the personal lives of many nobles as part of his duties, and he knew people of that class didn't live like this. The room smelled foul, too, a sickly sweet, rotten odor.

He poked around in the fall of silk on the floor with the toe of his boot and uncovered another blaze of color. He knelt to look more closely, pushing the crumpled fabric aside to reveal a Berani carpet. It was a large one, almost half the length of the room, deep red trimmed with black, with figures of stags and big cats and a whole bestiary of mountain animals picked out in gold and silver threads in exquisite detail. Rian whistled silently in appreciation.

These carpets came from lands far to the north and had to be carted over miles of frozen mountains before even coming within reach of the Sitanese traders, who paid raw gold for them. The Holder Lord of Markand, the biggest pig's ass in creation, had had one not a quarter this size and kept it properly hung up on the wall to prevent it being soiled. Rian knew what that one had cost, and this, with finer colors and so much larger, must be worth far more; it had to be one of those gifts from the Celestial Emperor they had heard about.

And she treats it like sawdust. Rian lifted aside a length of indigo silk to see a broken bowl and a large dried stain of brown sauce. That was the source of the foul odor. Ants had found it and a trail of them led away under the other debris. He stood, shaking his head. The Lady Marada was one thing on the outside and something else on the inside. That was worth notice in itself, but it still didn't prove anything. It didn't make her interest in the priest Veran anything other than sympathetic and it didn't mean she had killed him.

He started to search in earnest, sifting through the scarves and robes and the other litter on the floor and the bed. He sniffed the scent vials and checked the scattered collection of jars of creams and colored powders, but they seemed to contain nothing harmful. He searched the two chests at the back of the room, but they held only folded linen. The chest at her bedside was next and he shifted double handfuls of tangled gold chains, hair ornaments, arm and ankle rings off it before he was finally able to lift the lid.

It held more crumpled silk, more chains and armlets, a headpiece with jade lappets, and in the bottom a wooden box, inlaid with polished stone. Rian lifted it out and opened it, expecting more jewelry or another neglected Imperial gift. *Probably cracked sun-diamonds or spilled godwine, to judge by what she did with the carpet.* The box contained a ball of ivory or soft stone, carved with a complex design. It wasn't Kushorit, oddly enough. Every available stone or wood surface in the Empire had carving on it, and Rian felt he would have been able to recognize Kushorit work now if he was half-blind. This was unfamiliar. He turned it over thoughtfully. The lines were less elegant, the hand not as skilled as most Kushorit work. There were no flowers or people worked into the design, and it was strangely asymmetrical. The candlelight touched it, turning the dull surface to pearl, then to an opalescence that almost seemed to glow. Rian realized a heartbeat later that the light was coming from within the stone.

He closed the box and sat back on his heels. *That's . . .*

interesting. He hadn't known what he was looking for when he had come here, but now he had the strong feeling he had just found it.

He started at a sharp voice from the front of the house. His time had run out. He dumped the box and a handful of jewelry into one of the silk shawls and wrapped it up into a makeshift bag. If the thing was as important as it looked, they would miss it quickly; let them think he was a thief and it might buy a little time.

Rian bolted down the passage back to the nearest door, then out onto the veranda. He heard running footsteps from around the front of the house and vaulted the railing.

He hit the ground and fell, rolling to help absorb the shock. Ignoring the pain that shot through his right knee, he scrambled to his feet and ran for the palisade. The bundle slowed him down on the climb; as he reached the top someone grabbed his leg.

He kicked backward, connected with solid flesh, and was free. He hit the ground on the other side and heard shouting and a gate banging open. He ran for the other canal, away from the torchlit street and the more crowded avenue. Rian wondered how quickly the thief-takers would respond; considering this neighborhood was so close to the Palace, they would probably be here with dismaying speed.

There were large buildings fronting this canal, and in the dark they didn't have the elegant lines of the houses behind him. He ran between two of them and saw there were barges pulled up on the dirt under the pilings of the one on the right. The place stunk of fish and tar.

As he reached the muddy edge of the bank he heard voices and ducked down behind a piling. He eased forward enough to see the front of the building. Balconies overhung the water and another barge was floating at a lamplit dock that extended out into the canal. There were three men onboard, but they hadn't seen him. They were standing around a lamp mounted on the side of the barge, passing a jug and discussing the unreliability of other boatmen not present.

Rian glanced back up the alley toward Marada's house and saw figures with lamps and torches gathering in front of it. Marada might not have many servants, but she hadn't hesitated to rouse her neighbors in the emergency. He needed to get away from here, far away, fast. One of the men on the barge stepped off onto the dock and started to untie the mooring rope. The barge was about fifteen feet long, piled with baskets and bales. *It's better than nothing*, he thought grimly.

He opened the shawl and scooped out the jewelry, shoving it down into the soft mud near the beached boats for the boatmen or some lucky beggar to find. He wrapped the shawl around the box more tightly, then tied it around his neck.

The boatmen were pushing the barge away from the dock with heavy poles, creating ripples and splashes. Rian crept through the straggly grass to the bank, slid over the stone embankment and into the water, the noise of the barge's movement covering any sound he made.

He pushed away from the bank, toward the middle of the canal. The water was cool and at first he could touch the bottom, but it rapidly dropped off. The barge was drifting out from the dock and the lamp wasn't throwing much light over the sides. One man was poling at the front and the second at the back. Rian took a deep breath and went under.

He came up slowly at the side of the barge, just his eyes and nose above the water, and caught hold of the slimy surface of one of the pontoon logs. On the bank men were searching under the pilings of the building next to the shipping business. The boatman who had remained behind was running toward them with a lamp.

"What's all that?" a voice from the barge above his head asked.

"Who knows?" was the philosophical answer.

Rian relaxed a little. The barge had been caught by the slow current in the center of the canal and it would have taken forever to turn it and bring it back to the dock anyway. The box was bumping into his chin. He hoped the water didn't hurt it. Or break it. If the ball was like that grey glass bubble the enspelled boy had carried into their camp outside the city . . . *Then I'll be dead so fast I won't know it.*

The search party on the bank was left behind as the barge drifted smoothly down the canal. Buildings rose on either side, tall like the shipping house, some with lamps glowing in windows or on balconies. The barge reached the point where this canal met one running north-south, and both boatmen came to this side to pole off the bank. Rian clutched the box and ducked under the surface. He stayed under as long as he could, grasping the slippery logs and waiting for the barge to turn into the other canal. It did, just before he ran out of air, and he came up again as the barge straightened out and was caught by the new current.

Just as he decided he had put enough distance between himself and the search, the houses lining the banks began to show more light and there were suddenly people everywhere. There were torches on the docks and water stairs, and pleasure craft with awnings and flowers tethered near the bank. Music and voices drifted out over the water and the light outlined the shapes of trees in lush gardens between the buildings. The barge passed one house with four levels of balconies, all crowded with people, and the lamplight sparked off bronze and gold and bright colored silks. Rian sunk down until only his eyes and nose were above the water. Fortunately all the light on the bank would only make the center of the canal that much darker and the reflections on the water were sure to confuse the eye.

Rian was thinking of the wild river and the large number of dangerous things that inhabited it when he felt something twine around his thigh. He gripped the wet log and fought the urge to throw himself out of the water and up onto the barge. Then a large white flower bumped him in the head and he realized they were passing through a small underwater forest of lotus. Telling himself not to be an idiot, he shook his leg free and sunk down in the water again.

Then the buildings abruptly dropped away and the barge passed a short canal that seemed to lead into a vast area of empty water. Rian realized it had to be the western baray, the large square reservoir that was half water supply and half holy symbol of something or other. He let go of the barge and let himself drift toward the bank.

When the barge had passed on, he untied the shawl and set the box up on the stone embankment, then hauled himself up after it, the water weighting his clothes, making it an unwieldy process. Finally he was able to sit on the edge. The night breeze was cool and he pulled his shirt off and wrung it out, then drew the Holder Lord's siri to check the coating of oil on it.

There were stands of trees and several temple complexes around the baray, great dark mountains of stone in the night, only a few lamps or torches to mark doorways. Another temple stood on a stone island in the center, a round one with little towers topped by elaborate cupolas. It wasn't lit and looked tantalizing and mysterious in the night, the water reflecting back the moon-shaped portal of its doorway. Rian made plans to come back some quiet night and explore. It occurred to him that dark magic, demons that crossed ancient protective barriers, and the chance of being taken as a thief all notwithstanding, he was glad he had come to this city with Maskelle. Especially with Maskelle.

He eyed the little wooden box, sitting innocuously in the sodden shawl. He just hoped they hadn't come to it too late.

Much later Rian was trudging down the street that paralleled the moat on the Marai's east side, almost home. It was still an hour or so until dawn. He had avoided the whole area around the Baran Dir and the main gate into Kushor-An out of caution, in case one of Marada's servants had seen him running across the court. Consequently he had gotten lost. The lesser gate he had chosen led out into one of the suburbs where craftsmen and laborers lived, where the houses were much smaller and closer together, though most of them still had room for garden plots and breadfruit or banana trees. The streets didn't follow the even plan of the other areas, and the north-south canal he was using as a landmark was further out than he had thought. By climbing a tree he had seen the torches that burned high in the tops of the Marai's five towers and gotten pointed back in the right direction.

As he rounded the large house at the top of their street, he stopped abruptly and sank back into the bushes next to the palisade. Three men in breastplates and helmets stood under the gate lamps of the house across the way. They were talking to a sleepy porter, who was shrugging and pointing to another house down the street. *Our house,* Rian thought. Constabulary he might have expected, but not this. The crests on their helmets resembled those of the men who had come to the post compound after the Celestial One's entourage had arrived. *Something else going on here.*

On impulse, Rian ducked back between the houses, toward the canal. Near the stone bank was a small shrine dedicated to some odd little spirit with several arms and more heads. He had seen it in the daylight yesterday. It would have looked like a demon except that the faces on all the heads were smiling in far too friendly a way. Fumbling in the dark, Rian dug at the mud next to its base, making a hole. He worked the box into it, still wrapped in the damp shawl, and scooped dead leaves and grass over it.

Dusting his hands off on his pants, he started back to the street. He could have worked his way back along the canal and gone in through their back gate, but he didn't know if Maskelle was still at the Marai, and if they really were after him, he didn't want to lead them right down on top of her. He also knew from

Markand that if they were after you, avoiding them temporarily never did you any good. The only way to dodge trouble permanently was to run for the outer city gates and not come back, and there were too many reasons he didn't want to do that.

Rian went down the street without trying to conceal himself, stepping around the mud puddles left by the last rain. The night air was heavy with damp and the scent of wet greenery. The guards were gone from the gate of the house across the way, but a prickling on the back of his neck told him they hadn't left entirely. Morning life was starting to stir behind the palisades, and through the occasional open gate he could see sleepy cooks stoking the domed bread ovens.

He was almost home, crossing in front of a dark house with a closed gate, when a man stepped out from behind the corner of the wall in front of him, flicking up the shield on a lantern. Rian stopped, reached for his sword hilt, but then hooked his thumb on his belt instead, pretending to just now realize that this wasn't a footpad confronting him. He could hear two more coming up behind him.

The one facing him took a couple of steps forward, slowly, eyes narrowed suspiciously. He was no ordinary guardsman. He wore the wrapped silk trousers and open brocaded jacket that Rian had seen on the wealthier passers-by in the streets, but over it he had a heavy leather swordbelt studded with figured gold. The lamplight struck glints off the gems in his rings and the archer's wristbrace he wore. Rian read the combination of finery and utilitarian weapons and knew this man was of the warrior-noble class, who formed the officer corps of the Empire's armies. The man said, "You are the Sitanese who came here with the Voice of the Adversary?" He spoke the Kushorit words slowly and carefully, obviously expecting the barbarian not to understand.

"Yeah. What's it to you?" Rian folded his arms, not wanting to be stabbed from behind by some overeager recruit.

The noble said, "You will come with us."

Rian sensed one of the guards behind him reach for his sword-arm and he sidestepped, making the man stumble and curse. "Why?" Rian said, sounding startled. "What did I do?" Too many poor fools had given their guilt away to him simply by acting like trapped conspirators the first time they were confronted. He was startled, a little. He couldn't believe he had been recognized at Lady Marada's house. *You carried evidence out of there that she was a sorceress, idiot. You should have expected this.*

They stepped toward him again and Rian backed away. The odds were terrible. At the other end of the street he saw two more guards on horseback coming this way, moving at a slow walk until they were sure which direction their quarry meant to bolt. The noble lifted the lantern and said, "Cooperate and you won't be harmed." Something about the way he said it told Rian that he didn't quite believe it, either. Then one of the guards slipped the bow off his shoulder and notched an arrow.

That made the odds even worse. Rian calculated the man could get off three bolts by the time he ran to either end of the street, and maybe two if he tried to go over the wall behind him. Deliberately, he pulled the sheathed siri off his belt. One of the guards shifted warily and the bowman took a step back. Rian watched them derisively, then tossed the weapon to the noble.

The man caught it one-handed, and nodded. "Good decision," he said.

We'll see about that, Rian thought, submitting mostly graciously as a guard came forward to search him. He knew there were enough of them to beat him unconscious and throw him over the back of one of the horses if they had to, and he didn't intend to limit his already few options just to show them a good fight.

The court of the Marai was empty when Maskelle came out of the tower of the Rite again. She was bone-weary and her shoulders and back ached from leaning over. The searches of the other temples had so far turned up nothing. No suspicious activities, and certainly nothing so unusual as another Wheel. After much deliberation Vigar and the other Voices had decided to remove the unknown symbols from the Rite once again and continue. Maskelle still thought it was exactly the wrong course of action, but couldn't muster any argument good enough to convince the others. *And it isn't as if I've given them any good reason to listen to my advice lately,* she thought, sighing wearily. Standing in the dark, looking up at the lamps flickering in the gallery windows, she considered lying to them and saying that the Adversary had told her it was a terrible idea. *It wouldn't work.* The Celestial One would know if the Adversary started to speak to her again, and she couldn't rely on him not to expose the lie.

What if the lie were true?

She walked out of the Marai, down the long flights of steps to the causeway and across the outer court, then the silent stretch of black water with only the moon's reflection and the stone lions for company. When the causeway reached the plaza, she turned away from the streets that led to their guesthouse and instead went toward the Avenue of the Moon Rising. It led to the Illsat Sidar, the Temple of the Adversary.

There were still people on the plaza, some carrying lamps, some scurrying furtively in the dark. She supposed Disara might have sent someone to follow her again, if it was Disara who had sent the other one, but her mood was too fey to bother with that. And it was night, and the moon was on the wane, and the Adversary was strong. She could feel the city around her like a living thing, the beat of its heart in the stone under her thin sandals, its breath in the breeze over the water, its warm blood flowing through the canals.

The avenue led away from the plaza, past the smaller temples that marked the lesser sites of power and connection to the Infinite. She could feel them all in the dark, the ones set back from the avenue and separated from it by sacred and symbolic moats and flanked by libraries, the tiny ones of only one or two rooms, set low to the ground and close to the street where a passer-by could easily leave an offering of fruit or flowers or tie a fragment of bright fabric to the pillars. There were no houses behind or between these temples, no markets growing up on the small plazas in front of the larger ones, only stretches of grass with wild mulberry and ilex and red jasmine. There would be quarters for priests and penitents and the temple servants, but they were set far back from the street.

The avenue ended at the Illsat Sidar.

There was no ceremonial moat. The avenue narrowed to a walkway, passing between two long low buildings enclosing pillared courts, the temple's libraries. There was lamplight glowing from the windows of one, revealing late-night scholars, but Maskelle passed silently. The walkway became a broad stone stair that led up a hill that was part natural, part man-made, shored up with stone long ago when the city's foundations had been laid. She climbed the stairs to a wide terrace edged with knee-high statues of blackhead snakes, one of the Adversary's forms. There were two minor shrines facing each other across the terrace, now only shapes in the dark. A second, steeper stair led up to the central shrine, a larger building that if viewed from above would be in the shape of a lotus.

Maskelle stood in the entrance, breathing in the scent of the place, of cool dank stone and old incense. She moved further in, through the first court with its ceiling open to the dark sky, then to the inner sanctuary that lay just beyond.

A few candles had been lit in stone cage lamps, throwing gold light on the carvings and making the garuda birds and the other monstrous creatures seem to flicker with life. The effect was curiously like watching some of the Ariaden's smaller puppets on their shadowbox stage. In the center of the floor was a round gold plate, etched with ancient symbols of the Infinite too worn to read now, rubbed away with time and the softness of the metal.

Maskelle could feel the pulse of the city, the Marai, the Baran Dir, and the other temples, but of the Adversary's presence there was nothing. The temple had the feel of the Illsat Keo, an empty room, recently deserted. So recently she could almost sense the warmth of the departed body. Maybe anything else was too much to expect.

Except He gave you that dream. Dream, vision, warning. The Adversary's messages weren't usually so hard to understand. If you knew they were messages. She shivered, not from the dank air. *I won't make that mistake again.* A misinterpreted prophecy was what had gotten her into all this in the first place. The rest had been her own fault, compounding her original error. *I won't make that mistake again, but I'm so damn tired of being sorry for it,* she thought bitterly.

The figure stepped out of the shadows across the dark chamber, a solid darkness one moment, a man the next, the light touching dark-colored silk and gold. *Ah,* Maskelle thought, too used to the vagaries of the Ancestors to be surprised. *So that's what brought me here.* She said, "Sirot. Come to say welcome home?"

The man walked toward her, stopping not ten paces away. There was no dust on the stone tiles to be disturbed, or not disturbed, by the passage of his feet, but she felt that his body was not warming the air and his breath was not stirring it, despite the apparent substantiality of his presence. Sirot said, "So you returned after all."

He was exactly the same as he had been in life, an image caught in time without the mutability of memory. His long dark hair was caught back by a gold clasp, his sharp features harsh in the candlelight. His trousers and jacket were black, almost melding with the shadow except for the fine sheen of the fabric and the glint of gold armbands. Maskelle said, "It was only a matter of time."

"To face the scene of your defeat?" He smiled, his lips a thin line.

"I may be defeated, but I'm not dead. Pity you can't say the same." Shades had no power to touch the living, but she had never feared Sirot even when he was alive. She had loved him once, when she had been too young for judgment but old enough to mistake willfulness for certainty.

He laughed at her, a curiously flat sound that seemed to travel no more than the distance necessary to reach her; it didn't cast faint echoes off the stone walls as her voice did. He said, "My son has the throne. That's all that ever mattered to me."

"Yes, I found that out," Maskelle agreed. That, at least, was true. Sirot had never wanted anything except the throne of the Celestial Empire for his son. If he had wanted Maskelle once, that had given way to his ambition long before her false vision had made them enemies. It had been later that she had killed him, when she was older and no wiser. Killed him for nothing, for his son had taken the throne anyway and her vision of disaster had not come to pass.

"And what other wisdom has time revealed to you? Enlighten me." He spoke with that subtle edge of contempt that had once amused her when he had demonstrated it on others. He had been subtle and clever enough to hide his contempt for her until the final break between them.

Maskelle's shoulders ached and she was suddenly too tired for this, tired of ghosts and memory. She said, "Is that what you're here for? I've admitted that to the world, Sirot. I was tricked, fooled, lied to. The vision was false. You were right and I was wrong." Saying it to a dead reflection of a soul long gone to the Infinite was nothing.

His smile died, and his eyes stared into hers, flat and opaque. He said, "Was I right?"

That wasn't the answer she had expected. "What do you

mean?" she asked, before she could stop herself. It was never a good idea to ask questions of shades.

If this was a shade. Maskelle felt something stir in the temple, a restless flow of power. *The Adversary. . . .*

Sirot said, again, without expression, "Was I right?"

In the next breath he was gone. Maskelle cursed, buried her face in her hands. The sense of the Adversary's presence had gone with him. *No, it wasn't the Adversary, it was Sirot. He came to destroy what little calm you've managed to attain, only that.*

She lifted her head and sighed. The temple felt warm again, warm but empty. She looked at the gold disk in the floor. It marked the closest point in the temple to the Adversary, the carefully calculated point where this world came closest to the Infinite. Even people who had never explored the Path could receive visions by standing on it. *Let's test our resolve, then.* If the Adversary wouldn't speak to her there, she would know he would never speak to her again. Before she could think better of it, she stepped onto the gold disk.

Images struck her with breathtaking force. She saw the great stone buildings with their flicker of candlelight, the vast grey plain. But this time the dry cool air was suffocating, heavy with sharp fear and desperation so intense it choked her. *Soon, soon, soon,* her own voice whispered. *They will move soon. They can't afford to wait.*

Maskelle opened her eyes. She lay on her back, on the cold stone floor of the temple, staring at the arches carved into garuda birds. She sat up and grabbed her head. "Ow." She couldn't have been unconscious long. It was still dark out and the candles in the lamps hadn't guttered. *No answer would have been answer enough.* Now all she had was another puzzle.

The grey dawn light was filtering through the trees when Maskelle reached the gate of their house. She trudged across the muddy court to where Old Mali sat on a bench in front of the kitchen firepit, poking suspiciously at the oven. Maskelle picked up the pottery jug that was set to warm in the ashes, but it was empty. She asked hopefully, "Tea? Food?"

"In time," Old Mali growled. "I've only got two hands." One rheumy eye gazed at Maskelle critically. "You need a bath."

"Thank you, yes, I know." Maskelle started up the stairs. Old Mali snarled at her and, sighing, she stopped to take off her muddy sandals.

Upstairs there were unconscious Ariaden strewn around the common room and she picked her way across them carefully. She paused in the doorway to her room, staring at the empty bed, until her mind, trapped somewhere back in the past amid the patterns and symbols of the Infinite, registered what was wrong. Rian wasn't here. *He should be back by now. It's not that far to the west Palace district.* Unless something had gone badly wrong.

She checked the other rooms first, just to make sure he wasn't with anybody else, but Doria and Therasa were together and Killia was sharing a bed with her daughter. *An unworthy impulse,* she told herself. Perhaps seeing Sirot's shade again had shaken her more than she had thought. She went back downstairs and did a quick turn through the lower level of the house, but the storage areas and pantry were empty and the tiled floor of the bathing room was dry. She came out again and went to the kitchen, where Old Mali was putting lumps of dough on the baking stones in the oven. "The water jars are full," the old woman hinted again.

Maskelle ignored her. "Did Rian come back last night?"

"No." Old Mali glared at her. "He's with you."

"He's not with me."

"What did you do with him then?"

Maskelle started to reply sharply, then bit her lip and said, "I let him go to search the house of a woman who might've killed a couple of priests with magic."

Old Mali rolled her eyes and shook her head. Maskelle snapped, "Well, now I realize that." She paced, shoving her hair back out of her eyes. "Maybe he went back to the Marai and fell asleep waiting." She couldn't do anything until she looked there first.

Rastim staggered down the stairs, clutching his head as if trying to keep it from falling off. "What's all the noise?"

Maskelle started toward the gate. "Sorry, go back to sleep," she told him, then saw the gate at the back of the compound that faced the canal was swinging open. She stopped, frustrated. *I don't have time for this.*

The Celestial One's boat was docked at their water steps and the young priest-attendant was lifting the old man out. Maskelle cursed under her breath, but one couldn't ignore the Celestial One when he came to your own house, no matter who or what one was. She crossed the muddy court to meet him.

The attendant sat the old man down and he came toward her. Rastim hurried forward, trying to straighten up and not look half-dead, and Old Mali was standing ready with a mat in case the old man sat down. As Maskelle reached him, she said impatiently, "I'm in a hurry—"

"Listen to me." The Celestial One held up one hand.

Maskelle suddenly knew what this was about. Intuition or the Ancestors, it didn't matter. Her throat felt tight. She said, "He'd better not be dead." Rastim and Old Mali stared at her.

Deliberately, the Celestial One said, "I had a message from Hirane of the Baran Dir. Your friend was brought to the Celestial Home by the guard during the dawn meditation."

Maskelle nodded, looking away. *Rian was right,* she thought. She could see it now, just as clearly as she could see the dark eruption in the Rite. "That's all I needed to know." It hurt to talk and she realized it was because her jaw muscles were so tight.

Rastim looked at Old Mali, baffled. She hissed, "The Sitanese."

The Celestial One shook his head. "Let me deal with this."

"Oh, no." She smiled. "He's gone to all the effort of having

Rian brought to him, just to get my attention. I could hardly deny him what he has asked for, now can I?"

The Celestial One's eyes narrowed. "You will let me deal with this."

Maskelle's rage crystallized into a hard knot in her chest. She turned and strode for the gate. Behind her she heard the Celestial One shouting for his attendant and his boatmen.

10

The guards took Rian back toward the gate of Kushor-An, down the causeway of giant guardians. His first thought was that they were going back to the Lady Marada's house so someone could point and say, "It was him!" If she had used her magics to see who the intruder had been, there was nothing he could do about it. But they passed the way that led to Marada's house and continued up the broad avenue toward the Baran Dir.

The guards didn't know quite what to make of him. They had expected him to put up a struggle, so he had gone quietly. He had heard the man who had confronted him called Lord Karuda by the others, so he knew he was correct in his initial assessment. It was mildly annoying that they had found all his knives; Karuda himself still carried the siri. Like a trophy. *Careful, Kushorit lord; trophies like that come with high prices.*

As they walked, Rian saw Karuda half-draw the siri, examining the bare hilt and the ring, rubbing his thumb over the places where the figured gold had been removed. Rian eyed him warily. He suspected Karuda was too sharp for his liking. As they neared the great gate, the noble raised his hand, stopping them under a large brass lamp hanging from the harness of one of the giant elephant guardians. He stepped closer to Rian, looking him over thoughtfully, then said, "You're a *kjardin*. Which lord do you belong to?"

He had the pronunciation as right as his Kushorit accent would allow. Rian rapidly weighed the merits of claiming Riverwait or Markand and decided on neither. "No one. Not anymore." Let Karuda think he was a thief, an outcast, anything. *Just don't let him think it would be a good idea to send me back.* It hadn't occurred to him until now that that could be a possibility. *I'm not going back to the barrow. Not alive.*

Karuda's brow lifted skeptically. If he knew enough to look at the remains of the caste marks in Rian's ear and use a word which didn't have an equivalent in Kushorit, then he knew how unlikely it was that a *kjardin* had been allowed to leave his Hold without catastrophe or scandal. Karuda asked, "The High Lord?"

Relief at the wildness of this guess made Rian look honestly puzzled. "No. I was from Sorde." That was a small Hold even closer to the mountains than Riverwait and surely Karuda wouldn't know it.

"I went to the Sintane once with the Kushorit ambassador," Karuda said, eyeing him deliberately. "*Kjardin* don't leave their Holds."

Rian could have given him half a dozen ready lies, but Karuda would know them for it immediately. He said only, "This one did."

Frowning, Karuda only looked at the siri again, sheathed it, and moved on.

The dawn light was beginning to illuminate the Baran Dir, the faces that surmounted its many towers gazing in massive beneficence over the smaller temples and the sprawl of wealthy homes and gardens that grew up just outside its moat. It wasn't meant to look like an ever-rising mountain like the Marai, but it was built up on two high stone terraces that raised the central towers more than a hundred feet in the air. The stone was a lighter color than the other temples and glowed a rich gold in the dawn.

They couldn't be taking him to the Baran Dir. As far as Rian could tell it had something to do with hospitals and healing. The Marai was really the main temple in the city, though the Baran Dir seemed to occupy the most central location. It was hard to remember that Duvalpore was organized according to the invisible geography of the Infinite and not the real world.

Near where the avenue turned into a causeway to cross the Baran Dir's moat, they turned west on another wide paved street, skirting the edge of a large plaza which was nearly empty at this early hour. There were walls on the far side, all carved with elephants engaged in game hunts in the forest, the theme brought partly to life by the heavy band of trees and foliage visible just over the top. They were heading for a gate guarded by stone lions and some of the misshapen spirit creatures. Rian concealed his increasing bafflement; Duvalpore was laid out in a strange fashion, but he didn't think a prison could be situated anywhere near here.

Past the gate was a short paved avenue, this one lined with walls carved with festival scenes, shaded by palms and sycamore. Stone latticework showed they were actually on a causeway, crossing a stretch of water too large to be a canal. In Duvalpore moats were considered spiritual rather than defensive barriers; it was as if they were going into a temple's precincts.

At the end of the causeway they went up a set of steps to a large garden square. At the top Rian finally saw what had to be their goal. The square was enclosed on three sides by a rambling and complex arrangement of buildings. Sprouting long verandas and roofed balconies, some were as much as three or four stories tall and were built around enormous old trees. The peaks of the red-tiled roofs were ornamented with huge carved beams that pointed upward like horns at the ends.

As they led him across the garden, they passed plots all taken up with bright flowering shrubs, the vivid colors muted by the grey dawn light, and two large square pools, one deeply sunken into a stone basin with steps leading down into it. There were guards posted at intervals and a few workers fully occupied with cleaning a raised stone channel that watered one of the basins.

They were not going to the broad shaded portico of the main building, but toward an archway in the garden wall that led to an interior court with palms and other trees hanging over the wall. As they neared it he could see the arch was framed with polished and gold-tipped elephant tusks. Rian thought, *If it's a prison, then the Koshans and the Kushorit really are crazy.* He stopped at the base of the steps that led up to it, planting his feet when one of the guards pushed him. He said, "What is this place?"

Lord Karuda glanced back at him, his expression closed, and didn't answer. The biggest guard gave Rian another hard shove. He shifted his weight to keep his balance and stood his ground. Rian supposed that sort of treatment was always effective on the peasants in the market, though he would have thought any one of the porters who carried burdens yoked on their backs could have beaten the man into the ground one-handed.

Karuda pressed his lips together, annoyed. Rian had the feeling they didn't want to make a disturbance here. The aggressive guard uncertainly fingered his sword, contemplating further persuasion, and looked to Karuda for instruction. Finally the noble said, "This is the Celestial Home."

Rian just stopped himself from calling Karuda a liar. He looked at the large complex of buildings again, reluctantly admitting to himself that it did look a lot like a Kushorit palace. *All right, you only thought you were in trouble before.* The guard gave him another hard shove. Rian kept his balance and ignored it. Karuda shook his head, for a moment looking almost as puzzled as Rian felt, then turned and went up the steps. Rian followed without persuasion, much to the guard's annoyance.

Just past the archway the lush garden court was shaded by palms and ilex and a massive cypress whose roots had dislodged many of the paving stones around the square pool. The scent of flowers mingled with sandalwood incense. On the far side of the pool was a pavilion with a red tile roof supported by stone pillars. There were cushions on the polished wooden floor, and courtiers on the cushions, three young men, probably of the warrior-noble rank like Karuda, but in their silks and gold they looked as soft as doves. Standing to one side was a Koshan priestess, robed in blue and clutching a silver-wrapped staff. She was a small elderly woman with thin lips and a grimly determined expression.

Another young man who didn't look soft at all was pacing on the far side of the pavilion. His long dark hair was pulled back from a narrow face with sharp, handsome features. He was dressed in a simple open jacket and trousers of watered green silk, but his armbands, anklets, and pectoral were heavy gold. He stopped abruptly and turned toward them as Rian was brought in. Rian saw the man's face was dark with anger.

Karuda bowed, and though Rian wasn't practiced at interpreting the different levels of the Kushorit bow, he knew that one signalled an even greater degree of homage than the Celestial One normally received. *I know who this is,* he thought, feeling a shock that was like a punch to the pit of his stomach. The guard behind him kicked at his knee, and Rian knelt smoothly, back straight, sitting back on his heels. It was the proper etiquette for showing fealty to the High Lord of the Sintane, and even if they didn't know that, the gesture could hardly be interpreted as disrespect.

He hadn't expected the Emperor to be so young. He had thought of him, if he had thought of him at all, as somebody like the Celestial One, if not quite so ruinously old. This man couldn't be much above twenty, if that. "That's him?" the Celestial Emperor said, his full lips curling with contempt.

Uh oh, Rian thought. He hadn't accused Lady Marada of being a murderer to anybody except Maskelle; the Emperor couldn't have heard about that. *I'm either dreaming or dead,* he thought. *Probably both.* Even if had been obvious that he shared the bad opinion of Marada held by the servants attached to the

Marai, that couldn't have found its way to the Emperor's ears in so short a time, unless his spies had near supernatural abilities.

"It is, Your Majesty," Karuda said. His voice was colorless, only the tension it took to keep it so betraying any opinion. Rian didn't think Karuda was a possible ally, but he could tell the noble wasn't entirely happy with his role in all this. Whatever all this was.

The Emperor said, "Stand up."

Rian stood.

The blow caught him across the cheek. Rian saw it coming, rocked back on his heels to absorb the force of it. He felt one of the Emperor's rings open a cut under his cheekbone. *He doesn't hit nearly as hard as the Holder Lord used to.*

For just a moment the Emperor's expression was disconcerted, possibly at Rian's lack of reaction. He turned away, paced almost to the edge of the pavilion and stopped, fists knotted. He jerked his head at the courtiers and said, "Get out."

All three immediately got to their feet, gracefully, though not wasting any time, and made their bows. When they had gone, there was quiet for a moment. In the trees birds sang, greeting the dawn, and the tension stretched.

Then the Emperor turned his head and asked softly, "Where did Maskelle find you?"

At least he's not asking about Marada, Rian thought. At least not yet. He hesitated, but he couldn't think why the Emperor had the remotest interest in him. *If he really cares so much who Maskelle travels with, why aren't Rastim and the others here?* He said, "On the Great Road, two days south of Duvalpore, lord." He had no idea what the Kushorit called the Emperor when addressing him directly and knew that making a mistake would be a serious tactical error, so he used the Sitanese honorific for the High Lord.

Fortunately no one seemed to care. The Emperor faced him, staring. "Two days . . . Before she came to the city?"

"Yes."

"The implication is obvious," a new voice said. Another man stepped up into the pavilion from a hidden path through the foliage. Rian managed not to twitch at his sudden appearance. He was older, his dark hair greying and pulled back behind his head in an elaborate knotted braid, his face hard and calm. He wore enough gold to mark him as a noble, but there was no ostentatious display, and his air of power didn't require the support. "Our information was correct. She has made foreign alliances."

"What use would an alliance with the Sintane be?" the Emperor snapped.

True, Rian thought, just managing to keep his face straight. The warring lords of the Sintane made terrible allies for each other, let alone for the Celestial Empire, which they regarded with suspicion and fear. *They suspect Maskelle of making a foreign alliance?* It was all part of her past, the mistaken vision, the throne and her second husband's heir. *But they must have known she was here that first night, when the Celestial One came to the post house.* If they suspected her of treason, then why wait until today to fetch Rian in? Surely the Celestial One's presence would not have been enough to stop men under the command of the Emperor himself.

The Koshan priestess, standing forgotten on the other side of the pavilion, said suddenly, "The Voice of the Adversary has no need of alliances. Chancellor Mirak knows this."

That explained part of it, anyway. Rian remembered the priestess Barime, at the Illsat Keo, had mentioned Mirak as an enemy of the Koshans at court. Mirak gazed at the old woman with amusement and said, "This priestess has divided loyalties."

"So, now Hirane makes a foreign alliance? The Master of the Baran Dir and the Celestial One conspire against me?" The Emperor snorted derisively.

At least he's not a brainless lordling, Rian thought. The Emperor seemed more than able to make up his own mind. Not that that was likely to help Rian's situation. Though he had to admit he still had no idea what his situation was.

Mirak, wisely, didn't argue, and the priestess Hirane simply stood silently, though a grim smile played about her lips. The Emperor stepped up to Rian again, his face dark but thoughtful.

Rian made himself relax, expecting another blow, but the Emperor only said, "You weren't sent by the Sitanese High Lord, were you?"

"No, lord," Rian said, keeping his tone even but willing the younger man to know it was true.

"Are you warming her bed?"

Rian's eyes narrowed. He didn't answer.

The Emperor studied him intently. "She draws men to her. Then she kills them. She's done it many times before. She did it to my father."

He was trying to sound mocking, but was too obviously taut with anger to be saying these things for his own amusement. Saying *I heard about your father and he was a power-hungry little shit of a lordling who should have been gelded and hung out for the birds to eat* was hardly likely to improve the situation any, so again, Rian said nothing.

After a long heartbeat of silence, the Emperor stepped back. He glanced almost angrily at Karuda, as if it was his fault Rian was here, then said, "Take him away."

Karuda and his men led him down the stone-paved path through the heavy foliage. It was narrow, and with the trees shading it and the dim morning light, it was ideal for making an escape attempt. Except for the small fact that the Celestial Emperor was less than twenty paces away and the last thing Rian needed was to get himself and Maskelle accused of another attempt on the throne.

The path led toward the high log wall of one of the buildings, to an archway that opened into a high-ceilinged entrance hall, the woven lattice panels over the openings to the upper level balconies letting in light and air. The walls and pillars were carved with scenes of priests and warriors and more of the strange multiheaded spirit creatures, the designs touched with gold and pearl inlay. Rian began to feel conscious of the state of his clothes, not improved by climbing palisades and the swim in the canal. Prison he had been prepared for; this sent prickles of unease up and down his spine.

They went through more large, airy rooms, lit by bronze candle-stands or elaborate lamps that hung from the heavy beams over-head. Rian saw two guards posted at the end of a hall, dressed for show in breastplates and crested helmets with half-masks, and a few sleepy servants scrubbing tile on one of the upper galleries. They passed a hall where the walls were panelled in huge sheets of ivory covered with delicately etched scenes of clashing armies. He had been to the High Lord's Hold at Belladira and thought it rich beyond imagination, but this place made it look like a pigkeeper's hut. The Markand Heir, so greedily pleased with the treasures that had come to him when the Holder Lord had died, would have writhed in envy.

They went up a spiral stair of large stone blocks that had wide windows overlooking another garden court. The stairs led up to a landing with two guards posted outside the doorway. Rian tensed, knowing this must be their goal, but it was only a room, large and high-ceilinged, with a broad balcony looking down on the shaded garden court. Rian looked at Karuda, now truly baffled.

The noble said, "You're a guest here, not a prisoner."

"A guarded guest."

"Yes. For now."

Karuda didn't leave, but just stood there, watching him. Rian went to the balcony, saw that there were guards down in the court also, though it might be possible to go up the timbered wall and onto the roof. The room hung out over the court, so that would probably be easy. Rian turned back into the room. It was furnished like a Kushorit house with cushions, a few carved chests and a low table. There were doorways leading off into at least two other rooms, and the wall paintings and the carving along the doorposts and the lintels was of a high quality, inlaid with fine wood and stone.

Karuda asked suddenly, "Will she come for you?"

"That's the plan, is it?" The noble made no answer, and Rian knew he was right. He was being used as bait for Maskelle. *The sanctimonious bastards.* He was used to controlling his anger, had swallowed down rage through that entire impossible year at Markand, but this almost broke his control. He found himself smiling tightly, an expression which Karuda weathered but made the guard who had followed him into the room shift warily. Rian said, "You'll get more than you bargained for."

"She's an old woman—"

Rian laughed. Karuda stopped, and Rian could see the noble didn't believe his own words either. He repeated, "You'll get more than you bargained for."

Karuda hesitated, as if he wanted to say more, then turned and walked out, the guard following him. The others remained at the door.

Rian went to the balcony again and gripped the carved balustrade, letting out his breath. Marada and her possible plots, the Celestial One and the damage to the Rite, all suddenly seemed of little importance. *We're for it now,* he thought grimly.

Maskelle entered the Celestial Home through the Golden Door, the main entrance that lay across a short bridge from the Great Square of Kushor-An. She went down an avenue lined with mimosa, under stone arches that, like the Passage Markers on the outer approaches to the city, served as protective barriers. The cloud cover had set in and the morning light was diffuse and dimmer than it had been at dawn, though the early rain hadn't started yet. The walk across to Kushor-An had been a long one and given Maskelle time to think. That this was all part of some sort of trap was obvious.

The Golden Door was just that, a great golden gate balanced so exactly that it would swing open or closed with a touch. It stood open now. There were guards, but they ignored her, some staring nervously, some making what they thought were unobtrusive warding gestures. Beyond the Door was the steps up to the broad portico of the Great House, with three levels of galleries above it going up to the huge red-tiled roof. Built of heavy timber from the upland forests and supported by round stone pillars, this was the place that ruled the Celestial Empire. It was so familiar and so strange. Like returning to a well-known place in a dream or vision.

Speaking of visions . . . It was an obvious trap, but as to who was behind it . . . *That is not so obvious,* she thought. It was encouraging that she could still think. Anger had been a heady intoxicant and she had always enjoyed that sensation of being balanced on a blade's edge. Rage had always left her oddly clear-headed, but this time it was even more so; Rian's life might hang in the balance and she didn't intend to make a mistake. The awareness that if she wasn't careful she would deliver herself into her unknown enemy's hand helped as well, but it was less important. She was rather looking forward to confronting an enemy just now. Any enemy.

Arrayed on the portico were a group of Imperial guardsmen and a young warrior-noble she didn't recognize. Maskelle stopped on the paved path about twenty paces away, leaning on her staff, and counted guards. "Only ten?" she said, her voice sounding brittle and bitterly amused, even to her own ears. "That's an insult."

The noble stepped down toward her. "Revered, we're to escort you only—"

Maskelle stopped listening. She had expected contempt or impertinence at the very least from these young men who had been hardly more than children when she had left Duvalpore. The noble's air of determined resignation reminded her they weren't doing this of their own volition and saved all their lives.

There was a direct line of power running under her feet from the Baran Dir to the Arkad Temple, and through it she could feel the strong reverberation of the Marai, and further off, the subtle echo of the Illsat Sidar. She drew on it and used it to widen her perception of her surroundings, right up to the clouds hanging high overhead heavy with water. Stimulated by the contact with the power running through the earth, the power of the sky inherent in the clouds leapt out. Drawing on the temples for the strength she channeled it down to impact harmlessly on the stone pavement equidistant between her and the guards.

For an instant the world was raw light and sound. She gripped her staff and stayed on her feet, temporarily blind and deaf. The violence of the ringing in her ears made her teeth hurt. When her vision cleared she saw the guards were scattered, some sprawled on the ground from shock and terror, but all unhurt. Some had dropped their bori clubs and swords, and all were now dragging off their helmets. Heat burned into her palm from the silver in her staff, and she knew that all the metal within many yards was now hot to the touch. The air smelled raw and burnt. There was a dark steaming hole in the pavement where the power had struck. *There,* she thought, a little dazed herself. *Are you pleased? Every dark spirit within miles will be drawn up to the city boundary, waiting for you to leave.* She answered herself, *Yes, I am pleased. I reminded them of what I am and why they shouldn't trifle with me with no harm caused to anyone but myself.* Something wasn't quite right with that, but she would worry about it later.

The noble staggered to his feet, staring at her. He didn't try to stop her as she walked past him and climbed the steps to the portico.

She went through the ivory-framed archway into the entrance hall, quiet now and dim, with the clouds cutting off the morning sun and the lamps not lit. It was fragrant with the scents of the fine inlaid woods in walls and floor and the semiprecious stones set into the carving gleamed in the shadows. It was too quiet, even for this time of day.

As Maskelle passed the antechambers and rooms reserved for waiting supplicants and petitioners, all empty, she knew that they had been cleared because of her presence. They should have been full of officials on real business and people who meant to try to seek some personal favor or matter of justice from the Imperial secretaries, who also had their audience rooms in these halls. To clear this place quickly, without resorting to threats of violence which would only cause full-blown riot among the regional governors and high court advocates who were sure to be here, was an impossibility. Only one man could have emptied the place with a simple request. Maskelle's jaw ached from unconsciously grinding her teeth.

She came to a huge room, the ceiling going up the full four stories to the peak of the roof, with the center portion open to the gradually lightening sky and covered only by the giant skeleton of the heavy support beams. The floor was paved with fine white stone, with two steps down to a shallow pool in the center, directly under the open roof. The floor under the pool was mosaiced to resemble a natural pond, blue water laced with lotus and other languid flowering water plants. The illusion of an outdoor pond was increased by the presence of a dozen or so large graceful herons, standing or stalking elegantly about the shallow pool.

The wide doors just past it led into a large dark room, this one with the empty feel of a place normally bustling with people. It had a floor of wood inlaid with ivory and the ceiling arched high overhead, the sections between the carved beams painted a deep indigo and starred with gems that glittered like ice in the light from a few gold candlestands. At the far end, on a dais raised two steps off the floor, was a heavy gold bench.

Seated on the steps in front of the Throne, his staff across his knees, was the Celestial One.

Maskelle stopped a few paces from him, folded her arms, and said, "Why did you clear the halls? Did you think I'd kill everyone in my path?"

"I wanted no one to take the opportunity to interfere with you. Any further, that is," he said, sounding tired. "Your friend is well. I made certain of that."

The anger went out of her suddenly. She was tired, too, and her ears hurt. And it came to her that it had cost the Celestial One something to cross the city by boat to be here before her, to reach the Great House from the Celestial Home's canal dock and clear the halls before she reached it. She crossed the short distance between them and sat down beside him on the steps. "Well."

"I'm too old for these plots," he grumbled. "That was always your duty."

"Thank you. I think."

"I meant to deal with the plots, of course." He gestured in irritation. "Raith insists this was his own idea. Perhaps he even believes it. The boy is just as stubborn as you."

The Celestial One was one of the few people in the Empire who could use the Celestial Emperor's given name and talk about him as if he was an errant acolyte while seated three feet from the Throne. She asked, "It wasn't Marada?"

He frowned at her as though the question sounded mad. "Who?"

"A Court Lady visiting from Garekind. I saw you speak to her at the Marai, the day we arrived."

"Oh, her. I can't tell them apart anymore. She had requested an audience with me to gawk, the usual reason these foreign visitors do." He glanced at her sharply. "Why do you think she caused this?"

Maskelle shook her head. "She was the only stranger close

enough to Veran to . . . do whatever was done to him." There was so much she didn't know yet. She needed to find out if Rian had managed to get into the guesthouse, if he had found anything. "She's a favorite of Raith's."

"That will make matters difficult." The Celestial One rubbed his chin thoughtfully. "Is there any proof or only suspicions?"

"Just suspicions." *That is the thing I don't understand,* she thought. *Someone with dark power did this, that's obvious enough, but how did he learn so much about the Rite?* Even with access to the Koshan libraries in Kushor-At, theoretical knowledge wasn't enough. It would take practical experience with building and shaping the sand patterns of the wheel, and weaving it in and out of the Infinite to make that new section, and make it so quickly.

That knowledge might have come voluntarily from poor dead Veran, or maybe even the Voice Igarin, but . . . *But I doubt it,* Maskelle thought. Rian had found out enough about both men to support her gut instinct. As Igarin had grown older he had grown closer to the Infinite, as most Voices did. He had hardly left the Marai at all in the past few years. Veran had been well occupied with his studies and his instruction to younger Koshans; Lady Marada had been the only odd intrusion into his life. And the Temple Master and some of the Voices had examined the books and notes in Veran's quarters, and confirmed that there was no trace there of the unknown symbols. *Something used Veran, that has to be it. Something invaded his mind and used him like a tool, and Marada killed him to keep him from telling us.*

"And what about the Rite?" The Celestial One sounded like any querulous old man in the market, complaining about taxes and the price of rice. "Who is working on that while we chase each other across the city?"

"Vigar and the other Voices—"

"Balls," the Celestial One said distinctly. Maskelle, though more used to his eccentricities than others, almost fell off the step. "I wanted your opinion. I had Vigar's already."

"I don't know what my opinion is. It feels wrong to remove the . . . obstruction, but we can't leave it in. The Equinox is tomorrow, and if they all work on it together and no one trods on someone's sleeve and falls on the Wheel, they'll barely finish in time as it is." She rubbed her face. "I think the Adversary finally spoke to me again in the Illsat Sidar but what he showed me has nothing to do with the Rite." She wasn't going to tell him about seeing Sirot. "I think I've done something to myself, so I can't understand what he says even when he does speak to me. My first decent vision in seven years and I can't understand it."

He watched her worriedly. "That isn't possible."

"Just because something's never happened before doesn't mean it's not possible. It could be happening right now and we wouldn't know—" She stopped in confusion. She had heard a whisper just then, not the chiding voices of the Ancestors, but the strong tone of the Adversary. It lingered, like the taste of copper in her mouth. *A warning. Something is happening now, but we don't know what or where.* She swore under her breath. These warnings that made no sense were going to drive her mad.

The Celestial One was shaking his head. "Calm yourself. Meditation—"

"I'll try it," she said, standing up suddenly. She wanted to leave, now. Whatever the answer was, she was more likely to find it in the Illsat Sidar or the Marai than here. "Tell me where Rian is and we'll go."

The Celestial One's mouth twisted. "There is something more. Raith wants you to spend the night here. As a gesture of fealty."

"What? He must be mad!" She realized she had shouted the words. Anticipating that must have been another reason the Celestial One had cleared the place. "I should be with the Rite tonight, with Vigar and the others."

The Celestial One snapped, "I am as aware of that as you, I assure you."

"Then what's the point of this?"

"He believes this will demonstrate your reformed character." The Celestial One's expression as he said the words suggested that there was an extremely foul odor associated with them. "If the boy were a fool, this would be easier to stomach."

"He gives me an opportunity to start trouble and heartily wishes that I'll take it."

"That too."

"Doesn't he understand we don't have time for all this posing? I should at least be there when the Voices complete the Rite, just in case. . . . You did tell him about the Rite, didn't you?" she demanded.

"Yes. But he doesn't understand. None of them do. They have little awareness of the Rite. It has been with them their whole lives, their parents' lives, back to the time of the Ancestors, as constant as the sun or the air, and they think it will continue as always, with or without our interference."

Maskelle turned away, rubbing her aching temples. "I hope they're right."

As soon as Rian judged it had been long enough for the guards to relax their initial vigilance, he tested his theory about the roof.

It was relatively easy to reach the very edge from the balcony by standing on the balustrade and leaning out from the supporting post. Fortunately, the guards in the garden below did not look up, and the view of the others was blocked by a large palm. The tiles were slick enough to make it chancy as it was; if the rain started they would be as slippery as looking-glass. He managed to drag himself up onto the roof after a few breathless moments, then saw that this part of the building was overlooked by an adjoining structure, with jutting cupolas and a long gallery just under the eave of its peaked roof. Before he could move more than a few yards toward it, someone saw him and the alarm was raised.

Cursing, Rian retreated, dropping back down to the balcony. The guards at the outer door hadn't noted his absence, but the thump when he landed caught their attention. They rushed into the room, drawing bori clubs, only to stop when they saw him standing on the balcony, arms folded, glaring at them. After staring suspiciously at him, they finally went back to their post.

Rian paced impatiently, kicking one of the brocaded cushions. The effort of the climb had accomplished nothing except to open the scabbed-over cut on his forearm which itched and bled sluggishly. He knew it must already be too late to stop Maskelle from coming to the Palace, even if he managed to escape right now.

Suddenly a crack of lightning, close enough to make Rian flinch, reverberated through the room. He stepped to the balcony again while the echoes of thunder died, squinting up at the sky. It looked no darker than it usually did. *That was strange.* While it rained with dreary regularity in the lowlands, it didn't often storm except at the beginning of the rainy season. The two guards at the door were commenting on it in soft voices, as surprised as Rian was.

Wait, he thought. *That couldn't be* . . . Well, it could. He had warned Karuda himself.

There was no more lightning and Rian went back to pacing, telling himself she could take care of herself and it didn't matter that he couldn't get out to help her. Still, he had come up with several increasingly unlikely escape plans when he heard her voice outside in the stairwell.

He was at the door in a heartbeat, though the two guards hurriedly moved to bar his way. He started to shove past them, bori clubs or not, then saw Maskelle coming up the steps, with a stone-faced Lord Karuda trailing her. A moment later a young priest appeared carrying the Celestial One up the steps after them.

Karuda was trying to say something to Maskelle. She ignored him, using distracted pokes from her staff to nudge the startled guards out of the way as if they were sheep that had strayed into the road. She shoved her way into the room and said, "Are you all right?"

"Yes." Rian reminded himself he couldn't grab her and shake her and demand to know what in hell she thought she was doing here.

"What did they do, throw you into the canal?" she persisted, looking him over worriedly.

Rian had almost forgotten about the expedition to Marada's house. It seemed an age ago. With Karuda standing there watching both of them, he said tightly, "Can we discuss that later?"

Maskelle turned to Karuda, who had followed her into the room. "Go away. Take the guards with you. Now."

Rian had time to notice that Karuda looked the worse for wear himself, that he had removed his archer's wristbrace and had a new red burn on his hand in roughly the same shape. Stubbornly, Karuda said, "I have been ordered—"

He was interrupted by the entrance of the Celestial One, who had been set down on the landing by his attendant priest. The old man hobbled into the room, shaking his head. He was followed closely by Hirane, the priestess who had been with the Emperor in the garden, and two more priest-attendants. The Celestial One looked at Karuda sourly. "I know your orders, young one. Go to Mirak and tell him his plot is successful if he intended it to greatly inconvenience the Voices of the Ancestors and all the upper ranks of the Marai, and indeed, their servants and the lower ranks as well."

Karuda looked at the Celestial One as if he wanted to argue, then his lips set in a grim line and he turned to leave. Rian said, "My sword."

Karuda didn't stop, but a moment later one of the guards

came back from the landing with Rian's siri and all three of his knives. He handed them over quickly and withdrew.

Rian buckled the sheathed siri to his belt again and hastily put his knives away. "Is this over now?"

Maskelle shook her head, her face drawn and exhausted. "No, not yet."

Rian froze in the act of tucking the last knife into his boot, looking up at her. "What?"

"I have to stay here the night, apparently as some half-witted show of faith."

Half-witted is right, Rian thought. "What about the Rite?"

The Celestial One muttered, "That is what I would like to know."

"I did my best," the priestess Hirane snapped. "I only caught word of this because one of my sixth-level priests had a dawn mediation with the Chancellor this morning."

"This didn't go through the Imperial Secretaries?" Maskelle asked, frowning.

"It appears to have been a private act on the part of the Throne," Hirane replied, her pinched expression betraying what she thought of that. "I couldn't discover who was behind it. Mirak was in favor of it, certainly, but I couldn't tell if he instigated it or not." She looked at Maskelle, and for the first time her face softened a little. "It may be that the Throne thought of this for himself."

Maskelle muttered something under her breath and turned away, going out to the balcony.

The Celestial One looked after her for a moment, then shook his head. "We must get back to the Marai. Today will be critical." He gestured to his attendants and Hirane to follow him.

Rian was thinking hard. Whether this plot was Mirak's or Marada's doing was irrelevant at the moment; whoever it was was sure to try again. *And nobody's using me as bait again, either.*

Rian checked the landing and saw that the guards were gone.

He slipped out onto the stairs and moving quietly, went down to the floor below. The room there was empty as well, but he heard voices from the door that led out into the garden and stepped softly across to it.

Karuda was informing the guards in the garden of current developments. Rian heard the noble's footsteps crunch away on the gravel path, then one of the remaining guards muttered, "You should have seen it. She called lightning out of the sky."

Rian listened to a biased account of Maskelle's arrival at the Celestial Home, wondering how much of it was true. *It explains the lightning, at least,* he thought. When it seemed there would be nothing else worth hearing, Rian went quietly back up the steps and into the main room. Maskelle was still standing out on the balcony, leaning on the balustrade. There was much he needed to tell her, but he couldn't think where to start.

When she heard him behind her, she stirred restlessly, and without looking back at him, said, "Now you've seen for yourself."

He didn't have time to figure that one out. "They think the High Lord sent me to you, that you're in some kind of plot with him. One of them does, anyway," he added, remembering the young Emperor's reluctance to accept the suggestion.

This at least made Maskelle glance back at him, baffled. "I'm in some kind of plot with who?"

"The High Lord of the Sintane."

She snorted and turned back to the view. "Oh, as if that's likely."

Rian made himself take a deep breath. She was safe, for the moment, anyway; there was no point in letting their enemies' tactics get to him. He thought he knew what was bothering her and decided they might as well get it out in the open. He said, "The Emperor is your son, isn't he?"

She didn't turn around. "Yes. Not by law. I gave him up to his father's family. He had a better chance at the succession that way. And I didn't really want a child." She gestured around at the suite, at her temporary captivity. "So this is what I get for it."

Rian said, "I've got three."

"Three what?"

"Three children. In Riverwait."

Slowly she turned around, leaned back against the balustrade, and folded her arms. Frowning thoughtfully, she asked, "How many wives?"

"None. *Kjardin* aren't allowed to make bonding contracts. But we're popular with women who want children. And then I was the Lady Holder's favorite, so she—"

Maskelle held up a hand. "I think I have the idea." Her tone was somewhat cool, but at least she had lost that air of deadly introspection.

"There's something else—"

"I don't know if I can take anything else just now."

"I found something at Marada's house. A box with something like an ivory ball in it that glowed when I touched it. I took it so you could look at it. There were other things too, subtle things. The house didn't look . . . right. If you want to search it again, we don't have much time. They know somebody was there, but they don't know who." He added ruefully, "Or at least I thought they didn't, until this happened."

"An ivory ball that glowed? That doesn't sound like anything I've ever heard of before." She shook her head, troubled. "She's brought foreign magic into the city and it will be interesting, to say the least, to hear how she'll justify it. Where is the box now?"

He told her where he had hidden it, and finished, "I wanted you to see it before anybody else, especially the other priests."

"Yes, if it's priests she's after . . ." Maskelle said slowly. Then she grimaced. "Why do I have the feeling she already has what she's after?"

He leaned on the balustrade next to her. If there were guards left down in the garden, they weren't visible. "The Rite?"

"Yes." She massaged her temples. "I'm beginning to wonder if the second Wheel has to be on a power center after all. The Infinite is very close to our world right now. Maybe it's enough that a Wheel be on a line between two power centers. Or very close to one."

He nodded. "The canal between the Baran Dir and the Marai. We should find out who gave her that house."

"It was the Throne," Maskelle said, with a trace of bitterness. She shook her head with a grimace. "We need to pay Marada another visit."

Rian watched her worriedly. "But you think it's already too late."

"Yes." She nodded. "First let's get that box."

But when they went to the spirit shrine near their guesthouse where Rian had hidden the box, they found nothing but a ruined scrap of mud-stained silk—the scarf he had used to carry it.

Maskelle examined the silk, feeling a leftover residue of some magic clinging to it. It had a foul taste, sour and strange, and she couldn't quite remember encountering anything like it before. And with the number of dark powers she had encountered in the past few years, that was hard to believe. "You're sure they couldn't have followed you?" she asked Rian, who was searching for tracks along the mud and grass at the edge of the canal. Not that she thought it was much of a possibility.

He gestured in exasperation, sitting on his heels to examine a disturbed clump of grass more carefully. "They turned out half the neighborhood to catch me. Why let me get all the way across the city with it if they knew where I was? And they couldn't know I'd be stopped before I got it to you." He shook his head.

"Yes. She used magic to find it." Maskelle let out her breath. "Foreign magic." *In my city.* She remembered poor Veran and anger stirred, hot and welcome.

"She's a sorceress, this woman?" Rastim asked, looking from

Maskelle to Rian. He was poking a stick into the mud and searching around the base of the statue, as if hoping the missing object had merely been misplaced. He had seen Maskelle and Rian come down the street with the Celestial One's entourage and come out to see what they were doing.

"For her sake, I hope so," Maskelle said. She went back to the road, where the Celestial One's white palanquin waited, his attendants parting for her like a shoal of startled fish. He lifted the curtain and peered out.

"Proof?" he asked.

"No."

He closed his eyes and sighed, starting to withdraw into the palanquin.

She said, "I need a free hand."

He stopped, watching her, his rheumy eyes expressionless.

She lifted her brows. "You don't trust me."

His mouth twitched, not in amusement. "I trust you as far as you trust yourself."

That's a hard one to answer, she thought ruefully. She said only, "Remember the Rite."

He was still another moment, then nodded once and withdrew into the palanquin.

The procession moved away, the acolytes going to the front to clear the way with sistrums, and she walked back to the shrine.

"Did he say we could do something about Marada?" Rian asked, looking up at her.

"Yes." Maskelle smiled. *Something to do, at last.* "Tonight she'll be getting a visit from the Adversary."

The sky cleared toward evening and the sunset was bloodred.

The whole city would agree that it was an omen, though there would be much debate over what spirit or Ancestor it came from. With one look Maskelle knew it immediately; it was the Adversary's omen.

If there had been no sign, it wouldn't have changed her mind about what she meant to do; but it was good to have the confirmation.

It was evening now and the candles were lit in the bronze and gold stands of her palace suite, sending warm shadows playing among the gilded and inlaid carvings on the walls. In the jasmine-scented breeze from the windows there was distant music and mingled voices; the sound of one of the many banquets being given by high officials and courtiers in the Celestial Home's gardens tonight. If she had stood and looked out the window and over the garden wall, she would see lamps hung from low branches or floated on the pools in little islands of flowers. It reminded her that as far as the rest of the city was concerned, this was Festival Eve. Rastim had mentioned that the Ariaden were engaged not only for the official celebrations tomorrow but for a special kiradi performance tonight at the home of the Lord Portmaster of Telai, who was in the city for the festival and giving a party for a hundred or so of his closest friends. In a few weeks the puppet Gisar would be able to rejoin them, purged of its curse by the Marai's influence.

"This is a bad idea," Rian said, for perhaps the hundredth time.

Maskelle sat on the floor, eyes closed, her hands turned palm up in the meditation position. Her awareness was split, part of it in the room and the rest roaming the night outside. She could feel the damp breeze from the window lightly on her skin, and more strongly as it tore through her insubstantial spirit body.

The Celestial One had sent several young Koshan monks with them, to act as his witnesses and to perhaps exert a restraining influence on any of the Throne's impulses to stir trouble. They were camped out in the stairwell now, practicing meditation rituals, and she could hear the soft echo of their voices in the Infinite. Old Mali had also come with them, apparently feeling that if Maskelle was staying at the Palace she needed an attendant to lend her countenance. Maskelle had mixed feelings about this: she didn't want to put the old woman in danger, but Old Mali had come in handy, terrorizing and then driving away the servants who kept showing up on various pretexts. Most of them were undoubtedly spies sent by Mirak, Disara, or other old enemies, but there had been nothing for them to see. Rian had sent away anything in the suite that could possibly be poisoned, and from the extent of the list, Maskelle wondered how there was anyone alive left in the Sintane.

She could hear Rian pacing and knew he was doing it to deliberately wreck her concentration. Without breaking the trance, she said, "It would be better to do this in the Illsat Sidar."

The pacing paused. "Why?"

"Then I'd have help that would cooperate and keep its mouth shut."

She was trapped here for the night by her agreement with the Throne, or at least her body was. After telling Vigar about Marada and the strong possibility that the second Wheel was located somewhere in her house, they had made their plans for tonight. Then Maskelle had spent the day in the difficult balancing act of removing the dark portion of the Rite grain by grain while the other Voices continued with the rest of the design. The symbols she and Vigar had uncovered as they had taken off the outer layer of dark sand were even less encouraging. They were inexplicable patterns that seemed to hint at storms and ruin, and the Koshans who were searching the libraries had found no record of them so far.

Maskelle and Vigar had also confirmed the hypothesis that the patch of dark sand had been growing larger. It had been trying to creep out along the Western Ascension, and if it had managed to traverse that axis, it could have gone anywhere in this hemisphere. With the second Wheel destroyed, they would never know what the purpose of it had been, but Maskelle was willing to sacrifice that knowledge for safety.

The other Voices would be completing the last part of the Wheel now. If they hurried, it would be just ready by the culmination point of the Equinox tomorrow, and the climax of the Rite would take place as ordained. Maskelle meant to give them the time they needed. The Celestial One was spending the night with the other Voices in the Rite chamber. All of the lower ranks had been given special instructions to ward themselves against spirit possession—a precaution that was normally only necessary outside the boundaries of Kushorit cities and villages, when Koshans travelled in the deep forest or on the wild rivers, anywhere particularly strong dark spirits might be encountered.

The pacing had started again. Rian said, "Forgive me. I meant, this is a stupid idea."

"And your natural timidity kept you from saying so before."

"I did say so before."

Maskelle remembered that Rian had never mentioned how the old Holder Lord of Markand had died. She suspected strongly that it had been from exasperation. "How did the Holder Lord die?"

There was a hesitation, then suspiciously, "From a fit, why?"

"Just confirming a supposition. If you can't be quiet, go sit with Old Mali."

"If that old woman slaps me on the ass one more time—"

"Rian." Maskelle took a sharp breath, opening her eyes. "Come here."

He stopped on the far side of the room, watching her warily. "Why?"

"Just come here."

He came reluctantly, taking a seat on a cushion in front of her. "Why?" he said again.

"I'm going to show you exactly what I'm doing. Give me your hands."

When she held his calloused palms in hers, she closed her eyes again and said, "Listen to the wind in the trees. Think of nothing but that."

She extended the window in the Infinite to include him, knowing it might not work. Some people were simply blind to the Infinite. But after a moment she felt his tense grip on her hands relax. She shifted her awareness to the Infinite where her spirit body hung above the Marai in the dark and tearing wind. For an instant she felt him beside her, then he jerked his hands away.

She opened her eyes. He was giving her an indignant look. "You could have warned me."

"It's the twilight world, the connection between this world and the Infinite. Everyone sees it in a different way. Now do you want to come with me or not?"

"All right, all right." He gave her his hands again.

They were in the air high above the Marai. The wind was stronger here, tearing through their spirit bodies. The streets were dark canyons, the buildings insubstantial blurs, and the people were only moving smudges of color against the darkness. Many of the streets and plazas were lit by torches for the festival crowds, but they were dim red blurs, like banked coals. Only the temples, shrines, and the canals were sharply visible. They glowed with a soft inner light, the carvings standing out in such high relief they were almost readable from this height. The faces on the Baran Dir were warm and alive, and the smaller temples and shrines glowed like fallen stars. Except the Marai. The light around the Marai was not soft. It was sharp, outlining every stone of the temple in warm yellow fire, and it pulsed with the growing power of the Rite. The causeway across the moat was covered with what looked like a solid red glow: the procession of Koshans entering the Marai for the opening ritual.

She could feel Rian watching it. She said, "Marada's house," and guided his sight in the right direction.

Two seventh-level Koshans and several monks and temple guards from the Marai were watching Marada's guesthouse to-night. They might not have any proof they could show the Throne, but Rian had seen enough to make the Celestial One put the woman under observation. In spirit form Maskelle could see something that was invisible to the watchers, except perhaps for the seventh-level priests. There was a radiance around the house, a dull, sickly blue glow.

"What is that?" Rian asked. "What's she doing?"

"Watch. She'll have to move soon; they must be almost done with the Rite by now."

The Infinite hummed with power; whatever Marada was doing was nearing completion. Then suddenly the blue glow died, coalesced into a point of light near the center of the house.

"Now we get our proof," Maskelle breathed.

Something was leaving the house, moving down the gallery, drifting over the railing to alight gently on the ground.

Its outline was blurred silver, shifting and changing as it

drifted out of the house's compound and down the street. The people it passed did not react to its presence.

"It's like the water creature from the river," Rian said.

"Something like, something unlike. This wasn't what I was expecting." She saw that the two seventh-level priests didn't sense its passage either. It wafted past them, through the wall of another compound, through the house within it that was crowded with people, across the canal on the other side. It was making a straight line for the Marai.

Maskelle had known that there was some sort of spirit in the business when Rian had found the marks of a garrotte around Igarin's neck. But she had thought Marada was leaving her own body and taking spirit form, with the help of some special foreign magic that kept the high-level Koshans from sensing her presence. But whatever that was, it wasn't Marada. And it was utterly impossible for a spirit to progress in a straight line across the power pathways of Kushor-At and Kushor-An.

Maskelle cast around for a form to take and felt a bird spirit high overhead, drifting in the night sky. Bird spirits belonged to the Adversary: another omen. She called to it and felt it circle and then fall toward her.

When it came close she felt Rian almost break the trance. All razor-tipped green and gold feathers and flashing claws, it too closely resembled what he thought demons looked like. But he didn't let go of her hands. She explained, "My spirit self can't truly touch or move anything; this spirit can."

She felt a wing brush her cheek, opening up a line of fire as the sharp-edged feather cut her skin. *I need you,* she thought to it. *Just for a short time.*

It circled her warily. She knew it recognized her. *To watch?* it said.

To hunt.

It laughed and opened itself to her, and suddenly she was looking through its eyes.

Its vision was sharper than that of her spirit body. It could see the temples and the canals even more clearly than she could, but the houses and other buildings were still just big brown blurs, the people nearly invisible. It hadn't seen the creature moving away from Marada's house until she looked through its eyes. She heard it hiss in surprise. *Kill,* the bird spirit whispered in her mind.

Soon, she told it.

They watched the creature drift across the Marai's moat. Maskelle was still amazed by the temerity of the thing. She had to change her course to follow it, flying above the straight line of the causeway; even the Adversary's proxy had to approach the Marai through the correct passages.

Once across the moat, the creature moved through walls, again taking the straight path through the temple that should be impossible. Maskelle had to make each square of the inner and outer court before she could drop further toward the ground, buffeted along the way by the power entering and leaving the temple.

She brought herself down to the inner courtyard and felt her own toes curl in reflex as the spirit's claws touched the damp cool stone. The lamps here were dim orange glows, and there were strange blurred shapes that were all she could see of the people moving in the court. She stepped out of the bird spirit and it crouched, waiting.

Her quarry drifted across the paving stones, the silver nimbus around its form a little sharper now. The creature was moving toward the central tower, toward one of the blurs that stood near the archway. This blur was more well defined than the others, its presence in the Infinite stronger. Maskelle recognized the Celestial One. *So that's it.* She shifted to block the creature's path.

It stopped, then tried to go around her. She moved again and it halted, drawing back a little. It seemed to see her even less clearly than she could see it. It tried to go around her again, reaching for the Celestial One. Now she could see the cord in its hands.

Now, she told the bird spirit, *kill.*

With a shriek that echoed through the Infinite, the bird spirit leapt onto the creature.

They fought across the court, twisting and writhing, teeth and claws throwing back shards of light. Maskelle knew the higher level Koshans in the Marai would sense this; she felt the Celestial One's awareness slide across her.

Struggling desperately, the thing shook free of the bird spirit, throwing it halfway across the court. The bird spirit tumbled in midair, a dizzying ball of green and gold, then shot back toward its opponent like an arrow. She saw the thing try to wrap its cord around the bird spirit's neck and the spirit went insubstantial, laughing, to reappear again and tear lacy remnants of the thing's flesh away.

Watching in fascination as the bird spirit tore into Marada's creature, Rian heard a sudden urgent shout from behind him. He turned to look, but couldn't tell which of the blurs in the court it had come from. Then he heard it again, still coming from behind him, and realized he had heard it with his real ears, not whatever passed for ears here.

He looked at Maskelle, but a crash of wooden furniture decided him. In another heartbeat he was sitting opposite her in the room in the Celestial Home. The room wavered in and out; he took a deep breath and pressed his hands to his eyes, trying to adjust to the abrupt transition. The noise came from the anterooms where the monks were on guard. One of them was shouting for help.

That jolted him back to full awareness. He rolled back off the cushion, catching the siri up on the way and drawing it as he came to his feet.

In the doorway one of the monks was blocking the way, trying to hold someone off with a stool. Old Mali was at his back, armed with a heavy gold pot. Past them he could see a figure in dark robes with lacquered armor and a crested barred helmet disguising its face. One of the other monks sprawled unmoving on the floor.

Torn and bleeding, the spirit thing fled out of the Marai's court. Maskelle went straight up, almost losing sight of it as she and the bird spirit threaded their way out of the pathways of power around the temple. But the thing was fleeing straight across the city and she knew what its destination must be. It was going back to Marada's guesthouse, to its master.

Rian pushed Old Mali aside, caught a handful of the monk's robe and yanked him out of the way, just as a Kushorit short sword cleaved the air where the young man had been standing. Rian slung the monk behind him and ducked a second swordcut. He slammed into the armored man, knocking him back out of the doorway and across the stairwell.

There was one lamp lit in Marada's guesthouse, in the common room, the light leaking through the wicker of the closed shade panels onto the balcony. There were no walls of power around it, and Maskelle alighted on the balcony without resistance. By unconscious habit she used the partially open door to enter the house, the bird spirit slipping through the wall next to her.

She gave herself the semblance of a body so she could see more clearly, and the room swam into focus around her. Marada sat at a low table under a single candlestand. Several Kushorit books lay on the table, and in front of Marada was a glowing ball of light.

The armored man threw Rian off and he smashed into the carved panels next to the stairs. One of the monks must have gone for help; there were two lying dead or unconscious on the floor and three still standing, again blocking the doorway between the armored man and Maskelle. The one armed with a stool started forward, but Rian motioned him back. Realizing where the most effective resistance was going to come from, the man ignored them, striking down at Rian. He rolled away from the blade, slashing upward with the siri.

The blade sliced between the sleeve of the dark robe and the leather gauntlet, severing the wrist. The gauntlet hit the ground but there was no spray of blood and Rian almost died when the astonishment made him hesitate. The armored man's sword thudded into the wall above his head as he ducked and came to his feet. He had an instant to exchange a baffled look with the monks braced across the doorway.

Marada looked up at her, no expression on her lovely, perfect face. Maskelle could see her in sharp detail, something that should be impossible with spirit sight. She's not a person, *Maskelle thought.* She's a spirit, but she exists in the world and in the Infinite at the same time. *But that was impossible.*

"You killed Igarin with your shadow creature, and you somehow took possession of Veran's mind, and made him do your will. Am I correct?"

In her colorless voice Marada said, "You are correct."

Maskelle looked down at the books. They were works of Koshan philosophy. She brushed her spirit hand across the cover of one and said, "You should have included The Book of the Adversary *in your course of study."*

Marada watched her, a small cold smile lifting the corners of her mouth. "I didn't need it."

Rian parried two cuts and ducked and rolled again, slamming into the far wall to avoid the armored man's rush. His opponent was doing well for a man with only one hand. They were making an incredible racket and no Palace Guards had come yet. The monk who had gone for help might have to run all the way to the Baran Dir.

"Tell me who you are and why you did this, and I may let you live," Maskelle said.

"You can't stop us." Marada's eyes didn't waver. "It's too late. And your own philosophy will not let you harm me."

The bird spirit laughed, its amusement making the Infinite shiver around them. Maskelle said, "You really should have read The Book of the Adversary*." The glowing ball must be doing something, but Maskelle couldn't see any effect in the Infinite. Her spirit eyes could see shadows moving inside it. She felt Marada's creature behind her, saw the loop of cord come over her head.*

Maskelle stepped through it. "Is that its only trick?"

The armored man came for him again, backing him into the corner, and Rian parried the cuts, until one blow bashed the siri right out of his hands. He dropped to the ground under the return blow and kicked the man in the kneecap. The man hit the ground and Rian leapt on him, pinning his sword arm down. The body bucked and twisted under him, almost throwing him off, and then the handless arm punched him below the ribs, hard enough to stop his breath. The man's strength was close to supernatural. *I'm not going to be able to hold him.* Then a monk landed on the man's legs and another one was at Rian's side, helping him hold down the swordarm. "Get the sword," Rian said through gritted teeth.

Marada leaned over the glowing ball, whispering to it. It was a strange harsh language Maskelle couldn't understand, and certainly nothing that was spoken in the Garekind Islands. As if she needed more confirmation that the woman was an imposter. She could feel in the bones of her real body a growing resonance, coming from the canal that connected the Celestial Home with the Marai. The Wheel of the Rite was almost complete and Maskelle couldn't afford to wait for answers when she didn't know what else Marada might do to ruin it. She said, "One last chance."

Marada ignored her. Maskelle let out her breath. "I was lying about letting you live, anyway." She released the bird spirit and it flowed past her, eager for prey.

Marada might not be entirely human, but she screamed like one.

The third monk scrambled for the siri, as their opponent heaved and twisted to free himself. He didn't seem so much interested in getting away as in inflicting as much damage as possible. The monk trying to hold down the man's kicking legs wrestled with the handless arm, trying to keep it from punching Rian, but he could hardly hold it. Rian had already felt one of his ribs crack.

He grabbed the siri's hilt as the monk brought it up and sliced the blade down on the dark gap between the man's gorget and helmet. He felt an instant of resistance, then the blade jarred his hand as it struck the wooden floor.

Suddenly he was kneeling on the chest piece of an empty set of lacquered armor and robes, the greaves and arm pieces strewn around him. One of the monks gasped in astonishment and the other picked up an empty gauntlet, turning it over wonderingly.

Rian tipped back the helmet. It was empty. He shared a look with the monk who had brought the siri. "This sort of thing happen much here?" he asked.

Later that night, Maskelle paced in front of the balcony, distractedly braiding her hair while waiting for Rian, Hirane, and the others to return from Marada's house. They had gone there to arrest the woman's servants and to destroy the second Wheel. She knew Rian still wanted to search for clues to Marada's identity and purpose here, but that was a secondary goal. Destroying the second Wheel took precedence.

Maskelle could feel the tension still in her shoulders and back, and the knowledge that the last preparation for the Rite was underway only made it worse. The resonance of the voices of the priests, monks, and nuns echoed from the Marai, where they performed the chants which were the first step in the ceremony of the Great Opening, that would end when the Rite was culminated tomorrow. The Temple Dancers would be filling the outer court, moving through the ageless patterns in the light from scores of lamps, and hundreds of people would line the walls to watch.

The disturbance had woken the whole Palace and Maskelle had taken advantage of the sudden surfeit of servants to order a bath brought in, and now she was wearing her red Meidun robe, clean if not calm. Still disturbed herself, Old Mali bustled around like a hen with lost chicks, clearing up the debris from the fight and grumbling.

Hirane of the Baran Dir had sent a score of temple guards and a couple of seventh-level priests to make sure the rest of the night was undisturbed, but Maskelle knew there would be no further trouble here. The suite had also been infested with messengers, from the Imperial Secretaries down to the functionaries whose job it was to keep the stairs clean, all demanding to know what had happened. The temple guards were sending most of them off, except the ones with too high a rank. Maskelle was sending those off herself, with succinct commentary on the inherent dangers of being a guest in the Celestial Home. She hoped her comments were repeated to Raith's lackeys, and wondered what his reaction would be when he discovered just what his new favorite Marada had done.

The Palace Guards had not been able to come to their aid because of an invisible barrier that had formed over the stairs. Maskelle would have been inclined to doubt this, except that she had seen for herself how powerful Marada had been. And the monk who had gone for help had run straight into it and been unable to get through from the other side. Now there were guards everywhere in the garden outside their suite. *Now that they aren't needed,* she thought with an annoyed shake of her head. Marada shouldn't have been able to send one of her creatures inside the Celestial Home, any more than she should be able to send one inside the Marai. *Now if I just knew what she was, what she wanted, where she came from, and who sent her, everything would be fine.*

One of the monks had been killed defending Maskelle, and the thought made her want to kill Marada all over again. *I should have told the bird spirit to make it slow,* she thought, tying off her last braid and tossing it over her shoulder.

There were louder voices from the stairwell and she moved back into the room, waiting impatiently. The knot of guards at the door moved aside as Rian strode in.

Maskelle motioned sharply to the Koshan healer who had been waiting patiently in the corner. The woman advanced on Rian determinedly, already opening the wooden box where she carried her medicines.

Rian saw her coming at him and said, "I don't need any—"

"Let her look at you," Maskelle said. "The monks told me you were hurt."

"All right, all right." Rian stripped off his shirt, revealing a dark, painful-looking bruise on his right side, just over his ribs. He sat down on the mat and the healer knelt next to him, clucked her tongue and probed gently at the injured area with her fingers. Rian didn't wince, but Maskelle could tell it hurt him and so could the healer. The woman released him and began to dig through her box. Rian ignored her, telling Maskelle, "It wasn't there."

"Not there?" Aghast, Maskelle sat down on the cushions, burying her head in her hands. *I am so tired of being wrong,* she thought. "It has to be there."

"I know, but it wasn't." Rian's tone was brusk, but she could tell he felt it as much as she did. "No sand or anything else they could have made one with, either. They must have been hiding it somewhere else." He rolled his shoulder carefully and winced. "We caught everyone she brought with her, four women and seven guardsmen. None of them will talk, yet."

Maskelle shook her head, trying to make herself think again. She poured a cup of palmwine from the serving set on the table. Handing it to Rian, she asked, "Do the others still pretend not to understand Kushorit?"

He nodded. "I couldn't tell if they were faking it or not. Neither could Karuda or any of the Koshans." He drained the cup and shrugged, then grimaced at what the incautious movement had done to his injury. Maskelle lifted a brow at him and he gave her a disgruntled look.

"I don't suppose the priests could tell if any of her people were the same sort of creature as Marada," she said.

"That's what they want you for." The healer had taken out a length of bandage and started to wrap Rian's ribs. He lifted his arm to let her, looking annoyed.

"I couldn't tell that Marada was what she was, until she revealed herself," Maskelle pointed out. *Can't these people do anything for themselves?* she thought in irritation. *What did they do while I was gone?* "They didn't find out anything?"

He shook his head. "The priests are still searching the house. We brought that ivory ball thing back here, but it won't glow anymore." The healer tied the bandage off and Rian told her, "It's too tight."

"Good," the woman said sharply.

Maskelle got to her feet. The Ancestors were whispering that no good could come of this, but that's what they usually said. "Where are they?"

Marada's companions were being held in the Celestial Home's guard house. This was a long stone-walled barracks that stood back against the south moat wall, concealed from view of the pleasure gardens by a heavy screen of bamboo and breadfruit trees. It had its own watergate, causeway, and dock, where the prisoners had been brought by boat. They were being held now in the big common room, surrounded by guards and priests. The outer wall had open arches facing a little court and the greenery that shielded it from the gardens, though the air was still warm and dank.

Garekind Islanders were the same stock as the mainland Kushorit, and there was nothing unusual in the appearance of Marada's servants, except what were apparently habitual sullen expressions and a strange lack of fear at their arrest. They hadn't been harmed during their capture, though their clothes looked as if they had rolled in the dirt. They all wore rough plain trousers or wraps, no jewelry, like fieldworkers stripped for labor. It was odd that Marada hadn't chosen to equip them more lavishly; most of the wealthy in Duvalpore kept their retinues well dressed as another way of showing status.

"They are defiling the Celestial Home with their presence here," Hirane said, folding her arms. The priestess of the Baran Dir was grim, her thin form rigid with tension. The Celestial One was still occupied at the Marai with the other Voices. Hirane should be there too, but the protocols of tonight's ceremonies could spare her presence where it couldn't spare the others. Chancellor Mirak was also present, dressed in festival finery, with Lord Karuda a shadow at his back.

"It's a little late to worry about that." Maskelle picked up the ivory ball from the table where it rested. Except she didn't think it was ivory. The texture was wrong, and though it was hard to tell in the lamplight, she thought the color was off as well. She tried to feel it with her inner senses, to listen to it the way she could hear the currents of power in water or air or the stone of the temples. There was nothing. The power that had made it shine with light in this world and the Infinite might have died with Marada.

"These people should be taken to the prison," Hirane persisted.

Maskelle looked from the white ball to the face of the oldest servant. She was a stocky woman with grey hair, just as plainly dressed as the others. She had probably been Marada's chief maid. There was no defiance in her cold dull eyes, just a complete lack of interest. Too complete. "I'm not so sure that's true," Maskelle said, thoughtful. The woman's only jewelry was a wooden amulet with an earth spirit sigil on it. It was the kind of token worn by the village shamen who had helped people placate or defend against the spirits, before the temples had risen in the Celestial Empire.

Hirane snorted. She folded her arms and looked away. "By your own evidence they cooperated with that woman in an attempt to assassinate—"

Hirane was an intelligent, perceptive guardian for the Baran Dir, but she didn't like being argued with by anyone but the Celestial One. Maskelle didn't like being argued with either, but she explained, "Marada wasn't a woman. We don't know what she was." She stepped closer to the oldest servant and looked into her eyes. "And I don't think I'd call this cooperation."

"You're thinking of Veran," Rian said, watching her closely.

"Yes." She nodded slowly. *Poor dead Veran, who I should have watched much more carefully.* "He was a priest, trained in meditation disciplines. If he was close to fighting his way free of whatever controlled his mind and kept him from speaking to us, then that's why he had to be killed. . . . How would the same condition look on a person who wasn't trained, who had no way to fight?"

"You told the chief healer that Veran was possessed," Mirak said slowly, almost unwillingly. He took a step closer. "Possessed by what? And why can't the other Voices and the seventh-level priests see what you seem to see?"

"If I had those answers, we'd be further forward in this matter than we are now." Maskelle rubbed the bridge of her nose, tired and annoyed. "The only thing I can say is that this seems to be a deception only the Adversary has the knowledge to penetrate. That is why the Ancestors created him, to be their guide where they couldn't go." She turned the globe over again. *Maybe I should just break it.* The Adversary and the Ancestors remained stubbornly silent on the subject.

"Is it to be a philosophy lesson?" Mirak asked, his voice an amused rumble.

"If you're in need of one, I can send a fifth-level priest to supply it," Hirane told him sharply.

At least she's impartial in her irritation, Maskelle thought. She hefted Marada's ball again. "I'll keep this with me." Stepping closer to the oldest woman, she looked into her eyes.

There was still no expression there. She might have been staring into the eyes of a dead woman. Like Veran, this woman might be trapped inside her own body, struggling to get out. Like Veran, it might be possible to reach her, if only for an instant. Maskelle stretched out her power toward the woman, drawing on the Celestial Home's place in the network of temples. There was a barrier there, something of the Infinite and of the world at the same time, as Marada had been. Maskelle pushed at it, but it held firm. She felt power flow down toward her from the Baran Dir, from the Marai with the Wheel of the Infinite set into its heart like a great glowing jewel, and pushed again.

Suddenly she felt the presence of the Adversary, flowing through her, lending her a strength that struck forward into that barrier, shattering it like glass.

Maskelle caught the woman, then felt her own knees give out on the way down. They landed on the gritty floor together, but she managed to keep the woman's head from striking the stone. Dizziness overwhelmed her for a moment and it was all she could do not to keep from falling over on the woman in her lap. Looking down at her white face and the pain etched there, Maskelle thought, *Ancestors, she's dying.* She reached for the Adversary again, but felt it withdraw. It couldn't, or wouldn't, help her.

The woman's fingers dug into her arm and she gasped, "Listen. I was a healer and a shamaness of the old magic, until that woman came to our village on the coast at Iutara and trapped us."

"Trapped you how?" Maskelle asked. Rian was leaning over her shoulder and she could hear Hirane shouting for the guards' physician.

"With that ball. She made us look into it and it trapped our minds, made us do whatever she willed. There was something inside it, alive, it had a face. . . ." She shook her head wildly. "She made me— I know the old magic, the death magic. I never used it, but she knew I could. She made me bind a dead boy's soul to a curse, a tela worm ball, and she sent him after some-one— Warn—"

"It's all right, he was released. No one else was hurt."

A brief expression of relief crossed the woman's face. "There were others with her, she wasn't the only one. They look like people, but inside . . ." She gasped.

"How many others?"

"I don't know. I saw four . . . men." The woman's voice was a faint rasp.

"Tell us what she wanted. Tell us—"

The woman stiffened in her arms, then went limp.

Maskelle watched her eyes go still and set. She lowered the woman to the floor and let Rian help her up. She glanced around, and saw that Mirak had left the chamber hurriedly with his atten-dants. From their muted voices they were in the court outside the archway.

Looking grimly down at the woman, Rian said, "She didn't know anything else. If she knew why Marada was here, she would have said that first." Glancing up, he said, "We need to find that village."

Karuda said, "I'll send men tonight."

Hirane nodded to the seventh-level priests who had helped search Marada's house. "They will go with them, should those others she spoke of remain there."

I should go with them, Maskelle thought, then, *No, not until after the Rite is over.* Iutara wasn't near a power center, and the second Wheel of the Infinite couldn't be there.

"What about the others?" Karuda said, eyeing the other ser-vants who still stood impassive, surrounded by their guards.

Maskelle looked at Hirane, who shook her head slightly. She saw in the old woman's eyes that she knew as well as Maskelle did that it might be kinder to kill them. But Maskelle wouldn't give that order, not yet. "Lock them up, under guard," she said helplessly. "Maybe we can find a way to free them."

Seeing the faces of Karuda and the others, she wasn't the only one who found this doubtful.

12

The day dawned hot and clear, unusual for this season of daily rains. It would make it easy for the priests to judge the exact moment of the Equinox, when the Rite would draw to a close.

The chanting had stopped early this morning, but the Marai's stones still sang with it. Despite Marada's interference and her strange brand of power, the temple felt exactly as it should, even to Maskelle. She had risen before dawn and bringing Rian with her, had gone to the Marai to make certain everything was all right. The crowds had already been thick in the streets and the canals nearly clogged with boats, but any craft with the Imperial seals had right of way and they made the trip in good time.

Once there she had walked an abbreviated meditation ring over the whole Marai, eliminating the rituals but checking every cardinal point, every resonance chamber, every corner of each court. She could find no weaknesses in the structure, not in the physical or the spiritual realms. After the first hour, they had passed Vigar in the solar side of the inner court, on the same mission.

Maskelle had reached the far end of the gallery on the lunar side of the outer court when the steady growl of the festival crowds on the other side of the moat rose to a roar. "Maybe that's Rastim getting lynched," Rian commented, leaning on the balustrade in one of the openings between the pillars.

Maskelle glanced out on the court below and read the time from the length of the shadows on the walls. It was midmorning and the Ariaden should have been performing some time now, from what Old Mali had told her of the plans for the entertainments. "Hopefully it's the end of the play," she said. "I think they're doing *The Mask of Night.*" With help conscripted from the hundreds of workers the Warden of the Public Festivals had available, they would be able to handle the complex scenery movements and the big puppets.

"Did you want to see it?"

"Yes, but I'm sure if I ask nicely, I can get the whole thing repeated for me tonight. With a blow-by-blow description of the audience's reactions."

Smiling, Rian cocked his head at her, pretending to doubt it. "You think so?"

"I don't see how I can avoid it." She leaned her staff in the corner and stretched, easing the kinks out of her back. She had brought Marada's white stone to the temple, not liking to leave it behind in the palace. She had given it into the safekeeping of the Temple Master, to be stored in one of the cupboards in his quarters within the Marai. It might be only a focus for Marada's strange power, like the staffs used by the Voices when they were away from the temples, and would be empty and useless now that its owner was dead, but she wanted to keep an eye on it. "At least after the Rite culminates, I don't have to worry about anything else."

Then she saw a monk running toward her down the length of the gallery, his expression urgent, and thought, *Why did I say that?*

He stopped and bowed hurriedly to her. "Revered, your presence is asked in the outer court, in front of the third gallery gate, by the Celestial One."

"All right, I'm coming." She followed him reluctantly. She was a little surprised they were calling her to the outer court. If something was going to go wrong, it would go wrong in the heart tower, in the Wheel of the Infinite. The ceremonies surrounding the culmination of the Rite were complex, but worthless for anything but entertainment value. "What is this about? Has there been another problem with the Rite?"

"I wasn't told, Revered." The monk glanced back at her worriedly. "But Chancellor Mirak is there, and guardsmen from the Palace."

"But the royal party should already be in the inner gallery for the invocations." The ceremonies involved the presence of the Celestial Emperor, who had been brought here in a formal procession earlier in the day. Maskelle had planned her examination of the temple carefully to avoid the Emperor's ritual progress to the inner gallery.

"They are there, Revered."

She glanced at Rian and saw the significance of this wasn't wasted on him, either. *I exist to be tormented for the pleasure of the Adversary*, she thought.

They went down the steps of the entrance to the outer court. Maskelle saw the temple guards arrayed on the lowest step under the porch and read the tension in their stances. They made space for her to pass before she reached them and she stepped down onto the terrace.

The sun was bright on the two reflecting pools on either side of the stone terrace and a damp heat rose off the deep green grass. The scatter of palms around the large court provided no shade whatsoever. Standing on the cross-shaped terrace were the Celestial One, his attendant priest, and Hirane of the Baran Dir. Maskelle sensed Rian tense next to her and a heartbeat later she registered what he had already seen. They were facing Chancellor Mirak, Lord Karuda, and a dozen or so Palace Guards.

Half-surrounded by the Palace Guards were the Ariaden, still in their stage clothing and face paint. The children, except for Firac's two sons who worked puppets in the show, were not with them. They would have been left back at the guesthouse with one of the Kushorit servants attached to the place, since their help hadn't been needed with the props and other little chores. That was one small mercy at least. Old Mali was there, though her help hadn't been needed in the play. The old woman had an uncanny ability to involve herself in everything.

It explained the roar of the crowd. Kushorit theatricals tended to be freeform and would often go on for hours if the audience was still interested. The play must have been a success and the crowd had expected more of it, and been disappointed to see the actors leave the stage.

It didn't matter. *This is enough*, Maskelle thought. She was getting very tired of Mirak's interference. She walked past the Koshans, almost stepping on the Palace Guardsman who didn't move out of her way quickly enough. "Rastim, what are you doing here?"

"There's a little difficulty," he said, sounding embarrassed. Firac, standing at his elbow, moved uneasily and looked down at his feet. The sun was melting the white paint off their faces and they both looked awful, but she didn't think they had been hurt by the guardsmen.

Karuda stepped toward her and Rian shifted just enough to block his way. The noble started to speak, but Maskelle ignored him, saying, "Rastim, please, just tell me."

"We were arrested." He shrugged, apparently philosophical about it. "At least they let us finish the play. I don't know what they didn't like about it—"

"Rastim, they didn't arrest you, and certainly not because of the play," Maskelle said, she hoped patiently. Rastim was doing a good job of telling the story briefly for an Ariaden. "They don't bring criminals to the Marai."

"I'm pretty sure we were arrested—"

"Rastim, don't argue with me just at the moment." Maskelle took a deep breath. *Something going on here.* More than just court intrigue and the shifting politics of power. There was nothing wrong with the Marai, there was nothing wrong with the Rite and nothing likely to go wrong with it, surrounded as it was by the Voices as they did the invocations for the royal party. She could feel the growing tension as a tightness in her chest, but it seemed to be coming out of nowhere. She said to Rastim, "Stay here."

She had meant for Rian to stay there too, but he followed her anyway as she went toward the Celestial One and the others. They had all been watching her and she had the uncanny sensation for a moment of feeling like one of Rastim's puppets. She asked Mirak, "Why did you bring these people here?"

Ignoring her, Mirak turned to the Celestial One. He said, "You understand the necessity for this."

The old man's expression was less yielding than the stone faces carved into the temple wall behind him. He said to Maskelle, "Tell our visitors to go into the inner court."

She looked back at Rastim, jerked her head slightly. He caught the hint and started for the stairs up into the gallery, the other Ariaden trailing after him.

Mirak turned, about to gesture to Karuda to stop them. Maskelle felt a swell of tension that was sure to end in something rash, but the Celestial One said, "I don't recommend it, Chancellor."

Maskelle had heard that tone only once before in his voice and that had been when he had told her that if she wanted to move against the Celestial Throne she would have to kill him first. It sent a little shiver of cold memory through her and her own impulse to take action died.

Mirak paused and regarded the old man. The moment stretched. Then he let his hand drop. Karuda shifted uneasily as Rastim and the others made their way past the Temple Guards and into the shade of the enclosure. Mirak said finally, "You choose a strange cause in which to exercise your authority."

The Celestial One didn't bother to acknowledge the side issue. "Does the Rite mean nothing to you?" he said.

"I mean to make sure she and all those she brought with her leave the city when the Rite is over." The Chancellor betrayed no sign of anger or any other emotion except quiet confidence.

"Oh, I'll be leaving the city." Maskelle had no idea it was she who had spoken until she saw the Celestial One and Hirane staring at her. The words had come straight from the Ancestors. It was one of the more annoying forms of prophecy, when the spirits spoke as your own voice. The world was so close to the Infinite at this time of year that in holy places like the Marai the barriers became so thin as to be almost insubstantial. The effect would become worse as the Rite drew closer to culmination. She just hoped the Ancestors didn't decide to say anything particularly damning in front of Mirak.

"You take too much on yourself," the Celestial One said to the Chancellor. The old man spoke quietly, but Maskelle still heard the warning tone in his voice. She saw Hirane tighten her hold on her staff and sensed the older woman's uneasiness.

"I've always believed the Koshans had too much power in the Imperial system," Mirak said calmly. "As you know."

"When have I given the Throne commands? I give him advice, which he is free to take up or ignore as his own judgment suits him."

Maskelle suspected Mirak had been preparing for this test of his power for a long time, that her presence had only provided him with a much looked-for opportunity. It was the worst of bad omens to have this sort of confrontation between religious and secular authorities, at this festival during such an important Rite, and in the Marai of all places. Such things would not have escaped Mirak's calculation. But if he thought to wring concessions from the Celestial One by forcing him to capitulate rather than continue such an inauspicious disagreement, then he hadn't counted on the old man's stubbornness.

"The next to hold your office may have the ambition you lack."

The old man's lips thinned. "A man with ambitions cannot hold my office—"

Maskelle winced in anticipation of what was coming next.

"—unfortunately I can't say the same for your position."

"Perhaps you take too much on yourself," Mirak said, his tone amused but his eyes hard.

"This can be settled later," Hirane broke in. "The Rite is more important than this bickering."

Maskelle felt someone standing behind her and turned. She found herself looking down at the Celestial One. A glance over her shoulder confirmed the fact that the Celestial One still stood confronting Mirak and the others. She turned back to what was standing in front of her. She felt curiously hollow, distanced from reality, free of emotion. After seven years, here was the Adversary. Not just a half-vision that might be a dream, not a ghost hinting at doom. She said, "You need to choose a new Voice to take my place."

It looked up at her, an odd gleam of humor in the ageless eyes. "All right," it said, obligingly. "I choose you." The voice was the Celestial One's as well, but it sounded oddly flat and she knew she wasn't hearing it with her ears.

Suddenly she was inside the chamber of the Rite, but the shape of the room and outlines of the carvings on the walls were subtly distorted. She looked down and saw the world was at her feet, glowing with life. Mountains, rivers, deltas, the gulf and the sea, the oceans beyond, all in perfect detail. The Adversary stood next to her, still in the form of the Celestial One. It said, "The sacred mountain is at the center of the universe."

Puzzled, she nodded. "Everyone knows that."

"Not everyone." He pointed down. The world was revolving around the centerpoint of the Rite. "They don't know it. Those who covet this world. The center doesn't move."

Not again, Maskelle thought. Another vision she couldn't understand. "Those who covet this world. Marada and her people?" Dizzy, she had to look away from the spinning landscape at her feet. "Why can't I understand you? Is the fault in me?"

"No," it said. Its eyes tracked the progress of the rotating world. An expression crossed its face, a mix of confusion and regret, near panic. "The fault is in me."

Maskelle stared, feeling her heart freeze in her chest. "What's wrong?" she whispered. "What's wrong with you?"

"With me?" it said, its features smoothing back into blandness.

Maskelle shook her head slightly, bewildered. *Did I imagine that?* "You said the fault was in you."

The glowing world at their feet threw a dizzying reflection onto its face. It said only, "Ask the right question."

"That's the trick, isn't it. You never have to do anything useful, just make me guess." It didn't react to the bitterness in her voice; she had been foolish to even think that it would. She gestured helplessly. "So it was no use, killing Marada?"

"Marada spoke the truth, it was already too late." Its smile was almost gleeful, then its face abruptly turned serious. "You have both one opponent and many."

One of the nameless fears Maskelle had been prey to all day suddenly became solid and real. *I missed something.* She still couldn't see it. *I must be the most useless Voice of the Adversary in history.* "Can you tell me what I need to do?" she demanded, frustrated.

Its gaze went to her and it no longer had the Celestial One's eyes, but the eyes of something mad and strange. Then it stepped close to her and the rest of the room seem to fade into shadow, until there was nothing but its voice. "Stay in the Marai. Whatever happens, stay. You must be here. To leave would ruin everything."

She was in the court again, the hot sun on her back. She

leaned on her staff, trying to adjust to the sudden change. The Adversary had finally spoken to her again. She had wanted it for so long and now . . . She was a little afraid. *That was an odd vision.* Maybe more than odd. No, that was her own interpretation coloring the Adversary's words again.

Rian was watching her worriedly. She knew he had sensed that something had happened, that he might even have seen her spirit temporarily leave her body. It was odd that the highest-ranking Koshans in the Empire were standing on this terrace and only Rian had noticed. *He's the only one who sees me clearly.* The thought had the ring of the Ancestors in it too. Mirak was still talking, Hirane was playing arbiter, and the Celestial One stood like something carved out of clay. *He needs to get out of this sun.* That thought sounded more normal; she was fairly sure it was all her own. "I'll go," she told Mirak, "when the Rite is over. Not until then." Her own voice sounded hollow and strange now.

To the Celestial One, Hirane added, "You must go to the royal party. If the Great Opening is delayed—"

"I know," he snapped. He stepped close to Mirak. "Leave this place."

"I will." Mirak's gaze was calm. "If she returns to the Celestial Home."

Maskelle looked away toward the outer enclosure, smiling a little. Whatever was moving these events was using Mirak as its pawn, whether he was aware of it or not. She would not let it force her to leave the Marai. The Ancestors whispered in the back of her mind again. She couldn't understand all the words, but the meaning came through as strong as a prophecy and with almost enough force to weaken her knees. *It's not going to be safe here.* It wasn't going to be safe anywhere, but the Marai was at the center of the danger. *Dammit, I should have sent Rastim and the others out.* She would rectify that mistake immediately. But first . . .

She turned to Mirak. "I have to stay until the Rite is over.

But take Rian with you as proof of my good behavior." Behind the Chancellor she could see Rian's expression turn incredulous.

Hirane drew breath as if to speak, but said nothing. Maskelle could feel the Celestial One's eyes boring into her. He would know she was doing this for a reason. She just hoped he trusted her.

For the first time Mirak looked directly at her and Maskelle knew she had surprised him. She smiled again, knowing it wasn't a pleasant expression. "You've already taken pains to find out he's a valuable hostage to use against me; why waste another opportunity?"

Mirak lifted a brow, studying her. He couldn't refuse this offer without his motives being called into question though she could tell he wondered what game she was playing at. Finally he said, "Very well."

She met Rian's eyes steadily. She was counting on the fact that he wouldn't disobey her in public. Mirak turned away, his men closing around him as he moved down the causeway. Karuda waited for Rian.

Maskelle faced him for another heartbeat, then he turned and followed Mirak, Karuda falling into step beside him.

Maskelle drew a deep breath, now that there was no one to see it but Hirane and the Celestial One. *He'll hate me for that*, she thought. *But at least he'll be alive to do it.*

"What game do you play, daughter?" the Celestial One asked, eyeing her thoughtfully.

Maskelle shook her head. "Something is about to happen. I don't know what. The Ancestors and the Adversary are speaking in my head so loudly I can't tell their words from my thoughts. And none of it makes sense."

"I thought you could no longer hear the Adversary," Hirane said sharply.

"I had a vision in the Illsat Keo on the way to the city, another in the Illsat Sidar, and . . . one just now. He spoke to me." She admitted wryly, "He was obscure, but insistent."

"What sort of vision did you have?" the Celestial One asked, frowning.

"You said nothing of this to me," Hirane said to him. "If the Adversary has returned—"

"You didn't ask me," he told her abruptly. "Return to your duties; we'll discuss this later."

Hirane's eyes narrowed. "Go inside, old man." She started across the causeway, her attendants moving to follow her.

The Celestial One watched her walk away, his face unreadable. Maskelle offered him her arm as they started up the steps back into the Marai. Answering his question, she said, "The Adversary appeared as you, showed me the Rite, and told me to stay in the Marai, no matter what happened. I'm as imperfect an Oracle as ever." They paused in the shade of the gallery. "It did mention Marada's people, the people who 'covet our world.' "

The Celestial One looked weary. "The wall between the world and the Infinite is always thin on the days of the Rite. But for this Rite it seems almost nonexistent. I have word from all the Voices and half the seventh level in the city of visions and warnings. Perhaps it's only that this is a Hundred Year Rite."

"But you don't believe that. You—" Maskelle stopped. Somewhere power swelled and rose like a wave on the sea. She could feel it echoing down the canals and the sacred paths of Kushor-At. *But where is it coming from?* It had to be the culmination of the Rite, but . . . She stared at the length of the shadows on the floor of the open gallery. *They're too early.* Maskelle shared a startled expression with the Celestial One. The old man's face had gone grey. Without having to discuss it, Maskelle picked up the skirts of her robe and ran down the gallery, making for the inner court and the central tower.

The Rite was always brought to culmination at the Equinox; it had never, in all the years of Kushorit history, been executed at any other time. What this would do she wasn't sure; the voice of reason in her babbled that it couldn't be that bad, they were only hours away from the proper time. If it was some buried sabotage of Marada's, set to proceed even if she was no longer alive to reap the benefits, then Maskelle wasn't sure of the use of it.

She reached the end of the gallery and pelted across the second inner court. She lost a sandal on the steps up to the first gallery and had to pause to tear the other one off. The flow of power was stronger and the taste of it was acidic and unfamiliar, as if against every principle of Koshan philosophy and craft something else had invaded Kushor-At's reservoirs and was flowing over the city. It couldn't have been worse if the mud from the rice paddies had suddenly risen up to break the flood gates and stream into the canals. Every Koshan she passed was reeling under the shock of the onslaught. If it was the Wheel's culmination, then something had gone very, very wrong.

She reached the first inner court, running out into the open area toward the central tower. Then it hit.

It was like a physical blow, as if something heavy had struck her in the back. Maskelle staggered, then sunk to her knees, pressing her hands to her face. *It came from behind me; it's not the Rite.* Power swelled and raged like a storm, tearing across her body and her mind.

Rian walked down the bridge, trying to keep his expression controlled, but it was an effort. He could feel Karuda's eyes on him and hoped what he was thinking wasn't there to be read on his face. *I can't believe she did this.* He didn't know whether it was some plan he was simply too dense to see the logic of, or if she had suddenly gone insane.

He looked out over the water toward the low dike and barrier wall, feeling his gut twist. It was stupid to feel betrayed. This was just the way of the world.

At the midpoint of the bridge Mirak stopped and motioned

Karuda to come to him. "Return to the temple and follow her. Make sure she keeps her vow."

Without a word, Karuda bowed and turned away, going back toward the Marai's enclosure. Rian fought the urge to make a break for it. He had known this would happen and now he wouldn't even be there to do anything about it. Mirak looked at him, brow lifted speculatively. The Chancellor said, "Perhaps you're not as valuable a hostage as I thought."

"Try it and see," Rian said, meeting his eyes. He was tired of playing it safe. If Mirak wanted to have him killed, let it be for a good reason.

The Chancellor's lips thinned, but he didn't deign to answer. He started for the end of the bridge again and Rian followed, the guards closing in behind him.

A hot wind lifted his hair, sudden and strong, and he looked up, frowning. *There's a storm coming*, he thought at first. There was a grey cloud on the horizon, visible above the buildings and the walls of the city in the distance. Then he remembered this wasn't the plains of the Sintane and he shouldn't be able to see storms coming on the horizon miles away.

One of the guards swore. The group halted and Mirak stared at the rising greyness above the city wall.

Rian squinted, lifting a hand to shade his eyes, trying to understand what he was looking at. This wasn't a storm, it was a wall of clouds. . . . Not clouds, it was a solid wall, becoming darker as it drew closer. The noise of the festival crowd was dying out, the sound dropping away in waves. The black wave grew larger and Rian realized it was now on this side of the city wall. The sudden realization of how huge it was took his breath away and he realized he was backing up without conscious volition. Its shadow was travelling across the terraces to the broad plaza that lay before the Marai. Its shadow was blotting out the sun.

There were screams rising from the crowd now. Rian felt the stone of the bridge's balustrade against his thighs and knew he had nowhere else to go. Maskelle's words were echoing in his head: *It's more likely that in changing the shape of the land, what they actually did was change everything about it, its shape, its history, its reality . . . changed the whole region to someplace else, that looked a great deal like the places where the Sakkaran cities used to be. . . . Which is why we don't try to do that anymore.*

Rian turned and bolted back down the bridge, running for the temple's entrance. The wind hit him with sudden force, throwing him against the stone. He tried to stand and the next gust tumbled him over the balustrade. He struck the cool water hard, going under. Coming up sputtering and gasping for air, he looked wildly around for the temple enclosure. There was no one else on the bridge and he hadn't seen if the others had run or gone over the side. Then he saw the black wall had reached the outer edge of the moat.

That's it, Rian thought. There was nowhere to go. It had to be the Rite. *Something went wrong. Very wrong.* The darkness moved out over the water and seemed to slow, as if pressing forward against a steady resistance. Rian discovered he couldn't just float here and wait for it, not even if there was nowhere to go. He kicked away from the bridge and swam for the temple enclosure. The noise of the city had died away and the silence was complete except for the sound of his own thrashing in the water.

Rian was almost there when something lifted him up and flung him against the rough ground at the base of the enclosure wall. He struck it with stunning force and lay tumbled there a moment, gasping for air.

He pushed himself up on his hands and knees, shaking his head, dizzy and sick. Pain from his ribs stabbed him again and he clutched at his side, sitting back on his heels. Then he noticed the water was gone, replaced by giant paving blocks, each one of smooth grey stone. *Oh, no*, Rian thought. *I really don't want to know.* He made himself look up.

The sky was dark and roiling, like a summer thunderstorm,

and under that sky was another city. Buildings as mountainlike as the temples of Kushor-At and Kushor-An, but far stranger. The nearest, perhaps half a mile away, looked like a giant overturned pottery bowl. Others were cone-shaped, or like pillars with giant balls set atop them. Surfaces that the Kushorit would have used for giant stone canvases were mostly bare, marked only with one or two bands of geometric shapes. Trying to deny the evidence of his eyes, Rian looked toward the front of the Marai.

The moat and the bridge over it, the plaza and the walls and the city itself were gone; he could see the causeway that ran through the outer gate of the Marai's enclosure not far away. It dead-ended about level with where he had fallen, the stone chopped off as if by mason's tools.

He looked back out at the strange city. There were no people anywhere. The festival crowds that had surrounded the Marai had vanished with everything else.

Rian got to his feet, stumbling as his right knee tried to give out. He realized he was shivering, though the air wasn't cold. He wiped sweaty palms off on his shirt. Panicking was beginning to seem like an appropriate response. He wished he had screamed earlier when the wind or force or whatever it had been had thrown him into the wall; it seemed like self-indulgence to do it now.

He started toward the gate, limping, new bruises making themselves known. The only sound was the wind sweeping dust over stone, a whispering noise that seemed to echo with threat and loneliness and loss. Rian took a deep breath. He had come to the Celestial Empire looking for a different world right enough, but this wasn't what he had had in mind.

Rian reached the outer gate and leaned on the pillar. The court on the other side of the wall looked the same, except the color of the grass was dull and lifeless under the dark sky and the only sound was the stir of the palm leaves in the empty wind. A rustle in the grass that wasn't the wind made him freeze.

For a long moment there was nothing. *Maybe I've gone crazy and none of this is actually happening*. It was a heartening thought. Then he heard it again. He stepped to the edge of the causeway.

Karuda lay on the grass near the base of the causeway. As Rian watched he stirred feebly and groaned. Rian contemplated the unfamiliar sky in exasperation. *It would be him.* He swung over the low balustrade and jumped to the ground, landing awkwardly. Karuda groaned again as Rian rolled him over. The noble had a bleeding gash on his temple, but he blinked and opened his eyes.

Leaning over him, Rian said flatly, "Guess what."

Slowly, Karuda pushed himself up on his arms. He stared at the churning sky. "The Rite . . ." he managed to say.

"Yeah, the Rite. But at least that little problem with the Koshans having too much power in the Imperial system is all taken care of. Too bad Mirak isn't around to appreciate it." Rian turned away in disgust, limping toward the steps that led back up to the causeway. If Karuda had survived inside the Marai, the others must have too.

Maskelle's head hurt. She knew she was still in the Marai before she opened her eyes. The gritty stone under her cheek resonated with the temple's power, but something was terribly wrong. She pushed herself up on her arms, lifted her head.

The sky was grey, the clouds dark and angry, as if a storm had just passed. It was almost familiar.

The breath caught in her throat. Her vision in the Illsat Keo.

"Oh, no," she breathed. "Oh, no, oh, no." She laid her hand flat against the stone of the pavement and extended her awareness outward, through the courts of the Marai, inner, first outer, lunar and solar, to the outer wall just before the moat—there it stopped. "This isn't happening."

Rian was kneeling at her side then, one hand under her arm to hold her up. She stared at him incredulously. "What are you doing here? I sent you away from this."

He was looking worriedly up at the strange sky. "Just lucky, I guess."

She shook her head. Nothing worked, nothing. "Help me up."

He pulled her to her feet and she wrapped an arm around his waist. Leaning on him, she buried her face against his neck, breathing in the scent of warm human sweat. It was another connection to the world as it had been. She took a deep breath. "We're in trouble."

"I figured that out," he said into her hair.

She lifted her head and looked toward the end of the passage. "I need to see outside."

Running footsteps in the court made them both turn. It was Rastim, white-faced and anxious. "What's happened?" he said, low-voiced, as he reached them.

Maskelle shook her head. "I need to get to the first solar tower."

Rastim picked up her staff and tried to hand it to her. She shook her head. Cut off from the spirits and the power of the temples, it was only so much dead wood and silver now. His mouth twisting in distress, he leaned it against the wall.

All the lamps had gone out along the colonnade, and as they neared the corner tower it was almost too dark to see. Maskelle's knees were weak and she waited to feel the Marai's force start to fade. The temple would die around her until the stone was nothing but a shell.

They reached the entrance to the western tower and Rian started up first. The chambers off the stairwell were quiet and the air unnaturally still. When they came out on the gallery, Maskelle moved forward to lean on the parapet.

It was the plain of her vision, vast as time, stretching away into the dark horizon under the purple-grey storm-churned sky. In the distance a wind drove a wall of dust across the giant paving blocks that formed it, and from the height of the tower she could see a mountain range in the distance. The city she had seen rose like smaller mountains around them. The nearest structure was a strange bulbous shape, like three balls of stone perched atop each other. It was decorated only with wide bands of unfamiliar, meaningless geometric carving. It was so strange that it was frightening to look at, and Maskelle found it hard to draw a full breath until she turned away.

Rian asked her quietly, "The Rite brought us here, didn't it? Something went wrong, like you thought."

"The Rite didn't bring us here."

"You mean . . . it's an illusion?" Rastim's voice was hopeful.

Ariaden are the eternal optimists, she thought ruefully. She shook her head. "It's not an illusion."

"Oh." Rastim flattened his hands against the parapet uneasily, seeking reassurance from the familiar stone. "Then how . . . ?"

"This is our world. We haven't gone anywhere. They brought this to us. This is what the disruption to the Rite was for. It let them do this."

"No, really," Rastim said, as if hoping she would change her mind. Rian said nothing, looking out at the alien landscape.

"Yes, really." Maskelle touched the Marai's power again tentatively, waiting for the inevitable. But the temple wasn't dying yet.

It felt, in fact, a little stronger.

The center doesn't move.

She realized both men were staring at her, that Rastim had spoken again and she hadn't heard a word. She said, "I just heard the Adversary."

"And that means?" Rastim prompted worriedly.

She shook her head and turned back into the tower. Behind her, she heard Rian say, "It means we're not dead yet."

Maskelle went back down the stairs, down the gallery toward the inner court. She could hear voices, hushed and frightened, and when she came out into the open below the central tower, she saw a group of about forty people, huddled in the gallery and the portico around the tower. Some of the younger priests were on the upper level where they could look out over the plain. She saw one pointing, another shaking his head in disbelief.

And the Marai's stone throbbed with the temple's heartbeat, stronger with each step.

The rest of the Ariaden were there, and Therasa and Firac hurried toward her. "What's happened?"

The question was echoed by the others. It was a mixed group, most of them Koshans. "I'm not sure," Maskelle told them. What she wasn't sure about was whether she was lying or not. She was beginning to think she had misunderstood again.

She stepped past them, through the portico and into the tower. There was no one in the outer vestibule and she went around the wall to the chamber of the Rite.

Vigar and the other Voices were there, many of the older ones still lying on the floor in shock or unconsciousness. Vigar was just climbing to his feet with the help of a young nun. But Maskelle had eyes only for what lay on the chamber floor beyond him.

The Celestial One lay as still as a dead man, his head pillowed on a bundled-up robe, two of the younger Voices anxiously leaning over him. She went to his side and they made way for her. He wasn't breathing and she touched his face gently. She whispered, "I'm sorry." The Marai's power must be in her imagination, or it was some temporary state that would quickly fade.

She felt Vigar standing behind her. "He may come back when the shock is less," he said, his voice rough.

She didn't look up. "Come back to what?"

Vigar touched her shoulder and she finally looked at the center of the room.

The Wheel of the Rite was whole and almost undisturbed. A path was torn through the edge of the outer ring, through the border protection symbols and into the eastern rise. Someone must have been thrown into it when the shock of the change took place.

But that little disruption was nothing. The Rite was nearly intact and still waiting for its culmination. *I was right*, she thought. *It came from somewhere else, not the Rite. At least, not our Rite.* Maskelle looked at Vigar. "We didn't do this."

He shook his head. "No."

She felt a little of the tightness in her chest ease. She took a deep breath.

"Who did?" one of the other Voices said quietly. "That's the question."

We return to the basics of our philosophy, Maskelle thought. It was the first lesson of the first step on the Koshan Path. *When you seek an answer, first define the question.* She said, "That will do for a start."

Maskelle got to her feet and walked back out to the portico. The strange purple tint of the sky gave the carvings an unfamiliar cast, but the Marai was still itself. Rastim was with the other Ariaden, giving them reassurances she could see he didn't believe. Rian moved to stand next to her. "Over there," he said softly, nodding toward the west side of the court.

Mirak was there, in the shelter of the colonnade, standing with another man dressed as courtier whom she didn't recognize. "Ah, that's all I needed," Maskelle said under her breath. "I thought he was outside the boundary."

"So did I." Rian's expression was grim. "He must have run back down the causeway."

Ancestors, Raith is here too, Maskelle realized. The Celestial Throne and his most favored courtiers and advisors had been here for their part of the invocations. She saw Karuda, battered and bleeding, standing with three other Palace Guards. Most of the temple guards would have been outside in the crowd, but a small contingent of Palace Guards would have come with the Celestial Throne into the temple.

Vigar stepped out onto the portico and stood looking up at the sky. "The woman Marada . . . Whoever sent her . . ."

Maskelle nodded. "The disruptions to the Rite were part of this. There was a second Wheel, and those symbols were of this place."

"We have to know how they learned enough of the Rite to do this."

Maskelle couldn't argue with that. Knowing how meant knowing who. She could feel Vigar's eyes boring into her. Then he said, "You are the Voice of the Adversary."

"Only in name."

"In name and power."

"And authority?" She looked at him, lifting a brow inquiringly. She was holding her breath, half in dread, half in anticipation.

He stepped back and gave her the full ninth-degree bow, the obeisance and respect due to the chief religious of the Koshan temples and the Celestial Empire.

Maskelle's glance flicked around the court. They had all seen, the seventh-level priests, the two other Voices who had followed Vigar out into the court, Karuda and Mirak.

She nodded to Vigar. "Go back to the Celestial One. We can try to summon the Healing Spirits; that may help him return faster."

Vigar's brows lifted. "Can the Healing Spirits answer our call after what has been done?"

As if I know, Maskelle thought grimly. "I heard the Adversary earlier. If he can reach us, they can." Of course, the Adversary was far more persistent and far more ferocious than any of the other Ancestors. It might only be lingering after the others had gone. *No, don't think that.* Those thoughts were the first step toward giving in, and she didn't intend to give in. Not now, not while the Marai's heart still beat.

Vigar nodded, thoughtful, and turned back to the tower.

When he had gone, Rian said, low-voiced, "What was that about?"

"When the Celestial One is dead, the Voice of the Adversary is the chief religious of the Celestial Empire." She looked around the court of the Marai glumly. "The last part of which we seem to be standing on."

Rian stared. "The Celestial One's dead?"

"For now." She shook her head. "There's dead and there's dead. While the Marai is still alive, while I can still hear the Adversary, he may come back."

"So Vigar just told you you're in charge of this . . . this . . ."

"Disaster? That's what the Adversary is for." Her mouth made a dry smile. "The tasks no one else wants."

Rian let out his breath. "We're going to need guards, lookouts. Without the moat, the outer wall isn't much protection."

"You take care of that."

Rian jerked his chin at Karuda. "What's he going to say about it?"

"Whatever you tell him to." She motioned for Karuda to come to her.

He crossed the court toward them and bowed to her, to the correct degree. She said, "You take your orders from Rian now."

He inclined his head, and without waiting for further signs of acceptance, Maskelle went back to the central tower.

13

The dry wind tore at Rian's hair as he stood outside the Marai's low wall. In the distance he could see the unfamiliar shape of the mountain range. There were dark clouds so low over them they brushed the cone-shaped peaks. The nearest building was only a few hundred yards away. It was shaped like two giant stone balls standing next to each other, with three open bridges connecting them, the whole about as tall as the Marai's central tower. From here he could see an opening in the base of the nearer ball, large enough to drive four wagons through side by side.

Rian glanced at Lord Karuda. The Kushorit were afraid to approach the strange city. Rian couldn't blame them for it; he was terrified of the thought himself. Standing here, outside the low wall of the Marai, he could feel his heart pounding like one of the Temple Dancers' drums. Karuda's face was as immobile as a statue's, but Rian had the feeling the noble wasn't any happier about this than he was.

Karuda caught Rian's eye and made an "after you" gesture. Rian lifted a brow in appreciation, then started to walk.

After only a moment, Karuda followed, and after a much longer moment, the six Palace Guards who had been chosen to accompany them followed him. Only three of them had bows, the most useful weapon if anything came at them across the open ground. Most of the guards who had accompanied the Celestial Throne had only been armed with short swords. The temple guards had been outside the wall, helping keep the crowds in order, and there had been no need to have more than a ceremonial detachment of the Palace Guard inside the temple with the Throne.

Rian squinted, trying to see inside the dark opening in the wall as they covered the distance toward it. He wished that someone in the temple had had a distance glass; it would have come in very handy. More detail of the building's decoration was visible now. He could make out the angular designs on the bands of roundels carved on the wide part of the ball sections. There was no sign of life. No hint of Marada's people, if it had been her work that had done this. No birds, no insects even. The city was utterly quiet except for the wind and the noise they themselves made.

If anything did come at them, their only advantage was that they would see it across this open expanse. *And that's only while the light holds*, Rian thought. The sky, purple-grey with angry clouds, had been getting gradually darker for the past hour at least.

"We'll be perfect targets," Karuda said grimly, obviously thinking along the same lines.

"We're perfect targets anywhere in the Marai," Rian pointed out.

Karuda drew a sharp breath, then shook his head. "I know." They walked in silence for a time, then Karuda said, "So. Are we enemies?"

Rian didn't answer immediately, trying to gauge the man's intent. The wind pulled at their clothes and one of the men walking behind sneezed at the dust in it. Karuda was looking ahead toward the building and Rian couldn't read his expression. Finally Rian said, "That depends on you, doesn't it? And Mirak."

"Mirak is acting for the Celestial Throne."

"The Celestial Throne can't help us now." Rian jerked his head back toward the Marai, where Maskelle was. "She can."

Karuda didn't have to ask who he meant. "The chief religious of the Empire serves the Throne. Does she?"

"If she didn't, I think you'd know by now."

Karuda lifted an ironic brow. "That is probably true. Unfortunately."

Rian thought Karuda realized as well as he did that this was no time for Court machinations, when the Court no longer existed and they might all be dead within the day or the hour, but he couldn't give over all suspicion yet. *The problem is, some people are just that stupid, and Mirak may be one of them.* "What exactly does Mirak think she's going to do?"

Karuda looked into the distance and finally shook his head once, as if in dismissal. "Make an agreement with our enemy."

Karuda didn't sound certain at all, as if he wasn't any more attuned to the Chancellor's thinking processes than Rian was. Rian didn't find that terribly comforting. "We don't know who our enemy is."

"I know that."

"Well, maybe we'll know soon."

"Or we'll be dead."

"Then it won't be our problem."

Karuda's short bark of laughter held no mirth.

Even if they were never attacked, Rian knew they had only a limited time here. Unless the storm overhead broke, the only water was in the double reflecting pools on either side of the causeway and the other small basins in the temple courts. The first solar tower contained a storeroom with bags of rice and taro root and some bundles of sugar cane, which were used to pay the temple servants, and at the moment this was their only source of food. The Temple Master was sorting it out and tallying the amounts now, and soon they would know just how many days' supply they had. If this place even had days.

There was no way to approach the building subtly, no possible cover to take, so they simply walked toward the doorway. As they drew closer, Rian was relieved to see that appearances hadn't lied; the place did seem deserted. Grey dust had gathered in drifts along the edges of the walls, and this close he could see there were cracks in the carved roundels and some of the windows above them had pieces broken from the sides. Whatever lay beyond the wide doorway was lost in shadow.

Rian reached it first and stopped just inside the archway, letting his eyes adjust. This was the most dangerous moment, when something could come at him out of that darkness. But nothing moved except the dust and the wind.

The shadows lightened to reveal an open, empty chamber. *Well, it's not going to take as long to look through it as I thought,* he realized, not sure whether he was disappointed or relieved.

It was a vast space, taking up the whole of the building, the walls curving to the dome high overhead. Wan light came through the small windows, throwing odd speckled patterns on the grey mottled stone. The place smelled thickly of dust, age, dead stale air. Rian stepped inside tentatively, then moved to the side, following the curve of the wall. High in the far side, he could see the round openings for the bridges that connected it with the second part of the structure.

Karuda and the others fanned out, looking around, equally mystified.

Rian touched the stone of the wall. It was cool and the surface was rough, lightly pitted. He dug at the dust with his boot, exposing the place where the wall joined the pavement. The seam was as close as that between the paving blocks outside. He had thought the Kushorit were the masters of stonework, but whoever had built this city had obviously been even more skilled.

"Nothing," one of the men whispered, looking up at the height above.

"No bats, no birds, no spiders," Karuda said, glancing around at the dust-strewn pavement.

Rian knew that wasn't what the man meant. "No," he told Karuda. "No stairs, no ladders."

They returned to the temple, entering through what had been the north side water gate in the outer wall. Leaving the smooth paving blocks for the more familiar stone of the steps was a relief, and Rian rolled his shoulders, trying to shake the feeling of having a target painted on his back. Karuda paused to speak to the sentries posted at the gate and Rastim, who had been hovering nearby, hurried to Rian's side. The Ariaden had been brave enough to come out a short distance onto the pavement, which was more than most of the Kushorit were willing to do, but he hadn't quite dared to follow Rian and the others all the way to the first building. Rastim asked worriedly, "Did you see anything?"

Rian swallowed a sarcastic answer and said, "No, it was empty. Completely empty." Rastim was, in his way, trying hard to be helpful, though about the only thing he had been good for so far was keeping Rian company while he walked around and saw just exactly how terrible the situation was. Rian explained briefly what they had seen in the first building. The other half of it, the second ball that was connected to the first by the bridges, had not had an outside door.

Rastim rubbed his chin, puzzled. "Wood," he said. "The inner floors were all of wood, and it's been so long it's turned to dust."

"It's possible," Rian conceded. "Funny the trees haven't grown back after all this time."

"It won't help," Karuda said as Rian and Rastim reached the terrace that bordered the wall. The noble was watching the last group of sentries take their position in the low tower in the corner. "Anything could come over this wall."

To say the Marai hadn't been designed for defense was an

understatement so laughable it was almost imbecilic. The outer wall that was meant to border the moat was low and broken by four gates barred by nothing but broad flights of water steps that now invited entry from the open ground surrounding them. Rian didn't think much of their chances either, even with Karuda's men at each entrance and temple servants and monks posted as sentries in all the vantage points.

"Then what will help?" Rian asked seriously. "I'd really love to know." Rastim shifted, but managed to keep his mouth shut.

Karuda said nothing. No one had seen any movement or sign of life out in the city so far, but someone had built it, just like someone had brought them here. *Or brought here there,* Rian thought. No one was discussing it, but Maskelle and the other priests knew that the Marai had not been somehow snatched from its foundations and dropped in this strange barren world; the cloud that Rian had seen cover the city had brought this world within it, had laid it over the surrounding country like a carpet over floorboards. What they didn't know was why the Marai was still here at all, if it had been left intentionally or had somehow saved itself and anyone within its boundaries at the last instant. Though that might prove to be more a curse than a mercy, depending on what else lived in this place.

Karuda's gaze had shifted to the sky. Ignoring Rian's question, he said, "It's getting darker."

"At least that means there's a night," Rastim put in suddenly. "This place may not be as strange as it looks. If there's a night, there has to be a sun past those clouds somewhere."

Karuda just stared at him.

"If there's anything here," Rian explained to the Ariaden reluctantly, "it may be more likely to attack at night. And we won't see it coming."

Rastim drew a sharp breath. "Oh."

Karuda said, "I'll be in the inner court," and walked away

toward the front of the temple. As soon as he was out of earshot, Rastim said, "That one could make trouble."

"Thank you, Master of the Obvious." Shaking his head, Rian started across the court toward the steps up to the gallery.

"Don't get snappy with me, Sintane, I'm on your side," Rastim said, right on his heels.

"Oh, good."

Reaching the gallery, Rian heard a regular tapping echo down the pillared hall. He stopped at the top of the steps, frowning. "What's that?"

Rastim looked around, baffled. "Someone hammering on the stone?"

"No, that's wood." The walls threw back echoes, making it difficult to tell where the tapping was coming from. Rian drew his siri and slowly paced down the gallery.

The outside wall had openings between the pillars that gave a view onto the terrace and the grass court; the inside wall was solid except for the doorways into the second inner court. Anything could have entered the Marai during the confusion after the change. The tapping seemed a little louder and Rian knew he had chosen the right direction.

In the shadows at the base of a column he saw a long dark shape, but a cautious step closer revealed that it was only a wooden box. A familiar wooden box. Rian let out his breath. *This damn thing.*

"Gisar. I forgot all about it." Rastim blanched. "Oh, no."

"Oh, yes." Rian moved closer and circled the box, though he was careful not to touch it. At least the lock still looked secure. He supposed if it could do more than tap, the thing would have gone on a rampage by now.

"What are we going to do?" Rastim muttered, wringing his hands. "It could make someone let it out again. It could—"

Rian slid the siri back into the scabbard. "Rastim, if you're going to panic, pick something else to panic about. There's plenty to choose from, and this is the least of our problems."

The actor pulled himself together with a little shake and took a deep breath. "I suppose you're right." His brow furrowed with worry, he added, "But what about the noise? It might lure someone out here and trick him into releasing it. Will we have to put a guard on it?"

Rian had to admit the actor had a point. Thinking it was worth a try, he kicked the box. "Hey, demon puppet. Be quiet or we'll use you for firewood."

The tapping ceased. Rastim looked hopeful. Then a low, gravelly voice said, "Let me out."

"Yah!" Rastim leapt back a step.

Rian felt the hackles on the back of his neck itch. "Did it ever do that before?"

"No." Rastim shook his head, his eyes wide.

It said again, "Let me out."

There was a strange grinding note under the words, like wood grating painfully. The other Ariaden puppets had hinged jaws, so the operator could make them appear to speak. The image of the thing lying packed in its box, that fake jaw working, gave Rian a chill. To the puppet he said, "I don't think so."

"I can help you."

Rastim's expression went from horrified to incredulous. Rian snorted and said, "And we should believe you because you've been so much help in the past?"

"I'm not cursed anymore. The spirits of the temple came into me and frightened the curse away."

Oh, I'll bet, Rian thought. It might have sounded almost convincing had the thing's eerie voice not had quite such a coy note to it. Something had gotten into it true enough, but it wasn't any spirit that came from the Marai. It said again, "Let me out. I'll help you."

"Of course, we'll let you out." Rian backed away, motioning

for Rastim to follow him. The actor circled wide around the box, watching it as if Gisar might suddenly leap out at him. Rian added, "Just give me some time to find the key."

He led Rastim to the nearest door into the second inner court and said, "Wait here while I find out what Maskelle wants to do about this." Personally he was hoping for a bonfire. "Don't let anybody go near that thing."

"All right." Rastim nodded, his round face worried. He wiped his palms off on his shirt, glancing back at the box warily. "We can't really burn it, you know, unless this thing that's in it now is different from the original curse. Maskelle said destroying it would just release the curse and make it more powerful."

"That's good to know." Rian swore under his breath as he started away. Behind him, he heard Gisar begin to laugh, a painful wrenching sound that conveyed a fiendish amusement.

Rian found Maskelle in the central court. The place had begun to divide up into separate camps, which wasn't an encouraging development. The royal party was in the east side of the gallery, behind the central tower. The priests, assorted monks and temple servants, and the Ariaden were in the south side of the gallery and the court around the tower itself. The Voices were in the chamber of the Rite, repairing the portion that had been disturbed during the change, but so far they seemed to be able to cross back and forth between the two camps with impunity. Rian hoped it stayed that way, since it was Vigar who was the key to Maskelle's authority here.

The rest of the great temple was empty, except for the sentries posted in the towers and along the outer wall; everyone's instinct seemed to be to stay as close to the central tower and the heart of the temple as possible.

As Rian came through the passage into the court, he saw most of the priests were up on the second level of the gallery, heads bowed in a meditation position, chanting in that low, rhythmic way he had heard the night before. He couldn't understand the words; they must be from that special Koshan variant of Kushorit, but he still thought it sounded different from the chants last night. *Last night, before the world ended.* He shook his head and started down the steps. Last night seemed like years in the past.

Firac and Gardick caught him halfway across the court. Gardick had his customary suspicious scowl, but Firac just looked worried. "Any news?" he asked anxiously.

"Well, yes," Rian admitted reluctantly. He didn't want the word about Gisar to spread, but these two already knew most of it and he couldn't risk leaving Rastim alone with the thing for long. "Not good. Rastim's keeping an eye on something in the north side of the third gallery. Can you go and help him?"

Firac looked puzzled. "On the north side of the . . ." He had helped deliver Gisar to the temple and recognition lit his face. "Oh, no."

"Oh, yes."

"What?" Gardick demanded.

Firac caught his friend's arm and hauled him toward the passage, saying grimly, "I'll tell you on the way."

Rian crossed the court and stepped up into the south gallery. They had closed off one of the side passages by draping some of the white festival banners over the openings and made a bed there for the Celestial One. He picked his way past the little circle of nuns who were gathered around the entrance, murmuring to themselves in meditation, and lifted the drape to step inside.

The makeshift room was kept warm with a couple of braziers, though their supply of wood was limited. Rian had enjoyed ordering the temple servants to break up one of the royal litters for its wooden poles and supports, but he knew just how hollow a victory it was. There were two libraries in the second court and two in the third court, if they got desperate for firewood, but no one wanted to talk about that. It would mean admitting there was no way back. And Rian knew anyway there was no point to it; the supply of food would run out long before the supply of fuel.

The Celestial One lay on a pallet, his attendant priest and Old Mali sitting on the ground next to him. The old man was utterly still and looked as dead as the Voice Igarin had when Rian had persuaded the Temple Master to let him examine him. The young priest was deep in prayer or meditation, but Old Mali glanced up as Rian stepped in. She grimaced at him, an expression that might be either a welcome or a warning to keep his voice low, then wrung out a cloth over a bowl of water and placed it on the old man's forehead.

Maskelle sat nearby in the meditation position he had seen her use before, her eyes closed. Her face looked hard in the muted light and Rian knew the Celestial One's condition frightened her, though he was probably one of the few who could tell. And if he knew Court factions and intrigue, then on the other side of the gallery it was already being said that she wanted the Celestial One to stay dead. In the next few days, if things continued to go badly, the story would change to suggest that she had killed the old man herself. Back against the wall, wrapped up in a piece of sacking, was Marada's white stone ball. Maskelle had retrieved it from the Temple Master's keeping to examine it again, hoping that in this strange place it would provide some clue to their enemy's identity or location, but as far as he knew it had told her nothing yet.

The air was heavy with incense and Rian sneezed. Old Mali glared at him. Without opening her eyes, Maskelle said, "Come here."

He stepped across to sit on his heels in front of her. She was doing that spirit-walking thing again, the way she had last night, when the bird-demon had killed Marada. When she held out her hand, he took it.

As soon as Rian closed his eyes he was outside the Marai, in the alien city, feeling the unbelievably strange sensation of the wind tearing through his insubstantial body. He had expected to be high up in the air, but they were only a few feet off the ground.

Taking up his entire field of vision was a dark grey stone wall. After a moment he got the trick of moving and rolled backward to get a better view. The wall arched up and away and he realized it was the side of a dome. About midway up was a carved roundel, like the bands of decoration he had seen on the building to the north. The design was of concentric rounds of raised or sunken squares, with other geometric figures woven between them. In the ears of his real body Maskelle's voice said, "It doesn't look like writing. It's not complicated enough. Unless it's one or two symbols repeated over and over again."

Rian tried swinging around, noting that he couldn't see Maskelle's spirit body. After a couple of tries he managed to face the right direction to get a view of the Marai from a distance. It looked odd, framed against the nightmare storm sky and the strange city, ripped away from the other temples that should surround it. The wind carried a curtain of sandy dust across the stone between their position and the temple, but nothing else moved. He swung around to eye the strange building again, trying to estimate scale. If he was judging it aright, this was the squat, bowl-shaped one to the east. "What about the inside?"

"This is as close as I can get, and it was hard going to make it this far. The power pathways are all gone, no canals, no rivers, no roads, no croplines, no footpaths, no game trails, nothing. Not even any residue of where they were."

Rian felt a sick feeling settle in his stomach at more confirmation that this was their world. He couldn't afford to think about it now. He said, "I've got something to tell you."

She dropped his hand and abruptly he was back in the incense-heavy air of the Celestial One's sickroom. He sat back with a thump, startled at the sudden change, and Maskelle smiled apologetically at him. "Sorry." She stretched and shook out her hair. "Let me guess. Trouble with Karuda?"

Rian leaned back on his hands, waiting for the room to stop spinning. "No, trouble with somebody else. Gisar."

"Gisar?" Maskelle frowned. "Who the— Oh, him." She was puzzled. "What can he do? The curse should be almost gone now."

"It might not be the curse. It could be something else, or at least," he added ruefully, "that's what it said."

Old Mali shook her head and muttered under her breath.

Maskelle's brows rose. "It said?" At his confirming nod, she gazed up at the ceiling the way she did when she was cursing the Ancestors. She told Old Mali, "I'll be back soon."

Out in the open gallery, Rian thought the scent of impending storm in the air was stronger. Maybe it would rain. He stopped in the gallery to tell one of the temple servants to make sure anything that could possibly catch and hold water was set out in the open. As the man hurried off to organize help, Rian caught up with Maskelle, who stood out in the court, squinting up at the sky.

She said, "So it is getting darker. I thought my eyes were going."

Rian nodded. "It'll be . . . interesting to see what happens then."

"That's one way of putting it."

"Is the Celestial One any better?" Rian asked her as they went up the steps to the passage. The man looked dead to him, but all the Koshans were so determined that he wasn't, or that at least it wasn't a permanent condition, it seemed easier to fall in with their belief. And he really didn't want the old man to be dead. Rian wasn't sure what it would signify if the old man did come back, but the Celestial One was like the Marai itself, and his continued existence would somehow mean that not everything was as bad as it seemed.

"The same." She shook her head. "There's really nothing

we can do except wait and watch. When he comes back, it will be sudden."

They passed under the second gallery and out into the second court. The chanting of the priests sounded louder and was beginning to take on that low reverberation that had echoed all the way to the palace last night. "What are they chanting for? The Rite?" Rian asked her.

"No, it's something different. They're trying to make the Marai a little less vulnerable. It's a very ancient ritual the Temple Master knew of." She pushed a stray lock of hair back behind her ear. "We won't know if it works until . . . well, it works."

"What will it do?"

"It will make a wall around the temple. A wall we can't see, but that we can feel."

He supposed he had seen stranger things, especially recently. "All right."

She grinned unexpectedly. "Wait and see."

Rastim, Firac and Gardick were gathered in a tight little knot in the doorway, nervously watching the box that lay down the hall in the shadow of the pillars. Rastim glanced toward them as they crossed the court and the relief was evident on his face. He hurried to them and reported in a low tone, "It keeps asking to be let out."

"Of course it wants out," Maskelle said. She ran her hands through her tangled braids and sighed. "It can't kill anyone while it's inside that box."

"I hope not," the Ariaden muttered.

Rian followed Maskelle past Firac and Gardick. He could hear Gisar making little wooden chuckling noises to itself. She paced cautiously toward the box, stopping a short distance away and sitting on her heels to eye it thoughtfully. Rian circled around the box to stand opposite her.

Before Maskelle could speak, Gisar said, "Did you come to let me out?"

Maskelle lifted a brow, exchanging an ironic look with Rian. She said, "And why should I do that?"

"My curse is gone," it said, and the coy note was back. "I can help you."

"I don't think your curse is gone. But I think your curse may be finding it a little crowded in that wooden body right now." Her expression thoughtful, she added, "Help us how?"

"Help you destroy your enemies."

"I don't think so." Maskelle stood, starting to turn away. She added to the others, "These demons have no imagination."

"You don't even know who your enemies are."

Its voice was subtly different. Deeper, less coy, more sure. Maskelle paused, watching it carefully. Skepticism evident in her tone, she said, "And you can tell us?"

"They journeyed here from a dying place, to take this place for their own."

Maskelle's face went still. "This place . . . The Celestial Empire?"

"The Celestial Empire, the Sintane, the Ariad, and beyond."

Rian heard Rastim draw a sharp breath. He thought, *It knows who it's talking to.* He wasn't sure why the thought should give him such a chill of foreboding. Maybe because the demon had seemed more like something that was just reacting to them, randomly and maliciously. A knowledge of who they were and where they came from seemed to imply a more thoughtful intelligence. *Maskelle was right, it's not the same demon anymore.*

"They did this? They constructed a Wheel of the Infinite to transform our world into theirs? Their dying world?" Maskelle said slowly.

"What's the sense of it?" Rastim burst out. Maskelle squeezed the Ariaden's shoulder, signalling him to be silent, and Rastim jumped as if he had forgotten anyone else was there and muttered, "Sorry."

Ignoring the interruption, it said, "They miscalculated." It sounded balefully pleased, as if it delighted in the mistake. "They meant to bring their city here, to take the place of Kushor-At and Kushor-An, and from there to take the rest. Instead they brought all their dead world."

"But what can be done can be undone." Maskelle eyed the box, her expression thoughtful and a little predatory.

"And done again, while they have the second Wheel."

"We had thought of that," she said dryly.

"Well for you."

"Tell us where the Wheel is."

It didn't answer. They waited, and Maskelle asked more questions, but that was all it would say.

Gisar with a new demon, Maskelle thought wearily. And a demon that seemed to know far more about their enemies than they did. "I'm afraid Gisar may be a lost cause," she said to Rastim as they walked back through the gallery.

They had left Gardick to watch the thing, and Rian, not wanting to take any chances, had called in a couple of Karuda's men from the outer court to help him.

"That's all right," Rastim answered with a little shudder. "I really don't think we'd want him in the company anymore." He gestured helplessly. "But what are we going to do with it?"

"I'll talk to the priests. We'll put a guard on it, one of you," Maskelle nodded to the Ariaden, "and a Koshan, to make sure it doesn't play any tricks."

Rian folded his arms. "What do you think it is? Something like Marada?"

"Possibly. But why did it tell us about them?"

"To frighten us?" Rastim said with a grimace. "I think the less I know of what's going on, the better."

Maskelle smiled, shaking her head as she stepped back out into the court. "Maybe you can hide under a blanket and I'll wake you when it's over?"

Before Rastim could reply, Firac spoke, his voice rough, "So you think it will be over, then? Sometime?"

It was the question no one else had quite dared to ask. Rastim watched Maskelle nervously, waiting for the answer. She paused, standing down in the court, looking ahead toward the central tower where it rose over the galleries. Finally she said, "Oh, I think it'll be over. Whether we'll still be here when it is, I can't say." She glanced back up at them. "I'll tell you when I know."

Firac nodded. "Well enough."

The Temple Master met them as soon as they came through the gallery into the inner court. His face was drawn and worried, and he said, "The Throne wants to speak to you."

They gathered in the court outside the portico of the central tower. The Emperor had sent all his guards to help watch the gates and the outer wall. The courtiers who had accompanied him stood between the pillars or sat on the balustrades of the gallery, grim faces hiding confusion and fear. Raith himself sat under the portico on one of the padded seats taken from the royal litters. Maskelle was startled at how old he looked. His office had already etched fine lines of care around his mouth and his eyes were deeply shadowed.

Vigar paced impatiently near the portico, obviously anxious to return to the Wheel, where the other Voices still worked. Chancellor Mirak stood with Karuda on the gallery steps. The other Koshans, the temple servants, and the Ariaden were an anxious audience in the opposite gallery. The chanting of the priests in the upper levels rose and fell like the howl of the wind.

Maskelle moved to a position directly opposite the Throne's, with Rian and the Temple Master following her. Rastim and Firac moved to join the other Ariaden. A few people were talking, but all the voices fell away as Maskelle took her place.

Mirak started to speak, but Raith held up his hand for silence. The Emperor met Maskelle's eyes, and said only, "Well?"

Maskelle smiled tightly, admiring his calm and the way he had shifted the burden onto her. It was a gesture that said, *If you are the chief religious of what's left of this Empire, then act like it.* She folded her arms and said, "We've discovered something new, but the source is, at best, dubious."

There was a faint stirring of curiosity and unease through the crowd, as she repeated the gist of what the demon had said. Even Vigar stopped pacing. When she had finished, Raith shook his head a little. "Why would this creature betray its own people, if it is one of them?"

"That's the question," Vigar said.

Raith glanced over at him, frowning. "Do the libraries tell of anything like this happening before?"

A very Koshan question, Maskelle thought. Echoing her own words to Rian last night, Vigar said, "There are many places that touch the Infinite." He waved a hand, gesturing at the strange city beyond the walls and galleries. "We have the evidence of our own eyes that it's possible. If these people the demon speaks of learned the power to travel from place to place, in search of a new home to replace this one . . ."

Maskelle took a deep breath. "Believe it or not, the situation is the same as it was before this happened," she said. "We need to search for the second Wheel."

"Why? Why not simply begin the Rite, if you believe it will restore things to what they were?" Mirak protested.

Maskelle saw the flicker of annoyance on Raith's face and surprised herself with a small surge of pride. *He realizes it, too.* As Vigar drew breath to answer, the Throne said, "Our enemies have proved that they can create a Wheel of the Infinite similar to our own. If the demon didn't lie, they made a mistake in using it. Presumably they won't make that same mistake again. All they have to do is rebuild their Wheel and we will have no second chance." He leaned forward. "We must destroy their ability to use the Rite against us."

"Exactly," Vigar said before Mirak could speak. "It takes the combined power of Kushor-At and Kushor-An, and every other temple center in the Empire, to initiate our Rite. That power is stored now, in the Wheel and the Infinite, ready to be expended. It will take another year for us to rebuild our Wheel, and then it won't have the force of a Hundred Year Rite. We have no second chance."

"Which begs the question," Maskelle began carefully, "where is their power coming from? Not our cities or temples. And there isn't anything similar here, unless we simply can't feel it."

Vigar shook his head, unwilling to speculate.

Karuda stepped forward and said, "Will they know our Wheel is intact? If they do, they'll come after it."

Maskelle felt Rian shift beside her and knew he had drawn the same conclusion.

In his mild voice, the Temple Master said, "The Marai is no longer undefended." His arms folded into the sleeves of his robe, he nodded up at the priests in the upper levels. "The barrier is complete. What they do now is only to keep it in place."

"We'll send out search parties for the second Wheel," Raith said, standing. "Leave enough men behind to watch the boundary, but finding that Wheel must be our first task." He looked around at all of them. "Small groups, with a few trained warriors, and a priest or monk who knows what to look for. When they find it, they will send a message back for the others to make a plan of attack."

There was a murmur of agreement and relief through the crowd.

The Emperor glanced up at the darkening purple-grey clouds. "It seems night is coming. The groups should be ready to leave at first light."

Maskelle exchanged a look with Rian. The Emperor was right. No matter the urgency, they couldn't send anyone out to stumble around in the dark. The Temple Master added, "It will take time to teach everyone how to move through the barrier around the temple. That can be done during the night."

And we'll just have to hope that we're here to see the next day, Maskelle thought, taking a deep breath.

The sky was rapidly growing dark.

14

After the royal party had retired to their side of the Marai and everyone else had been dispatched to make the various preparations for tomorrow, Rian stood in the inner court of the Marai with Maskelle, watching the night fall. It was quiet except for the low chanting of the priests.

It was already so dark Rian could hardly see Maskelle standing at his elbow; it made the yellow flicker of lamplight in between the pillars of the galleries look as bright as the sun. He said, "If Marada and her people were from here, how do they live? What do they do for food, water?" He knew someone had laid the stone blocks on this plain and built this city. It just didn't seem reasonable that they could still be here.

Maskelle looked up at the now inky blackness of the sky and shook her head. "I don't know. I have a feeling Marada was an even stranger creature than we thought. I saw she seemed to exist in the Infinite and our world at the same time. Maybe . . . they don't need the same things to exist as we do." She shrugged. "Perhaps we'll ask about it when we find them tomorrow."

Rian hoped that was a rhetorical "we." If Gisar was telling the truth and Marada's people were here with their Wheel, then the search expeditions would be even more dangerous. With the Celestial One gone, they couldn't afford to lose Maskelle too.

How he was going to talk her out of it, however, was another question and not something he wanted to worry about right this moment. "Why wouldn't they come to us, that's what I don't understand. Whether they meant this to happen or not, surely they have to do something about us?"

She drew a slow breath, still lost in thought. "I don't know. I wonder . . . This place feels dead to me. Dead or dying."

Rian felt a coldness settle in the pit of his stomach. That was something else he hadn't been thinking about. The wind whipped through the court, carrying the scent of emptiness and dust. "Couldn't that be because of what it did to . . . the real world?"

He was looking at the east side of the gallery, trying to make sure no one was creeping out to listen to their conversation. Mirak and his faction had been ominously cooperative; Rian would have preferred a direct confrontation to force all the innuendo out in the open where it could be fought. At least the Emperor seemed to be in firm control for now.

Maskelle stepped close to him suddenly, turned his chin back toward her and kissed him. It was a deep kiss but quick, and if it was meant to distract him from his question, it worked. She stepped back and said, "We're not dead yet."

It was what he had said to Rastim this morning, he remembered, watching the white gleam of her robe disappear into the shadows as she walked back toward the south side of the court. He heard a light scrape, a sandal slipping against stone, from behind him. Rian turning, stepping back warily. A man was standing in the portico of the central tower.

"Something I want to show you," Karuda's voice said.

Rian hesitated, trying to decide if he smelled a trap or not. It was too dark to see the man's face. *One sure way to find out.* He nodded and followed when Karuda led the way across the court.

They went through the courts to the west outer gallery, then down it toward the corner tower. From the windows that looked out on the silent stretch of the grassy court, he could see three dim glows on the wall, the lamps of the sentries, muted to keep the light from ruining the men's night vision. There was a brighter light at the bottom of the stairs in the tower, where a lamp had been left burning. In its light Rian saw Karuda's expression was tense. The shadows made the carvings that spiraled up the walls look threatening, the sinuous Temple Dancers appearing more sinister than erotic.

As Karuda started up the stairs, Rian stepped sideways, looking up through the tower, but he couldn't see anyone lying in wait. Maybe things weren't bad enough yet for that kind of factionalized infighting; it was hard to tell with these Kushorit. Karuda glanced down but said nothing when Rian started up the stairs.

At the third level Karuda stepped out onto the balcony. There were three men crouched there, all of them temple servants. Rian didn't relax; he wasn't sure of the loyalties of all the servants, though most of them seemed to lean toward the priests.

One of the men stood, pointing across the plain. In a hushed, frightened voice he said, "There. It's getting brighter."

Rian looked where he was pointing and forgot his suspicions. On one of the massive dark shapes outlined against the sky, pinpricks of light glowed, the red flicker of firelight.

Maskelle leaned on the parapet, looking toward the flickers of red that hovered in the dark like stars. Mirak was standing just within the doorway behind her. The Temple Master had moved up next to Maskelle and Rian was sitting on the balustrade. The sentries had been sent down to the bottom level of the tower to wait.

Maskelle heard footsteps on the stairs and a moment later Karuda stepped into the doorway. He reported, "You can see the fires from all of the other towers." He added reluctantly, "It seems to go forever."

"If there were that many people here, we should be able to hear them," Rian said, sounding frustrated.

Maskelle took a deep breath and nodded. She didn't think the fires meant people either. At least, not the kind of people they were used to. "We'll wait until daylight, then go out."

" 'We,' " the Temple Master repeated.

She nodded. "I have to go." She could feel the Adversary pulling at her, more clearly than she had felt it in years. The Infinite was closer, somehow, even though the other Voices said they couldn't hear the Ancestors. *But the Ancestors have always been tied more closely to the land, the water, the air.* All that was different now. The Adversary had always been identified and personified by its Voice.

"And leave the Marai unprotected?" Mirak said. He had been uncharacteristically silent until now. *But he's always been a cautious man,* she thought, and he was outnumbered here.

"My duty is not to protect the Marai," Maskelle told him, turning away from the distant fires to face him. She couldn't see his expression in the heavy dark, but he would know she was looking at him. "My duty is to find that second Wheel and destroy it." She heard Rian stir restlessly, but he didn't protest aloud. She knew his present forbearance wouldn't stop him from protesting aloud later.

Mirak was silent a moment. "The Voice Vigar gave you the authority of the Celestial One."

"Vigar's duty is to protect the Wheel, with the rest of the Voices. If there is anything that will help us, it's the Rite. But it will be useless to execute the Rite while whoever did this still lives. If they've done it once, they can do it again." She looked at the Temple Master. "When I leave, you become the chief religious of the Celestial Empire."

The Temple Master sighed, sounding weary. "I thought you might say that."

Maskelle smiled to herself. *As long as we're carrying on the tradition of awarding it to the person who wants it least.* "Now don't go and make any sweeping decisions on the Reform of the Eighty-First Passage of the Water Invocations while I'm gone."

His voice dry, the Temple Master replied, "There go my plans for the afternoon."

"I see no cause for amusement in this situation," Mirak said, his voice brittle as glass.

"Neither do we, really," Maskelle said mildly. *He's close to the edge,* she thought. And he could fall, or be pushed, over. *Unlike those of us who went over the edge years ago and have been looking up at everyone else from the bottom ever since.* It worried her a little. She knew what he was likely to do in his right mind, and he was dangerous enough as it was. She didn't know what he would do if he was panic-stricken enough to break. "I would honestly like to answer all your questions, but I won't have any answers until we find these people and—"

And kill them.

"What is it?" Rian asked sharply.

Maskelle realized they were all staring at her. She shook her head. "I heard the Adversary again."

The Temple Master drew a sharp breath.

"How very convenient," Mirak said, his voice laced with vitriol.

"Oh, the one thing the Adversary never is, is convenient," Maskelle said under her breath. "Finding that second Wheel," she said aloud. "That's the first step." *But only the first step,* she thought.

"Sintane, I need to talk to you," Rastim said.

"Not now." Rian didn't bother to look up. With the help of a couple of nuns who had been doing duty as sentries in the taller towers, he was drawing a rough map of what he had seen of the layout of the city around them in soot on the flat pavement of the second outer court. The night was an absolute pitch black, carrying no moon, no stars, and no reassurance that day would ever return. *It's just the clouds,* Rian had told himself. There was a real sky up there somewhere. *I hope.* Working in the flicker of lamplight had given him a headache and he was in no mood to listen to Rastim. He had spent the last few hours with Karuda, organizing the guards and Koshans into search groups, then sending them out to the Temple Master at the edge of the barrier to learn how to cross back and forth through it.

Rian hadn't completely believed in the barrier until he had felt it himself, but it made a wall as impossible to penetrate as stone or wood. To cross it you had to walk in a pattern: Left three paces, straight two paces, right three paces, straight one pace, then turn left and out. Follow the steps in reverse to get back in. No enemies were going to stumble on that formula by accident. Rian had thought the chanting of the priests would become an annoyance after a time, but now it was reassuring, a calming counterpoint to the silence of the night and the lonely echo of the wind.

"It's important," Rastim said through gritted teeth.

Rian looked up at him. Only a few lamps were lit to conserve the short supply of oil, and the orange-yellow glows were as bright as stars on the railing of the second-level gallery, at the archway that led through into the central court, and scattered through the lower levels where the people were gathered. The lamplight threw just enough illumination onto the Ariaden's face for Rian to see his expression. Rian sat back on his heels, brows drawing together. "What is it?"

The two nuns looked up from a prolonged discussion over whether the building with the eight spires was behind or to the west of the one with horns, worried at his tone.

"Gisar," Rastim said grimly.

There were plenty of lamps in this section of the third court, their light flickering over the wall carvings and the pillars. They clearly illuminated the empty box, its lid carefully set aside. Rian

touched the wood where Maskelle had written the protective sigils. The ink had been burned away; he could see and feel where
the wood was singed.

"It must have spelled you to let it out, like it did at the camp
that night," Rastim said tiredly, wiping the dust from his face
with his sleeve. Rastim had said that when he came to relieve
Firac at watch, he had seen that Gisar was gone. Firac and the
Koshan priest hadn't been able to see the box was open until a
frantic Rastim had pointed it out.

Now the two men looked rebellious. Firac folded his arms
stubbornly and the priest began, "With all respect, I don't
think—"

Examining the locks, Rian shook his head. "No, it opened
this from the inside." He could see where the thing had forced
the locks apart. Running his fingers over the inside of the lid, he
could feel where the heat had started. "The sigils were burned
away from the inside, too.

Karuda swore, straightening up from where he had leaned
over to look at the lock. Rian had sent for the noble as soon as
he had heard Rastim's story. He had also sent one of the nuns to
warn Maskelle. The Kushorit said wearily, "This is all we need."

Rian couldn't disagree. He got to his feet. "So let's start
looking for it."

Karuda rubbed his eyes, then nodded sharply and started
away. "I'll organize a search."

Rian took the opposite direction, heading down the gallery
toward the arch that opened into the outer court. Though he
hadn't shown it to Karuda, he was grimly afraid. There was no
telling what Gisar would do. He wished he had some idea what
to do if he found the thing.

Rastim hurried to catch up with him. "Why are you going
this way?"

"If it's possessed by one of Marada's people instead of the
demon, it'll try to get back to them," Rian said, as they reached

the steps and started down. "It could be heading straight for the way out." All the creature would have to do would be to leave the third court by the middle stairs and head straight across the outer court to the gate. If it could hide itself from Firac and the priest, the sentries at the gate wouldn't have a chance.

"Oh, that's a point," Rastim said, following him.

Rian reached the bottom of the steps and started across the open area. The wide grassy expanse of the outer court was dark except for a couple of lamps on the water gate directly opposite the entrance to the gallery behind them. The ground was carefully even and free of obstacles, so it wouldn't be hard to cross, even when you couldn't see your feet in front of you. Rian took a deep breath, the smell of still damp earth and green temporarily blotting out the odors of dust and emptiness carried on the wind. Thinking it through, he said, "It won't be able to get through the barrier, but it'll be trapped between there and the wall—"

They were halfway to the gate when a figure rose up out of the dark suddenly. Rian shoved Rastim back and caught the blow in the chest, hard enough to make him stumble. He ducked the next one by instinct and drew his siri. He could hear a weird jangle, as if whoever had attacked them was wearing a lot of noisy jewelry.

He blocked another blow with the sword, feinted and drove it in toward what should have been his opponent's midsection. The return blow knocked him off his feet and he felt the siri jerked out of his hand. Rastim had gotten to his feet and now dove forward, trying to grab the thing from behind, but it threw him off again.

Rian scrambled to grab the fallen sword, then rolled up into a crouch. This couldn't be Gisar, this was big, big as a man. The sentries from the gate had heard the fight and were running this way, one of them carrying a lamp. The shape dodged forward, back toward the temple, and Rian threw himself at it in a tackle. He caught it around the knees and landed on a tangle of wood and metal wire. Rian floundered for a moment, trying to tell by feel what this thing was. It suddenly contracted under him and threw him off.

Rian hit the ground hard and looked up as the guard arrived with the lamp. The creature was standing over him and he realized with a shock that it was Gisar. Or that it had been Gisar.

He remembered the puppet from when it had walked out into the middle of the Ariaden's performance in the outpost. It had been a small thing, only waist high, with a brightly painted wooden body, the arms, legs, and head strung to the torso with wire, meant to be moved individually by the actor who worked it. Now the wood was distended and lengthened until it looked almost like diseased flesh. The wires had grown into a profuse tangle, standing out from its body like the spines of some sea creature.

Before they or Gisar could move, a howl roared over the court. It was the wind through the empty buildings, magnified to monsoon strength. Gisar whirled and knocked the lamp out of the astonished guard's hand. Rian felt rather than heard it run past him and made a grab for it, but the wires slipped through his hands. He scrambled to his feet and bolted after it.

Gisar was heading for the outer wall. Rian ran blind, guided only by the jangle of the wires and the thump of the puppet's feet. He hoped he didn't slam into one of the palm trees that dotted this enclosure, but he couldn't risk losing the creature. His dark vision began to return as he neared the low wall and heard Gisar scrabbling at the stone, climbing it.

With no moon or starlight and only the few lamps at the water gate further down the wall, Rian saw only an odd-sized shadow moving in the darkness about where he judged the top of the wall to be. He sheathed the siri and jumped, lost his grip on the weathered stone and fell back, then jumped again. He kept his hold this time, finding footholds in the carving and pulling himself up to perch on top, ignoring the tight pain in his side from his injured ribs. The wind had risen, tearing fitfully at his hair and clothes, and he couldn't hear Gisar anymore.

He dropped to the ground outside the wall, landing on the uneven strip of packed dirt that was all that remained of the moat that had surrounded the temple. He braced himself, half expecting Gisar to leap on him, but there was nothing but the howl of the wind. It was impossible to see anything in the empty dark of the plain stretching out from the temple. The pinpricks of light still glowed in the void where the strange city lay, but there was nothing . . .

Rian stared hard. The shadows had seemed to ripple, as if something moved out there, not far beyond where the priest's barrier lay.

He took a few cautious steps forward until he met the barrier. After hearing Maskelle's description of it, he had expected a solid invisible wall, but it wasn't that simple. It didn't feel different at all, it was simply a place that it was impossible to walk through unless you followed the directions of the priests. Experimenting with it earlier, he had discovered that if you pushed on it long enough it would start to push you back, but it didn't hurt you. He stopped there, leaning on it, trying to listen for the slight sounds the wind might cover and make shapes out of the darkness.

". . . this way . . ."

Rian stepped back, flattening himself down against the stone by instinct though surely whoever was out here couldn't see him either. Catching only snatches of words over the wind, he could tell the voice was a man's, the words Kushorit, but he couldn't recognize the speaker. He heard what might be a reply, garbled by the wind.

He crept slowly along the wall toward the source of the voices, putting one foot in front of the other with utmost caution. There was no way to tell if the speakers were inside the barrier or out. They could be from the Marai, braver than their fellows and willing to investigate the outside world in the pitch dark, or even a couple of priests performing some sort of task necessary for the barrier, but somehow Rian didn't think so.

He froze, hearing a clumping sound like heavy footsteps. He thought he could see movement in the darkness, but it was too jerky, too strangely angular. Whatever was out there, it wasn't human. It couldn't be Gisar either; for all that the puppet looked like an abomination, it moved lightly and naturally. *And this thing doesn't jangle,* Rian thought. He started forward again.

He heard a scrabbling, as if clumsy feet tried to find purchase on the dirt and rock along the base of the wall. *It's inside the barrier,* he realized with a shock, and pushed forward.

Six paces along the wall he ran into something heavy and sharp-edged, like a man wearing lacquered armor. It was halfway up the wall and he grabbed it, throwing his weight back to haul it down.

It was strong and clung like a monkey. He clawed at it, trying to find a head or a neck or any other vulnerable spot to injure, but it was armored all over and he couldn't find anything that felt like flesh. It batted at him, then suddenly twisted and kicked, sending him sprawling backward.

Blinding light suddenly blossomed over the plain. Rian flung up an arm to shield his face, scrambling back against the Marai's wall.

Spots flared before his eyes, but he made himself look. The light was coming from two swirling clouds that hovered above the ground on the other side of the barrier. They gave off a pearly, iridescent illumination that lit up the plain and cast the low wall into high relief.

It looked like their hosts had finally come to call. One of the whirlwinds moved forward, and in instinctive fear Rian pushed himself away from it until he felt the wall press into his back. But it stopped abruptly. He watched it try to press forward again, and again it failed. The barrier was holding.

The two whirlwinds began to move parallel to it, toward the front of the Marai and the corner solar tower. Eddies of that strange phosphorescence broke free with that motion, drifting down to lay in puddles against the stone.

He remembered the armored thing that had tried to climb the wall and looked wildly for it. It was gone.

The whirlwinds are a distraction, Rian realized suddenly. *So the thing that got in . . .* He pushed away from the wall and ran along it toward the gate, past the glowing clouds. He catapulted himself up the steps and inside so quickly one of the Kushorit guards on sentry there almost took his head off with a bori club and Rastim leapt back with a short hysterical yelp.

"Sorry," Rian muttered. Leaving the guards staring in alarm at the whirlwinds, he grabbed Rastim's arm and dragged him toward the temple. "What now?" the Ariaden gasped. "What are they? Something to do with Gisar?"

"Gisar is the least of our problems," Rian told him, breaking into a run once he was sure Rastim was following. "Tell Karuda to meet me where Maskelle is. Something's gotten inside," he called back to him.

He heard Rastim moan, "Oh, I didn't want to hear that."

Sitting in meditative silence in the quiet dimness of the little room they had made for the Celestial One, Maskelle thought she heard someone call her name. She opened her eyes.

The makeshift curtain over the archway was still closed, the dust caught in the folds undisturbed. The nun who was helping to watch over the old man lay curled asleep in her robe in the corner. Old Mali sat back against the wall, drowsing, but surely close enough to wakefulness to hear someone speak just outside.

Maskelle looked thoughtfully at the Celestial One's unconscious form, hope stirring. Then she heard it again.

She came to her feet. This time she recognized the voice. She stepped to the door curtain and drew it back. One lamp burned low in the gallery outside. By its wan light she could see Killia and Doria asleep by the wall, and three of the temple servants on the other side. She could hear nothing but their quiet breathing. Nothing. Not even the priests' chanting. The air felt dead and still, without a whisper of breeze.

Hah, she thought, lifting a brow. A barrier of power surrounded them, isolating this little part of the temple from the rest of the world. Finally, the attack she had anticipated. At least it was something she could get her teeth into; faceless, formless enemies were impossible to fight.

Leaving the Celestial One's side would be folly. She stepped back from the doorway to the center of the room. Making her voice mildly inquiring, she said, "Who are you?"

Old Mali and the nun didn't stir, and she knew something must be keeping them unconscious. Then the curtain stirred and lifted and Maskelle took an involuntary step back.

It was Marada. She wore court finery, a gold-shot silk robe and pearls braided into her hair. Maskelle knew what ghosts looked like and this wasn't one, but the colors of her costume, her features, seemed just slightly blurred. So it was only the host body Maskelle's bird spirit had killed; Marada, whatever she was, had survived. Keeping her voice mild, Maskelle said, "Marada, how kind of you to visit."

"I told you that you couldn't stop us." Wearing her odd stiff smile, she stepped further into the room.

Maskelle reached for the Adversary and felt nothing. It had picked a fine time to desert her.

Somehow Marada sensed it. She said, "Your spirits can't help you here."

Maskelle fell back a step, felt her foot knock against the white stone ball where it lay near the Celestial One's pallet. That had been the focus for Marada's power, though the lack of it hadn't seem to hurt her. It was the only weapon Maskelle had. "How did you get here? Did the second Wheel bring you, or did you travel here on your own? You must be capable of it; it's how you got to our world in the first place, isn't it?"

"I didn't come to answer your questions." Marada flexed her hands and Maskelle remembered the spirit-creature that had strangled Igarin.

"Let me guess, you came to kill me?"

Irony touched Marada's opaque eyes. "How did you know?"

Maskelle picked up the stone ball. "Are you sure you didn't come for this?"

Marada's expression didn't change. "That can do nothing to stop me."

Maskelle tested the weight of it in her hand. "Really?" She took a step forward and swung it at Marada.

Marada fell back, throwing up an arm to defend herself, but the stone glanced off her head. Maskelle felt her arm jar with the impact. More proof the woman's form was an illusion; whatever Maskelle had struck had been more solid than flesh and possessed of sharp edges.

Marada shoved her back, sending Maskelle crashing into the wall. She fell and rolled away, her shoulder aching from the force of the impact. She grabbed up the stone again. Marada started forward, reaching for her, and Maskelle leaned back to throw the stone.

Just before she threw it, she felt the Adversary's power touch her. Lightly, as if it wanted to remain unobtrusive. She channelled the force of it into the stone and let it go.

The stone struck Marada's chest and seemed to pass through her body, striking the wall behind her. Bouncing off the wall with a heavy thump, taking a chunk out of the Temple Dancer carved there, it fell to smash against the floor. Old Mali and the nun sat bolt upright with cries of alarm.

Maskelle looked up in time to see Marada's form waver and collapse in on itself. She started back as a number of other objects struck the floor with thumps and crashes.

The nun stared and Old Mali cursed. Maskelle told them, "We were invaded." She edged forward to examine the debris.

It was nothing but trash: fragments of flat building stones, rocks, shattered remnants of smooth dark-colored pottery. Litter, from that wreck of a city out on the plain, swept together to form a temporary shell for Marada's spirit. *Did the woman—if she was a woman—ever have a body of her own?* Maskelle wondered. Or was she dead and her spirit lingering, seizing whatever form was available when she needed to be corporeal? Perhaps that was why Maskelle had sensed death in this place. There were still people here, life of a sort, but they were dead, only their spirits left behind.

Sound from outside washed over her like a wave as whatever barrier Marada had placed around the room faded away with her death. Maskelle heard the low murmur of chanting and a babble of frightened voices, then Rian burst through the curtain, stopping abruptly when he saw the collection of debris on the floor.

"Marada," she told him. She lifted a twisted piece of the strange blue-tinged metal. "Her spirit was using this mess, working it like that demon worked Gisar."

Rian looked over the odd fragments, dismissed them with an annoyed shake of his head. He said, "Gisar got out. It led me straight to the place where this thing got through the barrier. And there's something else—"

Karuda shouldered his way through the others outside, casting a puzzled glance down at Marada's remnants as he pushed his way in. "You'd better come," he told Maskelle abruptly, looking a little startled at being inside the enemy's headquarters. "There's something outside."

Maskelle made it to the first solar tower and careened up the stairs, Rian and Karuda beside her. She was breathing hard when she reached the top and pushed past a group of guards to see the Temple Master, Mirak, and the Celestial Emperor standing on the gallery, looking out toward the captive whirlwinds that hovered just on the other side of the barrier. A furious wind tore at their clothes and hair, keening among the openings in the tower above them. Past them she could see movement in the deep well of shadow on the plain.

At first she thought it was people, a large number of them, moving out there in the dark beyond the wall. But the movement was abrupt and inhuman. *More of them,* she thought. Creatures— constructions, perhaps, like Marada had been.

She stepped forward and leaned on the balustrade, reaching for the Adversary. It was slow to respond, and she prayed it wasn't losing whatever hold kept it here with them. It was their only hope.

"Are they people?" the Temple Master whispered.

"No," Maskelle said, almost as softly. "They can get past the barrier. One already did."

Raith was staring at her. He turned back to look out at the dark. "They must know we mean to destroy their Wheel," he muttered.

"A traitor," Mirak said grimly. "We know the creatures can take human shape, imprison human souls. There's one here, with us."

Maskelle shook her head, frowning. *Something wrong there.* "Gisar, the demon has escaped. It's too much of a coincidence. It could have warned them." She saw Rian's sharp glance, but he said nothing. If by some trick of the Ancestors, Gisar was helping them, she didn't want to reveal it just yet.

"How?" Mirak asked sharply.

Raith spared a moment to give the Chancellor an annoyed look. "The same way a human traitor would have."

Maskelle stopped listening to them. She could feel the Adversary's presence now, hear its voice in her head though the words came too quickly to follow. She closed her eyes and felt it fill the space around her. Whatever those creatures were, they had been dead a long time. She felt a flash of contempt, bitter and hot, and wondered where it came from. Not from the Adversary, surely. She must have felt the emotion herself, and it was reflecting back to her from their tenuous connection to the Infinite.

She blinked and opened her eyes. She was sitting on the floor of the gallery, Rian supporting her. The Temple Master knelt in front of her, chafing her wrists. The Throne, Mirak, and the guards had left. The night was silent again; the howl of the whirlwinds and the creatures on the plain were gone. "What . . ."

"It's all right," the Temple Master told her. He didn't look as if it was all right. He looked as if he had seen something that had horrified him.

Rian helped her to her feet and she looked for the creatures. The whirlwinds had vanished, and there was no more movement out past the wall. She said, "They left?"

"They died," Rian told her. As she steadied herself on the balustrade, he pointed. She squinted, trying to see, and finally made out still shapes lying on the stone.

"The Adversary?" the Temple Master asked.

Maskelle nodded weakly.

"I didn't know it could do that," Rian said, sounding impressed.

15

As soon as the cavelike darkness began to lighten to grey, Maskelle went to the south gate in the outer wall and through the barrier with Rian and Rastim. After the attack last night, the priests had altered their chant slightly, just enough to change two vital steps of the path through the barrier. It would be changed again tonight, as darkness fell, and again every night they spent here.

The sentries on the gate watched them curiously, the older one pointing out to Rian that they couldn't cover them while they were outside the barrier. Maskelle didn't think that would be a problem; their opponents had shown no inclination to attack during the day.

The sky was still heavily clouded, but the air was warmer and smelled faintly of smoke. Despite the dimness of the morning light she could already see that the dark plumes over the distant mountains were larger.

The bodies of the creatures who had tried to attack still littered the ground outside the wall, but as Rian kicked one over Maskelle saw that, like Marada's remnants, they weren't bodies at all. Rocks, fragments of carved stone, smashed pieces of dark-colored pottery clung together in a roughly man-shaped form. It didn't seem to have a head, but then Maskelle supposed whoever had created it hadn't thought the creature needed one.

Rastim stared. "That's all that's left?"

Maskelle shook her head slightly. "That's all there ever was."

"Something just put them together out of whatever was lying around and sent them after us?" Rastim said in wonder, looking around at the debris. "Like puppets." He shivered in disgust. He was taking Gisar's activities very much to heart, and seemed to think that he and the other Ariaden were somehow responsible for the trouble it was causing. Maskelle didn't have the time to sit down and convince him it wasn't true, that no one could have anticipated any of this, especially not the bizarre change in Gisar's demon.

Even the Adversary hadn't been able to warn her; at least, not in a way she could understand.

"Like that armor in the Palace," Rian said, poking at the remains of the creature again. He sat on his heels to turn the pieces over. "Like Gisar. Or what it changed Gisar into."

Maskelle pushed her hair back and let her breath out wearily. Her skin was gritty with the wind-blown dust. "It would help if we knew if it led you to the spot where Marada was coming through the barrier by accident or design. And how Marada learned the way through at all." Gisar had been seen throughout the night in the outer court and the third gallery, sometimes as close as the lower level of the second gallery. It had hurt no one so far, only appearing long enough to make people chase it. Maskelle had been awake all night, bracing for a possible second attack from outside and trying to get the Adversary's help to track down their resident demon, but the Infinite had been unresponsive. Rian looked weary too; she knew he had gotten only an hour or so of sleep, sitting up against the wall outside the room where the Celestial One lay. He was as determined to catch Gisar as she was.

"I'm sure I heard another voice," he said. He shook his head, still staring down at the litter, though she could tell his thoughts weren't on it. "I think she knew the way through because some-one told her. Which means they know our plans."

Maskelle nodded grimly. They were still going to send out the search parties. There was nothing else they could do.

Rastim had moved over to the other heaps of debris that lay nearby, picking through the remains. Maskelle saw Karuda and a few guardsmen come out of the gate, make their way through the barrier, and stare around at the "bodies" of the creatures.

Rian got to his feet and absently rubbed his hands on his pants. "You can't go out with a search party," he told Maskelle.

Rastim looked up, his expression intent.

Maskelle stared from one man to the other. "Oh, so you two decided this?"

Rastim scratched his head and looked away. Rian sighed and stared up at the dark cloudy sky. "Yes, that's it. While we were tearing the place apart looking for a demon puppet, we've been plotting against you."

She rubbed her forehead tiredly. "That's not exactly what I meant."

"You can't go with us. All the priests are keeping the barrier up. If Gisar goes after the Voices, or the Celestial One, or the Wheel—"

"I know," she said sharply. "I know."

"I'm going," Rastim said conversationally. He stood, looking off at the buildings to the south, their spires and domes wreathed in mist. "Which direction are we taking? I think—"

Rian stared at him. "Who are you talking to?"

Ignoring that, Maskelle asked the Ariaden, "Are you sure you want to do this?"

Rastim tucked his thumbs in his belt uneasily. "I talked it over with the others and we're all going out, except for Mali and the girls." He told Rian, "I'm going with you." With a shrug he added, "It stands to reason. We're not needed here. And we want to pull our weight. Especially after the . . . Gisar incident."

Maskelle threw her arms in the air. "Chasing him last night was helping."

Rian eyed the actor-manager for a moment, then said, "If you go with me, what are you going to do?"

Rastim bridled. "Help. What else?"

"No. What are you going to do?"

Rastim hesitated. Maskelle folded her arms and looked at the ground, hiding a smile. Rastim huffed and finally said grimly, "Whatever you say."

"All right. You can come."

"Well, thank you very kindly."

"Now that we've got that settled . . ." Maskelle looked around, trying not to think about anything but this present moment. "Which way are you taking?"

"South," Rian said, talking to the ground. She was a little surprised to see it; he had won arguments with her before. She seemed to recall that he had won most of them. She realized he knew how she felt at being forced to stay behind, and sighed a little. He said, "There're three groups going out this way. We'll spread out to cover more ground."

Maskelle looked south, hoping for guidance. Her eyes passed over a tall structure with two spires standing up like horns, then came back to it. Something . . . No, she wasn't sure. She shook her head in annoyance. Since this had happened the Adversary was either too close for comfort or completely absent. "I'll follow you in spirit form as long as I can."

Outside the gate in the south wall, Karuda folded the square of paper that had their plan for the search drawn on it and said, "If you find it, no heroics. Send someone back for help immediately."

Rian nodded mock-solemnly. "I know. We agreed on that last night." The sky was only a little lighter and the men who would form the search parties for this direction were gathered around, checking their weapons, and curiously examining the remains of the creatures as he, Maskelle and Rastim had earlier this morning.

Karuda grimaced but didn't reply, tucking the folded parchment into his belt. The Kushorit noble had meant to lead one of the parties going to the east, but now he was staying behind to oversee the defense of the Marai. He didn't look happy about it. He looked, in fact, like the circumstance left him not only badly embarrassed but had irreparably injured his honor. Rian knew he must have been ordered to stay behind by Mirak or the Emperor.

The group Rian would lead had two Palace Guards, one temple guard, two temple servants, and a monk, plus Rastim and Rian. There were two other groups going out from this side and Rastim was helping with the others who were dividing up the supplies. By turning out the entire contents of the temple storerooms, they had scrounged up several coils of rope and enough candles and handlamps to go around. There were also water flasks for everyone and a ration of food. Everyone was armed, though some only with makeshift clubs.

Karuda said shortly, "Good luck," and walked away.

Rian turned to realize they had had an audience, that his men and the other two groups were watching them with concern.

"Lord Karuda is very proud," one of the Palace Guards said. Rian thought the man's name was Idoru.

"That's why he should be with us," Rian said, which made everyone happy except Rastim, who rolled his eyes and muttered, "Diplomacy, who would have thought it?"

Rian made sure everyone knew the altered steps to go back and forth through the priests' defensive barrier. After performing the maneuver for the fifth time, Rastim objected, "Look Sintane, I have sixty-three plays in my head. I can remember a few dance steps."

"All right, fine." Rian wiped dusty sweat off his forehead and gave in. He picked up one of the packs with their supplies. "Let's go."

He waved to the leaders of the other two groups and they started away in the same direction Rian and Karuda had taken yesterday. Rastim positioned himself at his side, talking cheerfully. They would be able to see and hear the other groups for a time, but the plan called for them to spread out as they searched, to cover more ground. As they neared the first building, the one they had examined yesterday, Rian glanced back at the temple and movement caught his eye. He stopped, gazing back at it, squinting against the blown dust.

Rastim kept walking—and talking—for a few moments before he noticed. He jogged back to Rian's side and asked with annoyance, "Did we forget something?"

"No. I thought I saw someone following us."

"Ah." Rastim shielded his eyes with his hand. "Perhaps it's just someone coming along for a little while, you know. Out of curiosity."

Rian turned to stare at him, incredulous. "What, like dolphins after ships?"

Rastim immediately became defensive. "Why not?"

Rian shook his head, looking back at the temple. He didn't see any movement now. Perhaps it had only been someone left behind and running to catch up with the other group. Or his imagination, or a trick of the light. *In this place? With our luck? Not likely.*

"That's me," Maskelle whispered in his ear.

Rian just managed to turn his alarmed twitch into a shrug and rubbed the back of his neck. He remembered that she had said she would follow in spirit and he hadn't really considered what that would mean.

Rastim was frowning at him.

"Come on," Rian said, settling his pack more firmly on his shoulder and smiling a little.

"I was going already, you're the one who stopped."

"High Revered?"

Maskelle's eyes were filled with the strange city backed by the smoking mountains. It took a moment of concentration to say the word aloud and not whisper it in Rian's ear. "What?"

"A person has come from the Celestial Emperor. He wishes to speak with you."

"The person or the Emperor?"

"The Emperor."

Ah, well. This had to happen soon enough. And at least Raith had chosen to make his request before the searchers had gotten too far into the city. She extended her spirit out toward them again and whispered, "I have to go. It shouldn't be long."

"We'll try not to have fun without you," she heard Rian say aloud.

"What?" Rastim sounded startled.

Smiling faintly, Maskelle brought herself back to her body. She blinked and rubbed her eyes, focusing on the nun who had brought the news. "Who came with the message?"

"A courtier, High Revered. I do not know him." The nun looked a little worried, as well she might; they had seen no one from the palace contingent except Mirak and Karuda and the guards.

"Well, I probably don't know him either." Maskelle stood and stretched, ignoring the twinge from her knees. She went over to check the Celestial One.

As she knelt beside him, Old Mali said, "Still dead." Despite the irreverence of her words, the old woman's tone was bleak, her brow creased with sorrow.

"I didn't suppose any different." Maskelle touched the old

man's forehead lightly. His skin felt dry and cool. *I could use some help here,* she thought to him. *It's not like you to hide from a fight.*

Maskelle stood and went to the door, brushing aside the makeshift curtain. In the gallery outside a courtier was waiting, being impolitely stared at by Doria and Killia. Doria was holding a bori club, though fortunately she wasn't actively threatening anyone with it. The man was young, not much older than Raith, and looked as grim and tired as everyone else; the only thing that marked him as a courtier was the silk brocade of his robe. He bowed to her and said, "High Revered, the Throne—"

"I know," she said. "I'll go with you."

Killia touched her sleeve. "Are you sure?" she whispered, speaking Ariaden. "What if it's a trick?" Doria nodded worriedly.

"It's all right," she told them, raising placating hands. "Really."

"You want us to come with you?" Doria asked, eyeing the courtier with wary suspicion.

"No, wait here. I won't be long."

She followed the courtier through the gallery and out into the central court. The courtier glanced up at the men and women lining the upper galleries. They were all still rapt in concentration, the soft murmur of their chant rising and falling in the dry air. He said, "How long can they do this?"

Maskelle glanced at him and saw the uncertainty under the veneer of grim determination. "As long as the food and water hold out."

He led her to the corner tower and the stairs that went up to the second-level gallery. She caught glimpses of the other members of the royal party in the tower rooms and the chambers to the side, their festival clothes showing the wear after the days of unaccustomed use. A few of Karuda's archers, left out of the search parties to guard the temple, were posted at regular intervals. Everyone watched her with the mix of curiosity and fear she was long accustomed to. Except now there was something else in their expressions. *Hope?* Maskelle wondered. That would be typi-cal. *They look to me for their salvation, and I have only questions, no answers.*

A room had been divided off from the gallery by a couple of festival banners, and outside it waited more guards and another couple of courtiers, these two armed with swords. One of the guards drew the curtain back and the courtier who had brought her here bowed and gestured for her to enter.

Maskelle stepped inside and saw Raith standing across the room, his back to her. The openings between the pillars had been draped too, but the curtains were pulled back now to let in the wan daylight and a little of the breeze. The room was sparsely furnished with a couple of makeshift pallets and a braiser. One of the young Court Ladies was seated on a cushion, holding a small lute in her lap. Without waiting for the Emperor's command, the woman got to her feet hurriedly, bowed, and stepped out through the curtain.

Maskelle took a deep breath and simply waited.

Raith turned to face her, his stony expression telling her noth-ing. "So." He still wore the silk and gold of the festival clothing, but he had put off some of the heavier pieces of jewelry. "Here we are."

"Indeed."

To her surprise, he looked away, biting his lip, forehead creased with some strong emotion she couldn't name. His voice thick, he said, "You were right, then."

Maskelle watched him a moment, aware how very little she really knew about him after all these years. "Right? About what?" *It happens so seldom, lately. . . .*

"This." He gestured down at the court bitterly, then up at the sickly purple sky. "If I took the Celestial Throne, disaster would result." He laughed sharply. "If I had known this was the kind of disaster you meant, I would have taken my own life."

Maskelle shook her head, suddenly unsure what to say. "This is . . . Raith, this isn't the vision I had. That vision was false."

"Was it?" He stared at her. "You don't call this disaster?"

"I call it disaster, but—" She couldn't continue. Raith was the one who had allowed Marada at court. But it was such a small mistake, to find a foreign courtier pleasing. Marada had fooled advanced priests and spoken to the Celestial One himself without revealing her intentions or her strange origin. How could Raith possibly be to blame? And even if she had never received admission to Court, that wouldn't have stopped her from living in the city, seeking instruction from Veran or some other unlucky priest. *I thought I killed her, and it still didn't stop this.* "We still don't know what happened, or who created the second Wheel of the Infinite. We've only a demented puppet's word that there is a second Wheel; it could be telling us only what we want to hear, mindlessly repeating the theory Vigar and I had. The Wheel wasn't at Marada's house, where we expected to find it." She rubbed her tired eyes. She couldn't stay here and console Raith for long; she had to get back to Rian and Rastim before anything happened to them. "I know now she didn't die when I thought she did, and she obviously had allies we knew nothing about."

Raith stood silently a moment, then took a deep breath, seeking control. He took a couple of steps to the balustrade and looked down at the court, where some of the temple servants were drawing water out of the basins. "So Lady Marada was some sort of spirit creature? Karuda said she was killed while trying to assassinate the Celestial One with magic, but then she returned to attack you last night."

He sounded oddly dispassionate about it, as if he had had no close relationship with the woman at all. Maskelle said cautiously, "Yes. And she was certainly the one who killed Igarin and Veran." She hesitated, and added finally, "I'm sorry."

Staring pensively out at the court below, Raith made a dismissive gesture. Then he glanced at her, puzzled. "For what? For Marada?"

Maskelle studied his face. She said slowly, "For Marada. I'm sorry it was her. I heard you were much attached to her."

He shook his head, still puzzled. "No. She was close to the Court, but . . ." He saw her expression and added, "Why? Were there rumors? There always are. But she was more attached to Chancellor Mirak." He snorted and looked down into the court again. "The gossips told me he gave her the richest of gifts. It was unusual for him, he wasn't one to succumb to beauty. I suppose he feels like a fool now."

Maskelle drew a deep breath. "I . . . see." *Oh yes, now I see.*

"It's funny how Gisar helped us last night," Rastim said as he plodded along, shielding his eyes as an eddy showered them briefly with dust.

"What?" Rian asked. They were working their way south through the city, the strange empty buildings rising like mountains all around them. They investigated doorways that opened into huge cavernous spaces and others that led only into rubble-filled warrens, all that was left after the upper floors collapsed. There were no paintings, no carvings except for the spare geometrical designs, no statues, at least none so far, though Rastim had found one place that had had several spots on the walls where it was apparent the carvings had been removed deliberately, and not simply worn away by wind and time. Rian wasn't sure what to make of it, though he supposed it might be something like when a rival lord seized a Hold and destroyed his predecessor's likenesses in the wall paintings.

The city felt even more vast under the sunless sky the further they got from the temple. In the distance the wind drove sheets of dust across the stone, sometimes creating whirlwinds that shattered against the massive stone buildings. They had been able to hear and catch glimpses of the groups to the left and right of them for the first part of the day, but for a while now they had been alone.

"And you know, if we hadn't run into him, we'd have gone outside the wall," Rastim continued. "Maybe even outside the barrier since it would have been safer to look for him from the other side, with him trapped inside it and unable to get to us. We'd have run right into those things."

"So?" Rian prodded, though he knew what Rastim meant.

"So it was lucky. And odd."

Damned odd, Rian thought, but there were no answers. He craned his neck to look up at the buildings around them. The one right above them had a bridge coming out of its dome, stretching across the plaza to a tall thin pillar. "Here's another one with a bridge." He turned and waved to the men across the square, who started back toward them.

Rastim sighed and looked back again at the heart tower of the Marai, just visible between the two buildings behind them, but made no other comment. Rian had been looking for a building with a bridge or balcony that they could climb up to and get a better perspective on the city but all those they had found so far had been unreachable.

As the others reached them, Rian stepped back, looking up again at the dark windows high overhead. "Come on, let's try to find the way in."

"Perhaps there isn't one," Rastim suggested hopefully.

Rian started away, following the curve of the wall. "Then in that case I hope you like to climb." He gestured up to the windows, a good fifty or sixty feet up the side. "What did you think I brought the rope for?"

"That was a joke, wasn't it? I ask, you know, because I wasn't aware it was possible for a Sitanese to have a sense of humor."

A few of the men hid smiles, which Rian ignored. Rastim was keeping everyone's spirits up, and though Rian hated to admit it, the Ariaden's comments were funny. They started to work their way around the building and found the doorway on the far side. It was square and large enough for a river cargo crane. All the doorways had been large; it made Rian wonder if what had lived here had been people after all.

The interior was dark and they had to pause and light the lamp before going any further. As the temple servant who carried it held it up, they saw that this chamber was filled with rubble too, but something had made it all fall to one side of the structure, so it made a rough ramp against one wall. Rian squinted, trying to see if the opening to the bridge was reachable. He could see it wasn't blocked by debris; there was a faint daylight glow coming through it.

"What did that?" one of the men asked, puzzled by the odd pattern of the debris. "The rest of the floor is clean, as if it's been swept."

Rian took the lamp and lifted it, seeing the man was right. He shook his head. More mysteries. He handed the lamp back and said, "Wait here. I'm going to see if I can get up to that bridge."

The Koshan monk, whose name was Aren, stepped forward. "I'll go also."

"Me, too," Rastim said firmly.

Rian didn't argue with him. Rastim had a need to prove his bravery, and Rian was willing to let the Ariaden do it.

They started to climb, Rastim scrambling agilely along. Occasionally their progress dislodged rocks or fragments that rolled down on the men watching below. Rian could hear them cursing as they dodged out of the way. About halfway up, he could feel a strong breeze from the bridge opening.

They reached the top of the pile and Rian could see the square door was just within reach. It was nothing more than a short tunnel through the wall of the building, then it opened up into the bridge.

As the tallest, it was easy for Rian to reach the opening, haul himself up, then help the monk, who turned back to give Rastim a hand. Rian went forward cautiously to the end of the tunnel and paused at the mouth.

The bridge was a slab of stone about twenty feet wide with a low balustrade, only a foot or so high. It stretched out to the pillar, but strangely there didn't appear to be a door on the other end. The view was just as incredible as Rian expected, and the city now lay before them.

He walked out on the bridge, mindful of the gusty wind, but it didn't feel strong enough to knock him off. The monk and Rastim followed carefully. Rian stopped at about the middle.

From this angle he could see round buildings, each like a giant bowl of dark grey pottery set bottom-up, stood in a line on the outskirts as if forming a boundary to the rest of the city. *Fortresses?* he thought, trying to puzzle it out. He supposed archers could fire on approaching troops through the small windows if they had to, but it wasn't practical. Maybe that was just the way these people put their cities together. Maybe the Kushorit cities with their straight lines and canals and avenues would appear just as baffling to them. *If those cities were still there,* Rian reminded himself. *Bastards.*

The monk Aren grabbed his arm suddenly and pointed. "There."

Rian looked. The man was pointing at the domed building with the horn-shaped spires. There was a broad avenue leading away from it toward the west, the only approach to it Rian could see. He started to ask the monk if he thought the structure was some sort of temple, then he realized what the man was actually pointing at. There were openings high in the dome and out of one of them poured something that looked like a distortion in the air.

"Those things, the clouds that came to the temple last night." The monk spoke so softly Rian could barely hear him over the wind.

And they were coming this way. "Down," he snapped.

Rastim yelped and dropped like a rock, covering his head. Rian and the monk crouched down behind the low balustrade. A sound rose above the wind, a low howling tone. It grew louder and Rian and the monk exchanged a grimace. The creatures were flying right toward them.

Rian risked a look. "Another attack. Do you see it, Maskelle?" The blurring in the air grew rapidly larger as it drew closer. Heart pounding, Rian pressed himself against the low wall.

"She sees it. Surely she sees it," Rastim muttered. He wet his lips nervously, looking around as if he hoped to see a convenient shelter spring up somewhere. "What do we do?"

"Don't move," the monk advised fervently.

The high thin howl that was unpleasantly familiar from last night grew louder, but it was high overhead. Then the tone changed and it faded into the distance toward the Marai. "Maskelle, did you see it?" he asked again.

I saw, her voice said in his ear. *I have to help the others now. I won't be with you for a while.*

"All right." Rian got to his feet, brushing his dusty hands off on his dustier pants.

"She heard you?" Rastim asked cautiously, still huddling by the balustrade.

"Yes. She said she wouldn't be watching us while she deals with the attack. Didn't you hear her?" Sometimes Rastim had been able to hear Maskelle's spirit voice, sometimes not. It seemed to unnerve the Ariaden, and it might be that he was somehow unintentionally blocking it.

"Not that time." Rastim got to his feet, looking nervously toward the Marai. "The barrier will hold, won't it?"

"It will hold," the monk said firmly.

"If it doesn't . . ." Rastim was still staring bleakly at the temple.

"Rastim . . ." Rian threw his arms in the air in exasperation.

"If it doesn't hold, we're all dead. Is that what you wanted to hear?"

"Sorry, sorry." The Ariaden shook himself briskly and shouldered his pack. "Being dramatic, force of habit. Let's go."

"Thank you." Rian started away. If they came all this way and found nothing, then returned to the Marai to find nothing . . . At least now they had a goal.

They climbed back down, the loose stone making it far more awkward than the trip up. Once there, he told the others briefly what they had seen.

"Well?" Rian asked when he had finished. "We could go back and report to the others, or push on and look over that place ourselves. We're so far out that if we return to the temple first, we wouldn't be able to get back out here before dark."

"Another day here," one of them muttered.

Rian felt the same way. "So we push on?"

There were general nods, and no grumbling or outright fear, though Rian supposed they were all as terrified as he was.

"What's the worst that could happen?" Rastim declared as they made their way to the door. "They could turn us into those stone creatures we saw last night."

"They looked as much like people as they looked like monkeys," Rian objected. "That doesn't count." The game—which they had been playing off and on through the day—was "most horrible thing that can happen." Rian had thought he was good at anticipating the worst, but Rastim was winning hands down. He hoped the others in their group were enjoying his defeat. He said, "All right, all right, I give up. Why don't you tell us a play?"

Rastim took the victory in good part, launching into the plot of an elaborate kiradi play about warring noble families. Rian found himself relieved that Rastim had made the decision to come along; it would have been easy to go mad out here with nothing to think about but the consequences of failure. *Maybe that's what happened to the people who built this place.* They had built their palaces and stripped the world bare with the effort of it, then gone mad in the solitude, leaving only demons behind them. A nice idea, but it didn't explain Marada, or how they had built the Second Wheel.

"Damn it," Maskelle whispered. She didn't need the distraction.

"Maskelle?" Killia's voice invaded her trance. "We found him."

She opened her eyes and stood, shaking out her robes. The Ariaden and Karuda were standing just inside the curtain. Maskelle said, "The flying things are coming back. We'll have to hurry." She had sent Killia and the other Ariaden to find Karuda, who had been directing the search for Gisar and seeing to the temple's defenses.

Karuda stared at her. "Another attack?" he asked sharply.

"I'll let you deal with them in a moment. I only need you to tell me one thing." She pushed past them out into the gallery, telling Killia, "Warn the Temple Master there's an attack coming."

As she hurried away, Maskelle started across the court to the central tower. Karuda followed, his expression baffled. "That wasn't why you summoned me?"

"No. I need to ask you something." She led him under the arch into the central tower, and Karuda, suddenly realizing she was leading him to the inner chamber, halted abruptly in the foyer.

Maskelle turned impatiently and he gestured at the carvings on the wall. "Are you sure—"

"Come on," she snapped.

Just inside Vigar waited. The other Voices were arrayed around the Wheel of the Infinite in meditation positions, their concentration and the soft low murmur of their chant forming a second barrier around the Wheel. The final repair had been completed on the Rite late last night, and since then it waited only for the destruction of their enemies' Wheel before it could be initiated.

Maskelle met Vigar's skeptical gaze as she stepped aside and motioned for Karuda to enter the chamber. She had had only a few moments to tell Vigar her theory, impatient as she was to get back to Rian and Rastim. Vigar had thought she was wrong. *Not the first time for that,* she thought.

Karuda stopped again, this time struck by the effect that the Wheel had even on those not well attuned to the Infinite. Maskelle looked closely at him and what she saw on his face made her heart clench. The Wheel of the Infinite wasn't kept deliberately concealed, but its fragility meant that few besides the Voices and the others attached to the Marai ever saw it.

Karuda's expression in the candlelight was more startled than awed.

Certain she was right, Maskelle took his arm and drew him nearer, past Vigar, almost to the edge of the invisible barrier formed by the other Voices. She remembered Rian saying that they should discover who had chosen that house for Marada, so advantageously placed near the canal that formed the direct line between the Baran Dir and the Marai. She had assumed it had been Raith. One wrong assumption which had led to disaster. "Have you ever seen the like of this before?" she asked.

Karuda nodded and Vigar hissed under his breath in shock and deep anger. His eyes met Maskelle's and she knew the chief Voice was her ally in this, whatever came next. Maskelle looked at Karuda again and asked quietly, "Where?"

The sky was starting to take on that tinge of dark purple that had marked the arrival of dusk yesterday, when they reached the avenue that led up to the horned building. Rian leaned around the corner for a cautious look. It was about as wide as one of the Kushorit processional avenues, and was lined with tall imposing structures with many balconies and galleries on their upper levels.

There was a huge doorway in the bottom of the horned building, large enough for an animate manifestation of one of the giant Kushorit statues to comfortably stroll through, but Rian didn't want to approach it so directly. They would have to work their way down behind this row of structures and come at it from a side or back entrance.

It wasn't that far from the Marai, so they wouldn't have a long trip back. He glanced around at the others. Rastim looked weary and a little white around the eyes and the others appeared exhausted as well. Rian was too accustomed to long days of travel or hunting to be very tired, but walking on the unyielding stone for so long was making his feet hurt.

He moved back to where the others waited and motioned them to follow. They made their way down behind the row and finally to a round structure that flanked the horned building. The wind whipped around the curving wall, blowing dust into Rian's eyes and tearing at his hair. Rian winced away and Rastim coughed and scrubbed at his face with his sleeve.

As they cleared the wall, Rian saw the side of the horned building was badly damaged. There was a great crack in the dark stone that had torn an opening at street level. It looked as if it had been struck by lightning, or a siege engine.

The opening was almost choked with rubble, but there was just enough room for them to scramble through. Rian paused as his eyes adapted to the dark, then he froze, a cold prickle creeping up his spine.

At the far end of the ruined chamber was a doorway into a corridor, apparently unharmed by whatever had collapsed this side of the building. Along the wall were a series of bowl-shaped lamps with flames burning in their center. "I think we found the right place," someone muttered from behind him.

There was a general murmur of agreement. "I want a look down that corridor," Rian said. "Then we'll take the word back to the others."

"Good," Rastim said under his breath.

They started to work their way across the ruined chamber. A low, mournful howl echoed from somewhere. It sounded like wind moaning through a cavern, but here there was no telling. *I hope it's the wind,* Rian thought, taking a deep breath.

"I'm going to write a play about this," Rastim declared, keeping his voice low.

From his tone Rian could tell he had heard the sound, too. But he only said, "Good for you. Are you going to include the part where you almost wet yourself when the flying creatures went by overhead?"

Rastim snorted. "What do you mean 'almost'?"

Rian bit his lip to keep from laughing. They were keeping their voices low from instinct; he didn't think anything would be able to hear them over the hiss of the dust against the stone.

"Is she back yet?" Rastim asked, serious now. "I haven't heard her."

"I haven't either," Rian admitted. He didn't know who he was more worried about, them or Maskelle and the others back at the temple.

"I hope it's nothing . . ." Rastim began, then shrugged. "I suppose we'll find out later. It can't be too important to us right now."

Then somewhere across the chamber Rian heard the distinct sound of a foot knocking against a loose stone.

One of the flying things wouldn't make noise.

Rastim bounced agitatedly and Rian waved him and the others back behind a pile of rubble. The Ariaden managed to creep back behind it quietly enough and Rian started to advance cautiously toward the sound.

Rian heard that whisper again, a faint scrape against the gritty stone, and this time he could tell where it was coming from. Whatever it was, it was waiting for them to come through that next doorway.

The other men were watching him alertly from the cover of the pile of rubble. Rian motioned for them to stay where they were. He looked at Rastim to make sure the Ariaden was paying attention, then gestured for him to head across the room, toward the outer door.

Rastim nodded sharply then stood and moved briskly toward the door. Their opponent took the bait as soon as the Ariaden broke cover, stepping into the doorway and levelling a crossbow at Rastim. *It's a man,* Rian had time to realize, *just like us.* He threw himself forward and the man sensed him at the last instant, swinging the heavy wooden weapon around to strike Rian in the shoulder.

They hit the ground and Rian tore the bow away, slamming his opponent in the head with the stock. Rastim was bouncing around them, bori club upraised, shouting, "Get him, get him!"

Rian rolled off the man and came to his feet, handing Rastim the crossbow as the Ariaden scrambled back out of the way. When the man staggered to his feet, he was facing Rian's siri. He stared at them, panting. He looked Kushorit, even as Marada had, and he was dressed in trousers, an open vest and sandals that wouldn't have gotten a second glance on any street in Duvalpore.

"Who are you?" Rastim demanded. As the others joined them, Aren the monk gaped in surprise. "That's Vanthi. He's with Chancellor Mirak's party."

The man grimaced in contempt and looked away.

"He's one of them," Rian said. In Mirak's party. Oh, he had a bad feeling about this. "Taken over by Marada, like her servants."

That name got his attention. The man glared at them, eyes narrowed. "You killed her, but your tricks won't stop us," he said, his voice low and grating.

"We've got more tricks in our bag than we know what to do with," Rastim said archly, "so you just better talk while you can."

Whatever that meant, Rian thought. "Tell us where the Wheel is. It's nearby, or you wouldn't have bothered to try to stop us."

A sudden howl of wind nearly burst their eardrums and the others ducked and scattered. The man used the instant of distraction and charged them. He bowled Rian over, but Rian threw him off and rolled away, coming to his feet again. Ducking a wild blow, he stabbed the man in the stomach, freeing the weapon with a jerk that turned the thrust into a disemboweling stroke. He didn't bother to watch the man fall, his attention caught by the wind rushing into the chamber, its force almost enough to knock him off his feet. The whirlwinds must be returning. They couldn't get out the way they had come in. Further into the building was their only chance.

Rastim had already come to that conclusion and was pulling at his arm. They bolted back through the archway and into a high-ceilinged hall. Running down it, they could see other corridors leading off. They came to an intersection of another, larger hall and Rian saw fading daylight at the end of it. "That way." He pointed and there were cries of relief from the others. They started toward it when Rastim grabbed Rian's arm.

"Look, that light," the Ariaden said, wondering. "That must be something."

Rian looked at the opposite end of the corridor where Rastim was pointing. There was a strange murky light, not flickering like firelight at all. Whirlwinds or not, Rian realized, they had to investigate it.

Rastim glanced back, then yelled something incoherent, pointed back down the corridor, eyes wide.

Rian turned. A miniature whirlwind was coming down the corridor toward them. It was grey-white with dust and a strange white mist, and this close he could hear the pebbles and other debris trapped within it scraping and striking the walls. "Run!" he shouted to the others just as it surged forward, cutting him and Rastim off from the branch corridor.

Rian turned to run down the other passage after Rastim, but the thing was too fast, and before he reached the archway he felt a freezing cold dampness on the back of his neck. A force struck him from behind, shoving him forward into the wall with a stunning impact. He remembered sliding down to the corridor floor, then nothing.

16

Maskelle stood in the doorway, watching the Chancellor. Mirak had made his camp in the second level of the east corner tower, in a large square room with an offering block in the center. The carving in this room represented the watery chaos of creation; the walls were covered with waves, churning waters, and every kind of sea creature. Monsters that were part crocodile and part bird loomed out of the corners. Mirak faced the window that looked out over the second outer court. He was staring into darkness, motionless, his face deeply shadowed by the single lamp.

He turned suddenly and saw her, his face going still and grim. "What are you doing here?"

"I came to let you know how the search was progressing."

"Ah." His voice sounded reassured, but the suspicion in his eyes didn't alter. "Have they found anything?"

"No. But, you already know that." She stepped further into the room. Raith had made few provisions for his comfort in his makeshift quarters, but Mirak had done nothing. The room was bare, without even a pallet or a brazier. The only luxury was a lamp set atop the jutting head of a water monster.

"What do you mean?"

"You were Marada's patron, not the Throne." She met his eyes, but his expression of wary inquiry didn't change.

He said only, "Who told you that?"

"Raith himself." She shook her head slowly, smiling. "The Throne is isolated from all but his closest companions and advisors, especially around this time of year, with so many rituals to attend, so much prepatory fasting and vigils. If he heard the rumors that the noblewoman from the Garekind Islands had become his new favorite, he wouldn't have cared anyway. There are always rumors."

Mirak stepped toward her. "Speculation."

"Marada had the woman from the village in Iutara to make death magic for her, and you knew the Celestial One had sent for me, and where I was likely to stop on the Great Road."

"You're under a curse. Death magic and dark spirits follow you everywhere." He stopped a bare pace away from her.

She could smell his sweat. His eyes were dark and opaque. She felt the tension gather in her muscles, her throat tighten with growing anger. "You weren't in the Marai when the change occurred, you were on the causeway. Rian and Karuda were closer to the temple than you, and they were both hurt when the wave knocked them against the wall. But when everyone assembled in the central court, there you were, uninjured. Last night, when Marada's people sent their creatures to attack, you said, 'Take human shape.' How do you know what they look like?"

"None of that means anything."

"And then Karuda saw the second Wheel."

Mirak's expression didn't change.

"Festival Eve, when you didn't give the banquet that you always give for the Equinox. He went to your palace quarters because he thought you should be there when we questioned Marada's servants. He didn't realize that you already knew all there was to know about them." Karuda had only caught a glimpse of the Wheel through a doorway, but it had been enough. In all the confusion that Marada's failure and the death of the body she had possessed must have caused, Mirak hadn't realized the noble had seen the Wheel at all, which was undoubtedly the only reason Karuda was still alive. It also explained how the creature that had tried to attack Maskelle in the palace had gotten in, and where Marada's other companions had hidden.

Mirak's eyes changed, the dark opacity giving way to something raw and powerful. Something alien, like Marada. His lips moved in a slight smile, and he said, "You shouldn't have come alone."

He grabbed her throat with snakelike quickness, his grip crushing. Maskelle didn't break eye contact, though she felt the last gasp of air leave her lungs and the pressure on her throat was terrifying. She wrapped her hand around his wrist and reached for the Marai's distant heartbeat. Unexpected strength surged up from it, laced with hot rage and predatory greed. It filled the room like oil poured into a bowl and the lamp flickered, the light taking on an unnatural cast. It was a spirit presence so strong that she felt its breath on the back of her neck. For an instant she thought it was something as alien as the thing that had taken Mirak's soul, something from this dying world, but it was in the bones of the Marai itself. The temple had no defense against it because it was part of it.

Her hand tightened on Mirak's wrist and he released her, stumbling backward, catching himself awkwardly on the offering stone. Maskelle gasped a breath, managing to stay on her feet only because that power, familiar as her own, willed it.

"I'm never alone," she said hoarsely, and heard the Adversary in her voice.

Mirak looked up at her, and she saw in his eyes that he wasn't trapped, like Veran and the unfortunate villagers had been. He wasn't there anymore at all. "You used us!" he spat. "For what? Why? You destroyed your own world."

Maskelle stared at him, horror growing in the pit of her stomach. He wasn't talking to her. He was talking to the Adversary.

She was laughing at Mirak without conscious volition. The Adversary had never been much for chat with its prey.

"Whatever it is, you can't succeed. If you try to stop us again, we'll destroy you," Mirak said desperately.

The Adversary didn't understand threats; it either killed cleanly or it allowed the prey to live, there was nothing in between. She heard herself say, "You'll be dead."

Mirak drew a shaking hand across his mouth; the thing inside him had been pretending to be human so long, the gestures came naturally to it. *How long?* Maskelle wondered. How long had Mirak been dead? Since Marada had come to Duvalpore and been introduced at Court? Or before, and it was actually the knowledge torn from Mirak's unwilling mind that had allowed her to pose as a noblewoman from Garekind. He said, "Is it another bargain? What do you want?" He tried another smile, albeit a desperate one. "You have us at a disadvantage. Ask for anything you want."

He said a "bargain," Maskelle thought. The shock of it was almost too much. *They made a bargain with the Adversary.*

"I don't need you to give me what I want," the Adversary said through her voice.

Mirak's face worked, from rage to terror and back again. He surged to his feet, coming at her, just as something dropped through the window behind him.

Maskelle flung herself back against the wall. It was Gisar, grown larger and more horrible, its mottled wooden flesh stretched to cover its new size. Mirak whirled around, faster than a man his age should be capable of, but Gisar was faster still. It ducked a wild blow and seized Mirak's head, snapping his neck.

It stepped back and let the body drop. *A cat with a vermin,* Maskelle thought, watching it. A born predator, killing with stark efficiency and not a little glee at its own prowess.

Mirak twitched, blood bubbling up past his lips, and impossibly managed to wrench his head around to look up at Gisar. "Destroy . . . you . . ." it gasped.

"Try," Gisar said in its hollow wooden voice. It didn't laugh. Dead prey was dull.

Mirak went limp. Gisar stood where it was, then suddenly wooden pieces were hitting the stone floor, the head, the arms and legs, the metal wires that held it together. It was ordinary painted wood, from a puppet only a few feet in height. Gisar as he had been, before the curse and the demon.

Something else stood in its place. It looked like Rian, but Maskelle knew the Adversary by its eyes. In her voice, hoarse but her own once again, she said, "You brought us here." It was too raw a truth to understand. "You did this."

"To destroy our enemy."

It sounded pleased with itself. Maskelle shook her head, baffled and aghast. Had it thought it was doing the right thing? "You're not supposed to think. You're supposed to show the way."

"This is the way."

She couldn't fathom it. "You can't make those decisions for us. You're supposed to advise me and—"

"You weren't there," it shouted at her, suddenly furious. "Why did you leave?"

She stared at it, as it stood there quivering with rage. She said slowly, "You sent me away. I was cursed, because of the vision. The false vision. That you gave me." *That you gave me. Ancestors, no wonder you wouldn't . . . couldn't talk to me.* She had heard the whisper of their Voices, but never clearly. Had they tried to warn her? Had the Adversary prevented them, making sure she only knew what it wanted her to know?

It blinked, the confusion crossing its face all too human. "When was this?"

"When? You're not supposed to understand time." Her voice broke. It was too much to take in. The Adversary was insane. "What happened to you?"

"I had to change. I have to change." It looked down at

Gisar's pieces and nudged the wooden limbs with a boot. It frowned, biting its lip. "That didn't work out like it was supposed to."

"What happened to you?" she repeated.

It showed her. They knew the Adversary was not like the other Ancestors. It hadn't been born, lived, and died as a human before it melded with the Infinite. It was part of the world, possibly older than the world, an integral part of it.

"All of it," it said, looking at her with familiar eyes. "Including Sakkara and the Aspian Straits."

Her breath caught. She had told Rian the old story the day they arrived in the city, about the decision by the Voices to prevent the invasion from Sakkara by closing the Aspian Straits. "They changed the world, and it changed you," she said.

It nodded, looking down at Gisar again. "Pieces."

Maskelle turned away, leaned unsteadily against the wall. "Don't panic, not yet," she muttered.

"All right," it agreed helpfully.

"I was talking to myself." *I am not going to scream.* She looked back at it, trying to understand. "You bargained with them, told them you'd give them our world, helped them build the second Wheel. Why?"

"I needed to be here." It looked around and she knew it was seeing through the walls of the temple, out at the city. "There's something I have to do here."

It said "I." Had she ever heard it call itself "I" before?

"I need to kill them," it added.

It wasn't the concept she found horrifying, but the fact that it was the Adversary advocating it. "They're our enemies, but they're still people. You trapped them into this."

"I need to kill them." The predator again, nothing else.

"They are people," she insisted desperately.

It paced toward her, braced one hand on the wall near her

head, and leaned close. She could feel the anger radiating from it like heat. It said deliberately, "They aren't my people."

Maskelle held its eyes, though it was an effort. "The *Book of the Adversary* says 'Those who are pleased to hurt living beings are to be punished without mercy,' " she quoted.

An expression flickered across its face, too quick to read. It said, "We remember." It stepped back from her slowly, then turned and walked away through the outer wall.

Maskelle stood there, feeling cold, staring at the place where it had vanished. Karuda burst in suddenly, stopping abruptly when he saw Mirak's body. The Temple Master pushed in behind him and came to take her arm.

Karuda looked at her, aghast. "We couldn't get in. There was a wall, invisible—"

"It was the Adversary," the Temple Master said quietly. He shook his head and looked away. "It was the first time I'd ever felt it."

Maskelle nodded. "It was in Gisar." She gripped his arm and straightened up, taking a deep breath. "Did the search parties come back yet?"

Karuda shook himself slightly, looked at Mirak again. "All but one. Rian's."

Maskelle swore and ran her hands through her hair. *Rian found it. I knew he would. Damn it!* "Keep everyone inside the Marai." She looked at the Temple Master. "Tell Vigar to give me until dark, then initiate the Rite. I'll destroy the second Wheel."

"You know where it is?" Karuda stared at her. "How could you?"

She nodded. "You told me." At his blank expression she explained, "This is still our world. The second Wheel was in Mirak's quarters at the palace. That's straight out the south gate of the Marai to the Baran Dir, then west. It's still there."

Someone called out from down in the court. Maskelle stepped back out from the gallery and saw it was the nun Tiar. She waved her arms excitedly and called again, "Revered, the Celestial One is waking! He lives!"

Maskelle pushed past a startled Karuda and the Temple Master and ran for the stairs. When she reached the room where the Celestial One had lain so quietly, she found most of the nuns dancing about in joy outside. She pulled the curtain aside and saw Mali kneeling by the old man, bathing his face with a cloth. Maskelle could see from here that he was breathing.

She knelt beside him, thankful for this one thing. The old man's face was sallow and pinched, but he was alive.

"Does this have something to do with . . . what happened up there?" the Temple Master asked her. He had followed her into the room, though Karuda had stayed outside.

She nodded. "Oh, yes." *The Adversary doesn't need me to stay at the temple anymore, so it releases the Celestial One. It thinks its plans are too far advanced for me to stop.* She buried her face in her hands, hoping the Temple Master would mistake it for a gesture of profound relief at the Celestial One's return.

Karuda argued, but Maskelle insisted, and told him that the Adversary would not let anything happen to her. She didn't know if that was still true or not. There was nothing in the Koshan wisdom to say what happened when a spirit went mad. But she couldn't afford to bring anyone with her. Anyone outside the boundary of the Marai risked being left behind when their Rite was initiated. If the Adversary allowed them to initiate it at all.

She set out from the south gate of the Marai, carrying nothing but her staff. Firac and Killia were the only ones to see her off, as all the Koshans were scrambling to prepare for the Rite. She didn't look back at their anxious faces as she wove her way through the protective barriers; she knew they were afraid for Rastim.

Maskelle was afraid for all of them.

The velvet purples and greys of the clouds were growing darker as she walked over the dusty stone in the shadows of the ruined city. She hoped she had judged the time right. The buildings rose high around her, blotting out much of the sky. The yawning entrances to some were dark, but there were others she could just catch glimpses of from between the dark grey mottled walls, lit by the dancing red-and-yellow light of those eternally burning fires. The dry air was unpleasantly sharp with the tang of smoke. She had left the Temple Master to explain to Raith about Mirak; she wasn't sure how he would take it. The truth was that the Adversary had killed a foreign creature from this world. Mirak himself had likely been dead for months.

The path she followed wasn't a straight one. The line between the Marai and where the Baran Dir had stood was occasionally blocked by buildings, some of very odd shapes indeed. She circled around one of the large bowl-shaped ones to find a tight group of five large circular pillars, stretching high up into the sky, all connected by open bridges, with what looked like balconies fringing the tops. *It must have been a beautiful city once, strange and wonderful instead of strange and dead.* They must have had art and philosophy and religion; how they had come to this, she couldn't understand.

During the meditation rings, Koshans had to walk Kushor-At and Kushor-An's power pathways by counting paces. Not being able to follow a straight line made it awkward, but Maskelle only had to find the approximate location of the Baran Dir, not its exact boundary. She reached what she was sure was the right place, now occupied by a bowl-shaped depression in the stone lined with rows of stone benches or steps that must have once been a theater or some sort of assembly area, and turned west.

From this angle Maskelle could see the top of a structure larger than the others, a dome with spires to either side of it. If she was judging the distance correctly, it was standing approximately where the Celestial Home should be. There were fires lit in the tops of those needlelike towers that glowed in the dusk, and she could see a haze of light around the dome, as though there were more fires burning below. She walked between the two low square buildings that blocked the rest of her view, and found herself standing at the top of a long avenue that led to the base of the dome. There were lit windows, bands of them, around the dome, and an open archway in the bottom that glowed from within. The building seemed to dominate this whole section of the city. Rian's group had gone to the south. They would have found this place. *Well, that answers that question,* she thought.

Someone was lightly slapping his face. It didn't do anything for his headache. Without opening his eyes, Rian swung a fist by instinct, felt a connect and heard a yelp. The yelp sounded a lot like Rastim.

Holding his aching head, Rian managed to sit up. Rastim was sprawled a few feet away, rubbing his jaw and glaring. The Ariaden muttered, "Well, thank you very much."

Rian lifted his head. They were outside, on a stone surface set about a Kushorit house's height off the ground. Looming over them was one of the domed buildings from the city. But the stone was lighter in color and the windows were square and undamaged. He stared around, knowing it was impossible. The sky overhead was blue, cloudless. The air felt cool and dry. He had lost his siri, though he didn't suppose it would do him any good here. "How did . . ."

"We're not actually here," Rastim said nervously. He looked around and took a deep breath. "When we fell, we were in a large chamber, with the floor all rubble, and a sort of cloudy mist hanging in the air. Then this started to happen."

"It's an illusion." Rian rubbed his eyes. This actually made him feel a little better. At least he knew he wasn't crazy. "Did you keep track of which direction the door was in?"

"Ah, no." Rastim sighed and wiped dirt and sweat off his brow. "I thought I was, then things seemed to turn around and—" He shrugged, looking weary. "I'm not much use."

Rian shook his head, instantly regretting it when a wave of nausea almost overcame him. He pressed his hands against his eyes until it subsided, then said, "No, they must have done that on purpose, to confuse you."

"They." Rastim looked around again, his expression uneasy. "They're here, aren't they? All around us."

Rian nodded. "They must be." He shifted to the edge to look down. He thought he could manage the drop without a broken leg, but he wasn't sure Rastim could. "Wait, you said when you first woke up we were in a room surrounded by rubble?" He tapped the stone of the platform. "Was this here?"

"No, we were on the floor, such as it was." Rastim's worried expression turned thoughtful. "You mean, you think we can just walk out?"

Rian looked down again. He had heard about illusions that killed you anyway, even if they weren't real, but he didn't think they had any choice. "If we—"

Rastim drew a startled breath, pointing at the other side of the platform. The air was thickening there, colors growing out of nothing, swirling into an almost familiar pattern. Rian passed a hand over his eyes, but the distortion in the air didn't vanish. "Uh-oh," he muttered.

Rastim scrambled hastily back, moving as close to the edge as he dared. "It's one of them," he whispered. "Like those giant whirlwinds."

Rian warily watched the thing. "I don't think so." The colors were the colors of the Wheel of the Infinite, brilliant and alive and constantly shifting. That was what was familiar; it made no sense at all, but his eyes insisted he saw the Wheel, though he couldn't pick out any individual shapes or symbols in the growing mass. Then the colors swirled into a pattern that resembled a face. The form coalesced suddenly and Rian swore and looked away, blinking hard. Rastim clapped a hand over his eyes.

Rian tried to make himself look at it, but he couldn't. Impossibly, he knew what this thing was. It was the original of the demon faces carved above Kushorit doorways, the thing that lived in the killing birds that were one of its symbols.

The words *Don't leave this place* hung in the air, but Rian knew he didn't hear them spoken aloud.

"It talked," Rastim whispered.

"I know," Rian said through gritted teeth. "I think it's the Adversary."

Images came then: the platform and death just beyond. The illusion was to confuse, to make them leave this protected spot, to expose them to the danger all around.

"That's good, isn't it?" Rastim asked hopefully. When Rian didn't answer, he persisted, "It's warning us. That means it's here to help us, doesn't it?"

Help us, or keep us alive long enough to be bait in a trap. Rian wasn't sure what had sparked that thought, but he knew it was his own, and not something from the creature confronting them. What was it doing here anyway, in the middle of their enemies? "Are you evil?" Rian asked it. Rastim gasped and elbowed him and Rian motioned him to be silent.

There was a hesitation, long enough for Rian to wish he hadn't asked the question and Rastim to fidget nervously. Then it said, *No.*

Why is that not reassuring? Rian said carefully, "Now, when you have to wait and think about it, that worries me."

Rian felt it drift closer, knew it was examining him thoughtfully, and resisted the sudden urge to throw himself off the platform. *I'm everything,* it said. *If evil is part of everything, I'm evil too. Like that answer better?*

It was gone, winked out like a candle.

Rian let out a breath and ran a hand through his hair.

Rastim sighed and stared at him accusingly. "If it comes back, do you think you can manage not to cross-question it?"

"If it comes back, I think what I do is going to be the least of our problems," Rian told him.

17

Maskelle was a little out of breath by the time she drew near the strange building. She had stayed close to the shadows at the edges of the avenue, but there didn't seem to be any circumspect way to approach the temple or palace or whatever the place was. *Just walk up to the front gate,* Maskelle thought ruefully, *it's always worked before.* She could hear what sounded like wind howling wildly in the distance, strongly reminiscent of the air spirit creatures who had attacked them. *It's probably full of the things.*

She paused behind a pillar at the edge of the avenue, near enough to see just inside the doorway. It looked like a large hallway, lit by bowl-shaped lamps set into the walls, going back toward a more brightly lit area.

"I told you whatever happened to stay in the Marai."

Maskelle flung herself back against the pillar, swinging her staff at the figure that had suddenly appeared beside her. The staff passed right through it.

She looked carefully at its face and realized it was her first husband, Ilian, dead years ago from foolishly trusting her. She took a calming breath, and said to the Adversary, "You told me a lot of things, and I'd be a damned fool to listen to you."

Ilian had only been in his second decade when he died. His face was handsome, free of the lines that trouble and character usually wrote, and his build was stocky and well muscled. He was dressed in a red funeral robe. She would have known that this was not him, even if the staff hadn't passed through him, because this creature had a determined expression and the temerity to argue with her. It said, "You have to listen to me, I'm the Adversary."

Maskelle sagged back against the pillar. *I trusted it, all this time, even after the false vision, I trusted it and thought the fault was in me.* She wasn't sure she could understand the enormity of what was happening. "Are you sure you're the Adversary?" she asked hopelessly. "You're not Gisar's demon, or an illusion, or one of these creatures in disguise?"

Its face was blank for a moment, then it shrugged and ran a hand through its hair in an achingly familiar gesture. Her memory of Ilian wasn't that accurate; this thing could take his form so completely only because it had been with her at the time, had known Ilian as well as she had. It said, "I could pretend to be, if that would help."

Maskelle covered her eyes for a moment. *Oh, Ancestors. For years I thought it was me that was mad.* "No, no, that's all right."

It watched her with Ilian's worried expression, his concern in its eyes. "It knows you, the thing that's waiting in there."

"From Marada, or from you?" She asked wearily.

"Both."

How can I do this when the Adversary is against me? Maskelle thought in despair, then told herself angrily, *It was always against you, you were always alone.* Suddenly she heard voices, human voices calling out in Kushorit. She pushed away from the pillar, looking toward the building. Seven men ran out of the great archway. Bearing down on them from behind was a whirl of light and dust: one of the wind creatures.

Maskelle ran forward, reaching for power from the Marai. The link was tenuous, the pathway that had connected the temple with this location torn asunder by the second Wheel. The creature reached the last man in the running group, tearing at him, sending him falling and flailing on the hard pavement.

It's going to get all of them, she thought desperately, feeling it push aside her strike at it. Then she felt the Adversary meld with her, felt it take her feeble attempt to disperse the thing and . . . She was raw power, raw will. It showed her how to look into the heart of the creature, to see past the screen of dust and wind and power into the living soul beneath. There was fear in that soul, more fear than anger and bloodlust. Desperation, a fierce desire to live. *This is one of them,* she thought, startled. The thing that was Marada, the one that had taken over Mirak. This was its true being. *No,* the Adversary told her, *it was like you, it had a form. They built this city, lived here in contentment when this world was new. But they took their search for power too far, and the world started to die.* Then the Adversary reached in to that fearful, desperate heart, and snuffed it out.

She blinked, lowered her staff as the whirlwind dispersed and dust rained down on her, all that was left of the dead creature. The Adversary was no longer standing next to her, though she knew it hadn't gone far.

The first of the fleeing men reached her. He was a young man, a temple servant, she saw as he stumbled to a halt. "Revered!" Breathing hard, he tried to explain, "We were tricked, it was a man sent by Mirak—"

"We know," Maskelle said. Two of the others helped the wounded man to his feet and they all gathered around her in a panting, anxious group. Even in the dim light she could tell they looked glad to see her. Rian and Rastim were both missing, she had seen that as soon as the men had reached the avenue. "Where are the others?"

The man looked around, as if noticing for the first time that the two men were missing. He pointed back to the temple. "They must be still inside."

Of course. The Adversary had said what was waiting there knew her. "Run back to the Marai, run fast. You have to be there by sunset." She nodded to the injured man. "Carry him."

The men stared at her. The first one protested, "But—"

"Go. The Adversary demands it. If you don't hurry, he'll appear and tell you so himself."

That did it. A few of them exchanged startled looks, then they gathered up their wounded companion and ran. Maskelle gave them time to reach the end of the avenue and get out of sight, then she started toward the temple again.

She felt a coldness pass over her skin as she crossed under the arch into the building, as if she had moved through some kind of boundary. The place smelled of dust and age and emptiness, like the rest of the city, but the air trapped here was dead and the scents were stronger. The lamps were high in the mottled stone walls, made of bowls of smooth pottery with the flicker of flame in their centers. What did they burn? There was no wood, no oil. It had to be power. *Their power is different,* she reminded herself. She had already seen enough evidence of that. Even the dark powers she had fought were all part of the Infinite, and used spirits and the force of water and earth, the forest, the mountains. What passed for power in this bare dying place would be like nothing she had encountered before.

She stopped abruptly, turning that thought over. *That's what they use. Death.* The dead boy they had used against her outside Duvalpore, that had been the first clue. They had forced the village shamaness to use the old spirit magic, the death magic, against Maskelle. They didn't use the Infinite. They moved through it, but perhaps they didn't truly see it or understand it. They used the force released by the death of their world and themselves to make their power.

I see, the Adversary said in her thoughts, an air of approval in the words. *Now we're getting somewhere.*

Stop saying "we," she told it angrily, continuing down the hall. It was only parroting phrases back at her again, with no notion of what they meant. *You're on the other side, remember?* There was another arch at the end, brightly lit. There were small branching corridors between here and there, but they were all dark and she passed them by. The sound of howling wind grew a little louder with each step.

She realized the Adversary was walking beside her again, and this time its form was Rian's. She said, "Don't take that form. I don't want to be confused about who to save and what to leave behind."

It shifted back to Ilian, apparently without taking offense. It said, *I convinced them to keep your friends as hostages against you and not kill them. Wasn't that good of me?*

"Oh, that's going to help a great deal." Before she could say more, she reached the end of the hallway and saw what lay beyond. It was a huge round chamber, perhaps taking up most of the space left in the great building. Hundreds of the lamps dotted the walls all the way up to the top of the dome. Most of the vast space was concealed by a great cloud of mist and air, drifting in a circular pattern. The damp breeze of it touched her face, almost gently, despite the howl and moan of what should be a powerful wind. The floor beneath the cloud was torn up and the ground below that dug out to form a shallow pit. Broken paving blocks, fragments of carving that must have decorated the walls once, bits of broken lamps, raw stone from the foundation were all jumbled into a spiral pattern as far as she could see through the mist. It was as if the wind had tried to draw every loose fragment in the city to this spot, and the constant motion had worn down the ground. *This is where it made the creatures it sent against us last night,* she thought. The creatures the Adversary had destroyed with an annoyed thought. *Are you more powerful now that you're mad?* she asked it.

Not powerful enough.

"You still speak in riddles," she said aloud.

You assume you're the only one who can hear me.

Maskelle knew she wasn't alone here. After the Adversary had shown her the trick of it, she could feel the minds of the beings who inhabited this place, all of them bundled together, the beings who had built this city and lived and refused to die here. They were combining what was left of their power and their resources. Huddling together for warmth? *You have both one opponent and many,* the Adversary had said. When they were like this, they were one.

She could feel their awareness roaming the dead city, touching the Marai again and being repelled by the barrier. They didn't know she was here yet. "Where is the second Wheel?" she asked softly, sure she already knew the answer.

In the center, the Adversary said.

Yes, I thought so. Maskelle looked into the cloud, then closed her eyes briefly, weary beyond measure.

I needed this. I had to get here, it said, somewhat reproachfully.

"You've said that before."

Then Maskelle felt the creatures' perception growing, felt them sense her presence and turn their attention toward her.

A voice, human enough to be understood, spoke out of the cloud. "You've brought her. You've decided to help us after all."

You taught me so much, the Adversary answered them, sounding sympathetic. *You taught me how to lie. I needed to know that. For that, I'll make your end quick.*

They didn't reply. *They're stunned to silence,* Maskelle thought. She started to laugh. "Your ally," she said to them. "Are you happy with it? Is this triumph everything you imagined?"

"Do not mock us." It didn't sound angry, as Mirak had at the end. Perhaps it wasn't human enough in this form.

"But it's so easy. The Adversary says you've destroyed at least two other worlds, using their own powers against them. It's your turn now. Try to accept it with a modicum of grace."

There was a pause, then it said, "The Adversary needs our help. It wants more power; it wants to destroy the other spirits and rule as your only god."

"Is that what it told you? It doesn't want more power. It doesn't need more power. The Ancestors can't do anything with it, or they would have done it before now. It wants to kill. It used to want justice, but now it just wants to kill." She laughed again, a bitter sound that startled even her. "It doesn't want your help; it wants to destroy you and it was willing to destroy us to do it."

The wind was rising, pulling at her braids. *You're making them angry,* the Adversary told her. Its pleasure echoed through the thought.

The wind hit her and she staggered and went to her knees, trying to brace herself with her staff and grabbing for purchase among the rough stones. For an instant she felt the Adversary within her and thought it meant to help her, but it did nothing. Struggling to stay upright, she managed to plant her staff and pull herself up, but the sharp edges of the rocks cut her hand and the blood made her hold slip. Her staff snapped in two suddenly and she fell backward into the cloud.

She tumbled over the rocks, the breath knocked out of her. The minds of the creatures tore at her as she fell past them, angry, desperate, terrified. Then she landed on flat stone.

She heard a startled shout. A familiar shout.

Suddenly Rian and Rastim were standing over her. Rian took her arm and pulled her to her feet. As soon as he touched her, she knew it was really him. She leaned against him, relieved, and he supported her with an arm around her waist. "What are you doing here?" he demanded.

"Where's here?" Maskelle said, baffled, looking around. She rubbed at her eyes, wondering if she had struck her head.

"I was hoping you knew," Rastim said nervously.

They appeared to be outside under a blue sky, standing on a stone platform perhaps thirty feet off the ground. Around them was the city when it was young. The sky was clear, the stone a lighter color, the buildings untouched by time. There were people moving among the buildings, at least she thought they were people. They were about the right size, but there was a distortion of the sight whenever you looked at them, so their forms were blurred.

"This is what their world used to be. They keep it preserved, inside themselves," Maskelle said slowly. Even with everything that had happened, it gave her cold prickles all over her skin. This was a dead memory, held in stasis until it had lost its reality.

"Why can't we see what they look like?" Rian asked her.

"Maybe they can't remember anymore. Maybe they don't want to remember." She shook herself slightly and looked around again, biting her lip thoughtfully. "We need to find the Wheel."

"You mean it's here?" Rian looked around, startled. "In this room?"

She nodded. "It has to be. Mirak was one of them. They built the second Wheel in his quarters on the palace grounds."

"We know about Mirak." Rian sounded annoyed.

"We found out the hard way," Rastim added. "But the Adversary said to stay here."

Rian threw him an impatient look. "Yes, that's the last thing it said before it couldn't decide if it was evil or not."

"That was because you talked to it." Rastim glared back at him. "I didn't think you should—"

Maskelle stared, then thumped Rian in the chest. "What about the Adversary?"

"It was here," Rian explained. "It acted a little funny."

Rastim snorted. "That's putting it mildly."

"That doesn't surprise me." Maskelle stepped away from him, keeping one hand on his arm but testing her balance. "This place is in the same spot where the Palace would be if it was still here, so the Wheel is here too. This illusion or memory is just keeping us from seeing it." Maskelle concentrated on what she had seen of the chamber, trying to make the veil lift. Fixing your mind on the reality was the simplest way to break an illusion, and the only way open to her now, cut off as she was from the temples. But this was no ordinary illusion.

Rian watched her uneasily. "When the Adversary was here, I had the feeling . . . We were bait in a trap. Was that what happened?"

"Unfortunately, yes. I'm just not sure if the trap was for me or—" She gestured at the blurred forms of the beings in the city. "Them."

"Isn't the Adversary on our side?" Rastim asked, nervously rubbing his hands off on his dusty shirt.

"It's on its own side now." Maskelle closed her eyes, pushing at the illusion around them. Nothing happened and she swore. She stepped further away from Rian and paced a few steps, thinking it over. "When you were thrown in here, did you see anything of what this place looked like before this appeared?" she asked them.

Rian shook his head. "I was out."

"It was . . ." Rastim hesitated. "There was a heavy mist, bluish-white." He looked at the ground and scuffed at one of the paving blocks with a boot. "And all this was jumbled up rocks. Then this place just gradually began to appear." He shivered.

Maskelle frowned. "That's what I saw. There has to be something else. If the Wheel is here, it has to be on a flat surface, like a platform or a dais."

"Does it matter if it's square or round?" Rian asked.

"No, as long as it's flat."

"If it was in Mirak's chambers . . ."

"Oh, wait." She ran her hands through her hair. "The surface under their Wheel should be the same as it was in our world."

"So somewhere in here there's a flat surface that looks like the floor in Mirak's quarters." Rian looked around at the illusion, eyes narrowed thoughtfully.

Maskelle closed her eyes. "It's been years. It was lacquered wood, large panels."

"What color?" Rian asked at the same time Rastim said, "Any carving?"

"Light yellow, carved with flowers. I think."

"What kind of flowers?" Rastim persisted.

"Just flowers." Maskelle glared. "Give me a moment, will you?" She tried to fix the image in her mind, but it had been too long. She had never been Mirak's friend and had only been to the extensive quarters he kept in the west building of the Celestial Home during the banquets he gave for the major festivals.

I remember, the Adversary whispered in her head.

Of course it could remember. It walked in and out of her memory at will. *As if I could trust you,* she told it bitterly.

The image that appeared before her eyes was of a light yellow lacquered wood floor, with colored inlay forming tiny round flowers on the edge of each square panel.

Why? Maskelle demanded angrily. *Why trap me down here and then help me?* She realized it was idiocy, asking reasons of a mad creature.

I'm not as mad as all that.

Of course you're mad. You let this . . . thing destroy you.

Funny, I don't feel destroyed. To do this we both had to be here, at their center.

"Maskelle?" someone said urgently.

She blinked and found herself facing Rian, who was watching her worriedly. "The Adversary," she said. How she was going to explain to him what the Adversary had done, she didn't know. She pushed it away from her now, fixing her mind on the image it had given her.

She split her awareness, the way she did when she used her spirit body. With her eyes she could see the relic of the living city, with her mind the image of what must really be here somewhere: the fragment of flooring with the second Wheel laid out on it, surrounded by the rocks and debris that filled the rest of the place. The Wheel would look like the fragment that had kept intruding on their Wheel, dark and dangerous, threatening storm and ruin. *Storm and ruin are the symbols of this world.*

The city in her eyes shimmered and began to dissolve.

The howling rose again, the angry wail of the creatures that had once been these people. Instead of distracting her, it firmed the picture in her mind and she remembered the dead smell of the chamber and the feel of the cold mist on her face. It was a battle of all their minds against hers, but she could feel she was winning. *If I was that strong, we wouldn't be having this problem in the first place.* The Adversary was helping her.

She could see two images now, the city and the chamber, cold and empty except for the debris and the Wheel. "Can you see it?" she asked.

"Not yet," Rian reported tensely. "But the picture is getting thin and flat. It doesn't look real anymore. I can see the walls of the chamber through some of the buildings."

She said, "Be ready. As soon as you see where it is, destroy it."

"Oh, that will make them happy," Rastim moaned. "What should we do to it?"

"It's only sand," Rian told him impatiently. "Just mess it up."

"Mess it up, all right."

The veil didn't fall, it ripped abruptly. Suddenly they could see the chamber, the swirl of living clouds around them, the rocky floor torn apart by the endless motion of the air, and in the very center the section of lacquered wood floor and atop it the Wheel. Rian flung himself at it, Rastim gamely struggling after him. Maskelle started after them, awkwardly stumbling on the sharp edges of the broken stone.

Rian was almost to the edge of the wooden platform when

he stopped abruptly and stumbled back. Rastim and Maskelle reached him a few moments later and Maskelle felt the invisible barrier, a hardening of the air around the Wheel. Rian swore and slammed his fists against it. "It's like the barrier they put around your room in the Palace that night," he said.

"No," Maskelle said grimly. "It's like the barrier around the Marai. This is the Adversary."

"Is there a way through it, like the one around the Marai?" Rian asked immediately.

"Probably not."

"Then . . . Now what?" Rastim asked helplessly.

Maskelle started to reply, but the howling of the winds was almost drowning their voices out. She looked back and realized there was a second barrier, this one around the outer edge of the chamber, preventing the creatures from reaching them. They flung themselves against the invisible barrier and she could feel their ravening hunger.

"Don't."

Ilian was standing next to her again. She said aloud, "I suppose you have a good reason that won't make any sense to me."

"You'll need it to get back home." He smiled.

She knotted her fists and wished she could hit him. "We're not going to get back home. We're going to die. You made sure of that."

Rastim muttered, "I'm glad we got that out in the open."

"It's here again?" Rian asked. Neither man would be able to see the Adversary in this form unless it wanted them to.

"It never left," Maskelle said, not taking her eyes off the Adversary.

Ilian stepped close to her and touched her face. His fingers felt cool. He said, "I have to remake myself. This isn't working. It's time for me to die, too."

It's still mad, she thought. *It can't die.* Humoring it, she asked, "Why didn't you do this before now? Why wait?"

"I needed them." It gestured around at the creatures cluster-ing against the invisible wall. "This will take all their lives." It looked back at her, must have read her expression and explained, "It's for the best. They're broken. They died long ago and they don't know it. I'm broken too. I need to die." It shook its head, gave Ilian's familiar shrug. "It's time to try something different. The next Adversary needs to be a spirit that was once human, like the other Ancestors. Then it won't need a Voice like I needed you."

She shook her head. *Is it serious?* "That's why you did this? So you could use them to destroy yourself?"

It stepped back, its expression turning angry. "You know why you don't want to trust me? Because I'm you. You've given me all your fears, all your pain, all your little betrayals. You can't trust me because you can't trust yourself."

"All right." She turned away from it. "Stop." She buried her face in her hands, searching for calm. "You say you want to re-make yourself and you'll kill these creatures to do it. Why didn't you say this before?"

Ilian's hands rested on her shoulders. "They would have heard me."

She took a step away, shaking him off. She didn't know what Rian and Rastim were making of all this. She said, "What's stop-ping you?"

"I need your help." When she turned to look at him. He shrugged, with an apologetic expression. "And I need another body."

"A dead one?" she demanded. "You should have thought of that earlier."

"This is getting worse all the time," Rastim commented to Rian.

"Not dead," the Adversary corrected her gently. "Living. Liv-ing is always better. Rian—"

"No!"

"It won't hurt him. It'll just be for a moment." Ilian's brows lifted. "You trust me with yourself, but not with him?"

"I don't trust you with myself, either!"

"What is he saying?" Rian demanded. "I heard him say my name."

"Nothing," Maskelle snapped.

"What did he say?" Rian repeated.

"I wouldn't harm a life from my world," Ilian said.

"You wouldn't?" Maskelle demanded. "What about Veran, what about Igarin? And Mirak and the others Marada killed or used. You could have prevented their deaths and you did nothing."

"And for that I deserve to die. 'Those who are pleased to hurt living beings are to be punished without mercy.' " Ilian stepped forward and took her hands. "So let me die."

Maskelle felt it touch her mind again and suddenly she was seeing the Adversary as it saw itself. It was a pattern in the Infinite like the Wheel, but its symbols were far more complex and their attachment to the real world was only tenuous. She saw it hadn't been lying to her; there was a section of the pattern missing, torn out as if by force, leaving an empty darkness in its place.

It was in the same place as the dark blot in the Wheel of the Infinite. *That wasn't a reflection of Marada's Wheel. It was a reflection of this one, of the Adversary itself.* It was a warning, an appeal for help.

It made a terrible sense. If this had happened when the Voices had tried to close the Aspian Straits to prevent that long ago invasion, if they accidentally sent the Sakkaran cities away, they had sent part of the Adversary with it. It hurt, she realized, a deep pain, an injury that never healed. It had allowed corruption to creep in; if it had been whole, Marada and her people would never have been able to enter the world. The Wheel of the Infinite had done this to the Adversary, and the Adversary would never have used the Wheel again if it hadn't absolutely had to.

And this, she reminded herself, *could all be a lie.*

"Is it helping us or not?" Rastim asked, frightened by what he had heard of Maskelle's half of the conversation.

She said slowly, "It needs help. It's been damaged, and it needs to die, so it can remake itself."

They both stared at her. Gesturing out at the creatures surrounding them, Rian said, "It could have picked a better time."

She shook her head. "It needs them. It's going to kill them all and use their power to do this."

Rian hesitated. "Then what's it waiting for?"

"It also needs my help, and it needs to be inside you for a moment."

Rian stared at her. "What?"

"Sorry you asked?" Rastim breathed.

Rian looked confused. He looked at the Wheel, past the barrier they couldn't break, and then at the creatures that were howling for their blood around the perimeter of the chamber. It was obvious they were running out of time. "Is that . . . Should I do it?"

He must have seen the anguish on her face, because he said immediately, "I'll do it."

The Adversary waited, and Maskelle closed her eyes. There was no other choice. *It brought us all to this point solely for this. I can stop you,* she told it. *All I have to do is refuse. I can pay you in kind for everything that you did to me.*

I've accepted my failure, it replied with brutal truth. *Accept yours. Forgive me. Or forgive yourself, it's the same.*

She opened her eyes and felt the tears. "I can't."

Ilian was watching her gravely. He gestured to the clouds of dust and hate, all that were left of their enemies. *Look at them.* His expression sour, he shook his head. *Trapped in the past. Is that what you want? I'm a mad, damaged spirit, and I choose death over that. What do you choose?*

She looked at them. "Not that."

Then let it go. Let me go.

Is that it? Maskelle wondered. *I don't want to let the Adversary die?* It had been there all her life. Hate, love; after so many years strong emotions blended into each other. Should she hold the Adversary like these creatures were held, trapped by memory and old pain? And condemn not only yourself to death, but Rian and Rastim too? *Let it go. Let me go.* "Then go."

Ilian vanished and the Adversary flowed into Rian's body. He looked startled, stepped toward her, then started to collapse. Maskelle stepped forward and caught him, feeling her legs tremble. The Adversary hadn't been in a real body before, only Gisar's wooden one, and the effort it was taking to dampen its power, to keep from hurting Rian, was terrible. *This has to be done quickly,* Maskelle thought desperately. She felt that it needed more contact between them to make this work. Holding Rian as tightly as she could, she kissed him.

All sound stopped and she could hear nothing, feel nothing. She felt the Adversary poised on the brink and thought, *Please don't let it betray me.*

No, it told her, *all that is over with.*

"We can make a bargain," the creatures said again. Melded with the Adversary, Maskelle could hear their individual voices, keening, unhuman. "We can give you—"

I don't bargain with otherworld demons, the Adversary said as Maskelle felt it flow through her. *I eat them.*

Someone was shaking Maskelle's shoulder. She opened her eyes to see an unfamiliar face leaning over her. It was a young face, a girl's face, no more than thirteen or fourteen years, with olive Kushorit skin and features, but the hair tumbling down around her ears was light brown, and her eyes were green. In a light voice, she said, "Is this my temple? Is it supposed to look like this? Do I have to stay here?"

Maskelle closed her eyes briefly. *Ancestors, he did it.* She said, "No, yes, and no. Help me up."

A strong hand under her arm hauled her to her feet. Maskelle looked around, trying to get her bearings. The great chamber was empty, silent, still. *They're gone, dead, every one,* she thought, still taking it in. Rian still lay sprawled unconscious nearby. Rastim was just climbing to his feet. "They're gone," the Ariaden said, baffled. "How did— And who's that?"

To the girl, Maskelle said, "Wait here," and went to kneel by Rian. She touched his face anxiously and his eyelids fluttered, but his breathing was shallow.

"I can fix that," the girl said.

Maskelle looked at her anxious face. "Can you?" When the Ancestors had been in human form they had all been great healers.

"I know how. My father told me."

Her father. For the first time Maskelle let herself feel the emptiness at the core of her being. For the first time since all those years ago in Rashet when it had first spoken to her, the Adversary was gone, truly gone. When she had been under the curse, she had thought herself cut off from it, but it must have always been there, an undercurrent flowing through her own thoughts, even if it hadn't spoken aloud and denied her the visions. Now she knew what its absolute absence really felt like. "Go ahead."

The girl looked down at Rian, concentration making her childish brow furrow. She held out one hand and Maskelle felt a surge of pure power as strong and sharp as when she had drawn lightning from the sky. It hadn't come from the temples, it had come from inside the girl, where all the power of what had been the Adversary was now stored. Maskelle blinked and shook her head.

Rian drew a sharp breath suddenly, though he didn't wake. He was already less pale.

"All fixed," the girl said happily.

Nervous, Rastim asked, "Is he all right?"

"I think so," Maskelle whispered. She brushed the sweat-soaked hair back from his brow.

Rastim stripped off his tunic and handed it to her. "For my sake?" he asked, his tone pleading, nodding toward the girl.

"What?" Maskelle took the garment automatically, staring at him. "Oh, yes." She handed it back to the girl and said, "Put this on."

She held it upside down, looking it over curiously. Rastim took it away from her, saying, "No, here," and managed to get it over the girl's head and far enough down that she caught on and pulled it the rest of the way on. "Who is she?" Rastim demanded again.

"She's what's left of the Adversary. It remade itself into her."

Rian stirred a little, then grabbed his head and muttered, "Ow."

The girl tugged on her sleeve. "It's happening."

"It's happening," Maskelle repeated vaguely. The Marai, the Wheel, sunset. "It's happening! Come on." Maskelle dragged Rian's arm over her shoulder and hauled him up, panic giving her the strength.

Rastim helped support him from the other side, asking tensely, "What do we do?"

"Climb up here," Maskelle explained, planting her foot on the fragment of wooden flooring carefully. "Don't touch the Wheel."

"I could fix," the girl said helpfully.

"I know you can, but not just now." With Rastim and the girl's help she got Rian up on the flooring. Maskelle sat down heavily, pulling her head into his lap, Rastim crouching on one side of her and the girl on the other. There was just enough room for them. "Everyone watch their fingers and toes," she breathed.

She could feel it coming, like an immense heart about to beat. Rastim started to say something, then time paused and stilled, silence filling the void. Then silence rushed away and Rastim said, "When is it going to . . ."

Scents flooded in first, incense and warm damp air. The roar of a faraway crowd, the chamber suddenly much smaller, only a few feet larger on each side than the wheel. Maskelle found herself staring at an exquisitely carved Kushorit hunting scene with warriors and nobles mounted on elephants, and a wicked-looking tiger stalking through wooden trees. They were in one of Chancellor's Mirak's rooms in the Celestial Home.

". . . begin," Rastim finished.

18

Rian would never have thought the hot damp air of Duvalpore would feel good, but now it was as welcome as a cool breeze.

They were at a trader's post on the very outskirts of the great city, outside the outer wall and across one of the barrier canals. Rian was sitting on a fallen log near the cold firepit while Rastim lay on one of the grass mats nearby. The post was mostly empty, with all the traders inside the city for the festival. They had a good view of the wall across the water, with the heavy vines creeping up stone stained red and gold by the sunset, and the high domes of the temples floating above it in the evening mist. The Ariaden's wagons were drawn up under a cluster of tall palms, and the actors were all mostly asleep, recovering from their ordeal and the precipitate exit from the city.

No one seemed to be aware of the change except for those who had been in the Marai and experienced it. As soon as Maskelle had spoken to the guards and servants still present in the Celestial Home, it was obvious that those two days spent in that strange place had gone by in a heartbeat for everyone left behind in the city. Fortunately there was no one in the place of a high enough rank to demand an explanation from the Voice of the Adversary as to what she was doing in Chancellor Mirak's private quarters.

Maskelle had commandeered another boat from the Palace docks so they could return to the Marai. Once there she had gone inside and sent out the other Ariaden, and Rastim had hurried them back to the guesthouse to collect their wagons and the rest of the group and then they had worked their way out of the crowded city. That was earlier today and Rian hadn't seen her since.

The Ariaden were still confused, and Rian and Rastim hadn't had much time for explanations for them; Rian still wasn't sure he understood what had happened himself. It was a little hard to comprehend that a few hours ago they had been trapped in a limbo with the whole world at stake, and now they were sitting in a trader's post in the warm twilight waiting for Maskelle to return.

Rastim, who must have been thinking along much the same lines, commented, "Hard to believe it wasn't all a dream."

"Well, we do have some evidence," Rian said wryly.

They both looked at the girl. *Going to have to think of a name for her,* he thought. She had been wandering along the edge of the treeline, investigating the flowers and ferns and admiring the insects and birds. As the twilight lengthened, she had come back to where he and Rastim were sitting. Rian thought she was watching the barges and boats go down the canal, but now she edged closer to him and seemed a little nervous.

He asked, "What's wrong?"

She gestured at the colors streaking the darkening sky. "Is this supposed to happen?"

He looked up at Rastim, who shrugged his bewilderment. Rian asked, "Is what supposed to happen?"

She pointed up again. "That. The light going away."

Rian realized what she meant and smiled, shaking his head a little in amazement. "It's night. That's supposed to happen." The Adversary had given her much of the knowledge it thought she needed to survive, but it seemed to have left out a few key facts.

"Oh. That's all right then." Reassured, she leaned against Rian's knee.

Rastim stood up suddenly. "There she is."

Rian looked up to see the Celestial One's boat coming toward them from across the canal, the white fabric of the awning drifting gently in the breeze.

"Who's that?" the girl said excitedly.

"That's the Celestial One," Rian told her as he got to his feet. He could see Maskelle now, sitting next to the old man, and felt relief wash over him.

"Trouble?" Rastim asked worriedly.

"I don't think so." There was no one else in the boat but the boys who poled it. The Celestial One hadn't even brought his usual attendant priest. "Wait here."

Rian went down the gentle slope of the bank to the post's dock as the boat was drawing up. He saw the "wait here" had worked on Rastim, but the girl had followed him, bouncing along happily at his side. He looked down at her, lifting his brows, and she said, "My father said if Maskelle wasn't here I was supposed to stay with you."

"Oh, he did, did he?" Rian let out his breath. The Adversary had apparently planned for every contingency.

One of the boys jumped out of the boat to tie it off, and Rian helped Maskelle lift the Celestial One out.

"Ah," the old man said, looking around and sniffing the fresh air. "It is good to be alive again."

The last time Rian had seen the Celestial One he had been a corpse. It was still hard to believe they had survived it all.

"This is she?" the Celestial One asked, eyeing the girl.

"No other," Maskelle told him.

The Celestial One took the girl's arm and let her lead him up the short distance to the camp.

Rian hung back with Maskelle, asking, "What did you tell them?"

She sighed and pushed her braids back. "That the Adversary was injured by the change, that it needs time to recover and until then there will be no Voice."

"They believed that?"

She shrugged a little, smiling ruefully. "They don't have a choice. Besides, it's mostly true." She said slowly, "When the Voices used the Wheel to close the Aspian Straits and made the Sakkaran cities vanish, they damaged the Adversary. The Ancestors are all spirits who were once people, but the Adversary was the world itself, the way the Wheel is the world. A part of itself went with those cities. It had to wait until now to remake itself, but it was growing weary, and a little mad. It didn't always remember what it was it had to do. It gave me a false vision and told me to destroy Raith so I would be exiled. So all the events it foresaw would fall into place. It spoke to Marada when she came to this world and pretended to need her help. She told me *The Book of the Adversary* was the one Koshan text she didn't need to read. She thought she knew all there was to know. But none of us knew."

Rian looked at the girl again. "So she's like one of the original Ancestors. When she dies . . ."

"Her spirit will join the Infinite and become the new Adversary."

Maskelle drew her robes around her and they went up to the Ariaden's camp. Rastim was a little nervous at being left alone with the Celestial One and looked relieved to see them. They took seats near the firepit and the girl moved immediately to settle at Maskelle's side.

"You have a great responsibility," the Celestial One said, looking up at Maskelle, his tone solemn.

"I've always had a great responsibility," Maskelle told him. "This is nothing new." She looked down at the girl fondly. "Well, it's a little new."

The old man snorted in annoyance, but only said, "What will you do?"

Rian looked at Maskelle. They hadn't exactly discussed this.

She shrugged. "I don't know." She gave Rian a faint smile and he realized that she didn't particularly care where they went.

The Adversary was dead, and though she had the guardianship of its successor, this was the first time in many years that she had been free. Rian smiled back.

"Stay with us for a time," Rastim said suddenly, leaning forward. "We can tour the larger cities in the Empire. The roads are good and the audiences love us. When things calm down in Duvalpore we can come back." He rubbed his chin and added speculatively, "If we're still popular, I'm thinking of opening a theater, a permanent one. We're all getting older and it would be nice to have a home."

The Celestial One shook his head. "She should stay close to the temples."

"She should have as wide an experience of the world as possible," Maskelle countered firmly. She lifted her brows and added, "That's what the Adversary wanted."

"Hmph." The Celestial One sat back with a disgruntled expression and looked inclined to argue.

Rian suspected this argument had been going on since Maskelle had returned to the Marai. Maskelle continued, "It wanted her to live as a person, to learn compassion and morality, the way the Ancestors did when they were human. And besides," she gave him an arch look, "she's half Sitanese, so it's not your decision. The Adversary is a warrior and she needs to learn about that from Rian."

Everyone looked at Rian, except for the girl, who, never still for long, was wandering back toward the patch of grass where the oxen were grazing. Rian tried to look enigmatic. He still wasn't sure how he felt about all of this, but even after only a few hours' acquaintance he liked the girl. He could see a great deal of Maskelle in her already, and the occasional glimpses he caught of himself were startling.

"You'll take care of her?" the Celestial One asked him, his voice gruff.

"Taking care of people is what I do," Rian told him.

The Celestial one sighed and folded his hands, looking away. "Well?" Maskelle prompted. "I was raised in the temples at a high rank and it didn't do me any good. With her power it would be worse for her."

"You have told me that it isn't my decision," the Celestial One said stiffly.

"I'm humoring you." She smiled.

He shook his head at her, but he couldn't keep the amusement from showing in his face. He asked "What will you call her?" and it appeared the decision was made.

Maskelle looked at Rian, who shrugged. He had never had to name any children before. She said, "What about 'Siri'? It's the Sitanese word for a type of sword."

The Celestial One eyed the girl, who was stroking the forehead of one of the oxen. He said wryly, "That will probably do very nicely."